S0-BTC-198

His Favorite Mistress

Also by Tracy Anne Warren

My Fair Mistress
The Accidental Mistress

The Husband Trap
The Wife Trap
The Wedding Trap

His Favorite Mistress

A NOVEL

Tracy Anne Warren

BALLANTINE BOOKS • NEW YORK

His Favorite Mistress is a work of fiction. Names, characters, places, and incidents are the products of the author's imagination or are used fictitiously. Any resemblance to actual events, locales, or persons, living or dead, is entirely coincidental.

A Ballantine Books Mass Market Original

Published in the United States by Ballantine Books, an imprint of The Random House Publishing Group, a division of Random House, Inc., New York.

ISBN 978-0-7394-8990-1

Cover illustration: Chris Cocozza

Printed in the United States of America

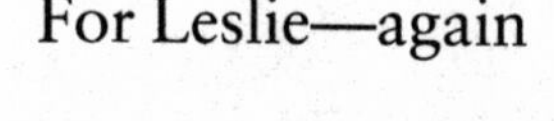
For Leslie—again

Chapter One

London
February 1815

ALL IT WILL *take is a single bullet straight through the heart,* Gabriella St. George told herself as she clutched the pistol inside her palm.

She was a good shot with confidence in her skills. After all, she'd been taught by the best—the Great Moncrief himself, who was known in entertainment circles as the finest sharpshooter in the civilized world. Her biggest concern was finding the courage to hold fast to her resolve and carry through with her plan—that and keeping her arm from shaking so violently that she fouled her aim.

She supposed she had good reason for her jitters, since before tonight the only lives she'd taken had been those of animals—rabbits and birds that she'd hunted for food as she'd traveled around England. She'd even been known to poach a deer on occasion in order to hold starvation at bay. But tonight would be different.

For tonight she planned to kill a man.

Easing deeper into the late evening shadows that painted the walls and corners of the study black, she waited, knowing that eventually he would come. She'd been observing him this past week and knew his habits, knew that he always stopped in this room for a few minutes each night before retiring upstairs.

Thanks to a maid who didn't mind chatting with a friendly stranger while out completing her errands, Gabriella had learned that, except for the servants, he was alone here in this immense townhouse. His wife and young children, so she had been told, were at his estate in the north of England.

The information had come as a relief, since she had no desire to involve innocents. After all, his crimes were his alone; he was the only one deserving of retribution. Even so, she couldn't completely set aside the guilt that nibbled at her like a school of tiny fish, aware that her actions tonight would bring grief to others. But she pushed aside her qualms.

One life, she argued, *in recompense for another.*

When she'd slipped through a conveniently placed window a couple of hours ago, she'd heard the low rhythm of male conversation, punctuated by sporadic bursts of laughter. He'd invited friends over, a small group of men gathered to share dinner, then drinks while they played a few rounds of cards. Having long ago learned the art of patience, she'd settled into a corner, gun in hand, and allowed time to pass.

At length, the house had grown quiet as his guests said their farewells and departed, the servants retreating to make their way to their beds. Only the steady ticktock of the room's finely crafted satinwood casement clock broke the silence, together with the gentle crackling of the fire she'd watched a maid refresh about an hour earlier. *Not long now,* she judged, *and he will be here*. Shifting slightly, she worked to ease the stiffness and pent-up tension that had gathered in her muscles and joints.

Another five minutes elapsed before she finally heard footsteps. Pressing her back flat against the wall, she sank deeper into the concealing shadows and watched him stride into the room.

From the moment he entered the study, he dominated the space, commanding his surroundings with not only his impressive size and athletic grace, but with the innate forcefulness of his personality. Despite the tenebrous light, she recognized the arrogance in his gait, along with an unmistakable air of noble authority she would have assumed was bred into him from birth had she not known otherwise. Before tonight, she'd only viewed him from a distance, yet he seemed taller up close, his hair darker, so deep a brown as to be nearly black. A trick of the late evening shadows, she assumed.

Shivering, a tingle whispered along her backbone, her heart pounded with the force of a hammer striking an anvil, a reaction she had never before experienced while observing the man. Likely the sensation was a product of the tension she felt, well aware the moment she had been preparing for was now nearly upon her. Gathering her nerve, she tightened her grip on the gun and let him come farther into the room.

Reaching the desk, he searched for a match and candle. Light flared to life moments later, illumination spreading in a comfortable yellow glow over the space. She forced herself not to tremble, holding her position as he stepped toward a nearby bookshelf and began to peruse the titles.

She moved forward, the pistol held straight out before her. "Rafe Pendragon," she declared in a clear, unwavering voice. "Prepare to pay for your crimes."

His shoulders stiffened before he slowly turned to face her.

Only then did she see him fully, her gaze riveted to his impossibly handsome face. Classically hewn cheekbones framed a long patrician nose, his forehead strong, his jaw and chin cleaved from a heritage of ancient aristocratic stock. His lips were blatantly seductive, as if nature had designed them to entice a woman into wanting to commit any number of earthly sins. Then there was his complexion—swarthy instead of pale, with a delicious evening's growth of whiskers that only enhanced his aura of masculine sensuality. Yet of all his attractive qualities—and they were legion—his most compelling physical feature was his eyes. Rich and deep-set, they were a pure, almost velvety blue, dark as midnight yet brilliant as a summer sea. Right now those eyes were gazing at her, full of keen observation and powerful intellect. *He is studying me,* she realized, *just as I am studying him.*

A soft gasp escaped her lips, but she held herself and the gun steady nevertheless. "You're not Pendragon!" she accused.

The stranger arched a dark eyebrow. "Indeed no, I am not. I trust you won't shoot me for disappointing you, Miss . . ." He let the sentence trail off. "You are a miss, are you not, despite your present choice of masculine attire?"

Earlier this evening, she'd decided to dress as a boy. After all, sneaking into a townhouse to kill a man was not easily accomplished while wearing a gown, stays, and petticoat.

She ignored his query. "Where is he?"

"Rafe, I assume you mean? Well, I am not likely to aid you by revealing his whereabouts. Why do you want to harm him, anyway? Is it money you're after?"

Her shoulders tightened. "I am no thief. If I were, I could have liberated a king's ransom from this room while the lot of you were having dinner. Yes," she offered when he tipped his head in unspoken inquiry, "I have been here for some while, waiting unobserved."

"A regular little cat, are you? Tiptoeing in on silent feet. A useful ability for any person, I will admit."

"I have many useful abilities, but I am not here to engage in a round of banter with you, whoever you might be."

"Ah, forgive my lack of manners," he drawled. "Wyvern at your service. I would make you a bow were I sure you wouldn't put a bullet in me while I attempted the move."

"I won't shoot unless you give me cause," she stated, inching the pistol higher. "In the interest of safety, however, I suggest you take a seat over there." She nodded toward an armchair that faced the desk.

"Thank you, no. I am perfectly comfortable standing."

"Comfortable or not, pray be seated."

At a height of more than six feet, he towered over her. Aware she needed every possible advantage in a situation that was suddenly not going at all as she'd planned, she knew he would pose far less of a threat were he ensconced in a chair. Despite his apparent affability, she didn't trust him for a second.

He met her gaze, then shrugged. "Very well, if you insist. After all, you are the one with the weapon. But first, tell me what grievance you have against my friend. He doesn't generally engender such a violent reaction, especially among the fairer sex."

Her breasts rose and fell beneath her threadbare linen shirt, a cold lump wedged deep within her chest. "He harmed me and mine, and that is all you need to know. Believe me, I have just cause for despising the man."

"Did your family fall upon hard times, then? Did you lose your home and decide to lay the blame at Rafe's doorstep?"

"Believe me, whatever blame I cast belongs at *no other* doorstep but his."

Wyvern crossed his arms over his chest and leaned a

seemingly negligent hip against the desk. "How old are you? You look little more than a girl."

She drew herself up. "I fail to see what difference that makes. I am a woman grown. Seventeen, if you must know."

"That old, hmm? It strikes me, though, that most young women your age would be tucked up tight inside their houses, far too afraid to venture out on their own, let alone go about dressed in male attire, and brandishing a pistol."

"You will find that I am not like most young women."

The edge of his mouth tipped upward, a twinkle glittering in his brilliant blue gaze. "Yes, so I am beginning to see."

A fresh tingle inched down her spine as if he had reached out and stroked a hand over her skin, the sensation having nothing to do with the peril of the situation, and everything to do with her awareness of the man himself. *Indisputably, he is the most breathtaking man I have ever encountered. But I have no business noticing such things,* she scolded herself, *particularly not now when I have come on a mission of vengeance. A mission I cannot afford to delay.*

"Now, Mr. Wyvern," she said, determined to move matters forward. "If your curiosity has been satisfied, I suggest you take that seat."

"It's Wyvern. Just Wyvern."

"Fine, *Wyvern*—"

"As for my curiosity," he continued, "you have done nothing but further whet my appetite. You haven't even told me your name."

"No, I have not," she stated emphatically.

He inclined his head. "As you prefer, then. Now, which seat is it that I am to take?"

Mildly surprised by the question, she hesitated, relaxing her stance a bit as she gestured toward the correct chair. "That one. Just there."

"Here?" He pointed, stretching out a hand.

She frowned, wondering if he might be hard of hearing. "Yes, there."

Quick as a flash, he reached out and seized hold of her wrist, yanking her off balance. She gasped, unable to recover from his trick before he wrested the gun from her grip and imprisoned her inside his arms. In the blink of an eye, she found the tables turned, going suddenly from captor to captive.

"Ooh!" she cried, wriggling inside his hold. "Let me go!"

He tightened his arms, her body pressed firmly against his own. "Tut, tut. Quit your squirming, girl."

She stomped on his foot, wincing as a rebounding pain jolted along her instep.

"Quit that, too," he admonished, a spark of amused annoyance gleaming in his eyes. "You're only causing yourself harm, since I have no intention of releasing you before I am ready to do so. In case you had not noticed, I am bigger and stronger and you are now entirely at my mercy."

Grasping her so tightly the air wheezed out of her lungs, he leaned back and set the gun atop the desk. Turning around, he moved the two of them a few steps away—too far for her to have any chance of recovering the weapon. Only then did he ease his hold enough to let her breathe normally again. On a sharp inhale, she filled her lungs with air, the movement pressing her breasts against the solid wall of his chest.

Gazing downward, he quirked a brow. "I must admit I have to agree with your assessment."

"My assessment of what?" she demanded in a winded voice.

"That you are a woman full-grown." He snuggled her

closer, and stroked a hand over her back and across her hip. "You may be young, but you are curved in all the right places. Considering our current proximity, you really ought to tell me your name, you know."

She squirmed against him. "Release me!"

He chuckled softly. "So you would rather have me use persuasion, would you, to force out the answer?" His gaze lowered to her mouth, his tone dropping to a husky drawl. "You will find I have a rare talent for persuasion."

"And you will find that I am well used to the blandishments of smooth talkers and confidence tricksters. I doubt your efforts will prove any more successful than theirs."

"A challenge, is it? I like challenges, especially ones issued by pretty little minxes like you."

Before she knew what he meant to do, his lips came down on hers. At first she stiffened inside his embrace, straining to be free despite the futility of the action. But even as she struggled, a part of her brain registered the captivating pleasure of his mouth moving against her own, the breath she'd barely managed to regulate becoming fast and shallow once more.

Still, with a last ounce of determination, she gave another wriggling push. To her dismay, however, her attempt did nothing but encourage him to reach down and secure her wrists behind her back before he slowly bent her body into his own, leaving her plastered to him, her breasts flattened against his hard chest.

She barely had a chance to adjust before he slanted his mouth and kissed her harder, compelling a response from her that she was helpless to resist. For in spite of having previously fended off unwanted advances from men, this was the first time she'd ever been caught by one.

The first time she had ever been kissed.

And what a kiss it is! she had to confess, her limbs turning warm and waxen as if they had a will of their own. Her brain might argue that she didn't want this—want him—but her body most decidedly did not agree. Ragged heat washed over her, a shiver following as he coaxed her lips to part.

Using his tongue, he painted her mouth with the lightest of strokes, a move that sent her heart racing at breakneck speed. Trembling from the almost shocking carnality of the act, she let him continue, let him delve inside her mouth to play there with a finesse that quite literally made her whimper.

Then, as suddenly as it had begun, the kiss ended, Wyvern lifting his head to peer down into her eyes. His own gaze was lambent, eyelids half-lowered as if he, too, was trying to recover from an unexpected surfeit of pleasure. Yet he didn't release her from his hold, obviously not so far gone as to forget why she had come into his possession in the first place.

"Have you had enough," he asked roughly, "or shall we try for another?"

Seeing his expression that was half challenge, half anticipation—as if he knew he would win no matter her answer—she decided it might be wise to acquiesce to his original demand. "It's Gabriella," she murmured. "My name is Gabriella."

His lips turned up on a smile. "It suits you. A pleasure to meet you"—Pausing, he shifted so their bodies rubbed together—"Gabriella."

Her breath caught on a sharp inhale, a quiver running like an electrical spark over her skin.

Easing his hold fractionally, he set an inch between them. "Well now," he drawled, "what am I going to do with you?"

Just then, footsteps rang out near the door as Rafe Pendragon strode inside.

"Sorry for the delay," he remarked. "I had a note from Julianna and wanted to write back despite the late hour. Did you find that book I . . ." Whatever else he may have planned to say, the statement dwindled off to nothing as his gaze landed on her. "What in heavens have you got there? Or should I more aptly say *whom*?"

"This," Wyvern declared, "is Gabriella, and from what she tells me, she came here tonight with the sinister intention of shooting you. As you can see, I have relieved her of her weapon. The pistol is just there on the desk."

"How extraordinary." Pendragon strolled forward. "Snuck in, did she?"

Wyvern nodded. "During dinner, it would seem. I should think you'd know better by now than to leave your windows unlocked. One never knows what might find its way inside."

"He didn't leave his windows open," she interrupted, struggling a bit again inside Wyvern's implacable hold. "I picked the lock. And I am not an *it* and do not care to be spoken about in the third person as if I were absent from the room."

"Fiery, isn't she?" Wyvern commented in an amused tone.

"And obviously determined." Pendragon lighted another candle then strolled closer, pausing to inspect her face. "So, child, why have you broken into my home? More to the point, what is it you imagine I've done that would lead you to wish me harm?"

"I imagine nothing, you murderer!" Anguish and fury burned like acid through her veins, along with the frustration of knowing her plans for vengeance had been thwarted. Considering what a heartless brute Pendragon was, she knew she had little time remaining until he had her arrested and cast into gaol. But before she found herself hauled off and tossed inside a dank cell—an idea she shivered to imagine—she vowed she would speak her piece.

"You deserve to pay for your crimes," she spat. "I may not be able to kill you as I'd hoped, but I want you to know the suffering you've caused."

Pendragon arched both of his dark brows. "Those are serious charges, indeed. And while I freely admit I have lived neither a pure nor blameless life, I can assure you I have not murdered anyone. Mayhap you have mistaken me for someone else."

"Liar!" she declared, "I know it was you. My mother told me what you did, how you drove my father to ruin, then lured him into the countryside so you could finally finish him off."

Pendragon stared at her. "Gabriella, did you say? Good God, I should have known straight away."

"Known what?" Wyvern questioned.

"That this girl you're holding captive is Burton St. George's daughter."

Chapter Two

Anthony Black, twenty-third Duke of Wyvern, felt his mouth drop open.

In the normal course of things, Tony considered himself an unflappable sort of man—calm under pressure, insouciant at the most astonishing of news. But given the magnitude of what Rafe had just revealed, he supposed he could grant himself a bit of latitude for the slip. After all, it wasn't every day a man found himself holding the daughter of his friend's most hated enemy.

Lowering his gaze, he studied her anew, searching for signs of resemblance to the deceased Viscount Middleton. Around the eyes perhaps, he decided, though the color wasn't the same at all. True, the viscount had possessed blue eyes, but Gabriella's were far more than mere blue—their petal-soft hue was a unique and unforgettable shade of violet. Instead of sandy brown, her hair was a dark sable, satiny and thick, the wavy locks straining against their tie as if begging to be set free. As for her face, it was nothing short of exquisite, her features framed in a perfect oval with an elegant nose; soft, full lips; and a translucent pink-and-white complexion that more than rivaled the finest porcelain. As for her body, well, he'd already had time to explore that for himself in close detail, finding her slender frame was lushly feminine yet surprisingly lithe and toned, as if she were used to a variety of athletic pursuits. In that, he supposed, she shared a trait with her father, since Middleton had never been a slouch. As for whether she possessed any of his other, less appealing, qualities, that remained to be seen.

Careful to maintain his hold, he shifted Gabriella to his side before turning his attention toward Rafe. "I did not even realize Middleton *had* a daughter. How did you know?"

"I made it my business, once upon a time, to be apprised of everything concerning St. George. It seemed safer that way." Rafe's gaze moved to Gabriella. "I knew of you, but very little more than your name. He kept you well hidden, so much so that I doubt even his closest cronies realized. Your mother is an actress, is she not?"

"*Was,*" Gabriella tossed back, her chin coming up as she shot Rafe a glare. "She is dead as well, because of you."

Rafe drew in a long breath. "I am sorry for her loss, but you cannot lay her death at my doorstep."

"Why not, since you are the cause!" she accused. "After Papa died, Mama grew despondent. She began to drink, and see men she would never, ever have considered entertaining in the past. One night, one of them beat her to death, and she let him. They said she barely put up a struggle, as if the effort was simply too much for her. Her heart was broken because of Papa's loss, because you killed him and left us with nothing."

"My sympathies as well," Tony interceded in a calm voice. "But you are blaming the wrong man. Rafe isn't the one who left your mother with nothing. He isn't the one who left *you* with nothing, making no provision for your future care."

"My father would have done so had he known," she defended, a sliver of doubt creeping into her voice. "He was still young. He had no reason to expect he might die."

Tony shook his head. "We, all of us, may die at any moment. A considerate man takes care of those he loves. Had Middleton not been a selfish bounder and heartless bully, he would have done so for you and your mama. As for accusing Rafe of murder, he is not the one guilty of that particular crime."

"Tony—" Rafe interrupted.

"If you want to know about murderers," he continued, "you have only to look to your own—"

"Tony, *enough*."

He shot Rafe a look. "She needs to be told, not go on laboring under falsehoods and delusions. Gabriella, you strike me as a bright young woman. Do you not wish to know the truth? Do you not want to have the veil of lies lifted from your sight?"

Her face hardened at his words, her gaze moving between the two men. "I know the truth. He murdered my father, stabbed him in the chest with a knife. You are simply trying to protect him because he is your friend."

"He *is* my friend and I would gladly protect him with my life, but what I say is the plain truth. I will swear an oath on it should you wish. Your father, I am sad to say, was not a pleasant man. He killed people, murdered them."

"He did not! I don't believe you!" Gabriella shot back, a defiant gleam flashing in her eyes. "My mother told me what happened, told me how Pendragon grew up hating my father because Papa was the viscount and the legitimate heir. How Pendragon let envy drive him to hound and torment my father, ruining him any way he could until he finally lured him to his death."

"And did your mother also mention that your father kidnapped Lady Pendragon?" Tony questioned. "That Rafe tracked Middleton out into the countryside in order to rescue his wife and the unborn child she carried? Did she know that your father demanded a ransom for her return, intending to use the money so he could flee the country? Or that he was desperate to recover journals that incriminated him in a number of crimes, the passages outlining many of his nefarious activities over the years? Acts that involved rape and murder, including the death of his wife, the brutal violation of an innocent girl, and even patricide."

She gasped, her eyes wide as blood drained from her cheeks.

"That's right," Tony pressed. "Middleton murdered his own father—*your* grandfather!"

Her lower lip trembled, a stricken expression on her face as though her whole world were being cleaved in two. And perhaps it was, Tony realized. She'd come here tonight seeking vengeance on behalf of a man she obviously loved, only to find out he was not the person she had believed him to be.

"No, it isn't possible," she argued, struggling inside his hold. "He wasn't like that. He would never have done the dreadful things of which you are accusing him." Her voice broke on the last word, her tone husky with barely repressed emotion.

"But he *did* do those things," Tony said. "Then afterward he killed one of his oldest cronies in order to cover up his crimes."

"You lie! You must be lying," she insisted, shaking her head in an effort to deny what she was obviously struggling not to see as the truth.

"A respected barrister has the journals," Tony continued. "I could obtain them for you and let you see."

"They must be false," she countered.

"The legal inquest into your father's death judged them valid," Tony stated. "Rafe fought with your father that day, and the two of them did grapple with a knife. But your father was the one trying to kill Rafe, not the other way around. He is the one who attacked first, then ended up being stabbed in the scuffle. Rafe did not murder your father."

"I have only your word. Why should I believe you?" Sudden desperation rang out in her voice.

"Why should you not? Do you really think I would fabricate such an elaborate story as that? That I would offer to produce proof written in Hurst's own hand?"

"Hurst, did you say?" She grew still. "I . . ."

"Yes. Did you know him?"

She shook her head. "No, but . . . my father mentioned him once. I overheard him say the man was a drunken fool who might . . . cause him trouble one day. That he might have to . . . do something about him. I never imagined . . . oh, God." She lowered her gaze to the floor, a single tear rolling over her cheek.

"Have you heard enough, or do you need more to convince you?" Tony asked in a quiet tone. "So far Rafe hasn't said a word in his own defense, but then he doesn't need to since right is on his side."

"Stop! Stop speaking. I cannot hear any more. I cannot bear any more," she exclaimed, turning her head away as if wishing she could hide.

"Yes, Tony, cease," Rafe stated in an uncompromising tone. "I let you continue because the truth had to come out, but enough now. She has confronted more than anyone ought to be forced to face in so brief a span of time. Release her. She must be weary of being held against her will."

"If you are certain," Tony replied, silently agreeing that Gabriella was unlikely to attempt any further violence at this point. As soon as he allowed her to go free, she bolted away, half-stumbling into a chair positioned near one of the room's night-darkened windows. For a long moment, he watched her cry, wishing he hadn't needed to be so hard on her. Then, remembering practicalities, he reached across the desk and picked up the gun, moving to set the pistol high onto a bookshelf, well out of her reach.

Rafe crossed to her. "You probably do not wish to speak to me," he said in a gentle voice, "but may I get you a glass of wine? Or some brandy perhaps, something to ease your distress?"

She shook her head, refusing to meet his gaze as her tears continued to flow.

"A handkerchief, then," Tony offered, joining them. Reaching into his pocket, he pulled forth a silken square. When she made no move to accept the cloth, he pressed it into her hand.

Moments later, she raised the handkerchief to her face.

"It's late, and all this has been rather draining," Rafe said, turning to address Tony. "My thanks for your help, but you might as well go home now. I can see to my niece."

Until Rafe spoke the words, the recognition that Gabriella and Rafe were related had not fully dawned upon him—though of course it should have, since he well knew that Rafe was Middleton's illegitimate half-brother.

"No, don't go!" Gabriella said, raising her face from the handkerchief to gaze at him. Despite her reddened, tear-stained appearance, she was still beautiful, her eyes the dewy color of wild, rain-drenched violets. "That is . . . I . . . I suppose it doesn't matter, since the runners will be here soon enough to take me off to gaol."

Tony scowled an instant before Rafe did the same.

"What runners? And who said anything about sending you to gaol?" Rafe demanded, asking the same question that came immediately to Tony's lips.

With clear surprise, she glanced between the two men before fixing her gaze on Rafe. "But I thought . . . I just assumed that you would have me arrested. I came here tonight with the intention of shooting you. If Mr. . . .

I mean, if Wyvern had not prevented me, I would have killed you."

"Perhaps," Rafe said in a quiet tone. "Still, I don't believe you would have gone through with it. You may genuinely have *wanted* to proceed, to take your revenge and shoot me, but in the end I do not think you would have done so."

"Why? Do you imagine I don't have the gumption?" she retorted.

One corner of Rafe's mouth turned up. "You appear to have plenty of gumption, but I don't believe you are a killer at heart."

Her lashes lowered for a moment. "According to the both of you, my father apparently was."

"Yes, but you are not your father. You are a distinct individual, who is entirely separate and unique from any other. From this moment forward, your actions and your path in life are your own to choose. So I grant you pardon, with no prison and no punishment for your aborted attempt to kill me."

Gabriella swallowed, her throat tight, almost raw, as she considered Pendragon's words. She had broken into his home tonight with hatred burning like a brand in her chest, convinced he was the very worst sort of villain—someone who deserved to be cast violently from this earth. Instead, she had discovered he wasn't at all the man she believed him to be, just as she had found out the same of her father.

Even now, she could scarcely believe what they'd said about him. Surely the man she had known and loved could not have been capable of committing the vile acts about which she'd been told. And yet, had she really known her father, or had she only seen what she'd wanted to see? What she had *needed* to see, given his infrequent visits and casual displays of affection? Had that colored her view of the man? Had it influenced her mother's perception of him as well? All she knew now was that Wyvern had given her serious reason to doubt the things she had always believed, his words ringing with a harsh yet convincing truth.

And what of Pendragon, the man against whom she had planned to enact vengeance? If her father's death really had been a case of self-defense, then she had no right to go on hating him. She considered his actions tonight and how he'd made no effort to come to his own defense, letting his friend speak for him as if he had nothing whatsoever to hide. More and more she was becoming convinced he did not—that he was the one innocent of wrongdoing, not her father.

Then just when she'd prepared herself to accept punishment for her attempt against him, he had shocked her once more by showing her the one thing she had not expected at all—kindness. Forgiveness. Compassion. "But why?" she asked, her voice sounding low and strained even to her own ears.

Her uncle met her gaze. "Because I know how it feels to lose everything and everyone you love. To find yourself alone in a world that suddenly seems very big and very cold. My parents died at an early age as well. I remember my own grief and rage, the sensation of wondering if life would ever feel right again."

Exactly, she thought with a kind of quiet surprise. She didn't know how, but he understood, as though he had peered inside her head and read her emotions, her thoughts. Glancing toward Wyvern, she noticed that he'd stepped back as if to give her and Pendragon a bit of privacy. Her gaze met his, sympathy clear in his deep blue eyes.

She looked away.

"Gabriella," Pendragon said, recapturing her attention. "This may seem unexpected, but you are my blood relation—one of the few I have in this world—and for that reason I would like to make you an offer."

Wary suspicion rose inside her. "What sort of offer?"

"A home, if you would like it."

"W-what?"

"Come stay with me and my family. Even with the children, my wife and I have plenty of room, both here in London and at our estate in West Riding. I am unaware of your present living situation, but I assume it is not so comfortable as what we can offer you."

Her shoulders drew back. "I manage ably enough." Actually she was barely managing at all these days, living on the last of the money she had obtained from pawning her mother's jewelry and clothing. Soon, even that small amount would be gone, despite all the measures she and her roommate Maude took to economize.

"Pray do not take offense, since none was meant," he continued. "I know I can speak for Lady Pendragon when I say that you are most welcome."

A frown creased her forehead. "But you do not even know me, and from all accounts detested my father. We may be related, but I find it hard to believe you really want me in your home. Are you not worried I might try to do away with you in your sleep?"

Pendragon laughed. "No, for the reasons I already gave you."

"And what would you expect should I agree? I have no wish to be a servant."

"Nor would you be. Should you accept the invitation, you would come to us as family."

"And should I decide to leave?"

He shrugged. "If you find you do not like our home, you may depart at any time."

His proposal sounded wonderful—a bit too wonderful. Having grown up in a touring company of actors, she was used to making do with whatever came to hand.

Being offered a home—and a luxurious one at that—sounded like something from a dream. Still, she had her pride, and no wish to be anyone's poor relation. She rose to her feet. "Thank you, *uncle,* but I fear I must decline. I . . . um . . . have prospects of my own that I plan to pursue."

"The theater, you mean?"

"Perhaps," she evaded. "Now, if I truly am free to leave, I believe I shall do so."

Pendragon nodded. "That, of course, is your choice."

"Gabriella," Wyvern interrupted, suddenly reentering the conversation. "Take his offer. Rafe is a good man and only means you well, even if I may think he is acting on foolish sentiment."

"Ah, now, Tony, you know I am never foolish and rarely act on sentiment," Pendragon drawled.

"You do since you married Julianna and had those babies of yours."

A contented smile moved over her uncle's lips.

For a moment she hesitated, silently reconsidering before forcing herself to discard the idea. "My answer is still no."

An expression that might have been regret passed over Pendragon's features, then was swiftly gone. "As you wish. The offer remains open, however. You are always welcome."

She stared at him for a long moment. "You really aren't at all as I expected, you know. I am sorry for trying to shoot you."

He smiled. "My sincere appreciation that you did not."

Turning, she glanced at Wyvern, then held out his handkerchief. "Thank you for this." As for all the rest that had passed between them this night—including the scorching memory of his kiss that even now had the power to make her tingle—she decide it best not to comment further.

She watched as his eyes landed for a second on the damp wad of silk in her hand. "Keep it, please. I have more than sufficient and shall scarcely miss that particular one. Now, if you will permit, pray allow me to escort you home."

Her heart picked up speed; ruthlessly, she willed it to slow. As tempting as the notion of allowing him to accompany her might be, she suspected it would be unwise to let him see where she lived. Plainly he was a gentleman, used to elegance in everything he did. Very likely he would be appalled should he view the shabby boardinghouse where she rented a third-story attic room.

"I will be fine on my own," she stated. "I know the city and how to reach home safely."

Wyvern's raven-dark eyebrows moved together. "Don't be foolish. It's nearly two in the morning and whatever you may say, the streets aren't safe, not even for someone as comfortable with the city as you claim to be. Come, we will go in my coach."

She shook her head with the barest hint of a smile. "Thank you, but no." Then before he could prevent it, she sprinted on lithe legs toward the door, dashing into the empty entry hall and disappearing from view.

From across the study, Tony watched in annoyance. Moving fast, he started after her. But Rafe reached out and stopped him with a hand. "Let her go. You'll only get into another scuffle with her."

He shook off his friend's hold. "She deserves another scuffle for acting like a peagoose."

"She's no peagoose. Stubborn and willful, mayhap, but as sharp-witted as they come. Dressed in boy's clothing, I am sure she will meet without harm."

"You do not know that."

"I do, since Hannibal is following on her heels, and to his credit she will never detect his presence."

As Wyvern knew, Hannibal was Rafe's trusted associate—a combination of servant and friend. Tall as a giant, Hannibal had a habit of scaring people the first time they encountered him, his bald head, as well as the fearsome scar that cleaved one cheek from temple to jaw, enough to give anyone a fright. Luckily, Gabriella would suffer no such anxiety tonight, since Hannibal was indeed far too skilled a tracker to ever be caught in the act.

His shoulders relaxed. "Well, if Hannibal is on her trail, she'll be safe enough, I suppose." Still, a part of him wished he'd given her back the pistol. From what he suspected of her current life situation, she might well have need of a weapon for something other than attempting to shoot Rafe. He didn't like to think of her in trouble, though she had told them she had prospects. For her sake, he hoped they were good ones.

A night watchman called three in the morning by the time Gabriella used her purloined key to let herself into the boardinghouse that stood a few blocks south of the Covent Garden Theater. After relocking the door at her back, she moved up the staircase, careful to tread lightly on the squeaky wooden steps so as not to wake the landlady. Thin-lipped and short-tempered, Mrs. Buckles would use any excuse to raise the rent again, exactly as she'd done last month when Maude made the mistake of cooking some sausages and onions in their room. After complaining about the supposed stench, Mrs. Buckles had threatened to toss her and Maude out, before she'd agreed to take a few extra shillings a month for their room and board.

The air grew increasingly chilly the higher Gabriella climbed, the temperature nearly as cold as the February night by the time she let herself into the attic room. Instantly, warmth surrounded her.

Bless Maude, she thought, *for adding an extra scoop of coal to the fire.* Although her friend was an actress and often worked late into the evening, Gabriella knew that she must be in bed by now. Slipping out of her borrowed jacket, she draped it over the back of a wooden chair, then turned on a yawn to seek her own slumber.

"For mercy sakes, where have you been!"

Gabriella jumped and nearly let out a scream. Glancing over, she found a nightgown-clad Maude watching her with accusing eyes. Laying a hand over her racing heart, she fought to recover her balance. "Heavens, you scared the life out of me."

The older woman tsked and wrapped her worn blue woolen shawl tighter around her shoulders. "It's no more than you deserve, creeping in here only a few hours shy of dawn without a word from you beforehand. I was worried something dreadful, imagining all sorts of scenarios involving thieves and scoundrels and the like."

"You know I'm far too light-footed to get caught by either variety of brigand. Truly, though, I am sorry to have worried you, since that was not my intent."

Crossing to the small fireplace grate, Maude bent down to light a candle. The pungent odor of tallow spread through the small room along with a weak yellowish pool of illumination. Raising the candle higher, Maude visibly inspected Gabriella, then released another loud tsk. "I suppose that's one of Joe's costumes? It's a good thing that suit hasn't been missed."

"Nor will it be," Gabriella replied. "I'll have it back to the theater tomorrow with no one the wiser."

"And what if someone has noticed?"

She shrugged. "I'll tell them the seams were frayed and in need of repair. Since I've been earning a few pence sewing for the company these last few weeks, no one will suspect a thing."

"Lucky for you." Maude moved to the far side of the room and opened the door to a small cupboard. "Have you eaten?"

At the reminder, Gabriella's stomach rumbled. With all the goings-on, she'd missed dinner, and breakfast had been a long while before that. "No, I haven't."

"Then sit down and I'll make you a bite. I'll put the kettle on as well. I could do with a cup of tea."

Having Maude offer her comfort in the form of food and drink just as she had been doing since Gabriella turned three—let her know the worst was over. Maude Woodcraft might bristle up sharp as a handful of straight pins when her sensibilities were offended, but she never kept a temper for long, unleashing her anger in a quick burst before letting it go.

The older woman tossed her long braid of graying auburn hair over her shoulder and fixed a plate, sliding the brown bread and cheese toward Gabriella. "So," Maude inquired the moment Gabriella's mouth was full. "I suppose you went over there to that man's house. I thought we agreed you'd stay away and forget this revenge of yours."

Gabriella took an extra few moments to chew and swallow. "I couldn't put it aside. I needed to confront him."

Maude laid a pair of clenched fists on the tabletop. "Please God, don't tell me you shot him, Gabby."

"No. But very nearly."

While she ate and drank, she told Maude about her encounter with Rafe Pendragon and how she had been caught and stopped by one of his friends. Wisely, she decided to omit the fact that Wyvern had stolen a kiss along the way—a very passionate, very intense kiss that she knew she would never be able to forget, and not simply because it had been her first.

"Well, I am glad Pendragon's friend had enough sense to take that pistol away from you before you could do any damage. Dear lord, if you'd shot him, you'd be in Newgate by now."

Gabriella pushed her plate aside, her hunger once more at bay. "I assumed that's where I would be regardless. Instead, he set me free. Oh, Maude, it was terrible hearing the things he and Wyvern said about my father! Even now I cannot entirely countenance the accusations they made." She met the other woman's gaze. "They told me Papa was a bully and a brute." A knot formed in her throat, her voice little more than a whisper. "They say he raped a woman and that he murdered people—more than one, including his own father. Do you think it's true what they said? Did you have any inkling my father could be such a monster?" Her heart gave a hard squeeze when she saw Maude's lashes sweep down, her response and the silence that followed speaking volumes. "If you knew, why did you not say?"

Maude sighed and met her gaze. "I didn't know it all—not about the murders anyway, though I'd heard mutterings on occasion about that wife of his and how odd it was she fell down the staircase and broke her neck. But I have to admit I never really cared for the bloke. Had a mean streak in him that came out sometimes, though thankfully never around you. Truth be told, he never really spent all that much time with you, dropping in every once in a while to cozy up with your mother for a few days, and give you a pretty trinket."

Memories of him flickered through Gabriella's mind—the big smile and the warm hug he would always give her before handing her a sack of lemon drops or taffy twists, and a china doll with a pretty face and elegant silk gown. She'd always assumed the presents were given out of love, but now she wondered. Had they merely been sops, pleasant distractions to keep her content while he dallied with Mama? The notion curdled the cheese and bread in her belly.

"You should have said, Maude," she murmured. "You should have told me what he really was instead of letting me make a fool of myself, and worse."

"I did try to stop you from hunting Pendragon, if you will remember. As for the other, the viscount had you and your mama so wrapped around that aristocratic finger of his, you couldn't see past his dazzle to the truth. Had I told you, you would never have believed me. Besides, I didn't want to hurt you. The man is dead and your mama is resting with the angels. You didn't need more pain heaped on like salt in a bloody wound."

For a long moment, Gabriella let everything she'd discovered tonight sink in, trying to adjust to the monumental shift in her reality. Suddenly, a terrible sadness engulfed her. "Lies," she said, "all of it lies."

Maude laid a hand over hers and gave a tender squeeze. "Perhaps in your papa's case, but all the rest is just as you knew it. Admittedly, your mother was wild and willful, but she loved you, more than any other person on this earth. That was real, and don't ever forget it."

Blinking back a few tears, Gabriella nodded. "I miss her, Maude."

"I know you do, dearie."

Gabriella paused, a dozen thoughts running through her mind. "He offered me a home."

Maude blinked in clear surprise. "What's this?"

"Pendragon. My uncle. He said I could come live with him and his wife and children. Of course, I told him no."

"Well, what in the world did you do that for?"

Gabriella's gaze flashed up. "Because I don't know

them, any of them." Her spine stiffened. "Besides, I have no need of his charity."

"Of course you do. From what I hear, he's richer than the king and a titled baron to boot. Just think of those fancy houses of his, better than this garret I'll say."

Gabriella had already seen his house, at least a small fraction of it, and knew the dwelling was indeed as *fancy* as Maude called it; it was the finest house in which she had ever set foot.

"Despite what he says," she argued, "they'll probably only want me as a servant, and an unpaid one at that, since that is generally what most poor relations become."

The other woman waved a hand. "Even if they do, it's an improvement over what you have now. And with Lord and Lady Pendragon, there's a chance you might meet a decent man, perhaps even be wed. I know you have no desire to follow in your mother's footsteps and tread the boards. Although that stage manager Hackett would cast you in any number of roles, including the lead, I suspect, if he thought he could gain your consent."

Indeed, I know he would, Gabriella silently agreed, fully aware of Mr. Hackett's eagerness to set her onto the stage. But as much as she loved the plays, and knew all the lines by heart after hearing them repeated for such a very long time, she had no intention of becoming an actress.

Mama's life is not for me. After a childhood spent roaming from city to town, with no real sense of home, she longed for permanence, as well as a feeling of truly belonging to a place. And Maude was right; she would like a family. A husband and children of her own, people upon whom she could depend, and on whom she could shower both her time and affection. Even more, hidden in a secret corner of her heart was a wish for love—for a man who would cherish her and whom she could adore in return. *But such notions are nothing but dreams. Aren't they?*

Without her meaning to, Tony Wyvern's devilish smile and mesmerizing blue eyes flashed into her mind. A tingle traced over her skin like a warm breeze, her pulse skipping a beat at the mere recollection of the man. After manhandling her as he'd done tonight, she ought to have been fuming, should have found herself affronted by his overly bold behavior. Yet what she felt was quite the opposite.

What a ninnyhammer I am! she decided, since she was alert enough to recognize a rakehell when she met one. Although her and Wyvern's acquaintance may have been brief, she could tell he was the sort of man who enjoyed women, relishing the pleasure their beauty and bodies could bring him. She sensed he was an elusive sort, more interested in flirting and flitting from female to female without ever pausing long enough to get ensnared by any particular one. Nonetheless, if a woman could succeed in turning the trick and capturing his unwavering attention, and if that woman could also secure his love, then she would find herself with a prize beyond measure. After all, as the old saying went, reformed rakes make the very best husbands.

But reforming Wyvern would have to be left to another woman, particularly since she doubted they would ever meet again. Aware of a resurgence of her melancholy mood, she turned her attention to back Maude.

"Take Lord Pendragon's offer, child. Don't be a fool like me."

A frown drew Gabriella's brows together. "What do you mean?"

Maude sighed, suddenly looking tired and a bit old, lines starting to fan at the corners of her eyes, skin sagging ever so slightly near her lips. In her late thirties, she was a beautiful woman still, and yet time, hard work, and poverty were wearing her thin.

"I mean," Maude continued, "that I had a choice when I was your age. A choice to stay on my parents' farm and marry one of the neighboring boys or run off and join the theater. I craved adventure and took to the road. I don't regret it, at least not in the main. The early days were fun and fine. I loved the attention and the fame, the pretty gowns and sparkling baubles received from one dashing lover after another, men who literally begged for my favors. I believe the same could be said for your mother in her prime—at least until she met Middleton. I don't believe she strayed too often after him."

No, Gabriella thought, her mother had pined for him when he was away, forever awaiting the moment he would reappear to sweep her off her feet once more.

Maude took up the pot and poured the last inch of tepid tea into her cup. "But as the years fly past, the acting roles get fewer and smaller—management makes you Nurse when you used to be Juliet, and you take whatever they'll give you and gratefully. And the men, well, they don't come around like they used to do, either. At least not the handsome ones, the wealthy ones who wanted to wrap you in silks and lace once upon a time." Glancing across, Maude met her gaze. "You know what I say is true. You've always known; that's why you've never succumbed to the lure of the footlights. Go to your family, Gabby, and be glad you have one. Let your uncle help you and don't begrudge."

A lump tightened beneath her breast. "But I can't leave you. We'll do well enough together, you'll see. I'll take on extra sewing and maybe accept a part or two from Hackett. He's always looking for a new Ophelia; I could play her in my sleep."

Maude shook her head. "I know you could, but you don't want to, and neither do I want you to." She paused for a moment. "I haven't said anything before now, but my cousin wrote to me."

"Josephine?"

The other woman smiled. "The very one. I always got on with Josephine, and well, she wants me to come to Shropshire and stay. She has those eight youngsters of hers, and she could use a spare hand. Since Hackett keeps cutting my lines and my pay along with it, I've been thinking of saying yes. I could always go out with the traveling troupe again, I suppose, but road living is hard, as you know, and I'm not up to sleeping in wagons and indifferent inns anymore."

"Oh. I hadn't realized," Gabriella replied, slightly deflated.

"Nor were you meant to. But with this offer from your uncle, well, I could go with a free heart knowing you were being looked after."

Gabriella swallowed against the mild panic that rose like a wave in her gut.

"You can come to me anytime," Maude said, as if Gabriella had spoken her fears aloud. "There will always be a place."

"I could come with you now. Surely with so many youngsters, your cousin could do with another extra set of hands."

Maude frowned. "The children sleep three in a room, and with Jo living on the soldier's wage her husband sends her, she hasn't the money to feed us both."

"But she wouldn't have to," Gabriella countered. "I would find work. With my sewing skills, I could take in mending, or even make gowns for the ladies."

"The local seamstress does that already, and I'm doubtful she would be hiring. The village is very small."

"A shop, then. Or a factory . . . there must be something I could do."

Her friend gave her a sympathetic look. "Yes, go to

your family. Working in a shop or a factory is no life for you. You'd be better off on the stage than that, and you know it."

Yes, I do know it, she thought, reality sinking in. Shropshire was no more viable a place for her than London. Maude would stay here in the city with her, of course, if she refused to go, but she would be a selfish girl indeed to stand in her friend's way, she realized. And despite her reservations, perhaps Maude was right; maybe she would be better off with her uncle. *Besides, if I don't like it,* she assured herself, *I can always run away.*

"Very well, I will go live with my uncle," Gabriella agreed. "But must I leave immediately? We have another two weeks left on the rent."

Maude smiled. "I'll need the two weeks to get ready anyway. Besides, I wouldn't give that harridan Buckles a farthing extra than she deserves. Come now, we're both tired. Let us to bed. Everything will look brighter with the sun."

Gabriella nodded, but unlike her friend, she wasn't nearly so optimistic—not about the new day tomorrow, nor any of the ones to follow.

Chapter Three

TEN EVENINGS LATER, Tony relaxed naked against a plump feather tick and pillow, the bedchamber warmed by a gently burning fire, the mellow glow of candlelight suffusing the space with an ambience he assumed had been arranged for seduction and romance. Jasmine oil perfumed the air, and a pair of half-drunk glasses of red wine rested together on a night table.

Reaching for one of them, he downed the contents, aware of a buzz inside him that had nothing to do with the spirits he'd just imbibed, nor the bout of recent, lusty sex. Beside him lay his mistress, Erika, her long blonde hair flowing over her pillow, one bare breast exposed to his view as she slept. He eyed the fulsome globe, but instead of interest, all he felt was ennui. He sighed.

London in February is a bore, he decided, especially with Rafe and Ethan Andarton gone from the city. Three days ago, Pendragon had departed for West Riding to join his family. As for Ethan, no one had seen the marquis or his new bride, Lily, since their Christmas wedding. They were still enjoying their honeymoon, no doubt, if the single letter he'd received from the man was any indication. Ethan had written a quick note saying that he and Lily were back in residence at Andarley, the marquis's country estate, and that both of them enjoyed good health and fine spirits. He had gone on to say that they were looking forward to seeing him at Rafe's estate in early March for the christening of the Pendragons' infant daughter.

Until then, Tony mused, *I am left to my own devices. It's what comes of watching friends fall in love and succumb to the bondage of the parson's noose!* Not that he had anything against their chosen brides—he quite liked both women, in point of fact. Still, the old carefree days were behind him and his two boyhood friends. Marriage and babies changed everything, as he had discovered, leaving those wise souls like himself—who preferred to avoid such entrapments—plagued in finding themselves at occasional loose ends.

Not that he had difficulty entertaining himself—he possessed a wide cadre of friends, and as much female companionship as he chose—but with most of Society still gone from the city, there were far fewer entertainments in the offing than normal. Of course, there had been that one scintillating incident in Pendragon's study, he reminded himself.

Now there is a tempting little morsel. Gabriella, he repeated, rolling her name silently on his tongue like some delectable piece of candy.

In sudden restlessness, he shifted against the mattress, his body awakening as he remembered her beauty. Her gamine face and exquisite violet eyes, and those luscious lips—he'd never tasted sweeter—sugary and delicious as a fresh baked cherry pie. Days may have passed since they'd shared a quick, stolen kiss, but the memory had in no way faded from his thoughts.

Damned shame she's Rafe's niece, he mused, *otherwise I might well have decided to pursue her.* But Rafe was a friend, and he knew better than to poach on the relative of a crony, especially when that relation was scarcely more than a schoolgirl. Gabriella might be daring and independent, cloaking herself in a façade of worldly bravado, but he knew an innocent when he saw one—and most definitely when he kissed one. Fiery and passionate she might be, with an innate eagerness to explore the sensual side of her nature, but nevertheless he could tell she was untutored in the ways of love.

Another shame, since he had a strict rule about avoiding virgins. Tempting though they might appear with their bright eyes and winning smiles, dallying with them had the potential to lead to all sorts of messy, unwanted complications—such as marriage. Many a perky debutante had tried to lure him, but he always managed to slip free of their traps. A confirmed bachelor, he had no intention of falling prey to matchmaking mamas and their eager daughters, who were wide-eyed and dreamy at the idea of becoming a duchess.

Instead he confined himself to experienced women—widows and wives who knew what he wanted and wouldn't cry foul when the affair was through. Erika was such a one, married and in the habit of taking interesting lovers. He was only the latest in a long string of affairs, her cuckolded husband unable to satisfy her extremely healthy sexual appetite.

At first, meeting for secret assignations had been amusing, especially since she was always ripe for him to take her in inventive ways and unusual locales—including one time among the library stacks at the British Museum. The games, however, were beginning to wear thin, no longer holding the same allure they once had. He was growing especially weary of avoiding her husband, Lord Hewitt. He almost felt sorry for the poor, deluded fool, cringing these days when he was required to witness the man doting on his wife with no idea what she did behind his back.

A sudden sensation of debauchery settled over him, leaving him with an urge to scrub himself with soap and lots of hot water. He cast a frowning glance at the woman curled at his hip. *I should be leaving,* he thought, aware of an abrupt longing for his own bed and clean, starch-scented sheets that didn't have so much as a drop of jasmine on them. Sitting up, he swung his legs to the floor.

Behind him Erika stretched and released a small, almost feline sound, his movement apparently having awakened her. "Hmm, where are you going?" she purred in a sleepy voice, reaching out a hand to stroke across his naked hip.

"Home. It's late."

"Not so very late," she complained, sliding her palm to caress his thigh. "Hewitt won't be back until tomorrow. Just think of all the fun we can have until then."

Instead of answering, he eased away from her touch and climbed to his feet. Crossing the room, he retrieved his discarded clothes from where they lay draped over a chair, then began to dress.

"What's wrong?" she asked, a childish pout in her voice that he had once found adorable but that now grated like a wood rasp on metal. "I haven't worn you out, have I?" she continued. "You're usually ravenous. One of the few men I know who really *can* go for hours."

He tucked his shirt into his pantaloons before fastening the buttons on both articles of clothing. "I find myself satiated at present."

"I'll bet if you come back here, I can persuade you otherwise." With a coy smile, she patted the mattress.

For a moment, he eyed the bed and the beautiful woman in it, then picked up his cravat and began tying the linen around his throat.

A set of tiny lines creased her nearly flawless face. "Why the silence? Whatever *is* the matter with you tonight?"

"Nothing. As I said, the hour grows late and it is time I

bid you farewell." Cravat secured, he slid his feet into his shoes and donned the remainder of his attire.

She gave another pout, then flopped back against the pillows. "Very well, if you must be stubborn about it. I shall see you at the opera two evenings from now I suppose," she said after a long pause. "Perhaps by then your appetite will have returned and we can find some way to appease it."

He waited, expecting a twinge of anticipation to catch hold. Instead he felt . . . nothing, only a sense of sameness—and yes, boredom. "Actually," he replied, speaking his thoughts aloud, "I do not believe I shall be at the opera."

Her scowl returned. "Oh. You have another engagement, then?"

"No. I just won't be there. Look, Erika, I wasn't planning to do this tonight, but there seems little point in dragging matters out." He slung his greatcoat over his shoulders and buttoned the frogs.

Her green eyes darkened. "Dragging what matters out? I'm not sure I comprehend your meaning."

"Oh, I think you do. Surely you have noticed a lessening of intensity between us lately."

Color flashed in her fair cheeks. "No, actually I haven't. And neither, it would seem, has that great staff of yours. From what I could tell, it didn't seem to lack for *intensity* when you were having your way with me here in this bed tonight."

He resisted the urge to sigh, at the same time putting aside any hope that matters might come to an amicable conclusion. But then breaking off affairs rarely followed a smooth course, since one party invariably wished to end the liaison while the other "did not." Clearly, Erika was in the 'did not' camp.

"I've enjoyed the past few weeks. You're a passionate

and exciting woman, but the time has come for us to part ways."

"Is there someone else?" she demanded.

"No. No one." As he said the words, an image of Gabriella whispered through his mind, her lovely face as refreshing as a warm sun on the first fine day of spring. Some glimmer of his inner musings must have been revealed, since a second later Erika's eyes narrowed, an ugly expression marring her features.

"So there *is* someone else. Tell me her name. I want to know who the little hussy is who's been diddling you behind my back. No wonder you weren't interested in me but once tonight."

"There is no other woman," he repeated in a measured tone. "But if there were, I fail to see your upset. Ours is hardly a monogamous relationship. I am free to take any lover I choose, just as you are at liberty to do the same. After all, as a married woman, you can hardly claim fidelity."

"Hewitt is of no importance," she stated, climbing out of bed, unconcerned by her nakedness as she crossed to him. "He is nothing to me, you know that. I married him for his title, nothing more. I love *you,* Tony. I haven't said it before, but I do. I . . . I would be willing to leave him for you. You have only to say the word."

He raised a brow. "Do I? So you would abandon Lord Hewitt for a life with me? And what of the scandal that would surely ensue?"

Her eyes came alive with undisguised hope. "I wouldn't care. Other couples have weathered such storms and come out all right in the end. Admittedly it would not be easy, but were I to divorce, we could truly be together. Forever."

"By *forever,* I presume you are thinking of a marriage between us? You'd like to be a duchess, would you?"

Wrapped up in the moment, she apparently missed the chill that coated his words.

"What woman would not? Oh, darling, are you asking me?" she cooed, stroking a hand over his chest. "Because I will wait for however long it takes to be together. For you, I would wait an eternity."

"I am sorry to hear that," he said, gently removing her hand, "because I have no interest in marriage. You should be well aware of my opinion on that topic. All of Society knows, I believe, since I have never made any effort to conceal my views."

She raised her chin defiantly. "All men make such claims before they are wed."

"Mine is not a claim."

"But what of children? Surely you want an heir?"

He raked her with his eyes. "My cousin can have the title and the necessity of breeding sons. I am content as I am."

"Then we will forgo children," she said with growing desperation. "It will leave us more time to be together. Just the two of us." She slid her arms around his waist.

Reaching back, he freed himself from her hold. "There is no 'two of us.' Not anymore. Erika, it's over."

Her skin paled. "Of course it's not over. If you d-don't want to marry me now, we can discuss that later. I'll send a note 'round tomorrow so we can arrange our next assignation. Perhaps one of the orangeries would be exciting. Just imagine making love among all those lush plants!"

He could imagine it. Just not with her anymore. "Good-bye," he said with a clear note of finality.

Her face changed, sudden fury sparkling in her gaze. "*Bastard!*" she spat. "I should have listened when my friends warned me what a cold, heartless beast you are. They said you relish crushing a woman's heart under your boot heel."

"Is that what they say?" he drawled in a bored voice. "As I recall, I never promised you anything more than pleasure, and that I have provided in abundance. As for being in love with me, we both know you're only in lust, though undoubtedly you would enjoy being a duchess. Despite your present anguish, I am sure you will have no difficulty finding another man to warm your bed. In the meantime, I'll send you a diamond bracelet. That should help soothe the wound, should it not?"

Glancing around, she picked up one of the forgotten wineglasses and hurled it at his head. Luckily her aim was poor, the glass and its contents shattering against the wall about two feet from him, burgundy dripping like rivulets of blood over the flocked yellow wallpaper.

He stared at the mess for a moment before striding toward the door and opening it.

She unleashed a small scream. "You'll regret this, mark my words! You'll regret what you've done to me, *Your Grace*!"

He quirked a brow at her threat, then made her an elegant bow. "Pray enjoy the opera when you next attend, Lady Hewitt."

A fresh wail and the sound of more shattering glass followed as he made his way from the house.

A week later—many miles to the north, in West Riding—the dog cart carrying Gabriella rattled to a stop at the end of a long, stone wall–lined drive. With interest, she gazed at the grand house and snow-covered fields beyond, the large edifice looking like a jewel nestled amid clusters of winter-bare trees and the rolling hills and dales that gave Yorkshire its distinctive appearance.

" 'Tis the Pendragon place on the rise just there," declared the driver, an amiable farmer who had agreed to give her a ride from the coaching inn. At the time, she had been attempting to hire some kind of conveyance—

no easy feat, considering she had only five shillings left in her pocket—when the man had overheard and offered to take her up with him. Fearing he might be her only means of reaching her uncle's house that day, she had gladly agreed.

Reaching now into her woolen cloak, she offered to give him her last few shillings. He waved the payment aside. "Keep yer money, missy. Baron takes good care 'un us around these parts. You a new maid, or some 'at?"

Or something, she silently agreed, although precisely what she was to become remained to be seen. Jumping on nimble legs to the ground, she reached up for her small traveling valise, the bag containing all her worldly possessions. With a wave, she watched the farmer set his horse and cart in motion and drive away. Swallowing against her nerves, she tightened her faded blue wool cloak to keep out the cold and started toward the house.

As she walked, she recalled her last days in London. Amid copious tears, she had bid a final farewell to Maude; only the sour expression on Mrs. Buckles's face at losing paying tenants keeping Gabriella from becoming completely maudlin. She and Maude had shared a last laugh over their disgruntled landlady before hugging, then parting to go their separate ways. Maude, of course, had promised to write; Gabriella swore to do the same, missing her friend the instant she drove away.

Heading in the opposite direction, Gabriella had gone to her uncle's townhouse, only to be informed by a gigantic ox of a man—the scar on his face worthy of a bloodthirsty pirate—that Lord Pendragon was not home. A bit of questioning produced the information that he had gone to his country estate in West Riding. To give the large man his due, he had asked if she would like to come inside and pen a message to his master. With a shake of her head, she had declined, slipping quickly away before he could prevent her.

In order to make the journey north, she had ended up pawning the last of her mother's jewelry—a gold bracelet with a single ruby heart she knew had been a gift from her father. With the knowledge of what he had truly been weighing upon her thoughts, she found she minded the jewelry's loss a great deal less than she feared she once might have done.

And so now, four days later, she was here at the Pendragon estate, about to begin a new chapter of her life. She only wished she knew whether the future would prove good or ill. Approaching the front door, she rallied her determination and forced herself to act. Drawing in a lungful of frosty air, she lifted her hand in its ordinary, knit woolen glove and rapped against the door.

A long minute later the portal opened, a very proper-looking manservant appearing in the entry. With a critical eye, the older man inspected her from the top of her plain straw bonnet to her comfortably scuffed, black leather half boots—pausing, she saw, to take note of the muddy, travel-stained condition of her cloak hem.

"Servants 'round the back," he stated without preamble. "Assuming you are here to apply for a position. I must warn you, however, that there are none to be had at present."

When he moved to close the door, she stopped him with a quick foot. "I am not here about a position," she declared. "I am come . . . I am Gabriella St. George, Lord Pendragon's niece." *Well, half-niece, and an illegitimate half at that,* she admitted to herself, but there wasn't any point in quibbling over such matters. "Please tell him I am here." *And please don't let him have changed his mind about welcoming me.*

The servant lifted a surprised brow, then stepped back to hold the door wide. "My pardon, miss. I shall inform her ladyship immediately that you are arrived."

Alarm squeezed like paste through her veins. "Oh no,

there is no need to bother her ladyship. I wish to see *Lord* Pendragon, my u-uncle."

"Lord Pendragon is out inspecting the tenant housing and won't return for some while. I shall inform her ladyship. In the meanwhile, you may have a seat in the drawing room. But first, allow me to take your luggage."

Take it where? she nearly asked, reluctant to let the valise out of her sight. "Umm, thank you, but no. I will keep it for now." *Just in case matters don't go as planned,* she thought.

The bridge of the man's nose wrinkled in obvious disapproval before he gave a faint nod and turned to lead the way. Gripping the worn leather handle of her valise in both hands, she hurried after him.

Moments later, she stood alone, the room's two great polished walnut doors closed at her back. After setting down her case, she turned in a slow circle, her lips parting as she inspected the elegant beauty of her surroundings. Decorated in soothing shades of green and blue, the refined furnishings were placed so as to capture the best of the late morning light. Fragrant warmth flowed from a massive fireplace—real logs burning in the grate instead of dirty, smoldering chunks of coal. And there were fresh flowers, masses of them arranged inside a pair of four-foot-high, painted porcelain urns. She stepped closer to admire the display, breathing in deeply to catch the scent of roses and lilies. *In February, no less!*

Behind her, the doors opened on silent hinges, followed by a whispering of silk. Turning, she beheld one of the most beautiful women she had ever seen. She wasn't sure how she had expected Lady Pendragon to look, but she knew it wasn't this exotically lovely woman with a curvaceous figure, deeply dark hair, and warm, coffee-colored eyes, with a gentle expression in them that caught Gabriella instantly off guard.

"How do you do," the woman began in soft tones, extending a hand as she glided across the plush carpeting. "I am Julianna Pendragon. Martin tells me you have come in search of my husband."

"Yes, I . . . am sorry to trouble you . . ."

"Oh, it's no trouble at all. " Lady Pendragon smiled. "I just put the baby down for her nap and my son is presently in his room killing Frenchmen—little toy ones, that is," she finished with a laugh. "Oh, but you must be exhausted from your travels. Please, please, have a seat."

Gabriella glanced behind her at the nearest chair, frowning as she saw the exquisite green damask upholstery. *I can't sit on that,* she thought, *not without fear of ruining the fabric.* "I am fine standing."

"Do not fret over a little travel dust, I won't. Though here, let me take your cloak. Martin should have seen to it when you arrived."

"Is that the man at the door?"

"Our butler, yes." With a kind yet implacable look, she waited, clearly expecting Gabriella to hand over her cloak. After a faint hesitation, Gabriella did, watching as the baroness carried the garment out to give to a servant in the hall. When she returned, Lady Pendragon motioned a hand toward the chair. "Sit, please."

Gabriella sat, trying not to be aware of the plain look of her serviceable, long-sleeved yellow wool dress beside the sophisticated cut of Lady Pendragon's gorgeous sapphire velvet gown.

Across from her, Julianna Pendragon took a seat as well, meeting her gaze for a moment. "So, you are Gabriella," she said in a quiet voice. "Gabriella St. George, did I hear Martin say?"

Her shoulders grew taut, well aware that some might say she had no right to bear her father's name, since he had never publicly acknowledged her. Yet for the whole of her life, St. George was what she had been called, her mother giving her the name when she had been a very little girl.

"*Just because your papa and I are not married doesn't mean you aren't entitled,*" her mother used to say. "*You are as much a St. George as any of the rest of that family, and a St. George you shall be.*" That and the fact that her mother had detested her own surname—Smollett—had decided the matter.

Although since learning of her father's past, Gabriella had considered changing her name—perhaps adopting one of her own creation like many in the theater did. Mama had done so, going by the stage name Annabelle LaFleur. But such flamboyant verbal plumage was not for her, and in the end she'd decided it easiest to stay with St. George. Besides, she thought, she'd never remember to answer to anything else. At least not until she married one day; then she supposed she would have no choice but to adjust to a new name.

Lifting her chin, she met Lady Pendragon's gaze. "That is correct. I am Gabriella St. George. My father was Burton St. George, Lord Middleton."

She waited for the condemnation, the superior look of a lady born in the sanctity of marriage toward one who had been conceived on the wrong side of the blanket. But none came, Julianna Pendragon's expression both understanding and accepting.

"Yes, Rafe told me of your visit to the townhouse. I am sorry for the loss of your mother. I know how difficult that can be. As for your father . . . well, I should probably say nothing."

"Did he really kidnap you?" Gabriella blurted without stopping to think.

Lady Pendragon paused. "He did, yes. And held me for ransom, though I rather doubt he ever intended to let me go free. He also tried to kill my husband. Your papa was not a nice man."

Gabriella lowered her gaze. "Yes, so everyone tells me." She clasped her hands in her lap. "Which is why I understand if you do not want me here. Lord Pendragon . . . my . . . u-uncle said I might come to him, but I can see that I should not have intruded."

"Why not? Rafe told me everything and I entirely agree. You are not to be blamed for the actions of your father, however dreadful they may have been." She paused. "Although I trust you did not come bearing a gun this time?"

Gabriella's eyes grew wide, her lips parting in surprise. "No, my lady, I did not."

"Good, then you are most welcome here. Though you should have let us know your plans, instead of running away from Hannibal that day you stopped by the house—yes, he wrote to tell Rafe. The large man with the bald head."

"And the scar," Gabriella added.

Lady Pendragon nodded her lovely head. "Just so. Had you only stayed, Rafe would have arranged for you to use one of our coaches. I hate to think of your having traveled all this distance by mail coach, and on your own, too, since you have no maid. Thank God you arrived without harm. You are well, are you not?"

"Very well, my lady."

"No more 'my lady.' You are family. From now on, you must call me Julianna, or Jules, as my siblings are wont to do. In Rafe's case, I suspect he would prefer you use his given name as well rather than uncle. Uncles, he'll say, are white-haired old men and he is far too young to be in his dotage yet," she finished, amusement twinkling in her dark, expressive eyes.

Gabriella blinked, her own eyes growing moist with unexpected emotion. Of all the things she had expected to hear, words of warmth and kind concern had not been among them. Suddenly, she was very glad she had come here, very glad indeed.

"Now," Julianna continued, "you must be hungry. Before I came downstairs, I asked Cook to prepare tea and a few cakes for us. The tray should be here any moment, unless you are too tired to eat and would rather have a lie-down? I'm having the blue room prepared for you in the family wing."

My own room in the family wing, Gabriella thought, more of her earlier fears evaporating. Suddenly a smile of genuine pleasure spread over her face. "Tea and cakes sound delightful, my lady . . . I mean, Julianna. To be honest, I . . . missed breakfast this morning." She decided not to say it was because she hadn't possessed the funds.

Julianna smiled back. "Well then, you must eat double the cake. In the meantime, you can tell me all about yourself. Rafe says your mother was an actress."

Two weeks later, Anthony Black stepped down from his coach, glad to be free of the vehicle's confines after long days of travel. The mid-March afternoon was brisk but sunny, the kind that lured people to defy the lingering chill in order to savor a long, invigorating draft of new spring air.

"Good day, Your Grace, and welcome," greeted the Pendragons' butler as he and a pair of footmen hurried forward to assist with Tony's arrival. "How was your journey? Uneventful, I hope."

"Too uneventful, Martin," Tony replied. "Downright tedious, in sections, especially given the mud that plagued us from Hertfordshire on north. But I am here now and fully prepared to enjoy the celebration. What of the others? Has anyone else made it past the morass?"

The butler smiled. "Only one other. Mrs. Mayhew, her ladyship's cousin, arrived yesterday and immediately took to her bed with a case of rheumatism. We are hopeful she will be feeling well enough to take dinner with company this evening. All the other guests are expected either today or tomorrow."

Tony nodded, then glanced around. "So where are Lord and Lady Pendragon?" Usually Rafe and Julianna came out to greet him when he arrived for a visit.

"His lordship is meeting in his study with a pair of investors who drove over from Leeds this morning. And I believe her ladyship is out taking Master Campbell for a stroll in the garden. Allow me to inform them you are here."

"No, don't trouble yourself," Tony said, waving aside the offer. "I'll just slip around back and announce myself. I know the way."

Martin inclined his gray-haired head. "As you prefer, Your Grace."

With a grin, Tony set off, hands tucked inside the pockets of his many-caped greatcoat, his boots sinking comfortably into the soft, cold ground beneath him as he walked. Birds chattered in the trees and bushes, one of them with lively yellow feathers pausing on a branch to complain about Tony's proximity, the bird's throat warbling as he sent his urgent call to the others of his flock. Amused, Tony watched for a moment, then continued on, the vast grounds of the garden stretching out before him. With the exception of a few rows of drowsy-headed white snowdrops and a handful of yellow daffodils brave enough to dare the weather, the flower beds stood dormant, green life waiting to burst forth at the faintest hint of steady spring warmth.

The garden appeared deserted—no sign of Julianna and her rambunctious two-year-old son. Moving onward, he continued his search, suddenly spying her dressed in a lovely dark green wool pelisse that blended into her surroundings like summer leaves against grass. Drawing to a halt, he stared, momentarily amazed by the sight of her most unusual position. Kneeling on the ground, her distinctly feminine posterior was pointed toward the sky, her head and shoulders stuck under an evergreen bush. Of all the situations in which he might have expected to discover Julianna Pendragon, this one would never have entered his mind.

"You may find this an impertinent question, your ladyship," he drawled, "but what are you doing down there?"

She jerked, a muffled murmur following before she began backing out from underneath the bush.

By sheer force of will, he resisted the urge to laugh. "I certainly hope Rafe doesn't know you're doing this. He wouldn't approve of finding his wife scuttling around on the cold ground on her hands and knees." He broke off as another thought suddenly occurred. "Cam's not under there, I hope."

"No," she stated in a voice that didn't sound at all like her own. Moments later her head popped out from beneath the bush, and she sat up on her knees. "I'm trying to rescue a litter of kittens. They're huddled under there and I don't want them to freeze."

Abruptly, his amusement turned to surprise as she tipped back her head—because the eyes that met his own weren't the brown he'd been expecting, but rather a stunning shade of violet.

Chapter Four

"YOU!" HE SAID.

Raising a hand to shield her eyes against the bright sunlight, Gabriella peered up at Wyvern towering above her. Even crouched beneath a bush as she'd been moments ago, she had instantly recognized his voice, the rich timbre and deep, whiskied cadence sending a warm tingle through her that fought the cold breeze tugging at her cloak.

As she knelt before him now, her pulse gave a funny little hop, an appreciative sigh rising to her lips that she managed to repress only by sheer dint of will. *I don't know how it's possible,* she marveled, *but I do believe he's even handsomer in the daylight than he was in the darkness that evening in Rafe's study.* His hair was still a dark, almost satiny black, and yet in the sunshine she detected strands of red that glinted like a simmering, secret fire. His midnight-blue eyes were mesmerizing, more vibrant and intense than before, while his classic, patrician features made her spin fancies, wondering if he might have stepped out of some great masterwork highlighting the gods. And though she knew it was likely just a trick of her present, awkward angle, he appeared taller than her memory of him, his shoulders seeming wide as a doorway beneath the fine, black wool of his greatcoat, his long feet and legs planted sturdy as a pair of oaks inside his polished leather Hessians.

"Yes," she replied, finding her voice. "Though you might do better to call me Gabriella or Miss St. George rather than 'you' during your visit here. I assume you have come for the christening." She had known a great many people would be arriving for the event, but hadn't realized, until now, that Wyvern would be among their number.

"Quite correct," he said, "I have come to witness the baptism. But pray allow me to begin again and greet you properly this time." He paused and executed a bow. "Good day, Miss St. George. May I say it is an unexpected pleasure to see you again."

"Thank you, Mr. . . . I mean, Wyvern—or should I perhaps call you my lord?"

A curious expression passed over his handsome face. "No, Wyvern will do at present. I must say I am surprised to find you here. I was not aware you had changed your mind and decided to take Rafe up on his offer after all."

She glanced downward at her hands. "Yes, my . . . um . . . circumstances changed and I decided this would be best." Her gaze rose once more to meet his own. "Rafe and Julianna have been very kind, more than I ever imagined or likely deserve."

A slow smile crossed his mouth. "Oh, I am sure you are quite deserving if for no other reason than you arrived unarmed this time. At least I am assuming you did," he teased.

"Hmm, yes. As I recall, someone confiscated my weapon. Although I am sure I could find a suitable firearm or two inside the house should such be required. Might I be requiring protection, Wyvern?"

A laugh burst from his sensuous lips. "Not at the moment, no, but if you do acquire another pistol, I could always be persuaded to disarm you again."

At his comment, she remembered how it had felt to be pressed against his body, as well as the heated, delectable slide of his mouth against her own. Suddenly too warm beneath her cloak, she pushed away such thoughts. "So, do I surmise that you came in search of Lady Pendragon? She took Cam upstairs to the nursery a couple of minutes ago."

"While you stayed here."

"Of course. I couldn't leave, not after finding these kittens. That's what persuaded Julianna to take Cam inside. He wanted to crawl under and get them." As if on cue, a round of high-pitched mews sounded from beneath the bush.

Wyvern bent slightly at the waist in an attempt to see, but the little cats were well concealed inside their thicket of greenery. "Surely their mother will return to care for them."

"I am sure she will, but I heard she took a fright this morning after one of the kittens was nearly trampled by a horse. That's when she moved them out of the stables and apparently stuck them here."

"If she's with them, they will be fine."

"Not if it snows this evening as Cook predicts," she pronounced with a firm shake of her head. "They must be moved where it is warm and safe. Now, hold out your arms."

He gave her an arch look. "For what purpose, might I inquire?"

"You will see. Arms, please," she persisted.

He raised an arrogant brow as if unused to being given orders, then with a slight twist of his lips, he stuck his arms straight out toward her.

"No, not like that," she corrected. "Fold them a bit."

Still on her knees, she demonstrated the shape with her own arms.

"Ah, I begin to see." Repeating the motion, he formed a kind of cradle against his chest. "Might I proffer a suggestion, however? Rather than use me as a basket, why do we not go inside the house and find a real one?"

Before Tony had a chance to say more, Gabriella ducked beneath the bush again and stretched out onto her stomach. In amazement, he watched her, unable to resist leaning closer to get a better view of her very attractive bottom as it wiggled beneath the folds of her cloak.

I suppose I ought not to notice such things, he mused, *since she is Rafe's niece and all. But how is a man expected to ignore such a fine show when the performance is going on right before his eyes?*

Agile as a cat herself, Gabriella emerged a few moments later, a trio of crying kittens tucked against her chest. "Here," she said, rising smoothly to her knees, then onto her feet. "Take them. There are more." Gently depositing the squirming noisemakers into his arms, she dove downward again.

"Good God!" he commented aloud, wondering how many more there might be. Holding the kittens, he hoped none of his little charges would try to escape. But the black-and-white balls of fluff simply meowed, terror shining in their small, round green eyes. "Hush, now," he murmured, "I've got you and there is nothing to fear."

"These are the last," she declared in a triumphant if faintly winded voice, when she reemerged a minute later. Cradled in her arms were two more kittens—one with bright orange stripes, the other gray with patches of white. Following their siblings' lead, they added to the chorus of high-pitched meows.

"Shall I take those as well?" he asked over the racket.

"Five seems rather much. I'll carry my two."

"And where is it we are headed? Back to the stables?"

Her eyes widened. "Gracious no! Their mama will only move them out again. No, I'm taking them into the house."

A laugh escaped him. "Are you sure that's a good idea? After all, with so many guests arriving, the staff isn't going to appreciate having a litter of kittens underfoot, to say nothing of Rafe and Julianna."

A momentarily wounded expression crossed her pretty face. "Rafe and Julianna like animals; Julianna told me so herself not twenty minutes ago. And the kittens won't be underfoot, not in my bedroom. I'm sure they will disturb no one there."

Her bedroom! He considered pointing out a few difficulties inherent in such an arrangement, but at her look decided he would be better off holding his tongue for now. "Lead on, then. I am yours to command."

She flashed him a smile that made his blood heat—leaving him suddenly glad his arms were full of kittens—before she turned and started across the garden. Managing his furry cargo, he allowed her to precede him toward a rear garden doorway. Just as he reached out to turn the knob, a streak of orange and black caught his eye. Glancing to his left, he found a calico cat seated a few feet distant, keenly monitoring their progress.

"Our missing mama cat, I presume," he observed in a low voice.

Gabriella nodded. "I knew Aggie would turn up. Leave the door open and we'll see if she follows."

Again, Tony held his tongue as they moved inside. He and Gabriella were halfway up the stairs when the cat darted in, trailing them at a run. She continued to follow a few paces behind all the way to Gabriella's bedchamber.

Inside the room, Gabriella carefully placed her two kittens onto the plush Aubusson carpet, far enough from the fireplace to protect them yet close enough to still give them some warmth.

"There you go," she cooed to the adult cat. "There are your babies."

Tony crossed the room and stood silent as Gabriella plucked the kittens out of his arms and set them, one by one, next to their siblings. As soon as all five were reunited, their mother joined them, purring out her pleasure.

"I'll find a basket and lay an old blanket inside for a bed," she said. "And a wooden box with some gardening sand inside should do for their personal needs until they are all old enough to go outside with their mama." Turning, she sent him another smile. "Thank you for helping me, Wyvern."

He smiled back. "You are quite welcome. Though you may not be thanking me when you awaken tomorrow morning with six cats in your bed."

"Oh, they won't be. They'll stay in their basket."

I wouldn't be too certain of that, he decided, casting a glance toward the large tester bed with its elegant blue counterpane. Unbidden, he envisioned her lying there beneath the fine linen sheets, her long, dark hair spread over the pillows in glorious silken waves, while kittens played around her, making her laugh. His loins tightened at the image, and he became far too aware how very much he would like to be here in this room to see if such a tableau actually developed. Abruptly, he forced himself back to the moment. "I should be going."

As if only then realizing the impropriety of being alone with him inside her bedroom, a light blush spread upward over her cheeks. "Yes, I suppose you ought."

But instead of leaving, he let himself enjoy the sight of her lovely face, her translucent skin dusted with pink—and something else, now that he took a good look. "You've a smudge," he remarked.

"Oh, do I? Where?" Raising a hand, she tried—and failed—to remove the mark.

"Here. Allow me," he urged. Stepping closer, he placed the tips of two fingers ever so lightly against the curve of her right cheekbone and stroked the spot. Meeting her gaze, he watched her pupils dilate, her lips parting on a nearly inaudible sigh. Tracing their movement, he wondered if her mouth tasted even half as delicious as he remembered, like the sweetest, most satisfying delicacy ever made.

How easy it would be to find out! he thought. *Only two inches closer and she would again be mine for the taking. But no, I cannot,* he sighed inwardly, forcing himself to recall his pledge to think of her as a little sister. Of course such a promise was the height of absurdity, since no matter how he tried, he knew he would never be able to think of Gabriella St. George as a sister. On the other hand, he supposed that didn't mean he couldn't at least make the attempt to treat her as such.

Dropping his hand he stepped back. "There you are," he said in a brisk tone. "All gone."

She blinked as if coming out of a momentary trance. "Oh . . . I . . . my thanks . . . Wyvern."

He made her a bow. "Your servant, Miss St. George. I shall see you at dinner tonight, I expect."

"Yes. Until then."

With a nod, he allowed himself one last look, then turned and strode out of the room.

"We give her the name Stephanie Charlotte," Julianna Pendragon declared, the maternal pride and happiness in her gentle voice ringing out through the parish church.

From her own seat on one of the wooden pews that held a number of invited guests, Gabriella observed the proceedings and the group clustered around the baptismal font. Among them were Rafe, Julianna, and their infant daughter, of course. On Julianna's right stood her sister, Maris, and her friend Lily Andarton, the Marchioness of Vessey, both women having agreed to serve as godmothers. Although only one was required, little Stephanie Pendragon would have two godfathers as well, Ethan Andarton, the Marquis of Vessey, and Wyvern, who looked suave yet respectfully somber attired in a crisp black tailcoat and pantaloons, his linen a pristine white.

"I baptize thee in the name of the Father, and of the Son, and of the Holy Ghost. Amen," the minister recited as he gently anointed the infant's head with water. Shocked at the wetting, the baby let out an indignant wail that echoed off the church's stone walls. Smiles and a few laughs ensued, everyone saying amen.

As the service continued, Gabriella watched the members of the christening party, her lips tightening whenever her gaze happened upon Wyvern—or should she say the *Duke of Wyvern*. Even now, she cringed to remember what had happened after dinner last evening.

The meal had gone well—fifteen family members and friends gathered around the table to enjoy delicious food and drink amid smiles and laughter. Gabriella had found herself surprisingly relaxed, amazed once again at how thoroughly she had been accepted into the Pendragon family. Since her arrival two weeks before, the entire household had taken her under its collective wing, from Rafe and Julianna, who treated her as if she really was family whom they had known forever, to the servants, who were always ready to assist her, even when she told them she could manage for herself.

Once dinner concluded, the entire party had retired to the drawing room, the gentlemen having decided to forgo a separate session of cigars and port on this occasion. Cordials, tea, and coffee were served, together with a tray of sweetmeats that Gabriella found herself unable to resist. She was savoring a particularly toothsome piece of pecan-laden divinity when the butler, Martin, approached Wyvern, stopping to offer him the snifter of brandy he carried atop a polished silver tray.

"Will there be anything further, Your Grace?" he asked.

"Not at present, thank you," Wyvern replied as he accepted the glass.

With a tiny frown, Gabriella laid the sweet she held onto her plate, then looked across at Wyvern. "Pardon me, Wyvern, but why does everyone keep calling you *Your Grace,* as if you were a duke or some such?"

An audible silence fell over the entire company before Julianna leaned forward from where she sat on the couch. "That is because he *is* a duke, my dear," she said in a kindly tone. "Did you not realize?"

Heat washed into her cheeks, her gaze dropping to the floor rather than see them all stare.

"There are many days," Wyvern quipped, breaking the silence, "when I sorely wish I was *not* a duke. Being toad-eaten, even when you're using the privy, can grow quite tiresome."

She'd laughed along with everyone else, and yet afterward a measure of her embarrassment lingered, a tight sensation forming inside her chest that she'd recognized as burgeoning affront. Undoubtedly she'd made a cake of herself by blurting out her question in such a public manner, but she would never have done so if Wyvern had been courteous enough to tell her who he really was. And it wasn't as if he'd lacked the opportunity to reveal his title, particularly considering she had asked him earlier that same day if she should call him "my lord."

Call me Wyvern, he'd drawled. *Wyvern, my eye!*

All this morning, she'd scarcely been able to look his way without ruffling up, reminded each time she did what a rube she had appeared before one and all. Everyone else seemed to have forgotten the incident, but even though she knew she should do the same, she couldn't erase it from her mind.

Glancing up, she tried to focus her attention on the final moments of the christening ceremony, but as she did, her gaze met his. To her consternation, heat crept over her skin, the tight feeling returning to her chest. Needing to look away, yet unable to do so, she watched as he lifted a single dark eyebrow in silent inquiry.

Her mouth firmed, and before she knew what she meant to do, she raised one of her eyebrows back, angling her chin in his direction with a challenging tilt.

His lips twitched, eyes widening in obvious surprise—and a bit of humor, if she was not mistaken. If he thought to intimidate her with his elevated status, he was in for a sad disappointment. *Duke or dustman,* she thought, *his title makes no difference to me.* If only she could say the same for the man himself, a shiver of sensual awareness rippling through her.

Luckily, the baby chose that moment to exercise her lungs by letting out another lusty wail. Breaking eye contact, Gabriella glanced down and studied the pale blue velvet skirt of her gown—one of five beautiful new frocks Julianna had ordered made for her during the past two weeks. Then, with a few last words from the minister, the christening was finished. Climbing to her feet with the other guests, she soon made her way from the church.

Later that afternoon, Tony stood in the Pendragons' drawing room, listening to Julianna's brother, Harry; her brother-in-law, retired Major William Waring; and his friend Ethan debate the finer points of horse breeding. Considering Tony owned a prosperous stable of his own—praised by many as one of the finest in England—he would normally have been immersed in the conversation. Instead he found himself distracted, his gaze and thoughts drifting often across the room toward a particular sable-haired female.

Swallowing a mouthful of robust red claret, he surreptitiously watched Gabriella where she sat talking with the ladies. After his silent, visual exchange with her at the church this morning, he'd assumed they would have an opportunity to speak. But each time he moved in her direction, she somehow moved in an opposite one.

He didn't think her elusiveness was deliberate, though he had taken note of the fact that they'd ended up with nearly the whole of the dining room table between them during nuncheon. Despite the distance, however, he'd caught her glance his way a time or two, in between bites of rosemary chicken, roast beef, and a wealth of delectable accompaniments. When he'd caught her looking again over a dessert of brandied ginger cake, he hadn't been able to contain himself. Licking a dollop of whipped cream off his fork, he'd winked, grinning as her cheeks grew dusky, her lips drawing together in the same adorable line she'd worn earlier in the church. Smiling around another forkful of cake, he'd made himself cease teasing her—for the time being, anyway.

"So what do you think, Tony?" Harry Davies, the Earl of Allerton, asked, breaking into his musings.

Blinking to clear his thoughts, he stared at the three men who awaited his answer. "Think about what?" he drawled, pausing to quaff another long swallow of claret.

"About taking in a round of shooting tomorrow, of course," the younger man returned. "Have you not been listening?"

Quite obviously he had not, since he'd completely missed the conversational shift from horses to pistols. Ethan gave him an inquiring look, which he returned with confident sangfroid. "Ah, well, so long as the winds hold fair and the weather continues to moderate as it seems to be doing, a bit of target practice sounds most agreeable."

Allerton nodded his approval. "Good. We'll gather the men in the afternoon, then. We thought the ladies might enjoy a spot of archery as well."

"A fine idea," he concurred.

Across the room, Gabriella rose to her feet. He watched as she crossed to the refreshment table, where a pitcher of lemonade and a decanter of wine had been set out for those not wishing tea or coffee.

"If you gentlemen will excuse me," he said, waggling his empty glass. "I find myself in need of a fresh libation."

With good-natured smiles, they waved him on his way as they returned to their conversation—politics this time. On the other side of the room, Beatrix Nevill's husband had Rafe cornered, engaged in a discussion of the economy, judging by the serious cast to Rafe's face. A self-made millionaire, Rafe was every bit as successful a financier as Rothschild himself. Well aware of Rafe's business acumen, Lord Nevill never missed an opportunity to pick his brain for investment tips. Strolling in the opposite direction, Tony made his way across the room.

At the refreshment table, Gabriella lifted to her lips the glass of lemonade she'd just poured. Overwarm after sitting near the fireplace, she enjoyed the cool, refreshing tang of the drink. As she took a second swallow, a tingle skittered over her spine, letting her know she was no longer alone. Lowering the glass, she turned her head and met the intense blue gaze of the Duke of Wyvern. At the reminder of his title, her mouth tightened again. *"Your Grace,"* she greeted.

"Miss St. George." He smiled, then picked up the crystal decanter from the table and filled his own glass. As he did, she caught sight of the ruby signet ring he wore on the little finger of his right hand, the stone's color reminiscent of the dark red wine in his goblet. "Enjoying a draught of lemonade, I see," he commented as he replaced the stopper. "I'm curious to know if the kitchen maid who prepared it failed to add enough sugar?"

She cast him a puzzled glance. "No, the lemonade is quite sweet. Why do you ask?"

"Just taking note of your countenance. The present set of your mouth denotes what one might describe as annoyance. Are you annoyed, Miss St. George?" His eyes twinkled, a teasing quality in his tone.

So he finds this amusing, does he? she thought, her jaw growing taut. "Not at all, Your Grace. Though were I annoyed, as you say, I should think you would have no difficulty recognizing the cause, Your Grace."

He raised a brow and sipped his wine. "Oh? How so? And pray cease adding 'Your Grace' to every sentence you utter."

She feigned innocence. "Why ever not, Your Grace? Is that not the proper manner in which I ought to address you, Your Grace? Since you are a duke, Your Grace. I have no wish to offend, Your Grace, none at all . . . Your Grace."

"Enough, minx," he said, setting his glass onto the table. "Your point is duly noted, though to my recollection you are the first female I have ever met who complained at discovering that I am a duke."

"Oh, do you often fail to inform women of your title? '*Call me Wyvern,*' " she said, pitching her voice in the lowest drawl she could manage.

He grinned at her attempt to imitate him.

"You might have mentioned that little fact, you know," she continued in her normal tone. "You might have said something before I acted the dunce in front of everyone here at the house."

A somber gleam came into his eyes, the smile disappearing from his mouth. "You are right, and for that, I most sincerely beg your pardon. But you see, I rather liked the novelty of you seeing me first as a man, rather than a title."

"Oh."

Such an idea had never occurred to her. Remembering his remark about being toadied, she supposed he must encounter many people who curried his favor and attention for no other reason than his status; such was the way of the world. How sad that he should be treated differently simply because of his elevated position in the nobility. Then again, she could feel only a limited amount of sympathy for him, since his privileged life gave him benefits the likes of which most could only dream. She was sure he had never been compelled to ration coal for the fireplace, nor skip a midday meal because there wasn't enough money for food that week.

Since coming to the Pendragons, she no longer bore those burdens either, she realized. Maude had been right to force her to get past her fears and accept their kindness and hospitality, just as Wyvern had been right to tell her the truth about her father, painful as that knowledge had been and continued to be. By rights, she should resent His Grace, the Duke of Wyvern—even dislike him, she supposed—yet somehow she found she could do neither. And if she held no grudge against him on such a grievous score, how could she possibly continue to do so because he had not told her he was a duke? With that realization, the angry knot inside her stomach began to unwind.

"Still," she persisted, returning to their discussion regarding the omission of his title. "You might have said."

"Yes, I might," he admitted. "But I did not lie when I told you to call me Wyvern. That is how I am known to those of my acquaintance, with the exception of a few intimates who use my given name, Anthony—or Tony, as I prefer to be called." A slow smile curved again over his attractive mouth, his voice lowering to a honeyed rumble. "You have my leave to call me Tony as well, if you like. Particularly when we are alone."

Her heart went *th-thump* inside her breast. Sternly, she willed the wayward organ to behave. "I do not imagine we will have much occasion for such a circumstance."

"Oh, one never knows." He gave her another smile that sent tingles rushing all the way to her toes.

Sipping her lemonade, Gabriella found herself rather hoping he was right.

Chapter Five

"WELL DONE, TONY! Another fine shot," Rafe declared the following afternoon. His assessment was quickly echoed by the five other men gathered on the lawn outside the house for their planned shooting match.

"Truly excellent," Lord Nevill stated. "Manton would be proud to see one of his pistols used to such fine effect." Considering the older man's inability to hit more than one out of every three practice wafers, his remarks were gracious indeed, Tony decided.

"Thank you, gentlemen," Tony replied, as he added fresh powder and shot to the barrel of his weapon. Wiping the gun clean with a soft cloth, he set the pistol carefully aside. "But I only won this round by a couple of points. The match could have gone to any of us. The outcome was no more than a rare measure of luck on my part."

"No luck about it," Ethan disputed, his and Rafe's second- and third-place scores having come in several points behind their friend's. "You, Tony, are what's known as a crack shot."

"Quite right. Wish we'd had you on the battlefield while we were fighting Boney," William Waring added, his own skillful aim apparently unaffected by the loss of an arm during the recently ended conflict on the Continent. "You'd have sent the French running."

"Undoubtedly," Harry concurred.

"Enough, enough." Tony threw up a hand. "Otherwise my head may puff up to the size of a balloon and explode."

All of them laughed, the sound drifting away on the mild breeze. Overhead the sun shone down out of a clear blue sky, the temperature was pleasant, requiring no more than light coats.

"The ladies seem to be having a fine time," Lord Nevill remarked, gazing a number of yards to the left where several archery targets had been arranged. "Good heavens, what a shot!"

"Who made it?" Tony inquired, turning to watch as well.

"From what I can see, the archer appears to be Miss St. George. By Jove, she's hit that bull's-eye dead on again."

Intrigued, Tony watched with the rest of them as Gabriella calmly loaded an arrow into her bow and drew back the string. Her third shot hit the target with the same perfect aim as its predecessors. Without waiting to discuss the matter, he set off toward her. At his back, the other men followed.

"Where in the world did you learn to shoot like that?" Lily Andarton, was asking Gabriella as Tony came within hearing range.

"Yes," Julianna said. "I've never seen anyone who could hit the target like you. I don't believe you have missed once since all of us began."

Gabriella relaxed her stance, lowering the bow she held to her side. "Oh, well, it is only because I have had a great deal of practice."

"Really? How did you come by that?" Maris Waring inquired in a curious voice from where she stood before her own target.

"My . . . um . . . mother's theater company sometimes played in the same town as a circus during the summers.

There was a man there who could shoot flaming arrows through hoops while he stood on the back of a galloping horse."

"My word!" Beatrix Nevill declared, setting her bow aside to join the conversation. "How amazing!"

Gabriella gave a tiny smile. "Yes, Mr. Stanley was quite a marvel. He was known as the Stupendous Stanley, and he could quite literally hit anything he wanted with his arrows. I watched him every afternoon for a week before I got up the nerve to ask if he would teach me."

"And obviously, he did," Lily said.

"Yes, though only after a great deal of cajoling. I was but ten at the time, and he was reluctant to waste his efforts on a girl."

Striding up to the group, Tony stopped. "Your abilities show that his attentions were far from a waste."

Her eyes flashed up to his own, their color luxurious and soft as pansies. "Hallo, Your Grace. What brings you and the other gentlemen here? I thought you were firing pistols."

"We were, but had to come see your remarkable prowess with a bow and arrow. May I say you are indeed a marvel."

A faint smile turned up the edges of her lovely mouth. "I suppose you may."

"And may I also inquire as to how far you can shoot? You have stirred my curiosity." *Among other things*, he couldn't help but add to himself.

She paused and glanced around at all the eyes upon her. "Oh, I wouldn't know. A few yards."

"From what I have observed, I suspect a few yards is an understatement. The targets are set now at twenty feet, I believe. Do you think you can do thirty?"

"Well, I—"

"Give it a try," he encouraged. "There is never any

harm in trying, is there? You, young man," Tony called toward one of the footmen who had accompanied the party outdoors. "Move Miss St. George's target back ten feet more."

With a nod of his head, the servant hurried to reset the straw bale.

"Your Grace, I'm not sure—"

"Wyvern," he reminded, lowering his voice. "And don't turn shy on me now. I only want to see what you can do. All of us want to see, I believe."

"I have to confess, I do," Rafe said, folding his arms over his chest. "Give it your best shot, Gabriella," he encouraged.

"Yes, yes," the others cheered.

She glanced around again, her gaze uncertain. "Well, if that is what all of you want, then I shall make the attempt."

In the distance, the footman finished his work and moved well out of the way. Lifting her bow, Gabriella assumed a marksman's stance and set her arrow. Slowly, she raised the bow and drew back the string, her arm held taut, elbow cocked appropriately as she sighted her aim. A second later, the arrow went flying, a solid thud resounding as it hit its mark dead in the center.

"Bravo!" Rafe said, several others murmuring their approval.

Tony studied the target for a moment. "I knew that would be too easy for you. Shall we try for fifty this time?"

Once again the target was set, and once again Gabriella hit the bull's-eye squarely in the center.

"One hundred feet!" Tony declared. "Can you do one hundred?" Meeting her gaze, he saw a spark of true competition glitter in her violet-blue eyes, her gamine face alive with an undisguised enthusiasm that showed she had warmed to the game.

"Move the target and we shall see," she agreed, flashing him a confident little grin.

A pair of minutes later, she made yet another perfect shot. She was laughing at her achievement and accepting another round of congratulations when Tony found himself challenging her once more. "Double it again," he said. "A real test of skill this time."

The chatter faded to an abrupt halt.

"I say, that seems a bit much, don't you think, Wyvern?" Lord Nevill protested. "Most men could not even reach such a distance. I believe all of us will eagerly attest to Miss St. George's superlative aptitude with the bow."

For a moment, Tony paused to consider. *Am I pushing her too hard?* Clearly, his dare was a mighty one, and there was a great chance she would fail this time. Yet, for some reason that not even he fully understood, he wanted to know exactly how good she was. Could she make the sensational shot, or was it beyond even her obvious talent?

"Two hundred feet," he repeated. "Unless you would rather not, Miss St. George. I leave the decision entirely up to you."

She tossed him a look he couldn't fully read, her eyes narrowed slightly in obvious indecision. "And if I win?"

"Ah, a wager," Harry chimed. "I love a good wager." At his statement, Rafe and Julianna both turned their heads to fix him with a look. "Not that I am in the habit of indulging in such sport," he stated in a rush. "Still, there can be no harm in watching others have a go, can there?"

"None at all," Rafe agreed. "Particularly when money is not in the offing."

Tony suppressed a smile. "In that spirit, I challenge Miss St. George to make one final bull's-eye at a distance of two hundred feet. If she succeeds, I will grant her the boon of her choice, payment of which she may collect from me at any time, as it suits her pleasure."

"And if I miss the shot?" she asked, her pretty chin angling up a notch.

Ah, if she misses? he mused. He knew the prize he'd like to extract from her—his blood warming imperceptibly at the notion. But he supposed demanding a passionate kiss wasn't the sort of bargain one made with an innocent young lady, particularly not in the presence of relations and friends. Besides, he really needed to exercise stricter control over himself when it came to the beautiful Gabriella St. George and cease this penchant for flirtation, no matter how sublime such a pastime might be.

He gazed upward, momentarily tracing the path of a meandering cumulus cloud as he considered the issue. "Well," he drawled as he lowered his eyes to hers, "if you fail to make your shot, you must promise to take a dish of tea with me tomorrow afternoon in the drawing room."

"Tea? That is all?" Her shoulders dipped, her eyes widening in apparent surprise—and if he wasn't mistaken, disappointment. *Precisely what,* he wondered, *had she been expecting me to suggest?*

"Yes," he replied, forcing down a roguish grin. "Just tea."

She stared at him for a long moment. "Well, in that case, I accept."

Excited anticipation traveled through the group as all of them waited for the straw target to be repositioned, a second footman trotting out from the house in order to aid the first man in his task.

"You can do it, Gabriella!" Lily urged, a spirited expression on her face that complimented the fiery color of her hair.

"That's right, we're behind you," Julianna agreed, clasping her hands between her breasts in eager expectation.

"If I am not mistaken, I believe I have just been slighted," Tony complained in teasing affront. "I assumed, based upon our long acquaintance, that you would support *me.*"

"Oh, we would under other circumstances," Julianna explained. "But we ladies have to stick together, since you gentlemen have a habit of winning far too often. I can't wait to see her put that arrow in the target."

"Nor I," Maris concurred. "We're all rooting for you, Gabriella."

"Go get 'em, Miss St. George," Beatrix Nevill added.

A fresh round of laughter ensued.

"Men, what say you?" Tony scanned his fellows. "Are you with me?"

"Of course," Ethan agreed. "Though I must admit I'd like to see her manage the shot."

Rafe shook his head. "I remain neutral and will gladly congratulate whoever proves the victor."

Although he remained silent about his feelings on the matter, Tony secretly hoped she made the shot too—though at such a great distance, the odds were decidedly not in her favor.

Gabriella grew deadly serious. Quiet fell as she studied the site, taking her time to evaluate the shot. She even went so far as to remove her pelisse so nothing would interfere with her aim before holding up a single dampened finger in order to test the wind. At length, she took up her bow, reached for a fresh arrow, and slid it into place. As she once more assumed the proper archer's stance, everyone held their breath, not so much as a bird daring to cheep. Drawing a deep breath, she drew back the bowstring.

Time slowed, each second ticking past in a syrupy flow.

In the blink of an eye, she released the arrow, the weapon making a hissing noise as it rushed toward the straw bale and the round target, which looked very small from where they all stood. The arrow struck with a solid impact. For a long moment, though, no one could tell if it had hit square in the target's center. A footman hurried forward to check, waving his arms a second later and shouting confirmation that she had indeed scored a bull's-eye.

A wild cheer exploded, the women hurrying to engulf her in a group hug. Gabriella came up laughing, an expression of happy amazement on her face. Not to be outdone, the men approached to bow over her hand, Rafe moving to pat her on the back with beaming pride and approval.

"By Jove, Miss St. George," Harry remarked. "You're a regular William Tell. If only we had an apple, you could shoot it off someone's head."

Gabriella chuckled. "I would be happy to, Lord Allerton, if one of you would care to volunteer." A wide grin teased her pink lips as she turned and found Tony's gaze. "Perhaps you, Your Grace?"

Gasping laughter echoed in the air. Good-naturedly, Tony smiled. "Admittedly your skill is impressive. However, I fear that is one wager on which I must pass."

"But what if that is my chosen boon?" she inquired.

The unexpected retort made him pause. "If that is the case," he drawled, "then I would beg your leave to go in search of an extremely large apple."

Laughter rippled among everyone again.

Happy excitement glittered like stars in Gabriella's eyes, her voice dropping to an almost intimate murmur. "Do not worry, Wyvern, I shall retain my boon for now.

One never knows when such a favor will come in handy."

"Very true," he replied. "I look forward to the day you decide to claim it."

A moment later, Lord Nevill stepped forward to interrupt. "What a superb display of talent, Miss St. George, quite extraordinary! I realize guns aren't in the common way for ladies, but have you ever had occasion to fire a pistol?"

Tony watched her gaze flash between his own and Rafe's before she turned to face Lord Nevill. "Actually, my lord, I have. The Great Moncrief himself taught me how to shoot."

"Good heavens! You truly are a marvel of your sex, aren't you? Is your ability with firearms at all comparable to your skill with a bow?"

"I've a fair aim."

"I'll bet it's more than fair. Oh, I say, you and Wyvern should have a match between you. I'd love to see that. What do you think, Your Grace?"

Before Tony could respond, Julianna broke into the conversation. "I think His Grace and Gabriella will have to schedule such a competition for another day. I have just been informed that our nuncheon is ready, and Cook will be quite put out if we are late."

Nevill, taking the hint, made a small bow. "Of course, Lady Pendragon. One dare not offend the staff, particularly one's cook. I hope Miss St. George will have the opportunity to delight us with her prowess at small arms at a later date."

Turning, all of them began to stroll toward the house, Lily sliding her arm through Gabriella's so she could question her further on her archery technique. Tony followed several paces behind, out of hearing range.

Rafe fell into step beside him. "Seems as if I owe you yet another measure of gratitude," Rafe said.

Tony raised a brow. "For what?"

"For disarming my niece that night in London. The girl shoots arrows like an Amazon princess. I tremble to imagine what she can do with a gun."

He chuckled. "As you said yourself, she would never have gone through with it."

"No. She's a sweet young woman. Still, I'm relieved matters transpired as they did, since I have the feeling Gabriella could shoot the cork out of a bottle and not break the glass."

"Now, there's a trick I'd like to see."

Rafe paused, tucking his hands into his pockets. "Perhaps I shouldn't mention it, but I could not help but notice the way she was looking at you."

"Oh?" Tony replied, striving for an even tone. "How is that?"

"With nascent infatuation. Tread carefully there, my friend. I do not wish to see her hurt."

"Don't worry, she won't be. She's far too young, Rafe. Besides, you know my rule about innocent, just-out-the-schoolroom misses. I steer well clear of such lures." *At least I always have before,* he mused, pushing aside the hint of guilt that whispered between his ears. "She's only testing her wings and having a little meaningless fun. I'm sure it's nothing over which you need be concerned."

"No, I suppose not." Visibly relaxing, Rafe gave him a solid pat on the shoulder. "Thankfully, I can trust you. Julianna and I have decided to bring her up to London next month, and let her have a Season. We're hoping she'll take, have fun at all the parties and entertainments. Who knows, maybe she'll meet a decent young man or two, someone confident enough that her parentage won't bother him. If she falls in love, mayhap she'll even make a match. Of course, that will be strictly up to her. We're in no hurry to lose her."

Marriage! He'd never even considered such a notion,

not in Gabriella's case. Still, he supposed he was being naïve, since girls her age married all the time. But why did he care? It wasn't as if he had any designs upon her himself. Even if she was one of the loveliest, most vivacious and charming young women he'd ever had the occasion to meet.

Lord, I need to return to London soon, he decided. Luckily, only three days remained and the house party would be over.

" . . . which is why I'm hoping I can count on you," Rafe was saying when Tony's attention returned to his friend.

"Count on me how?"

"To keep a vigilant eye on her, of course. Despite her worldliness on many matters, she is still an innocent and lacks in experience with men. In spite of her illegitimacy—or perhaps because of it—I fear there may be a few unscrupulous bounders hoping to take advantage. I want to make sure none of them has the chance."

"They won't," Tony promised, one of his hands curling into a fist at his side. "I'll be on the lookout to turn them away."

"Again, I owe you my thanks." Rafe smiled.

Reaching the house, they stepped inside the main hallway. As Tony walked upstairs to change clothes for nuncheon, he reviewed his conversation with Rafe, vowing again to follow through on his promise. But as he let himself into his guest bedroom suite, he found himself pondering a far more dangerous question.

While I am busy protecting Gabriella from other men, he wondered, *who will be protecting her from me?*

Chapter Six

TWO MORNINGS LATER, Gabriella tossed down her watercolor brush, then shoved the paper aside. "Faugh, what a mess! I give up."

"Oh, now, don't say that," Julianna told her. Glancing up, she paused in her efforts to re-create the magnificent flower arrangement she had set out in the morning room so that all the ladies could enjoy doing some artwork. "I am sure your painting is far better than you believe."

"No," Gabriella declared with a self-deprecating laugh. "It's not. Here, see for yourself." Lifting her painting, she turned it around to reveal a mass of disjointed blobs—runny pink and yellow ones that were supposed to be flowers, and a huge grayish-white splash that looked like a deformed rain cloud rather than a gorgeous Meissen vase. Even the sheep on the vase were unrecognizable.

Julianna stared, plainly searching for an encouraging response. The other women peered around their own paintings, their eyes widening before they gave her pitying little smiles and returned to their own work.

"It's a fine effort," Julianna stated in a bolstering tone. "You can't expect too much on your first attempt, you know."

"This isn't an attempt, it's a disaster. You are very

kind, but the sad truth is I am no artist and never will be."

"Keep practicing. You'll improve."

"In fifty or sixty years, if I'm very lucky." She sighed and reached for a cloth to clean a few paint smudges from her hands. "I think it safest to quit now, and save myself and countless others innumerable hours of pain."

"Well, as you prefer." Julianna glanced toward the clock, the hands reading half past nine. "I had envisioned us painting until nuncheon, but we can stop now and do something else."

"No, no, pray do not stop on my account. I won't hear of it."

"But we do not want you to be alone, dear," Mrs. Mayhew said, the older woman showering her with a concerned smile.

Lily, Maris, and Beatrix nodded their agreement.

"I shall be perfectly fine on my own for a couple of hours." Gabriella rose to her feet. "So none of you are to worry. Besides, there is a book I found in the library that I have been longing to read. This will give me just the chance."

Julianna's brows drew together on her lovely face. "Well, if you are sure. We can always put this away and find something else to do."

"No. Please keep painting, or else I shall feel horribly guilty for ruining your fun. Go on, and I will see you all at nuncheon."

"Very well, but do not forget our outing this afternoon," Julianna reminded. "We're driving to the village to shop for new trimmings and such. I hear the millinery has a fresh selection of Brussels lace in stock."

"I cannot wait." With a small wave, Gabriella let herself from the room. Once in the hallway, however, a sense of being at loose ends came upon her, for despite her assurances, she wasn't really in the mood to read. She could always take a walk, she supposed, since the weather was holding fair. Of course, that would require a trip to her bedchamber to retrieve her cloak, but what else had she to do? Strolling down the hallway, she made her way toward the stairs.

As she did, the Marquis of Vessey came striding out from one of the hallways in the rear of the house. Around his neck was draped a small towel that he was using to wipe perspiration from his flushed skin, his linen shirt sticking to his chest in a few places. He stopped when he spied her, a friendly smile coming to his handsome, blond-haired visage. "Miss St. George, how do you do? Please forgive my current state of undress, but I have just been enjoying a bout of fencing."

"Oh, swordplay! That sounds fun. So you did not ride out to view the home farms with my uncle, then? Julianna mentioned that he is giving the gentlemen a tour this morning."

He shook his head. "Impressive as Rafe's farms indisputably are, I have seen them countless times before. Tony has, too. That's why he and I decided to beg off and get a bit of exercise with the rapiers. I've just now come from the armory."

She paused at the information, her flagging spirits abruptly revived. "Ah, so the duke is here."

"That he is. Well, I had best be getting to my rooms. Have you seen my wife this morning? She said she planned to do some watercolor painting with the ladies."

"I saw the marchioness at that very endeavor not five minutes past. They're gathered in the morning room, by the way."

His smile widened, delight shining in his gaze at mention of his bride. "My thanks. Maybe if I make myself presentable, they'll let me in to see their progress."

She laughed. "Oh, I expect they might be persuaded."

"Until later, then," he said in a good-natured tone before turning away.

Murmuring a good-bye, she watched for a moment as he hurried up the stairs. As soon as he disappeared, so did her thoughts of him, instantly replaced by thoughts of Wyvern. *Is he still in the armory?* she wondered. *Dare I go find out?* Without giving herself time to debate the issue, she set off for that section of the house. After all, if she didn't hurry, he would most definitely be gone.

But she need not have worried, she discovered a minute later, when she found the duke still inside the spacious, wood-paneled room. The scent of beeswax polish, oiled metal, and a hint of clean, male perspiration drifted on the air. Breathing in the warm aromas, she moved to stand just inside the doorway.

Unaware that he was being observed, Wyvern continued his dancelike movements, wielding his rapier with an agile grace that was very nearly poetic. With each maneuver, his sword gave out a subtle hiss, the sharp blade cutting through the air like a shark through a calm sea. The room itself bore the stamp of lethal masculinity, the walls decorated with a collection of weaponry whose origins ranged from ancient to modern. There were rapiers, sabers, and short swords; broadswords, battle axes, jeweled daggers, and a few spike-studded maces. Several heavy pieces of chain mail hung in one display, while a suit of armor topped by a fearsome-looking helmet stood as if on guard duty in the far corner.

For a moment Gabriella imagined Wyvern dressed in the medieval steel suit, a mighty broadsword clutched in one of his fists as he prepared to protect his people and castle from invading marauders. She supposed his ancestors had done exactly that, having learned the other day from Beatrix Nevill that the first Duke of Wyvern had fought alongside William the Conqueror himself. As a reward for his loyalty and bravery, Édouard Black had been granted a dukedom, an immense duchy in the north of Bedfordshire. Since that time, the family had held the land against all trespassers.

She wondered if Wyvern had a room similar to this one at his own estate—guessing he did, since the Black family must have collected great numbers of weapons that had been handed down over the centuries. Yet in spite of the beguiling notion of Wyvern as a knight of old, she found she much preferred him as he was, with no need to conceal his powerful male physique and urbane grace in anything heavier than a thin white linen shirt and tightly fitting fawn breeches. She couldn't help but admire the sight of him. Not only was his fencing form excellent, his tall, powerful body was as well.

She must have made some small noise—an appreciative sigh, perhaps—since abruptly he ceased his movements and swung his head her way.

His deep blue eyes collided with her own. Barely winded despite his activity, he lowered his rapier to his side. "Gabriella."

She sent him a smile, her hands tucked against the folds of her white-and-caramel-striped day dress. "Hallo."

"I didn't see you before. Have you been there long?"

"Not very," she said. Rallying her nerve, she strolled farther into the room. "I happened upon Lord Vessey in the hallway and he mentioned you were here."

"Did he?" Crossing to a long table that stood against one wall, he laid down his sword, then reached for a small towel resting on a nearby chair. Using it first to wipe his hands, he then applied it to the hilt of his sword to remove any perspiration he might have left behind. Done, he turned back to her. "I thought you were occupied with the ladies this morning. Painting, was it not?"

"Yes, but a morning of water coloring has taught me a very valuable lesson."

One of his elegant dark eyebrows rose in inquiry. "And that would be?"

"That I am an utterly dreadful artist."

A smile broke over his face, eyes twinkling as a chuckle reverberated in his chest. "Surely, you're not that bad."

"No, I'm worse, believe me. And although Julianna tried her best to convince me not to give up, I know a hopeless cause when I see one. No, art will never be one of my finer accomplishments."

He set a fist on his hip. "Not to worry. You have myriad other talents, many of them quite exceptional."

"Though perhaps not always in the usual realm of ladies. My prowess with archery and firearms, for example. And I know how to fence as well."

"Really? And where did you happen by that ability?" Before she could answer, he held up a hand. "No, wait, don't tell me, another one of your circus performer friends."

Thrusting out her lower lip, she made a face at him. "Not at all." Ambling toward the table, she reached over and took his practice sword in hand, taking a few steps backward so she could safely slash the blade through the air. "I was taught by the sword master for our theater company, Monsieur Montague, who could slice a branch of candles in half and leave them all standing exactly as they were."

"Your Monsieur Montague sounds quite skilled."

"Indeed, yes. He was a French émigré who lost his home and family during the Terror. He never gave details, but we all believe he was the younger son of an aristocrat who watched his loved ones perish at the hands of the Committee and Madame Guillotine. He had an occasional habit of drowning himself in a few too many bottles of wine. Otherwise, he was an exceptional swordsman."

"And he taught you, did he?"

Another smile curved her mouth as she played the blade of the sword in a slow circle. Raising her left arm into the air behind her head, she assumed a fencer's stance. "En garde," she dared.

Managing a thrust in spite of her long skirts, she lunged forward three steps and set the blunted tip of the weapon against his chest. "Surrender, Your Grace!" she cried in a dramatic voice. "I have you at my mercy."

He cast a brief glance down to where the blade rested with innocent intent against his shirt. "So it would appear," he observed in a familiar drawl. "Though I must say this reminds me of another time we found ourselves in a similar situation."

The study in London, she thought. A small shiver rippled just beneath her skin, particularly when she recalled what had transpired between them that night after he had taken her gun. Without knowing she meant to, the edge of her tongue darted out and slid across her lower lip.

At the movement, she saw his gaze dip and hold, a dark gleam flashing inside his eyes. But an instant later, the look had disappeared, the only discernable expression on his face one of agreeable amusement.

"As I recall," she observed, "you tricked me that night."

"With good reason."

"Agreed. But that doesn't mean my pride wasn't wounded. A sporting man would give me the opportunity to repair it."

"By dueling with you?"

She nodded.

"Most of the sporting men I know would categorically refuse to fight a lady."

"But luckily you are not most men, are you, Your Grace?"

"Wyvern," he corrected. "And stop trying to appeal to

the unconventional side of my nature. Besides, how can I accept when I stand here at your mercy—you in possession of my sword, as it were?"

At my mercy indeed, she scoffed with silent mirth. Given he had half the room at his back, he knew as well as she that he could step free of his "capture" any time had he wished.

"There are a number of other weapons on the walls," she invited. "Choose one."

He tilted his head with arrogant refusal. "I prefer my own. I'm used to the grip on my rapier, you see."

Realizing he was right, she lowered the sword. "Fine. I shall choose one for myself, then." Flipping the weapon neatly in her grasp, she offered him the hilt.

He made her a small bow as he accepted. "My thanks, Miss Gabriella."

Moving toward the far wall, she began to inspect the swords. Behind her, she felt him watching.

"Surely you are not serious about this?" he asked after a moment.

"Of course I am," she returned. "I haven't had a chance to fence with a worthy partner in ages."

"All the more reason why you should not do so today. You are out of practice."

"A bout with you will help me refresh my technique. What do you think of that one?" Stretching out a finger, she pointed toward a likely sword.

"It appears to have good balance, but the rapier Ethan was using is better, particularly since its tip is already blunted."

"And which sword might that be, pray?"

He crossed his arms over his chest. "The answer scarcely matters, since we are not proceeding with this plan of yours."

Spinning to face him, she planted her knuckles on her hips. "Do you doubt my ability?"

"Not at all." In a sweeping motion, he raked her with his gaze. "Still, even you must admit you are hardly dressed for such exertions. You'll trip over yourself in that gown."

She shrugged aside his doubts. "I've learned to do more in a dress than you might imagine possible, so not to worry. Come on, Wyvern, fight me. Unless you're afraid of being bested by a girl," she added, hoping the taunt would ruffle his male pride enough for him to agree.

A laugh rippled from his throat. "You, my dear, have a very droll wit. No, the only thing of which I might possibly be afraid is for your reputation should we happen to be observed."

"But all of us here are family and friends. No one will mind."

He gave her a skeptical look. "I am not so sure of that. It's doubtful, for one, that Rafe would approve."

"Oh, surely he's not so stuffy as all that. But even if he is, why are you worried? After all, if I am not alarmed at the prospect of incurring his displeasure, then why should you be? Or do you only do the things of which my uncle approves?"

His smile widened. "Hardly, as well you know. I do as I see fit in accordance to my own rules and none other. Now, enough of your baiting, hoyden."

"But I am only longing to have a little fun," she implored, inwardly conceding the futility of her previous persuasion tactics. "Where can the harm be in that? It is not as if we are doing anything so very scandalous, is it?"

When he said nothing further, she continued. "Besides, who is to know, with everyone occupied elsewhere? My uncle and most of the men aren't even in the house, and the ladies are buried in their painting. Please, just fifteen minutes with the rapiers. No one will know but us," she finished, showing him her most winsome smile.

Like a star in a night darkened sky, a twinkle winked deep within his intense blue gaze. "You do not lack for persistence, I will say that much." Unbending, he gave a nod. "Very well, we shall have a bout."

Clapping her hands, she let out a small squeal and leapt up and down on her toes.

"But ten minutes only, not fifteen," he warned.

"Yes, Your Grace. Ten minutes and not a second more." She flashed him a mischievous grin. "Despite the limitation, that should give me more than enough time to defeat you."

He laughed again. "Outrageous minx!"

"Would you do me the favor of retrieving the sword Lord Vessey used?" she added in a light tone.

"But, of course," he agreed with a gallant sweep of his hand.

Once he had gone to find the correct sword, she moved to a nearby chair and dropped down onto the seat.

As he strode across the room, Tony shook his head, wondering what had possessed him to give in to her entreaties. Usually he had no difficulties resisting such feminine wiles, especially when they came from naïve little innocents. But as he was beginning to realize, Gabriella St. George was a genuine original. Of all the women he knew—and there were literally hundreds—he could think of none so daring and unconventional that they would challenge him to a fencing bout. He knew a great many men who didn't have the nerve to do so—not even for a practice round, since he was considered one of Society's most deadly swordsmen—but then she could hardly be expected to know that fact. But like a tiger indulging an adventurous cub, he would let her have her fun. As she said, what harm could come from a few minutes' sparring?

With Vessey's rapier in hand, he turned around—and nearly lost his hold on the sword. Lips parting, he stared wide-eyed with the sort of surprise he couldn't recall experiencing in a very long while. "Good heavens, your legs are bare!"

Glancing up, she tossed her skirts off her knees, the material instantly blocking the all-too-brief view he'd had of her beautifully turned knees and calves. Yet that single glimpse was enough to send his blood flowing faster inside his veins, and set his palms itching with the desire to uncover all that satiny-soft, alabaster flesh again so that his hands might go a-wandering. Such an interlude, he knew, would be nothing short of exquisite.

Down, boy, he reprimanded himself. *This is Gabriella, remember? Your friend's niece, who is strictly out of bounds.* Though even if she weren't Rafe's niece, she would still be out of bounds for all the usual reasons. Giving himself a firm mental shake, he pushed aside the fantasy. *Treat her like a sister,* he silently advised. Yet even as he focused on the thought, he realized the absurdity of it, a derisive laugh rising to his lips followed by an inaudible groan.

Plainly unaware of being the cause of any consternation, Gabriella tucked her stockings inside her slippers, then placed her footwear neatly beneath her chair. "This," she explained with a wiggle of her toes, "is one of the little tricks I've learned in order to compensate for dueling in a dress. Otherwise I really would stumble and do myself an injury." Springing to her feet—her very bare, very lovely feet—she padded toward him. "Ready to proceed?"

Swallowing down another groan at the sight of her loveliness, he passed her the sword with its protective, wood-covered tip. "Of course. I shall leave it up to you to begin."

He didn't have long to wait as she resumed the proper stance and brought her blade upward. He did the same.

"En garde," she called.

He let her make the first move and the first strike, the rapiers sliding against each other in a high-pitched whining of honed metal. With an easy, single maneuver, she knocked his sword to one side, then stopped.

"What was that, Wyvern? You're barely trying."

"I am allowing you to warm up. You said it's been a while since your last bout."

"A while, yes, but that doesn't mean I've forgotten everything I ever learned. Now, don't baby me. I want a real match."

He arched a brow. "Very well, I shall endeavor to do better." She gave a nod, then moved to once again assume the proper stance.

This time when she came at him, he countered with a bit more force. Still, he was careful to hold back, far too aware of his superior strength and the fact that it would take very little effort on his part to overpower her. Meeting a trio of her parries and thrusts, he allowed her to take the point.

"That was still too easy. Quit protecting me," she complained.

"And quit asking me to fight you as I would a man. You are *not* a man and when it comes to a contest of sheer strength, I will beat you every time."

"Perhaps that is true, but fencing isn't only about strength, it is also about cunning. Show me the courtesy of displaying more of your true ability and let us see how cunning I can be."

He considered her statement. Maybe he was mollycoddling her, and by doing so depriving her of the chance to actually test herself and her skills. He'd promised to give her a bout, but so far he'd done little more than condescend. "All right, Gabriella. You want the real me, then prepare yourself."

Lifting his rapier, he waited for her to move into position.

This time when they began, he didn't restrain himself—at least not too much. Moving with lightning speed, he lunged forward, their blades clashing in a series of parries that she valiantly struggled to meet.

One-two-three, their swords beat against each other.

Four-five-six, he waited for an opening in her defenses, quickly darting inside to tap her harmlessly on the hip and again on the shoulder.

Moving his sword out of harm's way, he stepped back. "Better?" he questioned.

Breath panted between her lips, her pretty eyes wider than usual. "Much."

"So? Do you wish to continue?" He waited, expecting her to concede defeat.

"Yes." Collecting herself, despite clearly having been shaken by the previous set, she lifted her rapier again.

On a nod, he moved again into place. "En garde," he declared.

Instead of assuming an aggressive tack by immediately engaging him, Tony noticed that she let him set the pace while she tried to study and anticipate each of his moves so she might have some hope of countering. The outcome was predetermined, of course, and took him scarcely longer than the first, but she held her own far more effectively than he might ever have expected.

"Not bad," he told her, genuinely meaning the words. Not only was she brave, he decided, she had talent—raw and in need of refining, but talent nonetheless. Mayhap that was the reason her first teacher, Monsieur Montague, had taken the effort to indulge her whims and teach a girl the rudiments of the art.

"Had enough?" he asked.

With a stubborn shake of her head, she moved into place once more. "Again," she ordered.

Having obviously been paying attention, she was able to hold him at bay for a few additional seconds before he once again slipped through her guard. "How do you do that?" she demanded the instant they disengaged.

"By waiting for you to leave me an opening. You drop your arm on the follow-through every time. Keep a tighter rein on yourself before you attempt a lunge, and don't make the move unless you know I cannot counter it."

"But you *always* counter it!"

"That's because you also need to be quicker." He tossed her a smile. "And you need to relax. Your stance is too tight."

Delicate, adorable little lines settled between her brows. "I don't feel as if it's too tight."

"Well, it is. Stop worrying and let your muscles do the work."

"That's what I thought I was doing."

"Only in half-measures. Your technique is a little rusty, but you know your form. Use it and have confidence, and stop overthinking matters. So, how are the kittens?"

She blinked, obviously nonplussed at his new query. "The kittens are fine—excellent, in fact."

"Playing well? Eating well?"

"Very well. They zip around like furry little balls of energy."

"No difficulties with the sleeping arrangements then?"

A sunny smile came over her lips. "Not a bit, if you don't count the dead mice Aggie brings me and the sandy paw prints Mama and babies are leaving on the carpet. The maids have been complaining about the mess, and since the weather has grown warmer, I've agreed to move the whole family down to a cozy spot in the stillroom tomorrow. That way they'll be able to run in and out of the garden at will."

"A most excellent plan." Suddenly he raised his sword. "En garde, Gabriella. Let's see what you can do."

Giving her only enough time to set her rapier in place, he came forward. This set she met him stroke for stroke, taking and repelling each of his moves. And when he dipped his blade in hopes of luring her into his usual trap, she held firm, maintaining her defenses like a seasoned warrior. Of course he won the point regardless, but unlike their earlier rounds, he had to actually work a little to achieve success.

"Well done!" he cheered once they broke off combat. "Wonderful improvement. Could you feel the difference? The control you gained by trusting yourself and relaxing?"

"I did!" she said with excitement. "I let my instincts lead me, just as you said. And I was careful not to drop my arm at the wrong moment. I held you off for a short while, anyway."

He grinned. "That you did."

Hurrying to resume the appropriate stance, she waited for him to do the same.

"Unfortunately," he continued, lowering his blade toward the floor, "I believe our ten minutes has expired."

Her sword dipped with disappointment. "No, we cannot quit now!" she protested. "Not when I'm just getting into the thick of it. Surely you cannot be so cruel."

"Is that what I'm being?" he queried, his tone rife with amusement. "Cruel?"

"Yes. Only an ogre would stop without giving me the opportunity to score at least a single point."

"Not to boast too highly of my own prowess, but we could be here a very long while if that is your criterion. Mayhap we might resume another day."

"But there won't be another day, not like this one. Please, Wyvern, three more tries. Just three and then I'll stop no matter the outcome."

Meeting her gaze, he saw the passionate entreaty shining within her eyes, strong emotion deepening their lush hue to an even more improbable shade of violet. The strength of her will hit him like a golden beam of sunlight, his resolve melting beneath the power of her youthful, heartfelt appeal.

"All right, three," he said in a voice that sounded as low and rough as gravel. "Then, win or lose, you'll cease without further complaint."

She held up a hand. "You have my most solemn word of honor."

The promise surprised him, since women didn't generally swear on their honor—that being the purview of men in their society. Yet somehow with Gabriella, the statement seemed fitting, both in light of the circumstances and of the girl herself.

His swordsmanship was such that he knew he could put a quick end to the entire matter in only a couple of minutes. Just the right maneuver and she would win the point, never realizing he'd lowered his guard deliberately in order to let her take it. But considering the earnest nature of her efforts, doing so seemed akin to cheating. He wouldn't battle her with every ounce of his skill, but neither would he intentionally let her win. If she took one of the three points, it would be due to her own skill and effort. Lifting his sword, he waited for their next engagement to commence.

Her first attempt rapidly proved to be a failure, lasting no more than the length of a few brief parries and counter-parries, his glancing riposte landing near her left shoulder for a strike. Acknowledging his win, she huffed out a breath, her disappointment clear as she disengaged. Yet she was undaunted, resuming the appropriate stance with a graceful swirl of her striped skirts, her determination unbowed, her sportsmanship impeccable—more admirable than that of a great many men he knew.

Giving her the right-of-way, he let her lead off. For many long, taut seconds, she gauged him, once more studying his technique in search of some visible weakness. Suddenly she lunged, her arm appearing to move upward only to reverse an instant later as she made a downward feint that she obviously hoped would outwit his skill. Reading her counter in time, he brought his sword down, the blades colliding in an echoing ring of steel-on-steel. His defense successful, they broke apart. At his ease again, he waited while she regrouped, her eyes alive with energetic intensity. They circled, her bare feet making quiet slaps against the polished wooden floor as she tried another feint, his shoes giving a few subtle squeaks as he parried her moves. Keeping up her attack, she increased her speed, searching for even the smallest of advantages, but in the course of their clash, he deflected her blade and moved around, and in, to score a touch and once more take the point.

"*Ooh,*" she exclaimed in plain frustration. "I nearly had you that time."

He gave her a sympathetic smile. "Unfortunately, *nearly* only counts in horseshoes and means naught on the dueling field. Shall we proceed to your third and final attempt?"

"Yes, and you needn't look so insufferably pleased about it."

"You mistake the matter, my dear. I am not at all pleased. Or would you rather I had taken it easy on you, after all, and let you have your victory?"

Her lips tightened, plainly insulted. "No, I want no false wins nor pitying gestures of gallantry."

"Just as I supposed."

Once more, she took her place. "Prepare to be beaten, Your Grace."

Smothering an indulgent smile, he made ready.

Gabriella extended her rapier at arms' length and began circling him. He circled back, the two of them watching each other like a pair of wary hawks battling over the same bit of prey.

"So tell me, Wyvern," she ventured in an even tone. "Do you have you any cats?"

"Cats?" He raised an eyebrow at her verbal sally. "Only of the barn variety. Why do you ask?"

"Just satisfying my curiosity, considering your earlier inquiry about the kittens."

"Ah," he drawled.

Their blades met, clashing in leisurely parries of three. One, two, three—disengage. One, two, three—regroup and circle.

"They'll be in need of good homes soon," she continued. "You should take one."

Her rapier struck his, his answering parry unleashing a cacophonous screech. "What? Take a kitten? Oh no."

"But you must." She flashed him a smile. "You cannot claim not to have the room. From what I hear, your country home is immense, and would provide a most excellent abode for a resident cat, or even two. They could keep each other company."

Adopt two kittens? Surely she is just trying to throw me off my stride with such talk, he told himself. "I have dogs," he retorted aloud. "Max and Digger would be most put out if I took in a pair of feline interlopers."

"Kittens are very adaptable and fit in anywhere. I am sure they would have your dogs wrapped around their tiny paws in no time at all. They aren't yet weaned, but you can pick out a pair before you leave. I'll make sure they're reserved exclusively for you."

A laugh escaped his lips at her outrageousness. The moment it did, she flew at him, beating her sword against his own in a violent flurry of movement. Definitely taken off guard, he struggled in order to counter, managing just barely to meet her parries and thrusts. With nimble footing, he leapt backward out of range as the tip of her rapier sliced downward in a move that would surely have struck him had he been a second slower.

Sensing his disadvantage, she continued pressing her attack. Once again, he took a defensive leap, but she followed, racing toward him with a huge pair of lunges as she thrust out her sword. Abruptly, a ripping noise split the air, her expressive eyes going wide as she stumbled forward and let out a cry of alarm.

Realizing that her feet must have tangled in the hem of her gown, he rushed toward her, hauling her tightly against his chest before she could tumble headlong to the floor. Cradling her close, he let her know by his touch that she was safe. On a shiver, she sagged against him, her rapier clattering harmlessly to the floor.

He dropped his sword as well, then brought his other arm up to enfold her more securely in his embrace. "Gabriella, are you all right?"

Tipping back her head, she met his gaze. "Yes. At least I think I am."

"Does anything hurt? Your ankle? Your toes?"

"No, nothing. I believe I am quiet well. But heavens, if you hadn't caught me—"

"Don't think about that now. You're safe."

"Thanks to you, Your Grace."

"Wyvern," he reminded, his gaze skimming over her face—her translucent skin flushed with color, her petal-soft lips parted as her breath soughed in and out. In that instant, he could not look away, mesmerized by her artless beauty and the sensation of her lithe feminine curves pressed snuggly against his body. Without full awareness, his arms tightened, his head dipping to breathe in more of the rich, honeyed fragrance of her skin, the scent wholly her own with no need of perfumed embellishments.

"Wyvern," she repeated, the sound of his name drifting over him in a seductive slide. Desire rose within him like some unstoppable tide. But even as he bent to claim her lips, he stopped himself.

No, he chided, *I can't. She's out of bounds, remember. Way, way, out of bounds.* But just as he was gathering the strength to set her from him, she undid all his good intentions by laying one delicate palm against the side of his face.

"Tony," she whispered, heartfelt longing plain in her eyes.

A deep tremor coursed through him as he fought his need. When she smoothed her fingertips along his temple and over his cheekbone, he knew he was lost. On a muffled curse, he took her lips with his own.

He felt her yield without an ounce of hesitation, accepting his kiss with an intensity that was both sweet and savage. Despite being pressed breast to chest and hip to hip, she wound her arms around his neck as if she needed to be even closer. Setting his hands at her waist, he lifted her up and placed her bare feet atop his shoes, taking her slender weight onto his own with a kind of sublime delight. Pleasure beat a crazy tattoo in his blood, a dull roar crashing inside his ears with a sound very like the quiet rush of the ocean inside a seashell. Coaxing open her mouth, he delved inside, plundering the hot, wet velvet of her lips and tongue. The taste and touch of her was intoxicating, more potent than the finest bottle of brandy he'd ever imbibed, her very essence leaving him drunk and a bit crazy.

Doubtless, that's exactly what he was—crazy, her touch driving him mad in a way he couldn't remember feeling for a very, very long time; not even as a youth in his first flush of passion, when he'd been a boy not so very much younger than Gabriella was herself.

Perhaps it was the startling remembrance of her age, or maybe the echo of a door closing somewhere in the house, but suddenly his reasoning brain switched back on. Breaking their kiss, he stared down at her for a moment, her eyes closed as if she were caught in a dream, her lips glistening and parted and clearly eager for more.

Christ, he cursed inside his head. As gently as he could, he moved to set her away, but the instant he did, her eyes popped open, her hands reaching out to grip his shirtsleeves and hold him in place. "Tony?"

He cleared his throat, his voice so rough he had to try twice before he could form more than a croak. "We need to stop."

"I'd rather you kiss me again instead."

Hmm, well so would I, he thought, an image of him dragging her to the floor while he worked open the buttons of her dress flashing in his head. Instead, he willed himself to be strong and sensible. "Can't," he said. "Our time's up."

"But I . . ."

"But nothing. Everyone will be readying themselves for nuncheon soon and it won't do for you and I to be found here together alone." Especially not looking as she did, with a rip in the seam that ran just beneath the bodice of her gown and her lips swollen, their color a violent pink as if she'd just received a very thorough kissing. Which anyone with a pair of eyes could see that she had!

"Go on now," he said as if giving instructions to a child. "Put on your stockings and shoes, then hurry along upstairs."

"Perhaps I don't want to."

"You haven't any choice." When she made no move, he realized she needed further coaxing. "Gabriella, this was just a . . ." He circled a hand in the air as he collected his thoughts. "A kiss, and despite the pleasure of it, the act means nothing." At her slightly crestfallen expression, he continued. "Whatever you may think you are feeling now, I assure you it is nothing more than simple infatuation and shall fade away directly. Now, do as I say and dress yourself. We shall pretend this never occurred."

"Twice," she piped, a suddenly mutinous gleam in her eye.

"What?"

"We shall pretend this never happened *twice,* or did you forget our other kiss?"

If only I could, he thought.

"I must confess I had rather put it from my mind," he said in a casual tone, striving to make the lie believable. "But not to worry, the memory shall fade soon enough for you as well."

Her lower lip trembled before she released her hold upon him and turned away.

Leaning down after a moment, he picked up the swords and carried them over to be cleaned and stored. He didn't look around when he heard her feet pad across the floor not long after, nor turn to watch her as she slipped from the room.

Impulse and infatuation, he repeated to himself. *Simple desire that could easily be put aside, that's all this has been.* Still, perhaps it might be wise if he left the house party early. No point continuing to set himself in temptation's path if he didn't have to. Besides, once he was back in London, among his old haunts and activities, he really would forget all about this unwanted desire he had for the luscious Gabriella St. George. By the time they met during the Season, he would see her as nothing more than Rafe's niece, just another pretty girl among many other pretty girls. He and Gabriella would each be occupied with their own circle of friends—happily separate, exactly as it ought to be.

Hurrying up the stairs as fast as her feet would carry her, Gabriella rushed through the house, grateful not to encounter so much as a junior housemaid as she made her way to her bedchamber. Shutting the door with a faint slam, she flung herself face-first across her bed and drew a deep, quavering breath as she strove to calm her pounding heart.

So my kisses mean nothing to him, do they? she railed. *So I am easily forgotten?* How could he say such things? How could he claim near boredom after the embrace they had just shared? The man had to be made of stone not to have felt even half of the delight she had experienced. And she knew he had enjoyed it too, pressed against his body as she'd been. Which could mean only one thing—he must have been lying.

She paused at the idea, replaying each one of his hot, hungry kisses, recalling the passion that had radiated from him like a blazing summer sun. Suddenly, she knew she was right. But why? Why would he turn dismissive and cold, then attempt to drive her away?

Because he doesn't want to find me desirable, came the answer. *Because he's a rake trying to do the honorable thing.* But why should he care? Why would he quibble when she clearly welcomed his touch? *His friendship with my uncle!* What other explanation could there be?

She supposed she should feel flattered that he would attempt to keep her at arm's length in order to preserve her maidenly sensibilities. Unfortunately, she didn't want him to stay away, at least not so far that he ended any hope for furthering a relationship between them.

And is that what I want? she questioned herself. *A relationship with Tony Black?*

Rolling over onto her back, she stared up at the ornate white stuccoed acanthus leaves scrolled on the ceiling above her bed. *Yes,* whispered the answer inside her head.

But what kind? Certainly not friendship; she enjoyed his kisses too much for any sort of platonic arrangement to ever work between them. On the opposite hand, she had no intention of following her mother's path and allowing herself to accept a carte blanche and become his mistress. So what did that leave?

Flirtation? Definitely.

More kisses and caresses? Oh, yes.

Courtship? Perhaps.

Marriage?

But why was she thinking that far ahead when she didn't even know her own feelings when it came to Wyvern? Though she supposed he was right on one score—she was infatuated with him. Never before had she met a man like the duke, so dashing and amusing and urbane. Nor had she ever felt any of the emotions he inspired within her. Dear heavens, just being in the same room with him made her pulse double its speed, his mere presence enough to draw her to him like a hummingbird lured to its favorite source of nectar.

If she wasn't careful, she could see herself falling in love with him. If she didn't guard her heart, she might lose it to him irreparably. Perhaps she should listen to his warnings and stay away. Maybe she should do as he told her and just forget about him.

But it was already too late for that, she realized. For good or bad, forgetting Wyvern was already an impossibility. Besides, she didn't want to forget, just as she didn't want to let him go, not without seeing where matters might lead between them if given a chance. Nor did she want to travel the prudent path and make sure her heart stayed whole. She wanted to know if she could feel more. She wanted to know if he might feel more as well.

And there was only one way to find out.

Chapter Seven

THE NEXT MORNING, not long after first light, Gabriella slipped out of bed and crossed to the huge mahogany armoire that stood on the far side of the room. Pulling out her new Bishop's blue riding habit, she began to dress, grateful that she didn't require the services of her maid since the garment buttoned in the front using a series of military-style frogs. After lacing her feet into a pair of sturdy black leather boots, she went to her dressing table and picked up her brush. A few quick strokes later, she twisted her heavy mass of hair into a knot, then artfully pinned the tresses atop her head. Pausing long enough for an appraising glance in the pier glass, she let herself out of her room and into the hallway.

A brisk stride soon brought her to Wyvern's guest bedroom door. Raising her hand, she rapped quietly before she had time to reconsider her actions. Shifting her feet, she waited. Perhaps he was asleep and hadn't heard her knock, she mused. She rather hoped that might be the case, imagining how delicious he would look opening the door all tousle-headed and barefoot, dressed in nothing but a thin silk robe. *Oh, I am a wicked girl!* she reprimanded herself. *But what is the fun of having an imagination if one never puts it to use?*

She was just raising her hand to tap again when the

door swung open to reveal a man—but not the one she expected to see. It was Wyvern's valet, an expression of curiosity lining his proper face.

"Who is it, Gull?" called the duke in his rich voice from somewhere inside the room.

"A lady, Your Grace," the servant replied, turning halfway around in order to address his employer. "Miss St. George, I believe."

A pronounced pause ensued, followed by the muffled sound of footsteps against the carpet. The servant stepped away as the door was pulled wide. And there stood Wyvern, fully dressed and obviously long since out of bed.

"Take those downstairs," he told the valet, pointing toward a pair of valises. "And if you would be so good, pray inform Hitchcock that I shall be along directly."

"Of course, Your Grace." Gull bowed, then moved to collect the leather cases. With a small nod to her as he passed, he left the room.

"Who is Hitchcock?" she inquired, taking a single step over the threshold.

"My coachman." He picked up a pair of leather gloves and pulled them onto his large, elegant hands. "What are you doing up and about when the rest of the house is still slumbering in their beds?"

"I am often up early. I find it the very best time of day." She cast a glance around the room. "But why is your luggage packed? Surely you are not leaving?"

"I am, yes." He looked away for a moment. "Unavoidable business at my estate."

A streak of disappointment went through her. *How interesting,* she mused, *that his "unavoidable business" has cropped up today, and at such an early hour, too!* Fleetingly she wondered if yesterday's spontaneous, impassioned kiss might have anything to do with his hasty decision to leave.

"Oh, well, that is too bad," she said in a casual tone designed to hide her chagrin. "I had thought we might go for a ride, since I wanted to try out my new habit. The village seamstress delivered it only yesterday." She held out her skirts to better display the garment.

His gaze swept slowly over her attire, an appreciative little smile playing across his mouth. "The gown is quite lovely, though by no means as beautiful as its wearer. As for the ride, I am sure one or more of the other guests would be happy to accompany you for a morning jaunt—once they're awake, that is."

"Doubtless you are right," she said. *So much for my grand plan to spend more time with Wyvern,* she silently bemoaned. She bit the edge of her lip as she cast about for a way to keep him with her for a little while longer. "Have you had breakfast? Surely you can remain long enough to take a meal."

"I already ate here in my room. Tea and toast with a hearty side of ham steak."

"Ah. Well then, I suppose I shall see you in London. You are coming for the Season, are you not? Julianna and Rafe have decided to sponsor me—whatever that might entail."

"A great many dances and parties, followed by balls and soirees and routs. *That* is the Season," he told her with apparent humor. "You shall have a splendid time, I am sure."

"I do like to dance," she confessed. "What of you, Your Grace?"

He shook his head. "I rarely take to the floor."

"That cannot please your hostesses."

"Over the years, they have learned to deal with the loss."

She considered his statement for a moment. "But surely you make an exception on occasion. If you will recall, you do owe me a favor."

One dark eyebrow swept upward. "Are you calling in my pledge in exchange for a dance?"

"Oh, it would have to be more than a single dance," she teased. "Two, at the very least."

A laugh rumbled from his throat. "Two dances, hmm? Well, I suppose I could be persuaded. And since I am not the kind of man to stint on his promises, I will be generous enough to make it a trio. How is that?"

She inclined her head. "A trio sounds most pleasant. I shall look forward to the occasions. Although," she drawled, "you could always dance with me and still let me retain the favor for later, you know."

"But then what might you demand?" he asked, a twinkle showing in his deep blue eyes.

She tossed him an impish grin. "One never knows."

He laughed. "If you will forgive me, Miss St. George, my journey is a long one and the hour grows late. I fear I must take my leave of you."

Her heart sank, the delight that had been floating inside her bursting like a handful of soap bubbles. Striving not to let her emotions show, she maintained her smile. "Safe journey, then."

"And to you as well, when you leave for London. Until we meet again." Executing a dashing bow that made her insides tingle, he tipped his hat and strode away.

"Yes, Tony," she whispered to herself. "Until next we meet."

"One lump or two, Miss St. George?"

From her perch on a silk-covered Sheridan chair in the Countess of Sefton's grand drawing room three and a half weeks later, Gabriella glanced up to meet the inquiring gaze of her hostess.

"Two, please," she replied, knowing better than to ask for the three lumps she really wanted, since such a request would apparently show a marked lack of refinement on her part.

While she waited for the older woman to pour, she met Julianna's eye, her friend giving her an encouraging little smile before turning away to respond to something said to her by the lady on her opposite side.

A moment later, Gabriella accepted the cup of gently steaming tea, murmuring her appreciation to the countess with what she hoped was a friendly yet gracious smile. Only after Lady Sefton went on to serve another of the ladies did Gabriella take a careful sip of her tea, forcing herself not to fidget lest she bobble her drink. After all, according to Julianna, today's afternoon call was of the utmost importance to her future in Society. Make a good impression here, she had been told, and she would find all of London's doors opened for her admission. Make a bad one, and . . . well, she didn't need to dwell on that, did she?

Earlier, Julianna had tried to alleviate any potential nervousness by telling her to think of the Season as nothing more than a very large house party. However, despite the advice and the ease with which she had fit in among Rafe and Julianna's titled friends and relations in the country, she was finding London Society an entirely different matter.

For one thing, she had never actually lived among the Quality—not as one of them, anyway—and despite being a natural mimic, she still found herself having to watch everything she did and said when out in company for fear of making a mistake.

Polite Society, she had rapidly learned, was an intricate maze of inflexible rules and obscure customs, a thorny thicket that seemed specifically designed to trip up those not raised within its lofty confines from the moment of their birth. And yet with Julianna's calm—and never critical—assistance, she was fast absorbing everything she needed to know. At least that's what she was trying to do.

One matter about which she had absolutely no complaint since returning to London was her wardrobe. From the moment of their arrival in Town, she and Julianna had descended upon the shops. Even now, she could barely believe her change of circumstances. For the first time in her life, she had truly elegant clothes—beautiful gowns the likes of which she had only dreamed, in luxurious silks, sumptuous satins, and delicate muslins in an array of stripes, patterns, spots, and hues. As if caught inside a happy whirlwind, she had found herself taken in hand, pinned and fitted and passed from mantua maker to milliner to glove maker and shoemaker—everyone working in concert to turn her into a true debutante.

To her private amazement, Julianna had seen to it that she was presented at Court, since a proper coming out would not have been possible otherwise. Now Julianna was working to get her admitted to Almacks, the Ton's most exalted inner sanctum.

Already she had received a veritable bounty of gifts for which to be grateful, her debt to Rafe and Julianna far more than she could ever repay. And so, despite her reservations about this particular afternoon call, she had vowed to make a favorable impression.

According to Julianna, the Countess of Sefton was the most affable and easygoing of the Almacks's patronesses, which is why she had chosen to approach her in hopes of securing the vouchers required for admittance into the assembly rooms. Sadly, if the countess would not consent, there was little chance that any of the other patronesses would agree to do so either.

"Cake?" the great lady offered.

Keeping a steady grip on the bone china tea saucer between her fingers, Gabriella took a moment to decide how best to answer. Somehow, an outright refusal seemed impolite, so she nodded her head. "Yes, thank you, your ladyship. They look quite delectable."

The older woman smiled. "Oh, they are. My chef makes the finest desserts in all of London, if I do say so myself. Though it is easy to indulge a bit too freely, if one is not careful."

"Then I shall have to content myself with only the one," Gabriella said, using a pair of silver tongs to place a single icing-covered square onto her plate. With the countess still watching, she forced herself to eat a small, delicate bite. As the sweet melted on her tongue, she couldn't help but give a completely honest reply. "Oh, you are right, this is wonderful!"

The countess laughed, an enigmatic smile crossing her lips. "Exactly so."

Gabriella patted her mouth with her napkin, then took a sip of her tea as the older woman finally looked away.

Had that been a test? she wondered. *More importantly, did I pass?* Unsure, she remained silent.

"So I hear Wyvern has decided to grace us with his presence at the Hoxleys' ball this evening," said one of the other women, her marriageable daughter at her side. "I do hope that means he plans to cease this nonsense of his and finally look for a bride."

Gabriella forgot all about her cake. *Wyvern at the ball tonight?* she thought. *Well, it is about time!* Taking another sip of her tea, she worked to conceal her interest in the news.

In spite of his promise to see her here in Town, she had not caught so much as a glimpse of him since her arrival. Initially, she understood that he had remained at his estate to take care of whatever business had drawn him home. But late last week, she had heard Rafe mention the duke, commenting that he and Tony had shared drinks and a game of cards at Brooks's Club together with some other friends.

The following day, she had waited with undeniable anticipation for Wyvern to put in an appearance at the townhouse. But he had not called. Nor had he called on any of the days to follow—not even to see Julianna, which as she had learned, was the polite thing to do. Surely the man could find a few minutes to drop by and pay his addresses. After all, how was she to test her feelings for him if he was never around?

But apparently the two of us will be at the same ball tonight! Suddenly anticipation lightened her spirits.

"So what do you think, Lady Pendragon?" the woman continued. "Your husband is a particular friend of the duke's, is he not? Maybe Wyvern has said something of his intentions to you?"

Julianna set down her cup. "About entering the marriage mart? No, to my knowledge, the duke has not changed his mind on that score. If I were you, I would not pin any hopes on tonight's entertainment."

"Nor would I, Lenora," Countess Sefton advised. "I have long had to count Wyvern as a lost cause. Now, if he starts frequenting Almacks, perhaps you might have some reason to hope."

Lenora huffed out an indignant breath, giving her daughter's hand a brief squeeze as if in consolation. "Well, I do not understand. *All* men have need of a wife and an heir. One would think he could put aside his distaste of marriage in order to propagate his line."

"Unlike us ladies, men have the luxury of being able to delay these matters," the countess said. "Besides, I have heard he doesn't mind if the title goes to a cousin."

"Despite all manner of pleading from his mother on the subject, I understand," confided another of the ladies. "Apparently the dowager asks him every year if he has reconsidered, and every year he says he has not."

"Well, I refuse to give up," Lenora declared. "One day he will change his mind and marry."

But only for a special woman, Gabriella realized. *The question is, could I be that woman? More importantly, do I wish to be?*

Not long after, the conversation moved on to other subjects, the remainder of the visit proceeding at an easy, undemanding pace. At the end of their allotted time, she and Julianna stood to make their farewells, moving with the countess toward the drawing-room door. Just past the threshold, Lady Sefton drew Julianna slightly to one side, but not far enough away that Gabriella could not hear.

"Your niece seems a charming, unassuming girl, Lady Pendragon," the countess said. "And despite the obvious flaws in her lineage, I believe she will take quite nicely. You may count on receiving vouchers for Wednesday next. I look forward to seeing you and Miss St. George at Almacks very soon. And perhaps your husband as well. We always have need of gentlemen for the dancing, even married ones."

Julianna paused, a twinkle visible in her eyes. "I believe I may be able to persuade him. I shall make a point of trying."

"Well, I cannot ask for more than that, now can I? Husbands being what they are and all." Turning, she smiled at Gabriella. "Until we meet again, Miss St. George."

"Yes, your ladyship." Gabriella dipped her knees in a curtsey. "Thank you for the lovely afternoon."

Lady Sefton's smile broadened. "It was my pleasure. Such a sweet girl you are! A shame your father turned out to be a villain and that your mother was an actress. But alas, we cannot choose our parents, now can we?"

Gabriella's shoulders stiffened, a defense of her family

springing to her lips. Instead, she forced herself to keep a pleasant smile on her face, lowering her gaze slightly so as to conceal the anger she knew must be burning in her eyes. "No, my lady, we cannot."

"Adieu, then," the countess called with a happy little wave.

Before Gabriella had time do anything further, Julianna stepped forward and hooked an arm through hers, drawing her out the door that was being held open by a waiting footman.

Only after they were down the stairs and inside their coach did Gabriella dare to speak. "Of all the nerve!" she said, fiery color warming her cheeks. "Did you hear her?"

"Yes, and I am very sorry for it. But I do not think she truly meant to be unkind."

"Do you not? Well, perhaps so, since she was good enough to grant me a voucher. Still, her remarks about my parents were rude."

"She was thoughtless in her choice of words, I agree." Julianna paused a moment as the coachman set their vehicle into motion, the wheels rumbling quietly against the Mayfair street. "But I would be remiss if I did not warn you that you may hear far worse this Season. The Ton can be quite severe in its opinions and cruel to those whom it deems lacking in matters of bloodline or wealth."

"Well, if those are the sorts of people with whom I must associate, then perhaps I do not care to keep their company after all. They can find someone else to ridicule and deem *lacking*."

Julianna reached across with a reassuring touch. "But you are not lacking, not in the slightest. You are a fine young woman for whom I have already come to care. And while it is true that you may encounter a few pompous sticklers who thrive on being hateful to others, do not ever let them hold sway over you. There are just as many people in Society who possess a good and generous nature. Seek them out and do not let the sour apples spoil your fun. And you *will* have fun, unless you quit the game before you have even begun it."

On an exhale, Gabriella released the worst of her temper and hurt. *Julianna is right,* she thought. *Why toss away my opportunities because of a few inconsiderate words?* And to be fair, Lady Sefton had spoken nothing but the truth.

Handsome and aristocratic as he may have been, she knew that her father had been guilty of some heartless and brutal acts, as much as the knowledge might still pain her to admit. As for Mama—well, she *had* been an actress; that was a fact. But though Society might look down on the profession, that did not mean she must do the same. She would always remember her mother as beautiful and kind, a woman with a healthy appetite for life who had shared that gift with her daughter and everyone around her. If she were still alive, Mama would have told her to be proud and do whatever it took to succeed.

"*Just look at you, Gabby,*" she would have said. "*My little girl rubbing elbows with the nobs like she were one of them. Going to fine parties and fancy balls, wearing gorgeous gowns and living in a big, grand house, and all without having to turn so much as a bit of ankle for the gentlemen folk. Now, there's the life, I'll say.*"

No, Gabriella decided, she was made of far sterner stuff than to let the Lady Seftons of the world deter her. Anyway, Julianna would be crushed if she did not follow through and participate in the Season. And she would feel horribly guilty over all the expense and trouble to which the Pendragons had already gone on her behalf should she withdraw. She couldn't let them down—or herself, she realized. *I shall stay,* she vowed, *regardless of what people may think or say of me.*

Glancing across the coach, she saw Julianna watching her with a concerned expression. "So, when do those vouchers arrive? I hope in time for me to wear my new gown with the seed pearls on the bodice. The dressmaker's sketch of the ensemble looked utterly divine."

A relieved smile broke over Julianna's face. "You're going to look a dream in that gown, I agree. The gentlemen won't be able to take their eyes off you."

Hopefully, Wyvern will be among them. Perhaps he might even experience a twinge of jealousy should enough men look my way, Gabriella mused. *Now wouldn't that prove interesting?*

"So, what are you wearing tonight?" Julianna continued. "The pink polonaise or the cream chiffon?"

Tony had missed the receiving line, the dancing long since underway by the time he strolled into the Hoxleys' crowded ballroom just a few minutes shy of midnight that evening. Keen as a fox, he had planned his arrival with premeditated precision, wanting to be able to slip into the party in a manner designed to attract the least amount of notice or bother.

And so far, his plan appeared to be working. All the eager, matrimony-minded mamas were ensconced in chairs as they busily gossiped with their friends, while their daughters whirled across the ballroom floor in the arms of their current partners, the girls' quota of available dances already promised for the remainder of the night. Which left Tony free to have a drink, talk to friends, and play a hand or two of cards—all without the nuisance of fending off unwanted feminine overtures.

Scanning the crowd, he looked for a few of his cronies, wondering if Ethan had decided to put in an appearance tonight. Or if Rafe might be there, ready to engage in their promised rematch at piquet. As his gaze roved over the sea of faces, though, his eyes stopped abruptly when he came across one countenance in particular.

Lord, she's even lovelier than I remember, he thought, allowing his eyelids to droop low so he could indulge in a long, surreptitious stare at Gabriella St. George's vivacious, raven-haired beauty. An answering heat formed in his loins, one he ruthlessly forced himself to suppress.

He supposed he should have known she would be in attendance tonight. Crossing paths with her here in Town was inevitable, and long overdue, he admitted. Since leaving the Pendragons' estate nearly a month ago, he'd kept himself busy, thoughts of Gabriella growing fewer and farther between, just as he'd assured himself they would.

For two weeks he'd gone home to Rosemeade, immersing himself in all manner of estate business—working with his secretary to review the accounts and answer correspondence, meeting with tenants about their various concerns, and answering a request from his mother to increase her quarterly allowance again. Once he'd finished with that, he'd literally rolled up his sleeves and set about the messy business of clearing a dam that had formed in one of the nearby riverbeds after a recent, violent rainstorm.

He could have let his groundskeepers see to the task, he knew, but he liked engaging in a bit of hard, physical labor every now and then, both as a way to clear his mind and to keep his sense of hubris in check. Having acceded to the dukedom at age ten, he knew how easy it could be to lose one's way among all the fawning posturers and false aggrandizements that came with the title. Clearing a dam or thatching a roof went a long way toward making everything seem less complicated and not nearly so important, after all.

The following week, he'd journeyed south to London,

spending his time riding and driving, going to his clubs, and visiting with friends. And although he could have called at the Pendragon townhouse in Bloomsbury, he had decided to let matters remain as they were, with Gabriella St. George out of his sight—and thus, out of his mind.

But now here she was again, dancing only a few feet distant, the mere sight of her enough to resurrect forbidden urges and dark longings that were best confined to private alcoves and candlelit bedchambers.

Angel or siren, he couldn't decide, Gabriella's dark, vibrant beauty and pert violet eyes a genuine rapture to behold. Draped in a length of pale pink silk, her slender figure showed to stunning perfection, a healthy wash of color gracing her cheeks as she performed the intricate steps of a country dance. Unaware of his observation, she tossed back her head on a laugh, obviously appreciating whatever remark her partner had just made.

He clenched, then unclenched his jaw, telling himself he was glad to see her so plainly enjoying herself. Just as he had known she would, she had let go of her initial infatuation with him and turned elsewhere. With all that London had to offer, she was clearly caught up in the whirl of the Season, relishing the chance to make new friends and strike up flirtations with gentlemen other than himself. Gentleman far closer to her own age; men who had marriage on their minds.

At least those young men's intentions had better be honorable, he thought. If they weren't, they would soon find themselves rethinking the matter—and seriously—or else face the consequences of his wrath. For in spite of his recent absence from Gabriella's side, he had by no means forgotten his promise to watch over her. True, he might do most of his watching from a distance, but he would watch nevertheless.

Shaking open the fist he found squeezed tight at his

hip, he turned and strode away, knowing she was well occupied for the next few minutes with the dance.

When the set ended, however, he tossed back the last of the wine he'd been drinking, handed his empty glass to a passing servant, and crossed the ballroom to where she now stood conversing with Julianna.

"Ladies, how do you do this evening?" he greeted, offering a bow.

The women turned, Gabriella's gaze immediately lifting to meet his own. "Your Grace," she murmured, a smile curving her lips as she curtseyed.

"Tony," Julianna said, accepting a friendly kiss on the cheek. "When did you arrive? I was beginning to think you were going to stay away tonight and make liars of all the gossips. You slipped in like a phantom."

He grinned, in no way hiding his lack of repentance. "Precisely."

"That is very bad of you, you know."

"Well, I strive to never be accused of being too good nor too predictable."

"Well, you succeed admirably on both counts. Do you not agree, Gabriella?"

"Oh, yes. His Grace enjoys teasing and taunting us all. Perhaps that is why we have seen so little of him of late despite his having been in the city for several days."

He raised a brow at her undisguised reprimand, seeing she hadn't lost the free use of her tongue since their last meeting. "Forgive me, Miss St. George. You are quite right to scold me for the omission. Though from what I hear, you've had no lack of callers since your arrival in Town."

"Thanks to Julianna's generous intercession on my behalf, that is quite true," Gabriella said.

"Oh, you don't do yourself enough justice," Julianna said. "I know the gentlemen certainly haven't been dropping by the house and sending flowers because of any urging on my part. Gabriella is taking splendidly. I won't be surprised if she has more than a few offers of marriage by the end of the Season. Whether or not she wishes to accept any of them is another matter."

Involuntarily, his hand tightened at his hip. "I am sure she will be greatly in demand. After all, Miss St. George is an exceedingly lovely young woman whom any man would be lucky to win." He met Gabriella's gaze. "Which is why I assume your dance card is completely filled this evening?"

"Actually, Your Grace," Gabriella said, "as it would happen, I have the next set free. And if you will recall, you did promise to stand up with me when we next met in Town."

Adroitly hoist on his own petard, he could do nothing but agree. Although, to be honest, he found he didn't at all mind the idea of dancing with Gabriella. "So I did. Miss St. George, may I have the pleasure of this next dance?"

Her lips tightened. Just for an instant, he thought she was going to refuse him, but then she smiled and inclined her head. "Thank you, Wyvern. I would be delighted."

"Julianna," he said, "I trust you will forgive the two of us for abandoning you?"

She waved a casual hand toward the dance floor. "Of course, go on and enjoy yourselves. It will give me an opportunity to find out where Rafe has gone. I suspect he is either playing cards or talking politics. Bonaparte is the most likely topic of conversation now that the little tyrant has escaped Elba and started the war raging again on the Continent. Have fun and I shall see you both in a bit."

With a parting smile, she walked away, leaving him and Gabriella alone—if one could view standing in a crowded ballroom as being alone. Yet oddly enough, that is how the moment felt, especially when she raised her gaze to his. The extraordinary depth and color of her eyes sent a rush of hot and cold over his skin, his pulse giving a hard kick as an unbidden fist of arousal once again lodged where it had no place being.

Tearing away his gaze, he held out his arm. "Shall we?" He waited while she laid a small palm against his black coat sleeve, then led her forward.

"So how are you finding the Season? Is it everything you had hoped?" he inquired as they took their places among the other couples assembling for the set.

She arched a brow. "Since I harbored no particular expectations from the outset, I must say it is everything I could have dreamt and more. I am continually amazed, much like a sparrow who finds herself thrust into a cage full of canaries."

He flashed her an amused smile. "You are hardly a sparrow."

"Well, don't tell anyone, but sometimes I feel like one masquerading in her fine new feathers. The Pendragons may have provided me with an array of gorgeous silks and satins, but I still remember when I had nothing but plain, serviceable cotton to wear."

"Silk or cotton, you look equally beautiful in either."

A warm gleam came into Gabriella's gaze and she opened her mouth to reply. But the moment she did, the music began and seconds later, the dance.

Due to the required movements, she found him moving away from her as often as he came near, her hands clasped inside his own for a few brief moments before he released her and stepped away. The experience was as frustrating as it was satisfying, a kind of sanctioned public titillation. At least that is how it seemed to her as she danced with the duke. Although she had to admit she had never felt this way with any of her previous dance partners.

"You owe me a ride, you know," she said when their

hands were joined again. "Considering how you had to hurry home that last day in the country."

His brow shot skyward. "I had business, if you will recall."

The dance forced them apart. Gabriella bided her time until they came together again. "It's all done now, I assume?" she commented in a lilting voice.

His eyes twinkled. "For the moment, though one never knows when it will once more rear its head."

"An ugly head, too, I would imagine," she quipped.

A laugh escaped him. "At times, though not all business is bad. On occasion it can be quite pleasurable."

"Many things can be pleasurable. Riding, for instance. I packed my blue habit, by the way. Though since arriving in Town, I've added a very smart lavender one to my wardrobe as well. Lord Carlow and Mr. Hughes both informed me the shade complements my eyes."

Wyvern's hand tightened around hers before he had to step away. She hid a smile, her heart thudding beneath her breast as she forced herself to continue dancing. From the opposite side of the line of dancers, she could feel his gaze, her skin tingling with awareness.

"So you've gone riding already, have you?" he demanded in a deep rumbling tone when the dance again brought them near.

"Just once. I have yet to christen my blue gown, though. You could help me break it in. Otherwise you never know who might be willing to do the deed."

His hand squeezed hers again, a heated flash darkening his eyes. "Be careful in choosing your admirers. Some of them may seem harmless but possess a set of hidden motivations underneath their exteriors."

"What of you, Your Grace? What hidden motivations do you have? Since a less harmless man I have never met."

A slow smile curved his mouth, the music and the

dance coming to an end. Yet he didn't immediately release her, his gaze locked upon her own. "You are right. I am far from harmless and you would do well to remember that. Don't play with tigers unless you're prepared to get scratched."

A shiver ran over her skin. "I'll do my best to take care. Though to my way of thinking, tigers are nothing more than great, big cats in wont of a bit of taming."

Another laugh rumbled from his throat before he offered her his arm. "Is that so? Come, minx. Let us find Rafe and Julianna."

"As you will, Your Grace," she demurred before laying her palm on his sleeve.

Chapter Eight

THREE DAYS LATER, Tony called at the Pendragon townhouse. As Gabriella had so aptly pointed out, doing otherwise would be rude. Rafe and Julianna were his friends, after all, and if he ceased visiting them in their home, they would surely begin to wonder why. Besides, it wasn't as if he was paying a specific call on Gabriella—since he most assuredly was not—but rather on the family as a whole. That's why he'd chosen late morning, the hour being too advanced for breakfast but too early for a regular social call.

Word had it the house filled with gentlemen in the afternoons, a collection of them gathering like a pack of hounds—all come to pant after Gabriella. The idea alone was enough to keep him away at that particular hour, since despite his promise to look after her, he had no intention of subjecting himself to such an appalling display. Julianna, he felt confident, was more than capable of acting as chaperone inside her own home. He certainly didn't need to add his efforts. Anyway, if he took to dropping by while Gabriella's coterie of suitors was present, Society might get the mistaken impression that he was one of them!

As he strode up the stone entrance steps, the door swung open, held wide by the Pendragons' butler.

"Hello, Martin," he greeted as he walked inside. "How are you this morning?"

"Very well, Your Grace. Thank you for inquiring. And yourself?"

Tony doffed his hat. "Excellent, all in all. Is Rafe available? In his office, I presume?"

"No, Your Grace, he left some time ago for a meeting at the Exchange. Bond merchants, I believe I heard him say."

"Ah. What of her ladyship, then? Is she receiving?"

"I am sorry, but her ladyship is out as well, along with Miss St. George and Lady Vessey. A breakfast party, was my understanding."

"Oh. Well, it would appear I have chosen a poor time to drop by." Placing his hat back onto his head, he reached into his coat's breast pocket for the small silver case that contained his calling cards. "Pray inform the family of my visit," he said, withdrawing a single white rectangle with his name engraved in black.

Martin had just taken possession of the card when a lilting laugh tinkled in the air beyond the open door. Tony turned at the familiar sound.

"You were right, my lord," declared Gabriella from outside. "Your carriage is exceptionally well sprung."

"You must allow me to take you out again, Miss St. George," came a deep male reply. "There is nothing better than an excursion around Mayfair on a sunny spring afternoon."

"Doubtless, you are right," she agreed as one of the footmen rushed to assist her from the vehicle. But the tall gentleman with her jumped down and brushed aside the servant's efforts, taking her by the waist to lower her to the ground.

A heavy scowl creased Tony's forehead. Without his full awareness, he strode outside to stand on the top step.

Apparently sensing his movement, Gabriella turned

and met his gaze, her eyes widening ever so faintly. "Your Grace, what are you doing here?"

"I might ask the same thing of you, Miss St. George. Where is Lady Pendragon? And Lady Vessey, for that matter, since I understand you three ladies ventured out together this morning."

"We did. But as you can see by the state of my dress, I had a bit of a mishap and decided that it was best to come home. Lord Carlow was kind enough to offer me escort rather than making Julianna and Lily leave and miss the rest of the garden party."

At her explanation, he raked his eyes over her white gown, only then noticing the large peach-colored stain splashed across the bodice and skirt. "What in the world happened? You look as if you were drenched with something."

"Indeed. A pitcher of orange juice and I had an unfortunate encounter. As you can observe, I lost."

One side of his mouth quirked upward. "That must have been unpleasant."

"And sticky." She tossed him a smile before turning to address the gentleman at her side. "My gratitude for your kindness, my lord. You are most gallant to have seen me home."

A wide smile split Lord Carlow's roguish countenance. "It was no trouble at all, my dear Miss St. George. Allow me to stay while you refresh your attire so that I might return you to the festivities."

"You are most solicitous," she said, "but I fear by the time my maid and I manage to repair all this damage, the party will long since have ended. Pray do not let me keep you any later. I have no wish to be the cause of you missing the entire event."

"Yes, Carlow," Tony called. "Let Miss St. George come inside and change out of her soiled garments. Otherwise, who knows what sort of pests she may start to attract."

Carlow shot him a hard look, as if he knew to what kind of *pest* Tony was referring. "The lady and I have matters well in hand, Wyvern. You know, Your Grace, you never did say what you are doing here."

Tony gave a casual shrug. "As a friend of the family, I am often here, and I am welcome whenever I choose. I can assure you, the lady's uncle wouldn't like you ignoring her wishes, nor having you keep her standing out here in the street."

The other man scowled, shooting him a narrow-eyed stare.

Tony raised a brow and stared back.

After a long moment, Carlow turned and took Gabriella's hand, making her a practiced bow. "Miss St. George, are you certain you wouldn't like me to remain? I shall not mind in the slightest."

"I know, and I truly do thank you for your generosity, but I feel I have burdened you too much already."

"It is no burden at all. Assisting you this morning has been my profound pleasure. And if I have not told you before, may I say what a vision you are. Your radiance and loveliness shine through like the sun. Your every word and movement a dream. Each minute in your company no less than a true delight."

Tony held back a snort. *Who does Carlow think he is? Byron?*

To his disgust, however, he saw that Gabriella didn't seem to mind the other man's effusive compliments. Instead, she gave another lilting laugh and showered Carlow with a smile. "You humble me, my lord. Now, I really should be going inside. Else I actually do start drawing bees or flies."

"Such creatures would only wing near so they might have a chance to bask in your honeyed sweetness."

She laughed once more. "Until we meet again."

"Until then," he said. "I shall be counting the moments."

Counting the moments indeed! Tony scoffed. *What a load of insipid twaddle!*

Folding his arms across his chest, he watched while Carlow made her another farewell, then sprang into his curricle. Tipping his hat to them both, Gabriella's admirer drove away.

Standing aside, Tony allowed her to precede him through the entrance. "What a fribble!" he muttered as Martin closed the door at their backs.

"Oh, do you think so?" she ventured as she strolled across the large entryway toward the staircase. "I find him rather charming."

"You call that charming, do you? He's full of so much treacle, I'm surprised you don't need a visit to the tooth drawer to pull out the cavity-laden teeth he's surely left behind."

Pausing, she ran her tongue over her teeth as if she were checking them. "All fine. Nary a caries."

"Very amusing."

On a grin, she started up the stairs.

After a brief hesitation, he followed. "Seriously, Gabriella," he said the moment they reached the landing. "You should be cautious about associating with the man. Despite the flowery drivel he spouts, Carlow has a decided reputation and not always to the good, especially when it comes to the ladies."

"Some might say the same of you, Wyvern, though not the flowery drivel part, I admit. Should I avoid your company, then, as well?"

"This isn't about me," he said with a glower. "Frankly, I cannot fathom why Julianna and Lily allowed you out alone with him. I should have thought they would take more care of your safety and reputation."

Her shoulders straightened. "I believe my reputation is capable of surviving an innocent morning ride in an open carriage with a gentleman of good character. As for my safety, I made it home in excellent health, as you can clearly see."

"But you might not have done," he insisted. "He—

Just then a maid came around one corner, a stack of clean linens in her arms. She stopped and curtseyed to them both, then disappeared as quickly as she had arrived. Not wishing for any more potential interruptions or eavesdropping, Tony cast a glance around and pulled Gabriella into a nearby room, which just happened to be the upstairs library. He closed the door at their backs.

"As I was saying," he began, "Carlow could have taken you anywhere in the city had he wished."

She made a dismissive noise. "One might say that of any of the gentlemen who asked me to drive out or walk with them. There is no difference between those men and Lord Carlow."

"Except that Julianna is not here at home awaiting your return."

"He brought me straight to the house without a single detour."

"Perhaps so, but he also wished to come inside, did he not?" he added.

"So he could wait for me to change my attire."

"And what else? How do you know he wouldn't have wanted more? How can you be sure he wouldn't have taken advantage of the fact that he would have had you alone?"

She shook her head. "He would not. And may I point out that you have a very suspicious mind, Your Grace."

"Not suspicious. Just experienced. Why do you think it is young unmarried ladies are never left alone with men?"

She paused, considering his words. "Even if you are

correct about Lord Carlow, I wouldn't have been in danger. Not with the servants here to protect me."

"So you think they would come to your defense?"

"Yes, I know they would," she stated, crossing her arms over her breasts.

"Maybe so, once they heard you. But the damage might already have been done by then."

"You are being ridiculous and this whole discussion is neither here nor there. Now, please allow me to pass so that I may go to my room and change."

Instead, he moved closer and blocked her way. "I think not. Not until you understand the need to exercise caution." Using his height and strength to his advantage, he stepped forward.

Having nowhere else to go, she stepped back. "Enough of this, Your Grace."

He forced her to step back again, maneuvering her so he had her neatly cornered against a bookshelf. "I'll say when enough is enough. Let's see if you can call for the servants in time."

"For what?"

"For this."

Before she could utter another word, or draw so much as a breath, he was kissing her, taking her mouth with a fierce, implacable possession that was almost savage in its determination and intent. He told himself he was teaching her a valuable lesson, one he would end in a few moments, just as soon as his point was well and thoroughly made. Yet the instant his lips touched hers, he knew he'd made a dreadful mistake. Somehow he'd convinced himself his memories of their previous kisses were in error, that she couldn't really taste as sweet and succulent as he remembered, that he must have dreamed the sheer delight of her touch.

But not only were his conclusions wrong, so were his memories, dulled by time and distance and, perhaps, a will to forget. The impact of her hit him like a blow, a heavy wash of desire turning his body hot and ready. He groaned and tugged her tighter inside his arms, wanting her in every possible way.

Dear God, he thought, *she is delicious, ripe and juicy as a just-picked peach.* And soft, so soft he wished he could tumble her down, wished he could toss up her skirts and stroke her naked skin, then bury himself inside her to see if she was even softer and sleeker there, as he suspected.

He willed himself to stop, giving himself a stern mental warning to let her go, and *now*! But even as he gathered the strength to do so, a devil whispered in his head to take just a little more—one more touch, one more kiss—and then he would put her aside. Angling his head, he coaxed her mouth open and slid deep to plunder and tantalize. Part of him hoped she would resist, prayed she would push against him or beat at him and end this insanity.

Instead, she wound her arms around his neck and kissed him back, darting her tongue forward to circle around his as if she were savoring a sugar-coated confection. He shuddered and kissed her harder, deeper, drowning inside the passionate duel they were now waging. A husky little whimper issued from her throat, the sound making him tremble. With an answering groan, he gave himself over to the pulse-pounding sensations.

Ravishing her mouth, he brought his hands up to cup her breasts. Resting them there, he let the ragged motion of her breath move her up and down against his palms. A moan vibrated inside his mouth as she arched even farther into his touch, unknowingly pressing her flesh right where he wanted it. Using the pads of his thumbs, he stroked her in slow, ever-widening circles, teasing her nipples until they were taut points.

But touching her through her dress just wasn't enough.

Reaching for her buttons, he loosened enough of them to drag down her bodice and stays so that she tumbled free into his waiting hands. Desperate to look, he broke their kiss and gazed down, his loins hardening painfully at the sight of her. Lush and pert, her beautiful breasts were worthy of a goddess, creamy white and tipped with pretty pink nipples.

A shudder ran through her as her gaze lowered to follow his movements. He saw her eyes widen, wondering if she, too, noticed how much darker and undeniably masculine his hands appeared cupped around her pale woman's flesh. A gasp puffed from her throat as he began to stroke her, his touches designed to impart equal measures of delight and torment. Pinching her gently between his thumb and forefinger, he teased her anew, her eyes sliding closed as her head lolled back against the books on the shelf behind her.

Suddenly he wanted even more. Bending, he opened his mouth and closed his lips over one breast, licking her with passionate skill. Her skin tasted just that much sweeter here, like sunshine and flowers, the flavor nothing short of heaven. Yet even as he increased the intensity of his touch, suckling harder while he finessed her other breast with his fingers, there was a niggling something about the fragrance that he couldn't quite place.

Oranges, he mused. *Hmm, that's it. She tastes and smells like oranges. But why is that important? Orange juice . . . spilled orange juice all over her dress.*

Good God!

He jackknifed into an upright position, Gabriella staggering slightly inside his arms as he pulled away.

What in the blazes do I think I'm doing! he questioned.

If not for the orange juice that had seeped through her clothes to her skin, he would have had her down on the floor and been taking her before too much longer. He'd been so far gone, in fact, that anyone could have walked in on them. Anyone, including Rafe.

The blood drained out of his cheeks at the idea. Without wasting another moment, he yanked up her stays and dress and began cinching her back into them.

"There, you're all set," he declared a minute later, fighting for composure as he slid a final button into place.

"All set for what?" she murmured, her voice husky and slow. She blinked, obviously still held within the grip of their mutual passion.

"For me to take my leave and for you to go to your room."

"Oh, you are departing then?" she asked.

"I think it best. With Julianna and Rafe absent, I shouldn't remain. Forgive my forwardness, Gabriella. I never intended our . . . kiss to go that far."

Her lashes swept downward. "I am sure you did not, but you certainly proved your point."

He frowned. "My point?"

"Yes, about how easy it is for a gentleman to take advantage of a lady when she is without a chaperone. I didn't let out so much as a single cry, at least not for help."

Until that instant, he'd forgotten all about the reason their embrace had begun. At her reminder, guilt clamped down like a sharp set of teeth. "You should have," he said. "You ought to have slapped me and made me stop."

"Probably so, but it seems neither of us can do as we ought today."

He opened his mouth, then closed it again, not sure what he wanted to say. Finally he settled on the simplest words of all. "Good day, Gabriella."

"Yes. Good day, Your Grace."

* * *

"May I bring you a cup of punch, Miss St. George?"

Turning, she gazed at the hopeful expression on the face of the young man with whom she had just been dancing. "Thank you," she agreed. "That would be lovely."

She watched for a moment as he walked away, finding herself alone for the first time all evening, and rather grateful for the respite. Actually the evening mirrored her life of late, the last two weeks so busy she'd scarcely had time to stop and take an extra breath between the myriad activities to which she was committed.

From morning to night, there was something to do. Breakfast and nuncheon parties, afternoon teas, promenades in the park, and more balls, routs, and soirees than she could safely keep count of. In between, she spent what seemed to her an inordinate amount of time changing her attire. Throughout the day, her maid would assist her, helping her switch from morning gown to day dress; day dress to walking dress; carriage dress to evening gown; and finally from evening gown to nightgown so she could crawl, exhausted, into bed. Ironically, she found all the frequent wardrobe changes oddly similar to the ones required in the theater; only now she felt as if her entire life were on stage.

The promised vouchers for Almacks had arrived as well; she, Julianna, and Rafe attended the coveted Wednesday-evening event with appropriate excitement. Despite all the anticipation, however, she'd found the assembly rooms surprisingly plain and uninspiring, the company prodigiously circumspect, with no hint of excess frivolity allowed.

As if that were not enough to keep her occupied, there were her usual callers, who continued to pay their respects at the townhouse. The gentlemen, including Lord Carlow, often arrived bearing a fragrant nosegay of flowers for her, staying to chat for a while before asking permission to take her driving or walking in the park.

The one person she did not see, at least not at the house, was Wyvern. Despite his assertion that he was a frequent visitor, he rarely called and apparently managed to time the few visits he did make so they would coincide with occasions when she was away from home.

At first, she didn't really mind his absence, grateful for a chance to steady her emotions after her passionate encounter with him in the library. Far too often during the day her thoughts would drift off, her senses leaping uncomfortably to life as she replayed memories of his exquisite kisses and sizzling caresses. Her cheeks flushed so frequently, in fact, she was surprised no one asked if she was coming down ill. And nights were even worse, her dreams plagued by heated fantasies in which the duke made torrid love to her, her body left aching and bereft when she awakened alone come the morning.

But as the days slid by with little more than an occasional glimpse of Wyvern as he passed through one ballroom or another on his way to play cards or share stories with friends, a simmering irritation began to build within her. *How dare he kiss me like that,* she fumed to herself, *then ignore me as if nothing had occurred! How dare he make me want him, then blithely walk away!*

Perhaps he was only trying to keep temptation at bay, since she admitted sparks did have a way of flaring between them when they were together. But one would think he could manage the trick without staying completely distant.

Part of her wanted to march up and confront him, but another part—the prideful one—urged her to let matters proceed as fate would dictate. After all, she had plenty of dashing suitors clamoring for her attention. She didn't need Wyvern chasing after her as well.

But you want him to, whispered a traitorous little voice. *And you want him to catch you, too.*

Suddenly in no mood for punch, she decided to seek out Julianna, whom she hoped would not mind going home early for once. Weaving through the throng of guests, and not paying strict attention to her steps, she moved around one woman only to bump into another.

"Oh, I do beg pardon," she said, reaching out a hand to steady them both.

Stiffening quite noticeably, the other woman shook off Gabriella's touch and peered at her through a pair of clearly disdainful blue eyes—eyes that oddly enough made Gabriella think of her father.

The stranger's lips pinched together. "Yes, you *should* beg my pardon, girl, and for far more than your graceless ineptitude. I suppose you did that deliberately."

Gabriella stared for a moment, her lips parting in astonishment. "No, ma'am. I am afraid I did not see you as I passed."

Tilting her elegant coiffure of light brown hair, the woman sniffed, then wrinkled her nose as though a foul stench hung in the air. "So you say. And I suppose next you will claim not to know who I am."

Gabriella stiffened, a mixture of confusion and insult traveling in a greasy slide through her system. Her senses tingled, alarm bells ringing out as she more closely studied the woman's face. Obviously, she thought Gabriella should recognize her, but to her knowledge, she'd never seen the woman before in her life.

Mayhap she is mistaken? Gabriella puzzled. *Mayhap she has confused me for someone else?*

But as she studied the woman—older than she by a decade or more—she began to see past the whole to the various features. Sandy-colored hair, blue eyes, and a nose that . . . *Good heavens, she has a nose that looks ex-*

actly like my father's! Gabriella determined. *A nose that looks remarkably like mine!*

"Ah," the woman drawled, "Is recognition now beginning to dawn?"

"Are you . . . are you my *aunt*?"

The woman's lips pinched even tighter. "I most certainly am *not,* even if you may claim to have my brother's blood running through your baseborn veins."

So this was one of her paternal relations. One of her two aunts, and who knew how many assorted cousins, who had never expressed so much as a passing interest in acknowledging her existence.

"I do not claim it," Gabriella said with quiet resolve. "My father was Burton St. George, Viscount Middleton. I have no doubt of that fact, since he visited my mother and me over the years while I was growing up and freely acknowledged me as his own. The last time I saw Papa was only a few months before his death."

Her aunt gave a soft hiss. "How dare you speak of the late Lord Middleton in such familiar terms! And how dare you have the temerity to use the St. George name as if it were your own! You haven't the right. Whatever your whore of a mother was called, *that* is how *you* should be called."

A collective gasp came from the people standing nearby. Until then, Gabriella had not known anyone else was listening. She felt her cheeks pale, her ears ringing suddenly as if she'd been slapped hard across the face. Before she knew what she meant to do, she heard herself speaking. "I am as much a St. George as you. *Aunt!*"

The other woman looked like the one who had been slapped this time, her eyes narrowing with obvious displeasure. "You are an affront to polite Society, you little guttersnipe. I cannot countenance why you have been allowed to parade yourself among the good people of the

Ton as if you belong. Despite your important friends, you should be cast out. I, for one, will never acknowledge you, nor will any other St. George. You, girl, have no family."

"She has plenty of family," interjected a commanding voice from just over Gabriella's right shoulder. She didn't need to glance around to know that Wyvern now stood at her side. Despite her recent pique with him, relief swept through her, along with the wish that she could turn and lean into his strength. Instead she held herself steady, her spine proud and straight.

"The Pendragons quite consider her one of their own," Wyvern continued in her defense. "As for the other, you are correct. Miss St. George does enjoy the protection of many influential friends, myself included."

Pausing, he gave her aunt a look of such arrogant ducal condescension that his expression made Gabriella want to shiver—Wyvern staring down the length of his long, patrician nose as if he'd suddenly discovered something repellent in his path. "You know, Lady Munroe," he drawled in a bored tone. "I cannot recall the last time I noticed you at one of the same entertainments as myself. I had rather imagined the Aptons to have better taste. Perhaps I shall need to take more care in choosing the invitations I accept in future."

A fresh round of gasps rose into the air, an entire sea of eyes now upon them.

As Gabriella watched, her aunt's face turned a telling shade of plum, her mouth opening and closing like a just-caught trout. "Your Grace, that is most unfair—"

Ignoring her, he turned and extended his arm to Gabriella. "Miss St. George, shall we take a turn around the room? I find the air on the other side far more refreshing."

Deciding that silence would be the most effective response, she laid her hand on the sleeve of his black evening coat and allowed him to lead her away. Once they were safely out of earshot, she leaned closer. "My thanks, Wyvern. It was very good of you to come to my aid."

"From what I observed, you appeared to be holding your own rather well, but you are welcome. I feel I must warn you, though, that your thanks may be a tad premature."

She lifted an inquiring brow. "Oh, how so?"

He angled his head toward her. "Your Aunt Phyllis is not without power in Society. Should she wish, she could cause you a great deal of trouble."

"But why? Heavens, before tonight I had never even met her."

Rounding a corner, he continued strolling with her along the room's periphery. "I suspect she sees you as a threat to her reputation. A visible reminder of her brother's indiscretions made public. That and the fact that she is an unpleasant, mean-spirited dragon."

As they walked, she couldn't help but notice the looks directed their way. Her way.

Wyvern apparently noticed as well. "Chin up and smile," he urged in a low tone. "It won't do for anyone to think you were affected by her venom."

Deliberately, she forced her lips to curve upward, showing him her teeth for good measure. "There! How is that?"

He laughed. "Excellent. Though if you aren't careful, you may blind some passerby with that amount of illumination."

"Very funny, Your Grace."

"The moment seemed in need of a spot of levity." His gaze met hers, warmth shining in his dark blue eyes. This time the smile she gave him was genuine.

"Now that's lovely." Reaching across, he squeezed her hand where it rested on his arm. "Don't worry,

Gabriella. You have done splendidly so far this Season and your success shall continue. We will not let tonight's incident be your undoing, I promise you that."

"Do you, Your Grace?"

He nodded. "Yes. If we act immediately, I feel confident we can quash whatever difficulties your aunt or her friends may try to stir up. My title alone lends me significant influence among the Ton. With support from a few other well-placed individuals, tonight's dustup should fade from Society's collective memory soon enough. I propose we begin tomorrow with a ride in the park."

A ride, is it? she thought. *I have barely seen him in the past several days and now he wants to ride with me in the park.* Despite knowing she should simply accept his offer and be grateful for his help, a sliver of her earlier annoyance returned.

"Ah," she stated, "am I to assume then that your social calendar has suddenly developed a few additional openings? I could not help but take note of how extraordinarily busy you have been of late."

A weighty pause followed, her statement obviously having caught him out. "My . . . um . . . schedule has been full recently. Yours as well, I must say. From my observation, you are never without your choice of escort."

She lifted her chin in a kind of silent retort. "No, I am not. Lord Carlow continues to call."

A scowl lowered over his brow. "Does he?"

"Indeed," she declared, striving for a breezy tone.

His jaw tightened perceptibly, his gaze hardening.

"I am taking care, however," she amended, "to avoid finding myself alone with him or any of my other suitors. As you so aptly demonstrated, such situations have a way of quickly getting out of control."

Memories of just *how* out of control matters had gotten between them when they'd last been alone flashed inside her mind. She wondered if such thoughts were replaying inside his head as well, since abruptly he stopped and turned her so his broad-shouldered body shielded her from the room. Maneuvering her back toward the wall, he created a veil of privacy.

"Exactly so," he murmured, his eyelids drooping. "I am relieved to hear you are exercising prudence."

Her blood beat faster, the noise and crush of the ballroom fading from her awareness. "Yes. It seemed wise."

Wyvern leaned nearer, his whiskied voice sliding over her like a caress. "Well, then, shall we take that ride tomorrow?"

For a second she wondered to what sort of ride he was really referring. *Horses, of course,* she admonished herself. *Nothing but horses.* Her lashes swept downward for a brief moment as she steadied herself. "Yes. All right."

He gazed into her eyes for another long moment before he slowly eased away. "If I am not mistaken, supper is about to begin. Why do we not share the meal together and plot our strategy?"

"So it is to be a battle, then?"

"Of course. If a thing isn't worth fighting for, it isn't worth doing."

She considered the sentiment, wondering if he would also apply it in the case of love. Shaking off such musings, she again took his extended arm. Together, they resumed their stroll.

Chapter Nine

"DID YOU SEE that?" Gabriella remarked the following afternoon as she walked her horse beside Tony's along Hyde Park's Rotten Row. "That woman ahead just turned her mount around rather than ride past us."

Yes, Tony thought, *I did see,* taking full note of the snub. Outwardly, however, he let none of his concern show, giving a nonchalant shrug. "She must be a friend of your aunt's. I wouldn't let it trouble you."

But that reaction, although by far the boldest, was not the only one to be cast in Gabriella's direction since their arrival in the park half an hour ago. Obviously Gabriella's aunt, Lady Munroe, had wasted no time in spreading more of her vitriol, aided no doubt by rampant gossip about last night's encounter between her and Gabriella.

While it was true that Gabriella's parentage had never been kept secret, neither had her illegitimacy been pushed so forcefully out into the open. The Ton as a group didn't like having their noses rubbed in scandal or impropriety, and being publicly reminded of both gave some of those previously willing to look the other way an excuse to rethink their opinion. Tony knew he could count on the support of his friends and those acquaintances who didn't dare risk his censure. But there were others—a few very influential and independent others—who had the power to either lift Gabriella above the fray or crush her beneath Society's heartless boot heel. Those were the people he and Gabriella needed to meet and win over to their side.

Whatever the gossip, however, Tony knew no one could find fault with her appearance nor claim she didn't look every inch a lady. Attired in a riding habit of willow-green satin, she looked as regal as a princess, her translucent complexion aglow with healthy color, her eyes soft as rain-washed violets. A dashing cut-straw hat with an impish white feather sat atop her lustrous upswept sable tresses, a few strands left to curl beguilingly against her forehead and cheeks.

What a beauty she is! he thought. *And not only on the outside.* As he well knew, her spirit was every bit as lovely as her face and figure, with the warmth and vibrancy of a perfect summer day. For that reason alone, he refused to let her suffer her aunt's wrath or endure Society's censure. After all, people don't choose their parents, only how they decide to conduct themselves throughout their life. And from his observation, Gabriella was doing an admirable job conducting hers.

Just then, she glanced over and caught him watching her, a small, intimate smile lifting the corners of her winsome pink lips. He smiled back, the impact of her innocent response shooting through his vitals. Hunger coursed through him rushing low to stiffen the flesh between his legs. Still gazing at her mouth, he fought the impulse to lean across and kiss her.

Now wouldn't that give the tattle mongers something to talk about!

Controlling himself, Tony straightened in his saddle and looked ahead, idly scanning the crowd of elegantly dressed ladies and gentlemen gathered in the park for

Fashionable Hour. That's when he noticed Dickey Milton riding their way.

A rising arbiter of fashion, Milton prided himself on being the new Brummell, now that the once great man had fallen from Prinny's favor and departed for the Continent. If Gabriella could earn Milton's support, his influence would go a long way to resecuring her place in Society. After a brief pause to speak to a couple promenading past, Milton reached them and drew to a halt. Tony and Gabriella did the same.

"Wyvern," Milton greeted, inclining his dark blond head. "How do you do on this fine day?"

"Quite well, thank you, Milton. I trust you enjoy the same."

"Oh, I'm in the pink as always, particularly now that Weston has finished tailoring my new coat." He tugged at a single dark blue cuff. "A quality cut, I tell you, that's the key. A man can't go wrong if he has a solid base on which to conduct his affairs. But enough about me when there is a lady present. Pray introduce us, Wyvern, if you would be so good."

Tony could tell by the gleam in Milton's eye that the other man was well aware of Gabriella's identity—and the whirlwind of gossip swirling around her. For her sake, however, he decided to play along. With a minimum of fanfare, he made the introductions. Once they were done, Milton raised his quizzing glass to his eye and swept his gaze over Gabriella from head to foot. Tony saw her stiffen slightly but maintain her composure with admirable equanimity.

"Do I pass inspection?" she inquired once Milton let the glass fall away from his eye to dangle at the end of a matching blue ribbon attached to his waistcoat. Up arched one of Dickey's censorious eyebrows. Tony wondered if her blunt comment had gone too far, half expecting a comeback cold enough to inflict frostbite, and the need to say their farewells and quickly move on.

Instead, Milton gave her another long stare. "That green is exquisite against your brunette coloring, brings out the pink in your cheeks. The style of your dress is excellent as well. You may give your mantua maker my compliments on her efforts."

Gabriella inclined her head. "Thank you. I shall convey your approval to her at my earliest convenience."

"So your mother was an actress, was she?" Milton continued.

"That's right, she was," Gabriella stated, pride ringing clearly in her voice.

"Hmm. Always been partial to actresses myself, don't you know. I find them full of fun and mischief, traits that I suspect may have been passed down to you. No aspirations to tread the boards yourself then?"

"No." She paused for an instant, her gaze unwavering from Milton's. "Actually, I find Society a great enough acting challenge all on its own. The stages at Drury Lane and Covent Gardens fairly pale in comparison."

A notable silence fell before Milton tossed back his head and released a booming laugh. "Quite so, m'dear. Quite so." He shifted his gaze to Tony. "This one's got wit as well as pluck, unlike the usual crop of dull-as-dishwater misses. I can see why you like her, Wyvern. I believe I like her, m'self."

Under Tony's watchful gaze, Milton tossed Gabriella a grin, then added an extravagant wink.

Gabriella laughed in reply.

Tony's fingers tightened fractionally on his reins. "You're right, Milton. I do like Miss St. George, which is why I hope you will do what you can to assist her. I presume you have heard the talk."

The smile eased from Milton's angular face. "Oh, I hear *all* the talk, however small or large it might be.

Sorry business that, what happened last night. My sympathy for any distress it has caused you, Miss St. George."

"Thank you," Gabriella said.

Milton inclined his head, then turned his attention once more toward Tony. "Of course I shall be glad to do what I can. Lady Munroe is a humorless sort for whom I've never particularly cared. Any opportunity to take a bit of the wind out of her sails sounds a fine idea to me."

"You believe it can be done?" Gabriella questioned.

Milton puffed out his chest with affronted pride. "I don't believe it, I *know* it. Never fear, Miss St. George. With Wyvern and myself here to lend you the combined strength of our consequence, your aunt doesn't stand a chance. Her efforts against you shall soon be put to rest."

Relaxing visibly, Gabriella sent Milton a smile.

The three of them chatted for another couple of minutes before Milton bid Tony and Gabriella a cheerful farewell. Once he had gone on his way, they urged their horses into a walk and continued their ride.

After only a few feet, Gabriella turned her head and met Tony's gaze. "Thank you."

He raised an inquiring brow. "Whatever for?"

"For everything. For accompanying me here today and for making a point of introducing me to someone like Mr. Milton. Given the chilly reactions I'm receiving today from some quarters, it would appear your concern about my aunt's influence is by no means exaggerated. No matter the outcome, though, I shall not forget your kindness."

Tony shook off the comment. "As I believe I once told you, I am never kind, so your gratitude is entirely unnecessary. As for the other, all will come right, you will see. Besides, any young woman brave enough to have once held me at gunpoint and who can shoot arrows with the skill of an Amazon queen is a woman perfectly capable of withstanding a bit of rough social weather. You will come clear of this. I shall make sure you do."

At Almacks the following Wednesday evening, Gabriella sat on a chair and watched the assembled couples whirl by. As they did, she assured herself she didn't mind sitting out the dance. Nor was she upset about her lack of a partner for the set that had preceded it. She'd danced several times tonight, and was in no way being relegated to the role of a wallflower.

Still, she couldn't help but notice the desertion of certain gentlemen over the last several days, her usual group of callers having dwindled to a numbered handful—a loyal handful—that included Lord Carlow and four slightly wild young men who were known for disdaining Society's edicts. And of course there was Wyvern and Mr. Milton, both of whom championed her at every opportunity. Were it not for their efforts on her behalf, she very much suspected her vouchers for tonight's entertainment would have been withdrawn.

As it was, people had taken to whispering about her, breaking off their conversations whenever she happened near. Often they would wait in silence until she moved away, then resume their tattling as soon as they assumed her to be out of earshot. She fought not to let their behavior trouble her; she'd dealt with far worse than snubs in her life. But she hated the distress such actions were causing Julianna, who had started hovering around her like a mother hen ever since the trouble with her aunt had begun. Lily Andarton and Maris Waring had joined the effort as well, all three women visibly determined to lift her spirits despite her assurances that she was fine.

Although tonight she wasn't completely positive she was fine, wishing mightily that she could leave early and put the evening behind her. Pride held her in place, though. Pride and Wyvern's admonition that she withstand this bit of "rough weather," as he had called it. If only he were here tonight! But as everyone in the Ton knew, the Duke of Wyvern did not attend Almacks—ever.

"Why do we not visit the refreshment table?" Julianna suggested from where she sat next to her. "Another glass of lemonade perhaps? Or a bite of cake? What do you think?"

"Yes," piped Lily with an encouraging smile from her other side. "Cake and lemonade sound delicious."

Gabriella knew they were trying to cheer her up. And their idea might even have worked if she hadn't already drunk two glasses of lemonade and sampled a slice of pound cake, which she'd found bland and a bit dry. She smiled and shook her head. "Oh, I couldn't, but you two go on."

A tiny frown settled on Julianna's brow. "You're right. Snacks now will only ruin supper. We shall sit here and enjoy the music."

"Yes. The quartet is in fine form this evening," Lily agreed.

Gabriella waved a hand. "Please stop, both of you. You are so sweet to keep me company, but it isn't necessary. Do go on and enjoy yourselves. Have some food, dance if you like, flirt with your husbands. I shall not mind in the slightest."

"But I *enjoy* sitting with you," Lily defended.

"As do I." Julianna sent her a smile. "Passing the time with you is never a hardship."

"Perhaps not," Gabriella said, "but we are here at an entertainment and I want both of you to be entertained, not sitting around nursemaiding me. Please, go have fun. I shall be quite all right on my own for a while."

"Well . . ." Julianna began, her hesitation clear.

"If you do not leave, I shall be very cross," Gabriella threatened. "Now, shoo. *Shoo!*"

"If you are sure," Lily stated, rising slowly to her feet. "But if you look at all blue-deviled, I shall be back in a thrice."

"As will I." Julianna stood. "I won't have you miserable."

"Not a miserable bone in my body," Gabriella declared, pinning a huge smile on her face. "Now, be gone!"

Their reluctance clear, Julianna and Lily made their way across the room. Gabriella maintained the happy expression on her face until she knew both women were otherwise occupied, only then did she release the sigh she had been holding inside.

The set ended, and not long after a new one began. Yet despite her hopes, no gentleman approached to invite her to stand up with him. As the music resumed, she cast a glance at the clock. Only five minutes to eleven. At the stroke of the hour, the doors would be closed and locked, no one else permitted to enter regardless of their status or explanations for being late. She was beginning to wonder if she should visit the refreshment table after all, if only to dispel her boredom, when she turned her head and felt her heart thump hard beneath her ribs.

Suddenly, there stood Wyvern framed in the entrance, his saturnine countenance as darkly handsome as the devil himself were he to assume mortal guise. As custom required, the duke was attired in black silk knee breeches and a cutaway coat, his starched white linen neckcloth tied in an urbane knot that emphasized the strong lines of his face and the masculine set of his jaw. "Magnificent" was the word that came to mind, and yet not even that description did him justice. He was . . . delicious—like a pot of the deepest, darkest, most decadent chocolate.

A shiver raced over her, so strong she placed a hand against her chest and forced herself to draw a measured breath. And then his gaze met hers and she forgot all about breathing.

A moment later, he strode forward.

Only then did she become aware of the hush that had descended over the room, some of the dancers actually stopping to stare. Lady Jersey and Princess Esterhazy stood with their mouths agape, their lorgnettes lifted to their eyes as if both women needed to make certain they were not seeing some sort of collective illusion. From the other side of the assembly room, Countess Lieven hurried across, waylaying the duke only moments before he would have reached Gabriella.

"Your Grace," the countess exclaimed, dropping into a full-skirted curtsey in front of him. "How do you do? May I say how delighted we are that you could join us this evening."

He paused and executed a crisp bow. "Countess."

When he said nothing further, the patroness continued. "I suppose it is no revelation to admit my surprise at your arrival. The other ladies and I had quite given up hope that you would ever attend one of our balls. Might I be so bold as to inquire what has changed your mind?"

"Who," he said in his low, whisky-tinged voice. "Who has changed my mind."

And then, stepping around the countess, he stopped in front of Gabriella and made her a low, elegant bow. "Miss St. George, a pleasure as always. May I say how lovely you look tonight. Although from what I have observed, you always look lovely."

"You flatter me, Your Grace," she murmured, aware of every eye in the room upon her as she dropped into a curtsey. Peeking up at him from beneath her lashes, she smiled as she returned to her full height.

"I speak nothing but the truth," he assured her "If you

are not otherwise engaged, may I have the honor of the next dance?"

She knew he was putting on a show for the assembled crowd, realizing his intent was to repair the damage her aunt had caused. Still, she couldn't keep her pulse from speeding faster, nor stop a surge of uncontrollable flutters from exploding like confetti inside her stomach. "I would be delighted." Then suddenly she remembered. "Oh, except the next set is a waltz, I believe, and I am not yet permitted to engage in that particular dance."

Graceful and urbane, Wyvern turned once again toward Countess Lieven, who had been unabashedly eavesdropping through the entire conversation. He sent the patroness a devastating smile, one whose power was so strong Gabriella felt the residual energy wash over her as well. "Surely you will not deny myself and Miss St. George the pleasure of enjoying the next dance?" he urged. "You have only to say yes. If I am not mistaken, I see a yes forming on your lips right now. Say it, dear ma'am. Please, just say it."

The great lady tittered, girlish color creeping upward into her cheeks. A moment later, she waved a hand. "Of course, of course. Yes, she has permission. Go on, you two."

"You are indeed everything gracious," he said. Making the countess another polished bow, he clasped Gabriella's hand and laid it on his sleeve.

As they strode toward the dance floor, Gabriella struggled to collect her emotions, not fully trusting herself to speak. Only after the new set formed and she was standing in the circle of his arms did she gaze up and into his midnight-blue eyes. "You are here," she stated.

His brow arched. "Did you think I would not be?"

She shook her head. "Truthfully no, since you never attend Almacks. You have quite set all their tongues a-wagging."

"I should certainly hope so. They'll wag even more when I dance with you twice tonight and with no other lady. I expect the event will make the Society column. You must be sure to cut out the clippings."

A laugh caught her. "You are very naughty."

"Of course. You wouldn't wish me any other way, now would you?"

No, she realized. She wouldn't want him to be anyone other than himself. Loyal, kind, and filled with a true verve for life. She longed to thank him again for everything he was doing to help her, but knew he would dismiss any further expressions of appreciation on her part.

Yet is that all I feel for him these days—gratitude? Hardly, she confessed to herself, her skin warm and tingly from his touch, her blood humming with an electricity she experienced only when she was in his company. She thought back all those weeks ago to her time in the country when she'd wished to explore her feelings for him. So much had happened since then, leaving her almost afraid now of what too much soul-searching might reveal.

Do I want to love him? she asked herself as he whirled her in his arms. He smiled and turned her knees to jelly. *Or, heavens above, is it already too late to have a choice?*

Chapter Ten

ON A WARM June night nearly three weeks later, Tony leaned his shoulder against a pillar in the far corner of the Eckfords' ballroom and watched Gabriella dance. Lilting strains of music floated on the air as couples glided in measured time and step. To his eye, though, none of the other ladies were half so enchanting as Gabriella, her every movement bespeaking refinement and grace—an opinion apparently shared by her current partner, the besotted expression on the fellow's face speaking volumes. If he wasn't careful, the young man was in a fair way to making a fool of himself. Although he wouldn't be the first, now that a new flock of gallants had flown to her side.

Just as Tony had promised, Gabriella had regained her standing in the Ton, the whole matter with her aunt having blown over so that it was now all but forgotten. Not that matters hadn't required a definite amount of finessing, but with diligent effort, the trick had been successfully achieved. In fact, she seemed more popular than ever, at least judging by the quality of the invitations that arrived daily at the Pendragons' townhouse.

He should be glad.

He *was* glad.

With any luck, she might still make a good match this Season. He just hoped she would have better taste than to choose one of the assorted young fops who hovered like slavering puppies at her heels, no matter how dashing she might find them and their smiles. Tossing back a swallow of the brandy his host had been good enough to dispense earlier, Tony averted his gaze.

He'd danced with Gabriella already this evening, leading her out for the first waltz before everyone's interested gaze. Until now, she'd needed his help and he'd been glad to lend it, dancing with her at balls, strolling with her during the interval at the opera and the theater, taking her riding and driving. He'd even introduced her to Lord Elgin, the scholar himself giving them a private tour of the collection of marbles he'd had shipped from the Parthenon in Greece. Tony had enjoyed that outing and many others, never the least bit bored in Gabriella's vibrant company. But now he supposed it was time their close association ended, time for him to start pulling away.

Speculation was already running wild, the betting books full of wagers predicting whether or not the two of them would wed. He'd even received a visit at Black House from his cousin Reggie, his heir apparent, who was curious to know if he should soon expect to be cut out of the title. Tony had given him a firm reassurance to the contrary, since his intention to remain a bachelor had in no way changed. Gabriella might be full of fun and an enthusiasm for life that made him see each new day in a different light, but that didn't mean he wanted to marry her. As for *wanting* her . . . well, that was another matter entirely.

Whenever she was around, desire inevitably rose inside him, a need he ruthlessly strove to suppress. So far he'd managed to restrain his baser urges. But if she'd been anyone other than Rafe's niece, he very much suspected he wouldn't have been able to keep from giving her a tumble, virgin or not.

Finished with the dance, she smiled up at her partner. Tony's fingers tightened on his glass as he watched them walk off the floor. Tipping back his snifter, he downed the rest of his brandy in a quick, burning swallow.

"Careful, Your Grace," purred a throaty feminine voice. "Or you just might do yourself a harm."

Turning his head, he encountered a pair of vivid green eyes framed within a lovely heart-shaped face. "Lady Repton. What brings you this way? I thought you were deep into a game of whist."

A sultry smile curved her lips as she gently fanned her face. "Oh, I find I am often deep into something, but for now, I have grown tired of it being cards. Are you in need of another?" she asked, inclining her head toward his glass as she took a step closer. "Or perhaps you have need of something else entirely."

He sent her a knowing look. "Ah, so I assume Lord Repton is out of town again."

"Yes. Off to Brussels over this dismal hullabaloo with Boney. He should be away for a month or more at least." Closing her fan, she slid the edge against his chest. "You could come keep me company. Remember all the fun we had the last time he was gone?"

"Of course," he murmured. "How could I forget? Or the time before that as well."

Lydia Repton laughed, her pretty face lighting with undisguised pleasure. But then that's the kind of woman she was, always up for a bit of dalliance whether it be with her husband or some other man who'd caught her eye. He and Lydia had been occasional lovers over the years, usually when one of them was bored and between steady partners. Taking her to bed would be wild and passionate, he knew, a quick, meaningless coupling that would slake the pent-up need simmering in his body.

God knows he had a hunger, since inexplicably, he'd been without a woman these past few weeks, practicing a celibacy that was completely foreign to his nature. Usually he availed himself of feminine company several times a week—sometimes every night. Yet he'd made no effort to find a new mistress, and he had no taste for the bawdy houses.

All he need do was accept Lydia's offer and escort her home. And if he didn't feel like waiting the hour it would take to get there, he was sure she would be perfectly willing to skip the preliminaries and find a convenient room here in the house so they could enjoy each other immediately.

He told himself to say yes. Why should he not, after all? He had no ties, no commitments to any female.

"Delightful as your invitation sounds," he heard himself say, "I am afraid I must decline." The moment the words were out, a ping of surprise resonated inside him.

What is wrong with me? he wondered. *She is beautiful and eager, a free-spirited bedmate who is more than willing to satisfy my desire. What more do I want?* Yet deep down he knew what he wanted, or rather *who* he wanted, and it wasn't Lydia Repton.

At his refusal, her lips turned downward into a pout. "Really? But why? From what I hear, you gave Erika Hewitt her congé weeks ago. She was none too pleased about it either, if the stories are to be believed. She claims she was the one to end it with you, but of course, everyone knows the truth. You aren't the kind of man women leave, not voluntarily anyway. Don't tell me the two of you are back together again?"

"No, we most definitely are not," he drawled with complete indifference. Since breaking up with his former paramour, he'd barely given her a passing thought.

"Hmm." Lydia unfurled her fan again and waved the painted fabric in languid arcs. "Someone new, then?"

He said nothing, deciding he'd be better off letting her interpret his silence as she chose.

A moment later, a fresh round of music filled the room as a new dance began. Without meaning to do so, he glanced over at the couples, his gaze seeking, and finding, Gabriella. Exactly as she had all night, she looked stunning in a gown of pale yellow silk, her luxurious sable hair pinned atop her head, her cheeks flushed with exuberant good health.

"Surely you are not serious about that girl you've been squiring around Town?" Lydia remarked, apparently noticing the direction of his gaze. "Despite the rumors, I had assumed it was nothing more than nonsense."

"It *is* nonsense," he stated, dragging his eyes away from the dance floor. "She is Rafe Pendragon's niece, and my recent attentions toward her are nothing more than a favor to a friend."

"Hmm. Interesting favor." Turning her head, she looked again in Gabriella's direction. "She is extremely pretty, I must say, though a bit long and thin for the current fashion. The gentlemen don't seem to mind, though, do they?"

A muscle tightened in his jaw. "I haven't noticed."

She laughed. "Of course you have. You notice everything despite those bored looks you so often enjoy affecting. Certain you are not considering making her an offer?"

"Quite certain," he said in a clipped tone. "I will never marry."

But clearly Lady Repton was not about to be put off. "Oh, don't say never. Invariably such a vow creeps up to bite the promiser in the . . . well, let us say a very delicate location."

His lips twisted into a wry grin. "I'm not worried."

"Not now perhaps, but then again most men don't think they'll wed, at least not until they find themselves sliding a ring onto their bride's finger. I shall be intrigued to see if you escape."

"I have all these years. The future shall be no different."

"Of course not, Your Grace." With a smile, she used her fan to tap him again on the chest. "Let me know if you change your mind about the other matter we have been discussing this eve. You have only to send 'round a note, and I shall see to it the side door to the library remains unlocked."

Smiling, he took her hand and dusted a kiss over its back before making her a bow. "My thanks, Lady Repton. You are far more generous than I deserve."

"Very true." Resignation settled into her green gaze. "But I can see you will not visit me. Adieu then, Tony. I refuse to say good-bye."

And yet in that moment he realized that is exactly what their parting was—good-bye.

Across the room, Gabriella watched the tableau unfolding between Wyvern and an utterly exquisite blonde woman whose name she did not know. Even as she danced, she'd found a way to keep them in her sight, her heart giving an uncomfortable squeeze at seeing the pair of them laugh and flirt together.

Who is she? Gabriella wondered, not liking how close together they were standing, nor the playful manner in which the blonde touched Wyvern every now and again, pausing occasionally to stroke him with her fan. Whoever she might be, it was obvious they knew each other well—*how* well was the question?

Surely she isn't his mistress? Gabriella thought, although once she considered the idea, she began to strongly suspect that might indeed be the case. Naïve of her, she supposed, to imagine that Wyvern wouldn't have a lover. A man like the duke undoubtedly had strong needs, and no lack of women willing to satisfy them.

Growing up as she had, she knew far more about such

matters than most girls her age, even if she wasn't familiar with all of the specific details of such arrangements. She realized as well that many married women and widows of the Ton took lovers, most seeing nothing amiss in sharing their sexual favors outside the bonds of matrimony.

So which one was the blonde—widow or wife? And what was she to Wyvern—his current mistress, or only a former one? Neither answer sat well with her, a bitter taste suddenly forming on her tongue.

To her immense relief, the dance soon ended. With a gracious smile, she allowed her partner to escort her from the floor. She was chatting with a group of gentlemen when Lord Carlow arrived.

He made her an impressive bow. "Miss St. George."

"My lord," she replied, giving him an easy smile.

"I have been waiting half the evening for our dance, and I believe the time has now arrived. If these other gentlemen will excuse us, shall we depart?"

A small round of good-natured complaints rose into the air as her coterie of admirers tried to dissuade her from accepting. Instead she laughed and showed them her dance card to prove Carlow right. With a trail of disappointed sighs, she took his arm and let him lead her away.

As he did, her gaze fell again on the mysterious blonde, the unpleasant taste returning to her mouth despite the fact that the woman was no longer standing with Wyvern. She scanned the crowd for him, a frown furrowing her brows when her search proved fruitless.

"Is anything wrong?" Carlow inquired. "You look a bit pained."

"Oh, no no, it's nothing," she lied. "Only a faint touch of the headache that comes upon me every now and again. I am sure it will pass directly."

"Would you be more comfortable if we did not dance? Perhaps a stroll instead?"

Glancing up, she met his open gray eyes. "A stroll would be pleasant, if you are certain you would not mind."

"Not a bit. Come, let us promenade."

They were halfway around the room when they came to a set of double doors, open to the night. Before she knew his intention, he drew her over the threshold and out onto the shadow-draped terrace.

"I thought the fresh air might do your headache some good," he volunteered. "The ballroom has grown rather warm and close, but if you would rather return—"

"No," she said, relaxing at his explanation. "You are right. A draught of air is most likely just what I need."

And the night breeze was refreshing, she decided, as they strolled at a leisurely pace away from the noise and light of the ballroom. The air was fragrant with the scents of earth and blossoming flowers rather than hair pomade and perfume. She breathed deeply, closing her eyes for a brief moment to better savor the fragrance. "Oh, just smell the lilacs! Are they not divine?"

"Hmm, they are indeed," he agreed as he drew to a halt. "But not nearly as divine as you."

Her eyes popped open an instant later as he shifted to take her in his arms. "My lord! What are you doing?"

"What I have been dying to do for ages."

She set her hands against his chest, intending to push him away, but then she stopped. Maybe she *should* let him kiss her. Maybe she ought to find out what it was like to know the touch of another man. After all, she had no means of comparison, only her experiences with Wyvern—devastating as those had been. Perhaps Lord Carlow would prove an even more adept lover than the duke, although she had her doubts. With thoughts of Wyvern and the gorgeous blonde still fresh in her mind, she let herself be convinced. With a shiver, she waited for Carlow's mouth to touch hers.

The moment it did, she knew she had made a mistake, as his lips moved with warmth and urgency against her own. Though his touch was pleasant and his technique quite skilled, no sparks sizzled through her bloodstream, no dizzying surfeit of pleasure rose up to cloud her brain and ease her inhibitions. Disappointment sank within her like a leaden weight. She'd so been hoping she would adore his kiss, but all she could think about was the duke and the fact that Carlow's touch could not compare.

Why can't he be Tony? Why can't I want him like Tony? But she did not, and there was nothing to do but put an end to the illusion. Sliding her palms upward again she pressed against his chest to let him know she wished to stop.

Only he did not stop.

Instead, he tightened his hold and kissed her harder. Her heart fluttered—and not with desire—as she pushed again, turning her head this time to break his embrace.

"Enough!" she said on a muffled cry. "Stop, my lord!"

Ignoring her, he once again sought her lips, but she eluded him so that all he was able to do was graze her cheek. Struggling, she fought to be free.

"You know you want me," he said, refusing to release her. "Quit the maidenly pretense and let that hot blood of yours flow. Give me what both of us want."

"What I *don't* want!" she cried. "I don't want you! Let me go!"

He laughed, the sound sending a quiver of dread along her spine. How could she have so misjudged him? How could she have allowed herself to get into this predicament? She opened her mouth to scream, then closed it again, realizing that once everyone came running, her reputation truly would be in tatters, absolutely irreparable. It wouldn't matter that he was forcing her, all Society would see was that she was in an improper embrace with a man. She would be ruined, her only hope marriage—to him!

Struggling harder, she lifted her foot and gave him a hard kick in the shin. He grunted in obvious pain, a sneer turning his handsome features cruel. His arms squeezed harder, cutting off part of her air, then his mouth took hers, forcing his tongue between her lips despite her attempts to extricate herself. She bit at him and wished she'd let out a good loud scream no matter the consequences.

Long moments passed, her heart hammering so loudly she could hear it inside her ears. Then without warning, she was free, stumbling back a few steps as Carlow was wrenched bodily away. Fists sailed through the air, the sound of flesh beating against flesh giving off sickening thuds.

"How dare you touch her, you filthy cur! I should kill you for this!"

Wyvern! Thank God it was Wyvern.

Despite the concealing darkness, she had no trouble making out his familiar form, nor that of Lord Carlow, who was now sprawled on the stone surface of the terrace.

"Get up so I can hit you again," taunted the duke, his fists clenched at his sides.

But Carlow stayed down, leaning over to spit out a mouthful of blood. Digging in his pocket for a handkerchief, he carefully wiped his lips.

"Coward!" Wyvern declared.

Carlow gave no argument.

"I should call you out for this," the duke continued, "but you aren't worth the scandal. Get up and go, else I change my mind and demand satisfaction, after all. Frankly, I'd relish a chance to have at you with a sword or a pistol. I don't believe you'd care for the outcome either way."

Carlow cringed, refusing to look at Gabriella as he climbed to his feet. Moments later, he melted into the darkness, moving around the house so he wouldn't have to return to the ballroom. Only then did Gabriella allow herself to react, shivers racking her body so she visibly trembled where she stood.

Wyvern stepped forward and drew her against one shoulder. "Are you hurt?"

She shook her head, leaning into his strength, her skin goose-pimpled with cold despite the warm night air. "I'm all right," she whispered. "At least I am now."

He held her for another long moment, then set her from him. "Of all the stupid ideas! What were you thinking? Coming out here alone with him?"

"I—"

"Did you learn nothing?" he stated in a harsh, low-pitched voice made all the worse for his control. "Especially after I warned you about him? What if I hadn't come upon you when I did? What if he'd managed to do far worse than steal a few kisses?"

"He brought me outside for some air, or so he claimed," she said, her lower lip quivering. "With the ballroom so near, I didn't think I needed to worry."

"Well, you did, didn't you? If he'd lured you out into the garden, he could have done anything."

Pressure built inside her chest, a tear escaping to roll down her cheek. Before she could prevent it, a second tear followed, landing in a salty splash on the bare flesh above her décolleté.

Wyvern cursed under his breath, then reached up to brush the moisture from her face. "*Shh,* don't cry. God, I hate it when women cry."

Another tear slid free. "I'm s-sorry."

He drew her once more against his shoulder. "Hush,

everything will be well." Reaching inside his coat, he withdrew a handkerchief. "Here," he said, passing her the silk square. "Dry your eyes."

Wiping her cheeks, she fought to get her emotions under control. Sniffing twice, she allowed one last tear to slide free before she successfully willed away the urge to burst into a watery torrent. A long minute elapsed, Wyvern's silence giving her more time to recover.

"Do you feel up to returning to the ball?" he finally ventured in a soft voice.

The ball? In the last few minutes, she had forgotten all about the festivities still taking place inside the townhouse. Some of her distress must have shown, since Wyvern continued before she could answer. "Don't worry," he said. "I'll send word inside to Rafe and Julianna and let them know that I'll be driving you home. We'll say you aren't feeling well, which, as it happens, is the truth."

"That would be most welcome . . . if you are sure you do not mind."

"Of course I don't. Now, let me take you out through the library. No one but the footmen will see us that way."

Less than half an hour later, Gabriella leaned back into a corner of Wyvern's sumptuously appointed coach, London passing by beyond the glass-paned windows, the blinds half drawn to keep out curious glances. With his usual easy efficiency, the duke had taken care of every detail, escorting her from the house without any need for excuses, then settling her comfortably inside his vehicle while he composed a brief note and sent it off with a footman for delivery.

Then they had been on their way.

He is still angry, she decided, given the fact that he hadn't said a word to her since leaving the Eckfords' townhouse five minutes ago. With a shiver, she leaned more deeply against the plump, velvet-covered squabs, their rich, sumptuous brown appearing black in the darkness. Sprawled in the opposite corner, Wyvern sat shrouded in shadows as well, only the lower half of his face visible upon occasion when they passed beneath the glow of a streetlamp, his square, heavily masculine jaw looking severe and unyielding in the subdued light.

Tears threatened to start again, but she refused to let them fall. There would be plenty of time for such weakness once she reached the safety of her bedchamber. What a little dunce she was to trust Carlow. And how lucky that Wyvern had stepped in to save her—again!

"I am sorry," she blurted, her voice slicing through the daggerlike quiet. "I am sure you are thoroughly sick of me, as I nearly ruined my reputation tonight after you worked so hard these past weeks to restore it. It was stupid of me to go with him. I have no excuse other than my own callow folly."

Silence descended once more, her chest aching a bit at his lack of response.

"Is that what you think?" he bit out abruptly. "That I am annoyed that you might have undone my so-called *hard work*? Were your success in Society not directly linked to your current and future happiness, I wouldn't give a flip about your reputation. Good Lord, Gabriella, I care about *you,* not some supposed slight to my pride. Carlow might have violated you, do you realize that? It makes me sick to think of the ways he could have harmed you."

"But he did not," she said, warmth spreading over her skin at Wyvern's concern. "Because of you."

After a pause, he reached out a hand. "Come here."

Without hesitating she stood, crossing quickly to sink down next to him.

He clasped her palm inside his own. "My heart nearly stopped when I saw you struggling with him," he told her in a thick voice. "The blackguard. I should have murdered him where he stood."

"No, you did the right thing. You stopped him and sent him away. I would not wish his blood to be on your hands. He isn't worth that."

"You're right. He *is* worthless. Still, I'll make sure he comes to regret ever laying hands upon you."

"But you said—"

"Don't worry. My methods will be completely nonviolent. There are more ways than combat to make a point."

A quiver traced through her, leaving her glad she was not on the receiving end of his wrath.

"So why *did* you go out there with him?" he demanded a moment later, his tone seemingly calm.

She paused before answering. "I told you. We went out for the air."

"Hmm, so you said. Nothing else?"

"No. At least not on my part. Honestly, I had no idea that was why he decided to take me outside. I thought we were only strolling."

"Did you let him kiss you?"

She flinched, wishing she didn't feel compelled to admit the truth. "I . . . yes, at first, but I wanted him to stop almost immediately. He . . . he was otherwise inclined."

"That much was apparent. You're too damned beautiful for your own good, do you know that? When you're at a ball, half the men in the room pant after you, while the other half wishes they could."

Her heart leapt at his words. "What of you? What do you wish?"

"Gabriella," he warned with a faint growl.

"*Your Grace,*" she returned. "And so, who was that blonde woman by the way?"

"Which blonde woman?"

"The one with whom you were talking. The one with

the decidedly flirtatious manner and the overly friendly fan."

His eyebrows lowered in a thoughtful scowl, then smoothed out again as recognition dawned. "Oh, her. Just an old acquaintance, no one with whom you need bother."

"Is she your mistress?"

"You certainly don't mince words."

Gabriella refused to be put off. "Is she?"

"No," he stated. "She is not."

"Was she ever?"

"Adam's apples, you're beyond bold! I do not believe I am required to answer such personal queries."

"Ah, so I am right, she was."

His eyes gleamed, their midnight-blue shade nearly black in the evening shadows. "Yes, she *was,* but it ended quite a while ago."

"What about now? Is there someone else?" she persisted, her pulse quickening with equal measures dread and determination. No matter the answer, she had to know.

A long silence hung in the air. "No, there is no one at present."

Relieved pleasure flooded through her veins. So he had no mistress currently. The question was why, and what might it mean?

"Now I believe you should return to your seat," he said.

From his implacable tone, she could tell he meant exactly what he said. She also knew he was not in the mood for further questioning. Deciding it easiest to acquiesce, she shifted forward to climb to her feet. Abruptly, the coach swayed, bumping her against the seat. Despite the excellent padding, a streak of pain shot through her upper arm and shoulder.

"*Ow!*" she cried.

His scowl returned. "What is it? What's wrong?"

Gingerly, she rubbed a hand over the abused area. "Nothing of import. Just a couple of bruises."

"Bruises? Where would you have gotten . . . why that bastard! Here, let me see."

"See what? The marks? I am sure they're under my dress. Besides, it's too dark to make out such a thing."

"Let me determine if that's true." Shifting, he caught her in a gentle grasp and leaned her closer to the window. With careful fingers, he pushed up the edge of one of her short sleeves. Mellow golden light from a passing streetlamp filtered inside, revealing an obvious row of finger-shaped smudges set in purple against her white skin.

Drawing a harsh breath, Wyvern stroked a thumb over her injured flesh. "I ought to go back and run him through. He deserves that and far, far worse. How dare he mark you!"

"They're only bruises. They shall fade."

"He should not have touched you. I don't know how you could have let him, even a little."

"I wanted to know," she whispered, her breath growing shallow.

His gaze lifted to meet hers. "Know what?"

"If I liked his kiss the way I like yours." She swallowed. "If I could possibly lose myself in another man's embrace."

A spark of hot blue fire flashed inside his eyes. "I don't want you ever taking such risks again, do you hear? In fact, you are to avoid kissing men."

Her lips parted. "*All* men?"

"Every one," he ordered in a rough tone, his gaze lowering to her lips. "Every one, that is . . . but me."

Before she had time to react, he drew her onto his lap and pressed his mouth to hers.

A ragged whimper caught inside her throat, pleasure streaking through her bloodstream in a fast, hot burn.

Acting on instinct alone, she kissed him back, curling her arms around his neck to draw him closer. His answering growl rumbled against her lips, making her smile before his tongue swept inside to play hot, wet, sinful games that made her belly clench and her legs turn to jelly. Needing more, she sank her fingers into the thick silk of his hair and cradled his head so she could better match his kisses.

A shiver raked her, one of his hands gliding low, then lower still to wander in bold, inviting circles over the rounded curve of her bottom. She arched when he gave her a gentle squeeze, his uninhibited caress driving a tiny cry of pleasure from her throat. Cradled against his muscled thighs, she became aware of another sensation as the rigid length of his arousal pressed with increasing insistence against her hip.

As though he sensed the direction of her thoughts, he shifted back against the seat and broke their kiss, breath soughing rapidly from his lungs. "God, Gabriella. You make me lose my head. Forgive me. You must think me no better than Carlow, kissing you like that."

"You are nothing like him. And there is nothing to forgive."

"I wouldn't be so sure of that, not where you are concerned."

She laid her palm against his cheek, his skin warm and roughed by a light growth of evening whiskers. "I am certain. I know if I asked you to stop, you would, whether you wished to do so or not."

His gaze met hers. "And do you wish me to stop?"

"No," she whispered, with a wicked little smile.

He laughed, but just as quickly his humor turned to a growl as his hold upon her tightened. With a muffled curse, he captured her lips again, kissing her with a raw, unstoppable possession that demanded her full participation.

She gave it, doing her best to match him, to please him as he was pleasing her. Torrid delight swam in her blood, her body engulfed with a longing she was helpless to resist—not that she in any way wished to resist, each moment being better than the last. Her mind grew hazy when he covered one of her breasts with his palm, his agile fingers gliding across her silk-covered flesh with an adept skill that sent sparks bursting like firework rockets along her nerve endings. Her nipples peaked, growing taut and aching.

"Too much?" he murmured in a husky tone as he pressed slow, open-mouthed kisses to her neck and cheek.

"N-no," she said on a broken sigh.

His hand moved again, thrilling her as he slipped his fingers beneath the bodice of her gown to stroke her naked flesh. Trembling, she bit her lip to hold back a quavering moan, but he wouldn't allow her to stay silent, capturing her mouth again to draw out the sound. Growling in obvious appreciation, he drank down her response, savoring their kiss as though she were a particularly fine draught of champagne. And heaven help her, she did feel giddy, drunk on a surfeit of sensual euphoria that left her wondering if the earth was actually spinning around her.

Curving her over his arm, he scattered velvety kisses across the bare, quivering tops of her breasts, while his hand roamed downward to explore. Completely enraptured, she didn't immediately notice as he inched up the material of her skirt. Her blood sizzled, though, when his hand glided over her knee and across the length of her naked thigh, liquid heat pooling between her legs in a way that made her want to twitch with embarrassment. A powerful ache rose in her feminine core, along with an emptiness that begged to be assuaged. The world melted away, narrowing down to nothing more than the glorious sensation of his touch and a desperate anticipation to find out where his hand might travel next.

Like a carefree adventurer, his fingers roamed up one thigh and across to the other, learning each contour and angle of her limbs with a thoroughness that bordered on torture. Applying the wide, warm surface of his palm, he caressed her bare belly, her stomach dipping inward in equal measures of surprise and elation as he inched upward as far as her stays would allow him to go.

Her nipples tightened into sharp points, the ache between her thighs growing more intense. Then, like a blessed rain in a desert, his mouth captured hers again, taking her with a drugging, seductive hunger that made her want to weep for its beauty. His hand glided low to gently part her legs. A moment later, she gasped, the sound muffled against his lips as his fingers brushed the curls of her femininity to caress the moist, wet heat she knew must be gathered there.

For an instant, she tensed, her earlier embarrassment returning. But he seemed to find nothing amiss, giving a rumbling male hum of appreciation low in his throat as he stroked her in the most intimate of ways. Amazement arced through her again when he slid a finger inside her, her inner folds clenching around him like a glove.

Gasping for air, she broke their kiss and buried her face against the linen of his cravat. Clinging, she sank her nails into his coat sleeve, while his hand urged her to spread her legs wider. She obeyed, incapable of denying him anything at this point. *And why would I want to?* she wondered. *Not when his every movement brings me pleasure the likes of which I've never dreamt possible.*

For a brief moment he withdrew his touch, a cry of complaint coming to her lips before he returned, tenderly easing two fingers inside her this time. Her hips bucked as he stroked, slow and deep and strong, building a need she didn't fully comprehend, driving an unfamiliar hunger that begged to be fed. Then he did something with his thumb that drove her mad, her mind going blank as an explosion of pure, unadulterated bliss burst like a fireball through her body. Shaking, half incoherent, she let him take her mouth in a rough kiss, grateful to him for muffling the harsh cry of pleasure his touch had wrung from her throat.

Her heart thundered in her ears, Tony's scent and touch surrounding her as she let him tangle his tongue with her own. Only then did she become aware that he was shaking too, his shoulders taut, his own need obvious, his arousal pressed rigidly against her hip.

Suddenly the coach gave a jolt and stopped. With her emotions still scattered, the cessation of movement made little sense—at least not at first. Tony seemed to comprehend well enough, though, muttering a small curse before he gently withdrew his hand and reached to toss her skirts back into place. After easing her off his lap onto the seat beside him, he levered himself up to place a couple of feet of space between them.

And not a moment too soon, she realized, as one of the footmen opened the coach door just a few seconds later.

Mercy!

She shot a glance at Tony, knowing her eyes must be wide and her expression vulnerable. "H–how do I look?" she asked, keeping her voice low so only he could hear. "Am I presentable?"

His gaze swept over her, his eyes heavy-lidded with latent desire. Leaning forward, he brushed his fingertips over one sleeve, giving the garment a subtle adjustment. "You are magnificent, Gabriella," he whispered. "Never fear. No one but the two of us shall ever know."

A reassuring warmth spread through her, along with a wish that he might kiss her again. After tonight, she realized she would want no other man—her passion was reserved exclusively for him. But she knew he could not touch her, at least not now, in spite of the reciprocal awareness shining in his gaze.

Taking an additional minute to compose herself, she allowed Tony to step out of the coach and help her down. Martin was waiting at the Pendragons' townhouse door, candlelight spilling outward from the interior. Taking her arm, Tony led her forward.

"Miss St. George is weary," he told the butler as they entered the foyer. "Pray have her maid attend her."

"Immediately, Your Grace."

"Well then," Tony said as the man moved away. "It would seem you are in safe hands, so I shall bid you good night."

She nodded. "Shall I see you tomorrow at the garden party?"

He hesitated for a moment as if he might be reconsidering their planned outing. Then his expression cleared, a smile spreading over his mouth. "I would not miss it for the world. Sweet dreams, my dear." Taking her hand, he pressed a lingering kiss against her palm.

"Good night," she murmured, curling her fingers over his touch as he turned to depart.

Yes, she thought, *I will dream tonight—but all my reveries will be of you and far too passionate to be sweet.*

Chapter Eleven

DESPITE A FEW half-hearted attempts, Tony found it nearly impossible to keep his hands off Gabriella over the next two weeks.

At first, he'd told himself he was protecting her. Who better than he to make sure she didn't again find herself in a precarious situation with an overeager beau? Who more determined than he to ensure she came to no harm? Yet as the days progressed, he knew himself for what he was, a rake always looking for a way to have her to himself—leading her into darkened alcoves and quiet, vacant rooms where they could share kisses and any number of delectable, forbidden caresses without being observed. Still, he was careful to maintain a strict level of control over himself, making a point to never let their love play progress to the point where he lost his head and ended up taking her virginity. Even so, he'd been giving her a bit of an education lately, finding Gabriella an apt and passionately enthusiastic pupil.

Meanwhile, word reached London that the war was over. Napoleon's final battle had been waged on the muddy fields of Waterloo in mid-June, the Duke of Wellington and his troops dealing the French a final, crushing defeat. Ever since, the city had been rejoicing.

When Gabriella heard there were to be fireworks as part of the victory celebrations, she had insisted Tony escort her. "Oh, but we must go!" she had urged him only a couple of days ago while they were sharing supper at a rout. "There is nothing quite as splendid as a fireworks display. All the sounds and colors lighting up the night sky."

"All the unwashed masses crammed into too little space, tipsy on drink and primed for mischief," he countered with a wry quirk of his brow.

"Do not be a curmudgeon, Your Grace," she had teased. "No one likes a spoilsport, you know."

"You seem to like me just fine these days," he'd murmured, enjoying the pink that had blossomed in her cheeks as he'd rubbed his calf against hers beneath the table.

Yet in spite of his supposed opposition to the outing, he'd been unable to deny her.

Arriving less than an hour ago, he and Gabriella had joined the noisy masses of revelers gathered in Green Park for the celebration. Rafe, Julianna, Ethan, Lily, and a few other family members and friends had accompanied them. Hannibal had come along as well—the huge, imposing servant with his glowering expression and piratical bald head precisely what was needed to scare the menace out of any would-be thieves and miscreants.

With night now fallen, the fireworks were expected to begin momentarily. Standing with Gabriella at the rear of their group, Tony used the darkness to his advantage, covering her hand where it lay on his arm. Silently, he stepped a fraction of an inch closer so that their hips all but touched. She shot him a quick glance, her lips curving into a smile before she returned her gaze, and presumably her attention, to the leisurely conversation going on between Rafe, Ethan, and the others.

He tried to focus, but found it nearly impossible with the honeyed scent of her skin teasing his nose. If he had any sense he would put *more* space between them rather than less, but ever since that night in his coach, he couldn't seem to shake his need to be with her. She was like a drug in his system, his craving for her growing stronger with each and every encounter.

The first round of fireworks exploded in a triple burst of light and noise, interrupting his musings long enough to draw his gaze upward toward the dazzling overhead display. Beside him, Gabriella oohed and ahhed along with the crowd, cheering as each fresh burst of pyrotechnics illuminated the night sky. He smiled as he watched her, far more interested in Gabriella than the light show above.

Suddenly she turned her head and their eyes met, her mouth parting on an indrawn breath he could sense had nothing to do with the jubilation around them. Abruptly he hardened, hunger suffusing his very blood and bone with need. He wanted her, or at least as much of her as he could safely allow himself to have. Clasping her hand, he eased her slowly back so that the two of them disappeared together into the intermittent darkness.

Having been to previous fireworks shows, he knew the display would continue for a few minutes more, giving him enough time to satisfy a measure of his passion, then return her without notice. And if someone did comment, he would simply say he'd taken her to watch the light show from another vista.

Several yards distant, he led her around to the far side of a large tree and pulled her into his arms, his mouth on hers before she had a chance to say a single word. Pressing her back against the tree trunk, he claimed her with an ardent intensity. Gabriella moaned softly and slid her fingers into his hair, caressing his scalp as she kissed him back with undisguised passion.

Cupping her breasts, he stroked her, bringing her nipples to taut peaks. He heard pounding inside his ears, but didn't know if it came from the explosions going on around him or the ones going off inside his body. Sliding closer, he let her feel his erection, shuddering when she rubbed herself against him in reply, arching forward like a warm little cat wanting to be pet.

And pet her he did, his hands roaming, even as his mouth left hers to dapple kisses over her cheeks and temples before grazing the lean column of her neck. Rolling her head to one side, she sighed as he scattered a line of kisses from her jaw to her collarbone and below.

Another series of pops and whistles sang through the air, together with fresh roars of excitement from the crowd. Drawing a deep breath, he forced himself to break away, the effort a truly wrenching one. "Enough," he panted in a reprimand to himself. "We'll be missed if we don't go back."

"Oh, must we?" she sighed. "Just one more kiss, hmm?"

Her breathy suggestion shot straight to his groin, the hard ache there urging him not to be so hasty. With a groan, he leaned forward. *One more kiss, as she said,* he mused. One more sweet taste despite the danger and the fact that her touch would only leave him more sexually frustrated than he was already. *I'll worry about that later,* he decided as his mouth met hers, letting the pleasure take him once again.

Soon, the pounding returned to his ears, her touch and scent an aphrodisiac of which he couldn't seem to get enough. Her tongue swirled around his, her small hands pressed enticingly against his chest. In some dim corner of his brain he heard the crowd roar along with another round of fireworks. But then the noise changed, punctuated by shouts and exclamations . . . and the high-pitched whinnying of a horse in distress. Suddenly someone bumped into him, feet hurrying as they stumbled past.

What in the blazes? His head jerked up, his arms going protectively around Gabriella as he looked to see who had collided with him. His eyes went wide as he made out the shapes of people moving in the darkness—men, women, and children being jostled amid an increasingly erratic mob.

Suddenly a gunshot rang out, followed by a woman's chilling scream, then more shouts and cries.

Good Christ, he realized, *a riot!*

"Stay close to me," he told Gabriella. Cradling her against his side, he drew her away from the tree and started forward, scanning ahead for signs of their party. Despite flashes of light from the fireworks still exploding in the sky, he couldn't make out so much as a trace of Rafe and the others, not even Hannibal, who was so tall he towered over Tony's own six-foot-three-inch frame. Shoving down the glimmer of alarm that squeezed in his belly, he held tightly to Gabriella and struggled forward another couple of yards. But he realized their effort was hopeless, as the crowd surged toward them like an unstoppable tide of human flesh.

"We'll have to go the other way," he told her, his voice raised so she could hear him above the mob, people jostling and pushing against them as they forced their way past.

Meeting his gaze, she nodded, amazingly calm given the situation. "Just don't let go of me."

"Not a chance," he vowed, hugging her even closer to his side. Careful of their footing, he turned them, making sure they didn't fall and risk being trampled. Abruptly, he and Gabriella merged with the flowing crowd, moving ahead with no tangible idea of where they were being led. The pace was challenging, just short of a trot at times. Several feet in the distance, he saw an old man stumble and cry out as he disappeared into the seething mass. Tony wanted to go to him to help, but there was no possible way to reach the man. Pushed onward, he could only pray Gabriella had not seen the old man's plight.

Long minutes passed before the crowd finally slowed

and began to thin as people found their way to freedom. Overhead, the sky was black, the fireworks silent, only an occasional distant shout left to punctuate the air.

Leading Gabriella to a vacant spot near another tree, he halted, then tugged her firmly against his chest. Saying nothing, he simply held her, while she did the same.

"We made it," she said after a long minute. "Thank God."

"Yes." Scanning the darkness, he searched for a recognizable landmark, but found none.

"Do you think Rafe and Julianna and the others are all right?"

"I am sure of it. Rafe and Ethan have cool heads. I can't believe they didn't manage to get everyone to safety."

She drew a breath. "Julianna will be worried."

"Of that, I'm sure as well. But she and Rafe must realize we were together and that I'll keep you from harm."

"I would have been quite terrified without you, you know."

"You'd have managed. I can't think of any other lady of my acquaintance with your calm resilience."

She gave a wry laugh. "An act, Your Grace. It was all an act."

He smiled. "As much as I would enjoy continuing our conversation, I believe we ought not linger any more. Thugs and pickpockets are known to roam the park at night and I would rather we did not encounter any of their sort."

A slight shiver ran through her. "No, this evening has proven eventful enough already. Let us be on our way."

He took her hand, and they walked forward. As they traveled, many others passed by, some wandering dazed and lost, a few bearing injuries, while more were simply weary and eager to reach their homes. After ten minutes or so, the two of them finally came to the edge of the park. Reassessing their surroundings, Tony realized they must have traveled toward Piccadilly, some distance from where the fireworks celebration had taken place.

Exiting the park, they stepped out into the city, the mostly residential streets quiet at this time of night. Given their location and the late hour, he knew finding a hackney would be a virtual impossibility. He could always knock on the door of a nearby home, he supposed, and ask that a footman be sent to Black House for a coach. But as he and Gabriella were so obviously alone together, he was reluctant to exercise that option. Better to make the journey on foot, then get her safely home to Rafe and Julianna with no one else the wiser.

"Are you up for a walk?" he questioned.

She nodded. "I wore my half-boots; I shall be fine."

Keeping her hand secure inside his own, he and Gabriella started forward, the surrounding darkness broken only by the light from a few house lanterns. They had been walking for nearly fifteen minutes when the rhythmic clip of horses' hooves rang out behind them. Pausing, Tony turned to watch the approaching coach. He was debating the wisdom of flagging down the vehicle when it slowed of its own accord and drew to a halt. The window closest to him and Gabriella slid down with a quiet snick.

"Gracious, Wyvern, is that you?"

He held back a groan, his jaw tightening as he met the gaze of the last person he could possibly have wished to see. "Good evening, Lady Hewitt."

"Whatever are you doing out here?" she questioned, sending an arch look in Gabriella's direction. "Has there been an accident with your coach?"

"A small riot, actually, during tonight's fireworks celebration in Green Park." He said nothing further, taking up a position just in front of Gabriella in the forlorn hope that his ex-mistress wouldn't be able to clearly identify her in the darkness. But as he knew, such a hope was indeed ridiculous.

"How frightening!" Erika said with exaggerated concern. "And now you and poor Miss St. George . . . that is Miss St. George just behind you, is it not? . . . are being forced to walk home. Well, providence has decided to shine upon you," she said, opening the door. "Come let me take you up. My coachman shall have you home in no time."

For an instant, Tony considered refusing, but he knew the gesture would be useless since the damage, as it were, was already done. Sliding Gabriella's hand over his arm, he led her forward.

"Thank the stars both of you are all right!" Julianna exclaimed nearly an hour later as Tony, Gabriella, and Rafe stood with her inside the Pendragons' entrance hall. "We were all so worried when we realized the two of you weren't with us. I assume you were pushed away from our group when the fighting broke out?"

Tony and Gabriella exchanged a quick look before glancing away.

"Something like that," Tony offered. "Everything happened so fast. It's hard now to recall."

This time it was Rafe who shot him a look, his friend's arms crossed over his chest, a speculative frown on his face. Julianna, however, didn't seem to notice, reaching out to give him and Gabriella yet another hug. "Well, whatever the details, it is of no consequence now. All that matters is that you are returned safe and unharmed."

"Yes," Gabriella piped. "Were it not for Wyvern, I don't know if I would have escaped unscathed. I was dreadfully frightened."

"If you were, you certainly didn't show it." Tony sent her a smile. "You were amazingly fearless."

"I didn't feel fearless. Inside I was a veritable bowl of jelly."

"The loveliest jelly I've ever seen," he murmured, losing himself for an instant in her expressive violet gaze. When he glanced up again, Rafe and Julianna were watching; there was a smile on Julianna's lips, while Rafe had an even more pronounced scowl on his brow.

Tony cleared his throat. "Yes, well," he stated, "the hour grows late and considering all of tonight's excitement, I suppose I ought to say my farewells."

"Yes," Rafe stated. "Good night, Tony. I expect I shall see you tomorrow at Brooks's."

He returned Rafe's gaze with apparent equanimity. "Likely so." Turning, he nodded to the ladies. "Julianna, rest well knowing everyone is safe. Miss St. George, may your dreams be deep and filled with the comfort of angels."

"May yours as well, Your Grace," Gabriella said, offering him her hand.

"Oh, I doubt that shall come to pass," he replied, curving his fingers over her own. "Seraphim and their like haven't been on speaking terms with me for years."

Rafe gave an audible snort, his lips twitching with amusement in spite of his taciturn mood. Making Gabriella a bow, Tony released her hand and stepped away. Wishing them all a collective good night, he exited the townhouse.

Late evening shadows stole around him like a dark cloak, the neighborhood silent except for the muffled bark of a dog several streets away. He was expecting to find one of Rafe's coaches waiting for him. Instead, standing before him was the same vehicle in which he had arrived. The horses advanced a few paces at his arrival, stopping so the coach door was directly opposite him.

Lady Hewitt leaned forward, her face framed in the lamplight that shone into the open window. "It's about time you left that house. I was beginning to wonder if you planned to stay the night."

He slipped his hands into his pockets. "What are you still doing here, Erika? There was no need for you to wait."

"Oh, I know. But how could I depart and cut short our chance to visit a bit more?" Satisfaction gleamed on her comely features, her expression reminding him of a vixen who had just located a henhouse full of plump, unsuspecting chickens. Given the twinkle in her eyes, he wouldn't have been surprised to see a telltale feather or two floating on the air.

"I assume you sent Rafe's coach away?" he questioned.

"Of course. Why go to the bother of two vehicles when one will do? Come along, Tony. The hour does grow late."

Hesitating only a moment more, he stepped forward and entered the coach. Relaxing back against the well-appointed seat, he waited for her to begin.

"It's been a long time since last we met," she ventured as the horses drew the coach into a gentle motion.

"An hour at least, I would guess."

She made a face. "Don't be glib. You know what I mean."

"My pardon. You are right, my attempt at humor was poorly done. Surely, however, you didn't ask me here to talk about old times."

"I suppose not, although I must say one can never entirely forget old times, can one?" she observed with a bitter tinge to her words. "Despite a person's best efforts to do so."

"It is true that some matters are more easily set in the past than others."

"As are some people. You seem to have had no difficulty forgetting *me,* for instance."

He restrained a sigh. *Ah,* he mused, *this is the trouble with encountering old lovers, especially those for whom the breakup was not mutually desired.* He rubbed an idle thumb against his trouser-clad knee. "I have not forgotten you, Erika. How could any man forget a woman like you?"

She made a slight noise of mollification, but said nothing more.

"I have simply moved on," he continued. "As have you. I understand you have been seen with Lord Plympton lately."

She rolled her shoulders in a graceful arch. "Hmm, noticed that, did you? He can't keep his hands off me, you know. And what inventive hands they are, too, I must say!"

If she thought her remark would spark some glimmer of jealousy in him, she was doomed to be disappointed. Although, as he well knew, she had yet to state her real objective for this conversation.

"While you, Your Grace," she went on, "have been dancing attendance on that young miss, that Gabriella St. George. It's very naughty of you to be dallying with such an innocent, especially beneath the noses of your good friends, the Pendragons. I assume you haven't taken matters too far beyond flirtation, since a man of your prodigious appetites couldn't possibly be satisfied with an inexperienced little chit like her."

His fingers tightened into a fist, disliking even the sound of Gabriella's name on her lips.

"Most unfortunate about this evening." She paused, trailing a hand across her long silk skirt. "Had someone else come upon the two of you wandering alone together in the dark, I fear they might have been tempted to rush home and start sharing such titillating news with their entire acquaintance. I mean, on the face of it, the girl is compromised, and what with the way the Ton can be, I worry that poor Miss St. George would soon find her reputation quite in tatters should word get out."

So now we come to the heart of the matter, he thought, waiting to see what further threats she had to utter.

"Given the previous aspersions cast upon her character by her aunt," Erika observed, "I do not see how she could possibly survive another round of scandal. What a tragedy that would be to find oneself driven from Society because of a circumstance not at all under one's control!"

He held his temper. "Yes," he replied in a deliberately casual tone. "That would be most regrettable indeed."

"Of course, I have no intention of breathing a word. It shall be our little secret."

"Will it? How generous of you!" he drawled with a faintly mocking undertone.

"Why, thank you, Wyvern," she mused aloud, a little smile of self-congratulation riding her lips. "I think so, too. And generosity deserves a reward, do you not agree?"

He clenched his hand tighter, in no other way allowing his emotions to show. "Just what sort of *reward* did you have in mind?"

She let out a brief laugh, the sound raking over his system like a set of nails across a slate. "You! I want you back."

His arched a single brow. "Do you really? What of Plympton?"

"What of him?" she shrugged. "He is amusing and serves his purpose, but despite his skills he lacks your unique finesse. Of all my lovers, I have yet to find one who comes close to matching your talents in bed. Of course, I wouldn't take you back without some additional recompense."

"Such as?"

"A good bit of groveling to start. Literally on your knees for a while, I believe. Although I can think of many other ways you can pleasure me while you're on your knees, can't you, Your Grace?" she purred, quite clearly enjoying the moment. "And there would be a few other rules as well. For instance, I would decide when and where and how often we meet."

"Would you?"

"Hmm-hmm. And most important of all, I will be the one to end the affair. You will be mine until *I* decide we're through. And when I have had enough and want to kick you out, it will be done in public so everyone can see me toss *you* aside. I'll expect you to grovel then, too, and beg me not to end things between us. I might even insist on tears. You can jab a needle into your palm if you can't conjure them up on your own."

"You've spent a lot of time thinking this out, haven't you?"

"You have no idea," she spat, her repressed anger suddenly showing.

"Then again," he said, "if you had considered all the angles, you would realize that I am not a man who begs—not for you, not for anyone."

"Not even for the sake of that poor, innocent girl you've led astray? And what of yourself? After all, think of your reputation should word get out. Since I am sure the last thing you'd ever want to do would be to actually sacrifice your freedom and marry her. Compromised as she is, there would be no other honorable way to rescue her."

He drew in a long, deep breath and held his tongue.

"No, I know you, Tony, and you'd rather be branded a cad than saddled for life with some debutante, however intriguing she might presently be. Although given that you're a rake already, the scandal would likely do nothing but add to your cache. Yet what of your friends, Rafe and Julianna? How would they feel, knowing you had brought shame and dishonor upon them and theirs? Why Rafe Pendragon might even feel the necessity to call you out! A tragedy to end a decades-old friendship over a girl. And you do not have to," she purred, leaning across to slide her hand over his thigh. "Just come back to me on my terms, and my silence is yours."

Her hand glided higher. He brought his palm down hard on top and stopped her progress. Restraining the urge to fling aside her touch, he curled his hand around her own, wondering in that moment how he could ever have wanted her. With a Machiavellian determination, he hid his disgust and raised her hand to his lips, pressing a kiss against her perfumed skin.

"You're very clever, my dear," he murmured. "But then you always were."

"I'm glad you noticed."

"And it would seem you have me at your mercy."

She showed her teeth, gleaming white even in the dim night shadows. "Just the way I like my men."

"It is late, however, and in case you were not aware, we have arrived at Black House."

She tossed a surprised glance out the window. "So we have. Perhaps I should come inside?"

"Not tonight," he said on a shake of his head. "After all, I could never be brought to grovel properly in my own home."

She laughed. "I suppose not. So we are agreed then?"

He stroked his thumb over her hand, then made himself kiss the inside of her palm again as if he savored the act. "We shall talk more on the morrow . . . but wait, I have an engagement tomorrow evening that I cannot break. Would the day after be agreeable? That way I can make certain arrangements to see to your pleasure."

Her eyes narrowed. "Your aren't trying to deceive me, are you?"

"To what end? As you pointed out, you leave me no other options."

He watched as she considered his statement, the smile returning to her lips. "The day after tomorrow will be acceptable. But be sure whatever it is you have planned for us will be creative enough to surprise even me."

"That, dear lady, I can safely guarantee."

Chapter Twelve

FROM HER PLACE on the divan in her bedchamber, Gabriella turned a page of the novel she was reading, a volume from the Minerva Press that Lily Andarton had lent her the last time she'd called here at the house. Rain drizzled in rivulets against the windows, the day a gloomy one that seemed to suit everyone's subdued mood.

After last night's troubles in the park, she and Julianna had decided to cancel their engagements and remain indoors for the rest of the day, the weather only reinforcing the wisdom of their decision. At present, Rafe was out on business while Julianna had gone upstairs to the nursery to feed baby Stephanie and play for a while with her precocious two-year-old son, Campbell, whose new favorite word was "no."

Turning her attention back to her book, Gabriella tried to focus, but despite the heroine's perilous situation, her thoughts soon began to drift again. Although Rafe and Julianna hadn't said anything further about her and Tony becoming separated from the group last night, she couldn't help but think there might still be repercussions from the event.

Her uncle's words had certainly carried an uncharacteristic edge to them, while the pointed looks he'd given Tony had been impossible to miss. For her part, Julianna had clearly been relieved by their safe return. This morning, however, Gabriella had caught a faintly worried expression on her friend's brow—an expression that disappeared the moment she'd noticed Gabriella looking.

And then there was Lady Hewitt.

On the surface, her offer to take Gabriella and the duke in her coach had been a generous one, her conversation during the journey congenial and often amusing. Yet the more Gabriella considered, the more she wondered if there might have been some other, underlying motivation at work. And although many of Society's rules still eluded her, she knew enough to realize that she and Tony should not have been alone together—at least not *discovered* alone together. Still, any reasonable person would surely understand that there had been extenuating circumstances. They'd been caught in a riot, for heavens sake!

Besides, she silently shrugged to herself, *what is the worst that could happen?* If anything were said, the talk would blow over in a few days' time. With her mind a bit easier, she returned to her book. Five minutes later, a knock came at the door.

"Come in," she called, marking her page with a finger.

"Pardon me, miss," said one of the housemaids. "His Grace is here and has asked if you would join him in the drawing room."

Tony is here? Setting the novel aside, she rose to her feet. "Of course. Tell him I shall be along shortly."

The maid bobbed a curtsey and withdrew.

Crossing to the pier glass, she checked her hair and smoothed a crease from the skirt of her apricot-and-cream-sprigged muslin gown. Deciding she looked presentable, she walked from the room.

She expected to find him already talking with Julianna, but instead he was alone. He turned as she entered the room.

"Good morning, Your Grace," she said, crossing to him. "I had not expected to see you so early and on such a dreary day. Why, it isn't even ten o'clock yet."

"Miss St. George." He executed a polite bow, looking even more urbane than usual in a dark green cutaway coat and fawn-hued trousers. A few errant droplets of rain glistened in his thick, night-dark hair, his eyes startlingly blue against the natural tan of his complexion.

"If you've come to see Rafe," she offered, "I am afraid you have missed him. Julianna is upstairs with the children. Why do I not send for her—"

"No," he interrupted. "Let her remain where she is. Actually, it is you I have come to see."

"Oh," she declared, tucking her hands at her back. "Have you really?"

An intense expression flickered in his gaze. "Yes."

She trembled, thinking of his kisses and caresses, including the ones they had shared only last night. Despite their increased intimacy of late, he had never before approached her here at home, as if the townhouse were forbidden territory—which, in a way, she supposed it was.

Striding past her, he went to the door and closed it with a nearly silent click of the lock. Then he returned to take up a position directly before her.

What is he about this morning? she wondered. *Why has he come to see me in such a seemingly clandestine fashion?* An uncharacteristic wave of shyness ran through her as she met his penetrating gaze.

"Miss St. George . . . Gabriella, I have come to ask you a rather important question."

"Oh? And what might that be? This doesn't have to do with last night, does it?"

He raised a brow. "In a way, but that no longer matters. Gabriella . . ." He paused, leaning forward to take her hand, which he enfolded securely inside his own. "Forgive me if I do not have precisely the right words at my disposal. I have never done this before, so I hope you will excuse me if I fail to say everything you might wish to hear."

And what would that be? How could I possibly know when I can't even fathom the question?

"This may seem unexpected," he continued, "but I assure you I have given this matter a great deal of thought and believe it to be the best thing for us both. You and I get along well, do we not?"

She stared for a moment at his query. "Of course, but then you know that already."

"And physically, we are extremely compatible." Moving closer, he stroked his free hand over the curve of her hip, letting his palm rest against her waist. "I don't think I am wrong to say that you would welcome me into your bed."

The air rushed from her lungs, her pulse throbbing in a mad rhythm at the base of her throat. "Y-Your Grace, I . . . I," she began, her words sounding strangled.

"A simple yes or no will suffice." He stroked his thumb against the underside of her palm, sending hot and cold shivers racing across her flesh, her nipples puckering beneath her bodice.

I should not tell him, she thought. *I should not admit to having such wanton, impassioned emotions inside me.* And yet, he already knew her answer, particularly since she had made no effort to deny his touch over the past couple of weeks. Under his steady gaze, she gave in to his silent demand. "Yes," she whispered, only then realizing the enormity of what she had confessed.

"Good. We'll do well together."

What is he saying? Surely . . . Good God, surely he isn't asking me to be his mistress? She didn't want to be any man's mistress and yet . . .

"Gabriella St. George," he said in a deep, velvety tone.

"Will you do me the great honor of consenting to be my wife?"

Air left her lungs in a great *whoosh,* as if she'd hit the ground hard. She blinked against the dizzying sensation. "Did you say *wife*?"

"I did."

"But you don't want a wife! Everyone in the Ton knows that."

One corner of his mouth turned up. "It would seem, then, that everyone is wrong."

For a long moment she could barely think as she tried to digest what he'd just said, wondering if he was truly serious. Over the past weeks, her emotions had been jumbled and unsure, setting her caution aside as she let herself drift day-to-day on the sea of excitement and pleasure she felt when she was with him.

Yet deep inside her had dwelled a secret wish, a hidden hope that he might one day ask her to be his bride. Still, she'd never really thought he would propose. Now here he was, asking her to be his wife. Had she, Gabriella St. George, really brought England's most elusive and sought-after bachelor up to scratch? So it would appear. Despite everything that had happened between them, though, his conquest somehow seemed too easy.

"So, what do you say?" he coaxed.

Say? She wanted to say "yes," she realized, but something held her back. A tiny frown furrowed her brows. "Why?"

He scowled back as if he had been expecting her unquestioning agreement. "Have I not just said? We are well suited. And in case you haven't noticed, I desire you. Badly." He drew her closer so their bodies were pressed together, his arousal plain.

His bold display left her in no doubt of his truthfulness on that score. But did he desire her so desperately he was willing to marry her in order to have her in his bed? And what of love? He'd said nothing of such tender emotions.

Her heart clenched at the thought, a flood of awareness washing through her, along with a realization she had denied until this very moment. *Good heavens, I love him! Truly love him. And with only a single word, he can be mine.*

Even so, she hesitated. "This isn't about last night, is it? You aren't proposing because we were seen together? Because if it is, then—"

"Then what? Then our getting married makes even more sense." He slid his hand along her back, circling his palm in gentle, soothing strokes that made her long to arch against him like a contented cat. "Let me make you happy, Gabriella. I can, you know, if you'll give me the chance. Let me make both of us happy."

Cradling her as close as nature and their clothing would allow, he bent and took her mouth, his lips moving over her own in a heated, seductive glide. Her mind turned fuzzy, as it always did at his touch, her breath thinning into shallow, unsteady puffs.

"Marry me, sweetheart," he murmured against her mouth. "Tell me you'll be mine."

Be his. Oh, how I want to be! she thought. *Yours and no other's.*

She'd met so many men since coming to London, some of them quite compelling. But none, not a single one, could begin to compare with Anthony Black—not in looks or demeanor or temperament. He possessed all the traits she most admired in a man: intelligence, compassion, and courage. And above all, an ability to see the world with humor, and never take anyone or anything, including himself, too seriously.

He spoke of happiness—hers and his. Surely that must mean he felt a measure of love for her, did it not? She knew there were men who couldn't express the words, not even when they felt quite deeply. Perhaps he was such a one, showing her what he could not bring himself to say.

"Well?" he asked again, dappling her lips with soft kisses. "What is your answer?"

"Yes!" she declared. "It's yes! I will marry you!"

For a brief moment, he eased back, his eyes turning a kind of dark, intense blue she'd never seen before, an expression in them of satisfaction and something else she didn't entirely understand.

Then she didn't have time to think at all, his mouth ravishing hers with heat and raw, unfettered need. She clung, answering his passion as fully as her innocence would allow. Moaning, she opened her lips wider to let his tongue inside where he dipped and dived, his skillful play leaving her aching and half desperate for more. His hands moved low, stroking over her buttocks before clutching her hips to lift her higher. Spreading his thighs, he set her between them, unabashedly allowing her to once more feel the blatant strength of his desire. She arched, unable to control herself as she curled her arms around his neck.

He'd just palmed one of her breasts, her nipple an eager peak beneath his questing fingers, when the familiar sound of an opening door echoed through the room. She paid it no mind, too caught up in the glorious sensations assailing her body to give the noise much heed.

"If you weren't my friend, I'd call you out!" said a masculine voice in a hard, ringing tone. "Then again, I just might make an exception since you were supposed to be protecting her, not helping yourself to the goods. Let her go."

Tony stiffened against her, his arms tightening for a long, lingering moment. Slowly, he broke their kiss, turning her gently so she was held in the protective curve of his embrace. Only then did he look across at the other man. Peeking through her eyelashes, Gabriella was alarmed by the expression on her uncle's face.

"You unprincipled rake!" Rafe charged. "I should have known leaving her with you was like handing a baby chick to a wolf. You just couldn't keep your hands to yourself."

"No, it would seem I could not," Tony stated. "But there are mitigating circumstances, if you would care to listen to them."

"Listen to what? How you've seduced an innocent girl? I knew last night there was something going on. If I hadn't trusted you, I might have realized it sooner."

"Realized what?" demanded a lilting voice as Julianna glided into the room. "What is going on?" She paused, taking in the view of Gabriella standing inside Tony's embrace. "Then again, perhaps I don't need to ask."

"That's right, they were fairly caught," Rafe explained. "*En flagrante,* you might say."

Tony quirked a brow. "Hardly that, since Gabriella and I don't have so much as a loosened shoelace between us."

"You'd have had half your wardrobe loosened up soon if what I saw was any example."

Gabriella felt her cheeks heat despite knowing she and Tony had nothing for which to feel ashamed.

"Now, Rafe," Julianna soothed, laying a hand on her husband's arm. "It can't be as dreadful as all that. Why don't you give them a chance to explain."

"Explain what? What can they tell us that I haven't seen with my own two eyes? And why are you taking up for them? Did you know about this?"

"No, not directly," she said, "but I confess I had my suspicions."

"And yet you said nothing?" Rafe looked offended, his jaw tightening in a dangerous way. "We'll talk about this later, madam."

Julianna waggled a dismissive hand. "Don't *madam* me in that tone, Rafe Pendragon. I did what I thought best, since I knew you would react exactly as you are now. Well, Gabriella, Tony, what do you have to say for yourselves?"

"Yes?" Rafe growled, crossing his arms over his chest. "What excuse can you possibly offer?"

"*Hmm.* You know, somehow all this furor makes our announcement seem rather dull by comparison, does it not, my dear?" Tony drawled, addressing himself to Gabriella. "But I suppose we might as well tell them."

"Tell us what?" Rafe said through his teeth.

"Why, the news that Gabriella has just consented to be my wife. We're getting married."

Rafe's arms dropped to his side, Julianna's mouth falling open before she recovered enough to close it. Apparently, even she hadn't considered such an idea. Julianna recovered first. "Married!" she exclaimed. "Are you really?"

Gabriella nodded. "Tony just asked me a few minutes ago."

"Oh, but isn't that wonderful!" Rushing forward, Julianna enveloped first Gabriella, then Tony, in an exuberant hug, her bubbling excitement making Gabriella bubble in return.

Rafe wasn't quite so instantly overjoyed. "Why?" he said, voicing the same question Gabriella had asked herself.

Tony met his friend's gaze as he looped an arm around Gabriella's shoulders again. "Because it's the right thing to do. And because it's what both of us want, is it not, sweetheart?"

Leaning down, he brushed a kiss against her temple that made her melt again. "Yes," she said, gazing into his eyes. "Most definitely what we want."

Only then did Rafe unbend, striding toward them with

his hand outstretched for Tony to shake. "Well, if that is the case, then I am happy for you both. My blessing is yours, of course. May you be as happy as Julianna and I."

"We will," Gabriella said, unable to contain her smile of beaming happiness. "I know we will."

Chapter Thirteen

STANDING BEFORE THE gilded cheval mirror in Julianna's dressing room, Gabriella watched as Julianna's maid pinned a sheer, waist-length white veil onto her elegantly coiffed tresses, then stepped back to study the results. "Oh, Miss, you look a right dream, if you don't mind my saying so," the servant declared.

"Doesn't she though, Daisy," Julianna concurred. "Sheer perfection."

"Do you really think so?" Gabriella asked, casting another quick glance at her reflection before turning to face her two matrons of honor.

Lily nodded with an enthusiastic smile. "The moment Tony sees you, he won't be able to look away. And he'll have a deuced hard time keeping his hands off you, too, if I don't miss my guess."

"I am sure you do not," Julianna remarked with an indulgent expression. "I've rarely seen a more eager bridegroom. Imagine giving us only five days to prepare for the nuptials. The household has been in a complete frenzy ever since."

As Gabriella knew first hand, her friend was right. After Tony's stunning proposal of marriage, he'd given her a second jolt a few minutes later by announcing that he wanted them to be wed by special license within the week. Julianna had exclaimed that it could not be done, given all the details to be arranged—not to mention the guests. Lily had tossed in her objections once she heard the news, both of them beseeching Tony for more time, but he'd held firm.

"Why bother delaying?" he'd told Gabriella once they were alone. "I want to marry you. And now that my mind is made up, I see no point in waiting. To be honest, even five days is too long. Were it feasible, I would wed you tomorrow."

She hadn't been able to keep from melting at his words, and to be honest, she hadn't really wished to wait either. She loved him and wanted to be his wife, some niggling part of her afraid if she insisted on a long engagement, he might change his mind and decide he'd made a mistake after all.

"Still, we managed," Lily pointed out. "Even Gabriella's dress turned out splendidly despite our having to improvise."

Gabriella watched as all eyes turned to study her wedding gown of lustrous white glacé silk with an overskirt of pale, semitransparent tiffany. Delicate Mechlin lace was stitched along the hem and the edges of her half-sleeves, the lace's pattern of entwined leaves and flower petals a regal complement to the cluster of tiny white rosebuds threaded into her dark curls. "No one would ever guess that gown was once one of your coming-out dresses," Lily continued.

"I know," Gabriella said. "It turned out so splendidly. Thank you both for helping me with this lovely gown and the cake and the decorations and, well . . . everything. You've made my special day absolutely perfect."

Gabriella watched as Julianna sniffed back a sudden tear before her friend moved forward to give her hug. Lily followed suit and did the same.

"With all this fuss, I feel a bit like a princess," Gabriella confessed a moment later.

"Well, a princess you are not," Julianna said with a glance at a nearby ormolu clock. "But twenty minutes from now you'll be a duchess. I assume that will suffice?" she teased.

A smile curved Gabriella's lips, nerves making the inside of her stomach quiver. "It will more than suffice, since Tony is to be my duke."

"Shall we go find him?" Julianna urged.

Gabriella gave an enthusiastic nod, then let the other women lead her from the room.

Inside the drawing room, Tony stood near a small, flower-covered bower that had been set up for the ceremony, morning sunlight dappling the room's interior with a cheerful brilliance. The fragrance of roses and lilacs perfumed the air, and harp music was being played in soothing tones. At his side were Rafe and Ethan—his friends having gladly agreed to serve as his groomsmen. The white-haired minister stood thumbing through a few pages in his prayer book, while a select group of guests sat in three narrow rows of chairs, chatting quietly as they waited for the bride to arrive.

Tony straightened his waistcoat, then twisted the ruby signet ring he wore on his little finger around in a circle. He'd taken care in selecting his attire this morning, opting for the traditional wedding garb of a dark blue tailcoat, light gray breeches, and snowy white linen with polished black dress pumps on his feet.

Only a few minutes more, he thought, *and Gabriella will be here. A few minutes after that and I will be a married man.* His chest tightened briefly at the thought, despite his certainty that he had made the right choice by deciding to marry Gabriella.

Actually, it had been the only choice, given the trouble Erika Hewitt could still cause. He'd managed to put her off again by sending her a huge bouquet of flowers and a diamond bracelet to make up for having to delay their assignation yet again. An unavoidable emergency, he'd told her in the note he'd sent to her townhouse. She'd written back, granting him two days more—but only two, or else her tongue would begin to wag.

Somehow, he'd managed to keep the engagement quiet, determined that Erika wouldn't find out about the wedding until after the deed was done. He'd invited only friends he knew he could trust, explaining that he and Gabriella wanted a private ceremony free of Society's scrutiny. In fact, he'd sent the notice to *The Morning Post* a mere half hour ago in order to ensure that he and Gabriella would be married and in his coach heading out of the city before anyone learned of their union.

The Ton would be agog, he knew, the wedding the talk of the Town for weeks to come. As for Lady Hewitt, he imagined she would be crimson with fury come morning, shredding her copy of the newspaper until all that remained were tiny flecks of paper and smudges of ink on her hands. Her screams might even be loud enough to be heard all the way up to his small estate in Norfolk, where he and Gabriella planned to honeymoon.

Convinced of the need to act quickly, he'd hurried the wedding along this week in spite of everyone's surprise and dismay over his haste. Convincing Gabriella had proven surprisingly easy, and Julianna and Lily had fallen in line with his plan once they realized he could not be swayed from his chosen course. Rafe, however, had been suspicious.

After dinner that first evening, Rafe had pulled him aside to ask if there might be any other "pressing" reason why he was in such a rush to wed. One, Rafe suggested, that might raise eyebrows in a few months' time? But he'd reassured his old friend that there was no such necessity and that Gabriella would come to her marriage bed a virgin—as innocent as the day she was born. He'd even offered to swear an oath on the subject should Rafe insist. Rafe had not, satisfied with his answer. Tony knew the other man still wondered at his reasons, sensing they were not driven solely by affection for his niece, but Rafe had said nothing further, clapping him on the back when he'd ask him to stand with him as best man.

Now, here he stood, waiting for Gabriella. He was just about to check the time on his pocket watch, when Lily appeared in the doorway. She signaled the harpist, who abruptly switched to a different song, then nodded to Rafe, who strode out of the room to join her in the hallway beyond. Tony's pulse gave an odd kick as he tugged once more at his waistcoat and moved to take the correct place at the altar.

Lily entered first, a small basket on her arm out of which she scattered pink rose petals as she walked. Julianna came next, a nosegay of larkspur held in her gloved hands. Her eyes twinkled as she assumed her place on the opposite side of the minister. Then Gabriella appeared carrying a bouquet of white roses, her other hand atop Rafe's arm as he led her forward.

Breath stilled in Tony's chest, his gaze riveted on Gabriella while the rest of the world grew suddenly distant. She was a vision in white, quite literally the most beautiful sight he had ever beheld, beatific as an angel come to life. She glided nearer and nearer still until she stood beside him as Rafe handed her gently into his keeping.

Casting him a shy glance from beneath her lashes, she gave him a little smile that went straight to his loins. Abruptly he found himself fiercely glad they were to be wed. *If she is my reward,* he thought, *then the sacrifice of my bachelor's freedom seems a small price to pay.* Knowing his lustful musings had no place during their wedding ceremony, he tamped them down, and concentrated instead on the words the minister was speaking.

When his turn came to recite his vows, he said them in a calm, clear voice that rang out across the drawing room. Gabriella did the same, though her words were more quietly spoken. Her hand shook slightly inside his own as he slid the plain gold wedding band onto her finger to join the glittering, square-cut diamond he'd given her four days ago. Moments later, the minister pronounced them husband and wife.

Uncaring of being watched by the assembled guests, he drew her into his arms and claimed her lips—claimed her—taking her mouth in a long, deep, thorough kiss that made his head buzz and the blood in his veins run thick and hot. Gabriella gave a small, muffled whimper and opened her mouth to let him take more, touching her tongue to his. Before he could respond to her silent invitation, a large male hand nudged his shoulder.

"Hey there, save something for tonight, will you?" Ethan said with clear amusement in his voice. "You're making the ladies blush. And if I'm not mistaken, your bride as well."

Tony broke off the kiss, Gabriella blinking up at him with a rather dazed, but radiant expression on her face. True to Ethan's prediction, her cheeks colored up seconds later when she realized everyone was watching—good-natured laughter ringing out at Tony's unrepentant shrug.

Tucking her hand over his arm to keep her with him, Tony led Gabriella forward, knowing they were supposed to partake of the wedding feast. *I'd rather feast on Gabriella,* he thought, but decided he would have to content himself with food and drink for the time being.

Several hours later, Tony assisted Gabriella from his traveling coach, afternoon sunshine beaming down from the clear blue sky above. The front door of a cheerfully appointed red brick house flew wide, a middle-aged woman emerging, her shoes crunching fast on the pea gravel as she bustled across the drive.

"Welcome to Thorne Park!" the housekeeper declared, pausing to dip into a respectful curtsey. "What a pleasure it is to have both of you here! Everything has been arranged to your specifications, Your Grace. The rooms are all aired and cleaned and the larder stocked with the best the local farmers can provide." She broke off and gave a short laugh. "Well, listen to me rattle on when I'm sure you're wanting to come inside. So, come, come. I've made peach lemonade and biscuits with ham, if you've an appetite. Or there's wine and spirits, Your Grace, if you'd care for something stronger."

Tony sent her a polite smile as the three of them crossed into the house. "Actually, a glass of your lemonade sounds quite refreshing, Mrs. Lamstead. But first, why don't you show my bride upstairs so she can have a moment to relax."

"I've been relaxing for hours in the coach," Gabriella reminded him with an indulgent smile, her good humor intact despite their day's travel. "But I could do with a basin of water and a fresh gown, I must admit."

"Of course, of course," the housekeeper invited. "If you'll just follow me, Your Grace, all will be as you wish."

Tony watched as Gabriella stood motionless, her gaze darting for a long moment between him and Mrs. Lamstead. Suddenly her eyes grew wide. "Oh, you mean me, do you not!" She let out a self-deprecating laugh and laid a palm against her chest. "I don't know how I shall ever grow used to being called 'Your Grace.' It seems quite peculiar."

"One grows accustomed," he said.

Gabriella arched a brow in his direction. "Well, I am sure one does after hearing it for practically the whole of one's life. I, on the other hand, have never before experienced anything loftier than 'Miss' or 'hey, you.' This other shall take some getting used to, I must warn you. Perhaps I should tell your staff to just call me Gabriella and save us all a great deal of confusion."

Tony laughed, then laughed a second time when he noticed the housekeeper's gaped-mouthed expression, the woman apparently amazed by Gabriella's unusual candor. Taking Gabriella's hand in his own, he brushed her palm with a kiss. "My staff is now also your staff, and I do not believe they would be comfortable referring to you by your given name. So, I fear you will just have to muddle through."

"A muddle it will likely be, but I shall do my best."

Folding her hand inside his own, he laid his lips against her knuckles. "Of that, I have no doubt. Now, go along with Mrs. Lamstead and I shall see you at dinner." Stepping nearer, he bent to murmur into her ear so only she would hear. "And get some rest while you can. Seeing this is our wedding night, I plan to keep you up late this evening. Very, *very* late."

Color burst like blossoming peonies on her cheeks, her eyes gleaming with a clear mix of nerves and anticipation. With a small nod, she slipped from his embrace and moved away to follow the housekeeper.

He watched until she disappeared, enjoying the graceful sway of her slim hips as she walked up the stairs. His loins grew heavy, carnal hunger urging him to follow her and take her now instead of waiting until tonight. But he'd lasted through the ceremony and the wedding breakfast; he could restrain his needs for a few hours more. Although to be honest, he'd been restraining his needs for weeks now, Gabriella the only woman he could recall ever waiting so long to possess. And possess her he would, slaking his deep thirst for her as often and as long as he wished—now that he could, now that she was his wife.

God, I can barely wait to have her! he thought, his arousal aching between his legs.

Turning on his heel, he strode down the hall to the study, where he knew he would find the Scotch decanter. Taking down a tumbler, he poured himself a healthy draught, deciding he was in need of something stronger than lemonade, after all.

Married! he thought as he tossed back a long swallow. *For good or bad, Gabriella and I are now irrevocably joined.* Still, he was looking forward to spending the next month here at Thorne Park alone with her. He rarely used this minor estate, purchased years ago on a whim as a bucolic retreat. However, when he'd been considering places where he and Gabriella might honeymoon, this property had come to mind—the remote, tranquil location seeming just right. Undisturbed, he and his bride would be able to sleep late, go to bed early, and laze their days away as they reveled in each other to their heart's and body's content.

Tossing back the last of his drink, he thought again of this morning's ceremony and how enchantingly lovely Gabriella had looked. *My wife,* he mused, *to have and to hold for as long as our passion burns.* And when the desire cooled, as it inevitably must, they would rub along together well enough, he assumed, no more miserable than most married couples. For the present, though, there was nothing remotely cool about him, impatience and barely controlled arousal riding him hard.

Maybe that's what he needed, he considered, a bit of exercise to take the edge off the worst of his pent-up energy and tension. He'd ordered a pair of his favorite steeds sent over from Rosemeade as part of the honeymoon preparations so he and Gabriella could ride if they wished. Perhaps a good gallop, followed by a cold bath, would relax him enough to get him through the next few hours until finally, it was time for bed—and Gabriella.

Either that or I'll be drinking a whole lot more of this Scotch, he realized. Somehow, he didn't think she would appreciate dealing with an inebriated bridegroom on her wedding night. Abruptly making up his mind, he set down the crystal tumbler and strode from the room.

Peering out one of the four master-suite windows, Gabriella watched Tony gallop across the yard below, the hooves of his coal-black stallion tearing up clods of earth and grass as they raced past. *How magnificent they are,* she thought, *both man and beast!* Moving as if they could outrun the wind, the pair headed for a grouping of trees and quickly disappeared beyond, the green foliage concealing them from view.

She sighed, wishing Tony had asked her to join him, since heaven knows she could have used the distraction. He probably assumed she was asleep by now, resting up for the night to come. But how could she possibly rest! Especially after he'd made that brazen promise that he planned to keep her up late. *Very, very late.*

A tremble chased over her skin at the memory of his lips whispering against her ear, her eyelids sliding half closed—not from nerves, but rather a surfeit of anticipation.

Shameful as it might be to admit, she was looking forward to tonight, eager to finally discover the mysteries of the sex act. Already, Tony had brought her to dizzying heights of pleasure when all they'd done was kiss and touch. She knew there was more, but she couldn't really imagine how that could be better than what she'd experienced up to now. Still, she was anxious to find out. Until then, however, she had time. Too much time, she was finding.

A glance across the room revealed the peach lemonade and biscuits Mrs. Lamstead had brought up. But despite the delicious-looking repast, she found she had little appetite. Hopefully that would change by dinnertime; otherwise, the meal was destined to be a very long one indeed.

A yawn caught her a moment later. Smothering it with a hand, she wondered if Tony was right. Maybe she should make an effort to lie down and rest. She certainly had the right to be tired, considering the hectic pace of the past several days as well as the nervous excitement of this morning's ceremony. She still hadn't fully recovered from the torrid kiss he'd given her there on the altar, her need for him in those moments making everything else fade away.

Later at the wedding breakfast, she'd fiddled with her meal, too powerfully aware of Tony seated next to her to be interested in food. Nonetheless, she'd forced herself to swallow a few bites here and there, then eat half a piece of the splendid wedding cake Cook had gone to so much trouble to create. Afterward, she'd changed into her traveling dress and said her good-byes, letting Tony assist her into the coach amid boisterous cheers and warm good wishes.

Finding it all a bit unreal even now, she stared for a moment at the rings on her finger, their sparkle and weight assuring her that none of it had been a dream. And later tonight she would become Tony's wife—not only in name, but in all the ways there could be.

Trembling again, she crossed the room and pulled the bell. A warm bath might soothe her, she decided, the fragrant lavender-scented soap she'd packed making her skin smell sweet and clean for his touch. She would even wash her hair. A good towel-drying and a few minutes in front of an open window should see it dry in time to dress and go down for dinner. Suddenly invigorated, she toed off her shoes and waited for her maid to appear.

Chapter Fourteen

"MORE WINE?" TONY inquired in a voice as rich and smooth as the merlot they had been drinking with dinner. He leaned forward and reached for the decanter.

"No," Gabriella said, laying a hand over the top of her glass. "No more, or else I am afraid I may end up tipsy."

He paused before relaxing back into his chair. "I wouldn't worry, since I am sure you would be adorable tipsy. But for now, I suppose, you are right. Shall we move on to dessert, then?"

She nodded in agreement. "Although I don't see how I can possibly eat another bite. Everything was so delicious."

He watched her over the rim of his glass, the intensity in his eyes sending invisible tremors coursing over her skin. Touching the goblet to his lips, he sipped the beverage as if he were imagining something else he'd like to taste. She swallowed and gave him a smile.

Abruptly he set down his wine. "Perhaps you would rather retire? I can tell Mrs. Lamstead to save our dessert for later."

A wild flutter brushed the inside of her belly, nerves she hadn't felt earlier rushing to the fore. "Yes, all right. W-will you join me?"

His eyes darkened. "In a few minutes. I'll stay and finish my wine."

She nodded, then slowly rose to her feet. As she made to move past, he reached out and caught her hand. Before she could guess his intentions, he tugged her down onto his lap and wrapped her snuggly inside his embrace.

His mouth took hers, his kiss both bold and hungry, as if she were what he really wanted for dessert. His tongue skimmed across her lower lip, then did the same above, before delving in between to capture her flavor. Curling her palms against his shoulders, she kissed him back, forgetting everything in that moment except him. Then he stopped, the interlude over almost as quickly as it had begun.

"Why did you do that?" she asked, breath panting from her lips.

"Impulse. I thought we could both use a little something to tide us over." He stroked a hand across her hip. "Go upstairs. I won't be long."

Her body humming, she let him place her back onto her feet. For a moment, she wondered if she was steady enough to walk, but somehow she managed.

Tony gazed after her as she departed, wishing he'd kept her in his lap where he'd had her only moments ago. Reaching for his wineglass, he drained it.

Ten minutes, he decided. He'd give Gabriella ten minutes, then go up to change in the adjoining dressing chamber, where earlier he'd bathed and dressed for dinner after his ride. Twenty minutes more should give her enough additional time to ready herself while he stripped out of his garments, slid into a robe, shaved one more time, and brushed his teeth. Rising to his feet, he went in search of Mrs. Lamstead.

After thanking her for a most wonderful dinner, he made her eyes widen by informing her that she needn't arrive at the house tomorrow until well past midday. When she protested that he and Gabriella might awaken hungry "come the morn," he agreed she could set their uneaten dessert, along with a plate of cold foodstuffs suitable for breakfast, in the larder. She could also ready the kettle on the stove and arrange the makings for a fresh pot of tea. Otherwise, he and his new bride, he assured her, would do quite well on their own. Leaving the half-scandalized woman to finish her duties and lock up the house, he made his way up the stairs.

Meanwhile inside her bedchamber—*their* bedchamber—Gabriella stood in a thin, white silk nightgown and slippers waiting for Tony to arrive. She gazed at the bed, a huge affair with carved cherry posts and dark green damask hangings. The sheet and counterpane were turned back in silent invitation, the draperies drawn to create an atmosphere of seclusion and comfort. After helping her undress, the maid had bid her a smiling good night, then let herself out of the room to make her way to the servants' quarters, which were housed in a small, detached wing.

Alone now, Gabriella shot a glance toward the door that led to the dressing room, a few faint noises letting her know Tony was on the other side. A tremulous quaver fluttered in her belly. *I wasn't nervous earlier today,* she mused, *so why am I now? It's only Tony, after all, a man I know and trust. The man I love—my husband!*

The thought made her breath grow shallow, memories washing over her of all that had passed since that first momentous evening when Tony had caught her in Rafe's study. How long ago that night seemed now, as if half a lifetime had passed, instead of only a few short months during which she and Tony had become friends and so much more. And always, there had been the unassailable pleasure of his touch, his every caress and kiss making her sigh with delight. Even now, the heat of the impassioned kiss he'd given her downstairs in the dining room lingered on her lips, making her long once again to be in his arms. And she would be. Soon.

So then, of what exactly am I afraid?

Suddenly her anxiety eased, her old sense of anticipation rising again to take its place. Gazing around the room, she wondered if she should continue to wait where she was, or instead take a seat on the sofa. Of course, he might be expecting to find her already in the bed. Or was such an idea too bold, especially for an untried virgin on her wedding night? Pondering each choice, she quickly made up her mind.

Checking his pocket watch, Tony snapped the gold lid closed, then set it aside. *Forty-five minutes.* In deference to Gabriella's maiden state, he'd given her an extra measure of time, concerned she might be suffering from a case of bridal nerves. If he didn't mistake the matter, she'd seemed a bit reticent at dinner, although her kiss had certainly been sweet as ever.

Despite his own needs, he'd already decided to take their lovemaking slowly—or at least as slowly as he could stand—and ease her, hopefully without fear, toward the consummation of their union. Taking a breath, he turned the knob of the connecting door and stepped into the room.

He'd expected to find the bedchamber swathed in near darkness, with only one or two candles left to burn. Instead, there were half a dozen at least, their combined illumination providing enough brightness to drive off the heaviest night shadows and leave the entire chamber swathed in what he considered a rather seductive, golden glow.

In spite of the candlelight, he didn't see her immediately, his gaze moving first to the sitting area before roving farther afield. His pulse gave a sharp kick when he did discover her—in bed, her long, raven hair spread across the pillows in a dark, luxurious cascade. *Dear Lord, how exquisite she is!*

Approaching, he barely noticed the soft texture of the thick, wool carpet beneath his bare feet. Moments later, he halted beside the bed, his gaze going to hers.

"Hallo," she whispered, her gentle greeting trailing like a blaze of fire through his system.

"Hallo." He drank in the sight of her, tracing the purely feminine shape of her delineated beneath the sheet. At the foot of the bed lay a length of white silk. He studied it for a moment, puzzled at first before understanding dawned. His pulse kicked again. "Are you naked under there?" he demanded, his voice low and rough as sand.

She nodded, her lashes lowering slightly in an unconscious display of seduction. "You don't mind, do you?"

Mind! His arousal throbbed out his answer. "No," he croaked. "I don't mind."

Her lush violet-hued eyes warmed with obvious pleasure.

A long moment elapsed, then she pulled back the sheet and revealed herself fully to him—her invitation clear.

Given his age and experience, he wouldn't have thought there was anything left in this world that could shock him, but watching his young bride display herself in such a daring and unguarded way left him momentarily speechless. His body suffered no such difficulties, however, his shaft thrusting forward as if it hoped to reach her, nearly managing to part the folds of his robe in the effort.

When he said nothing, she hesitated, her shoulders suddenly curving inward as she reached to cover herself again.

"Don't," he ordered.

She froze and gave him an uncertain look.

"Just lie back," he commanded in as gentle a voice as he could muster. "Just let me look."

Visibly forcing herself to relax, she did as he asked, settling back against the mattress and feather pillows to let him gaze his fill. And he did, tracing over her alabaster skin, across her lovely shoulders and arms, then on to the ripe thrust of her generous breasts, their pink nipples drawn into tight little berries beneath his inspection. Gliding downward, he surveyed the convex dip of her flat belly and the gentle flare of her hips before moving to the shapely length of her legs and the dark triangle of curls between. Even her feet were fashioned as if wrought by a master hand. In all his life, he'd never seen anything so exquisite, nor wanted a woman with such raw hunger and unbridled lust.

"*God,* Gabriella," he said in a harsh tone. "Not even in my dreams did I imagine how beautiful you are. I am humbled to know you are mine."

The smile returned to her mouth—a mouth he was abruptly desperate to kiss. "Would you . . ."

He raised a brow. "Would I what, sweetheart?"

"Might I see, too?"

One of his eyebrows went up. *So she's curious about me, is she? About the way a man is fashioned. Well, I shall be more than happy to oblige.* A grin spread across his face, suddenly realizing he was in store for what should prove to be an exciting night. After a brief pause, he reached for the tie on his robe.

Gabriella waited, her heart beating so hard and fast it was a wonder the organ didn't explode from her chest. She couldn't believe what she'd done, shocking herself, and at first, she thought, Tony as well. But he didn't look shocked anymore—quite the contrary, the expression on his face was one of unrestrained delight.

Peeling off his robe, he tossed it to the foot of the

bed where the black silk joined the white cloth of her nightgown, the two garments puddling together in a kind of intimate embrace. Yet she had only a second to consider such matters before her attention turned completely to him, her eyes riveted as saliva pooled against her tongue.

Like her, he hadn't bothered with night attire, his body bare—gloriously, spectacularly bare! He stood before her without an ounce of modesty or shame, apparently content to let her inspect him at her leisure. And why should he not when he was so superbly formed?

She'd known he had broad shoulders and a long, strong frame, but she'd never before realized how powerfully built he was, his body taut, all bone and heavy muscle. He radiated vitality and strength, his skin carrying the same golden hue as his face so that he had an almost burnished glow in the mellow candlelight.

A swath of black hair curled over his magnificent chest, spreading outward before narrowing down into a line that ran across his lean, flat stomach. Dark hair dusted his extremities as well, over his arms and along the breadth of his solid thighs, then onto his firm, muscular calves and long, tapered feet.

Giving her an indulgent look, he made an easy turn, slowly revolving in place so she could see his back as well as his front. Her breath caught, her lower lip caught between her teeth as she took in the new view. From his sculpted shoulders down his lean spine her eyes roved, her gaze pausing for long, long moments on the firm, twin globes of his finely shaped buttocks. Then he finished his turn to face her once more, leaving her only one final part to inspect.

Jutting out from his body, his staff was thick and heavy and long, its shape angled at a high, almost arrogant tilt, as if it knew just how impressive a beast it was. She marveled, amazed by the sight, as well as by the realization that he was fashioned so very differently from her. Superlatively so, in her estimation.

Without knowing what she intended, she lifted a hand. "May I . . . touch?"

His flesh twitched, seeming to grow even larger, as impossible as that seemed, a shiny drop of fluid suddenly forming on its swollen, reddened tip. And abruptly his face darkened, all earlier displays of indulgence gone. He gave a tight nod, his eyelids growing heavy. "Yes. Touch me," he agreed, his voice a near growl.

Her own body ablaze and trembling, she scooted closer, then wrapped her hand around him—or at least tried to, since he was too large for her fingers to meet. She gasped at the sensation, his staff hard and warm, yet soft at the same time. Unsure where she found the courage, she stroked him, gliding her hand upward in an untutored caress.

He stiffened more, hips arching forward subtly to slide her fingers higher. Her grip loosened in surprise, but before she could retreat, he grabbed her hand. "God, don't stop. Here, like this," he said, gently showing her exactly how he wanted to be touched.

After a minute, he released her hand, giving her the choice of whether or not to proceed. She did, each caress growing longer and firmer and more certain as her confidence built. She increased her grip just a fraction and stroked. As she did, a harsh moan escaped his lips, a full body shudder raking his frame. "Jesus, Gabriella," he said, pulling slightly away. "Are you sure you're really a virgin?"

She blinked and withdrew her hand. "Of course, I am! Why would you think otherwise?" She stared at him, scooting backward against the sheets as a terrible thought occurred. *Is my behavior too brazen? Have I disgusted him before we've even consummated our marriage?* "Are you saying I am immodest, indecent? If you don't like it, I can—"

"Of course, I like it," he told her, his midnight-dark eyes intensely blue. "A great deal, obviously, since you nearly made me lose control. The last time I did that was during my own first time when I was nothing but a randy, imprudent youth. And no, you're not immodest. You are passionate. Uninhibited. Bold."

Some of her unease faded. "And is that all right?"

"Of course, it's all right. Better than all right. In fact, I wouldn't want you any other way. Promise me you won't change, Gabriella. Swear you'll stay the same warm, spirited woman you are right now."

A tremulous smile curved her lips. "I shall endeavor to do my best." Lying back, she held out her arms. "I want you, Tony. Come and make me your wife."

"You're already my wife," he said, planting a knee onto the mattress as he moved into her embrace. "After tonight, you'll be my lover."

With a ravishing passion, his mouth came down on hers, his fervor seeming to hold back nothing as he plundered her lips, his hands making skillful forays across her naked body that set her aquiver. She returned his kiss with equal ferocity, giving him as much as she knew how, his every caress broadening her experience, deepening her sensual awareness and understanding. Confident now that he enjoyed her touch, she gave herself permission to roam, letting her hands glide over his taut, muscular flesh, smiling when she felt tiny tremors vibrate beneath his skin.

He kissed her harder, longer, practically eating her up in his obvious need to give as much pleasure as possible. Desire burned deep, a now familiar ache forming between her legs. But tonight her hunger was heightened, her ardor stronger and more insistent, the slide of his bare flesh against hers creating a friction that was half bliss, half torment.

On a whimper, she clutched him tight, urging him on even though she didn't know exactly what to expect. She understood enough of the basics, though, to worry that they might not fit together, especially after seeing proof of his impressive width and length. Tony, however, seemed to have no such qualms, and so she pushed aside her doubt and let him lead her wherever he willed.

His mouth captured her breast, scattering her thoughts as he drew the tip inside to suckle against his tongue and teeth. Moaning, she shifted, the ache within her growing sharper, keener. His hand covered her other breast to rub and caress. Her sensitive nipples tightened to hard points, a throaty groan rolling from her throat when he gently bit one delicate tip and pinched the other, moving quickly to soothe each with warm, wet swipes of his tongue.

Her hips bucked, moisture gathering low. His hand found her there, a finger sliding inside. Her hips rose again as he stroked her, her thighs parting in readiness for more.

"That's right," he murmured, kissing her ear and throat. "Let me in. Let me help you find your pleasure." And he did, working within her until she thought she might shatter, until all she knew was craving and hunger and need.

Just when she thought she couldn't stand any more, he pushed her onward, his mouth closing over one nipple again to draw hard, then harder still. The edge of his teeth raked her flesh as he eased a second finger inside her, stretching her full. Seconds later, he finessed her with his thumb, and she was lost.

She shook as an unstoppable tide of pleasure surged through her, her spine arching as rivers of delight pooled and eddied, her mind dulled to everything but Tony and the mesmerizing power of his touch.

He scattered kisses over her breasts and in between before trailing lower. Over the flat plain of her stomach he roamed, astonishing her when he paused to dip his tongue into the indentation of her belly button, swirling around the edge in a way that made her quake. With his fingers still lodged inside her, he continued to stroke, in and out in a compelling rhythm, as he leaned downward and used his free hand to caress the sensitive skin of her inner thighs. Tenderly, he eased her legs even farther apart, then settled his large frame between, resting on his knees.

Peering upward across the length of her prone body, he met her gaze, his eyes glittering sharply with desire. "You're still not as ready as I'd like."

I'm not? she wondered in confusion. Though far from experienced, she didn't know how she could possibly get any *more* ready, not with need sizzling through her bloodstream, her heart pumping as if consumed by fire. He'd brought her to a peak, but had never let her desire cool, reviving it instantly with his continued kisses and caresses. For a moment she thought to question him, but then he leaned down and sent her senses whirling skyward.

Her eyes flew wide at his first touch, his lips burying themselves in a place she had never imagined he might kiss. Or suckle, she marveled, his mouth and tongue drawing upon her with a suction that made her shift and whimper. A protest rose in her throat that died almost as quickly, his hand going to her hip to hold her steady for his delectation.

And he did seem to be enjoying himself, guttural masculine noises of satisfaction drifting to her ears as he feasted on her moist flesh. His tongue swirled and dipped and lapped, driving her instantly mad. Flames engulfed her body as the delicious torture continued, every pore growing damp with perspiration. No longer in control, she writhed in his embrace, a flood of wetness pouring from between her legs that might have embarrassed her were it not for the desperate state of her need.

As for Tony, he seemed to approve of her reaction, driving her ever upward with the relentless caress of his mouth and hands, his fingers continuing their sleek, internal massage in a way that left her helpless and panting for completion. Then, just when she thought she was on the brink, needing no more than a tiny push that would topple her over to the other side, he stopped.

She cried out a protest and reached down to his head in hopes of making him continue. Instead he eluded her, rising upward, his frame large and powerfully male as he leaned back on his haunches. Sliding her forward, he draped her spread legs over the hard musculature of his thighs, then with a careful, final positioning, clasped her hips between his hands and thrust inside.

She felt his entrance all the way to her toes and yet there was no discomfort, only a unique feeling of fullness and warmth. With a little smile, she relaxed, comforted by the fact that she had indeed been wrong about their ability to fit together. Her gaze went to his, surprised by the tension she saw in his jaw line, a faint tremor riding just beneath his skin as if he were holding himself under a very tight leash.

Then he moved again, pressing forward to gain more purchase. A glimmer of pain twinged within her inner muscles, her gaze flying to where he was joined with her. Only he wasn't joined, she saw with a gulp, realizing that no more than the very tip of him was lodged inside her.

Staring, she studied his length and felt her pulse trip with sudden fear.

"Tony, I—"

"*Shh,*" he hushed in a soothing tone. "You'll be fine. Relax and trust me."

Trust him? How could she, when the pain was increasing with every move he now made? Thrusting again, he gained what felt like yards but was probably only an inch or two. She bit the edge of her lip and closed her eyes, forcing herself to endure when all she wanted was for him to stop. Twice more he thrust, rocking against her in increments that seemed almost cruel. And yet the rational part of her knew he was trying to be gentle, to allow time for her body to adjust. Only she couldn't adjust, his penetration stretching her so much she feared he might rend her before this was over.

A tear leaked from the corner of her eye.

With a whispered apology, he leaned forward and brushed his lips against her temple, kissing the drop away. As he did, his new position pushed him deeper, lodging him far more fully than before.

"Almost there, sweetheart," he encouraged. "Here, wrap your legs around my back, high as they'll go." Reaching down a hand, he helped her reposition her hips. "There, you've got it." And then, with one last push, he slid the rest of the way in, his possession complete.

Is that it? she wondered. *Is that all?*

He kissed her, taking her lips in a slow, tender mating that made her love him in spite of the pain. *If this gives him pleasure,* she thought, *then I will bear it. Somehow, I will find the strength—for his sake.* But as he continued to kiss her, as his wonderful hands glided again over her body, something changed, the pain fading away beneath a rising surge of desire.

Moments later, he began to move, drawing nearly out, only to plunge back in again. His tongue met hers, tangling in a glorious slide as their bodies did the same. She arched, wrapping her arms over his shoulders to hold on tight as he increased his relentless pace.

Her breathing grew ragged, each stroke better than the last, deep then deeper still, as he buried himself in her time and time again. As if attuned to her very thoughts and wishes, he leaned up to palm one of her breasts, rolling her aching nipple between his fingers before taking it into his mouth. He drew upon her with a sweet, wet suction that left her completely enthralled—literally his to command.

And command her he did, encouraging her to meet his thrusts with tentative ones of her own, her enjoyment growing as a delight she'd never known ripened in her core. That's when she felt it, an impossible rapture held just out of reach, driving her ever onward toward completion. He must have felt it too, plunging faster as their ardor increased to an almost frenzied pace.

And suddenly her world flew apart, a keening cry of ecstasy ripping from her throat as draught after draught of stunning pleasure shook her in its grip. She quaked, helpless beneath the onslaught, her mind going temporarily dark and blank.

As sense trickled back, she became aware of Tony moving within her still, his large hands clasped on her hips as he drove himself fast and deep. Perspiration dotted his skin, an expression of naked arousal on his face as he fought to claim his own satisfaction.

Abruptly he stiffened, a harsh shout leaving his lips as he took his release, one that shook him, long and fierce. When it was done, he sank downward and buried his face against hers.

On a groan, he gradually levered himself away. "I'm too heavy."

"No," she denied, loath to let him go.

But she need not have worried, as he rolled her with him to tuck her snuggly against his side. Brushing back her hair, he kissed her temple. "Sleep," he urged.

Moments later, she did.

Chapter Fifteen

BRIGHT SUNSHINE FLOODED into the bedchamber the next morning, rousing Gabriella from a weary slumber. "Tony?" she mumbled, sliding her hand across the feather mattress in search of him. But instead she found only a cool expanse of empty sheet.

Opening her eyes, she surveyed the room and realized she was alone. With a sigh, she tugged his pillow into her arms and buried her face against its softness, letting her eyelids slide closed again as she breathed in the comforting masculine scent of him that lingered on the cloth.

Despite Tony's admonition for her to sleep, he'd given her scant opportunity to indulge in such an activity, awakening her twice more during the night and once this morning to make love. That last time he'd taken her from behind, her drowsiness falling away as he'd palmed her breasts in his wide hands and inserted a thigh between her legs. Parting her woman's flesh, he'd rocked them together, bringing her to a long, slow, shattering release. Yet sleep had claimed her quickly afterward, his still partially aroused flesh linked with hers.

She shifted now, her body protesting the energetic use her muscles had received in the past several hours, an unmistakable soreness lodged between her legs. With another sigh, she burrowed deeper against his pillow and let sleep claim her again.

Her nose twitched when she next awakened, stirring to the aromas of hot tea, yeasty bread, and fresh, sweet peaches. When she opened her eyes this time, she found Tony seated next to her on the bed, a laden tray of foodstuffs positioned on a small table across the room.

"Good morning, sleepyhead," he said with an indulgent smile. "Or I suppose I should say *good afternoon,* since morning expired some time ago."

She pushed a strand of hair off her cheek and gazed up at him. *Mercy, he is so handsome!* she thought, even with his hair mussed from sleep and his cheeks dark and rough with unshaven whiskers. She gave him a lazy smile, the full import of his words only then sinking in. "Afternoon?" she exclaimed. "Good lord! What time is it?"

A chuckle rolled from his chest. "About one-thirty or so, I believe."

"Gracious, I never sleep this late."

"No, I don't imagine you do," he drawled. "I do not generally make a habit of it myself, but one can surely be permitted to make allowances for special occasions. We are on our honeymoon, after all." Leaning forward, he pressed a warm, openmouthed kiss on her lips, one that made the blood thrum faster in her veins. With lingering slowness, he drew back. "Are you hungry?"

For a moment she thought he meant for him, aware of her desire but unsure if her body would be capable of accommodating him again so soon. Then she realized he was talking about food, and felt a faint flush stain her skin.

"Now, don't I wish I was a mind reader," he teased, trailing the side of one finger over her cheek. "Whatever is it you are thinking, Your Grace?"

"I am wondering if that is a pot of tea over there," she retorted, wishing suddenly to change the subject.

He laughed again and climbed to his feet. "Here, let me pour you a cup."

"I can come over to the table."

"No, stay right where you are. It shall be my pleasure to serve you. I rather like the thought of you eating in bed."

In reply to that she decided it best to say nothing. Sitting up, she gathered the pillows into a stack at her back, tucking the sheet snuggly over her breasts.

He made two trips, one to set their cups of tea on the night table and another to bring a plate heaped with a delectable-looking array of breads, cheeses, and fruit—including one of the lusciously scented, golden peaches she'd already noticed. And if her eyes did not deceive her, a thick slice of chocolate cake.

"I thought we'd share," he told her as he set the plate between them.

"Did Mrs. Lamstead prepare all this?" she inquired, reaching for a hard roll he'd broken in two, then slathered with butter and jam. She bit in, savoring the rich, sweet tang.

"Hmm, last night," he explained. "I had her leave everything out so we wouldn't be disturbed."

"But what about the tea? Did one of the maids make it?"

"No, I made it." He ate a bite of cheddar.

"You!"

He swallowed and raised a brow. "Yes, me. You needn't look so astonished, you know. Even I can set a kettle to boil."

She stared for a long moment, then smiled. "Well, fancy that, a duke who can make his own tea. I dare say there are country squires who wouldn't know how."

"Quite right, and you'd do well to remember it. I am an eminently resourceful fellow. Here now," he said, "drink your tea."

Leaning forward, she reached out to accept the offered cup and saucer. As she did, the sheet fell to her waist, revealing her naked breasts. "Oh!" she said, pausing in indecision over whether to cover herself again or take the cup. But as she sat there, his gaze glued to her chest, she wondered why she was being so shy. God knows he'd seen everything last night and done a great deal more.

"Don't cover up on my account," he said with a smile she could only describe as wicked. "I'm quite enjoying the view."

Deciding a display of modesty would appear ridiculous now, she left the sheet where it lay, then took the cup. Carefully she raised the tea to her lips.

"So," he questioned after a long moment, his gaze finally lifting to her face. "What shall we do today? I suppose horseback riding is out of the question, since I assume you are sore."

She shot him a look. "Are you always so indelicate?"

"Just being honest. What is the point, after all, in dissembling about such matters?"

She ate the last of her roll, then broke off a small bite of cake and popped it into her mouth.

"I would suggest staying in bed," he continued as he used a knife to cut the peach in half. "But that won't do for the very same reason. I'd never be able to keep my hands off you." He sank his teeth into the fruit, then chewed and swallowed. "We could take the carriage into Swaffham. There's a fine old church there you might enjoy seeing."

"That sounds nice, though isn't the town a summer retreat of sorts for the Quality?"

"Quite true. And I'm not much inclined to share you with the world at the moment." In contemplation, he sipped his own tea.

"We could go fishing," she suggested. "If there is a pond or river nearby. Do you like fishing?"

He paused. "I do. I just would not have thought *you* would. Though come to think again on the matter, I suppose one of your performer friends taught you how to dive in and wrestle the fish from the water using nothing but your bare hands."

She made a face, then laughed. "No. I learned how to fish the ordinary way, with rod and reel." A silence fell for a moment. "Actually, it was my . . . um . . . father who taught me. Angling was one of the sports we enjoyed doing together." When he said nothing, she set her tea aside. "I am sorry. I should not have mentioned him."

Tony placed his cup next to hers, then tucked a finger beneath her chin so she was compelled to meet his gaze. "No. It's fine. Whatever he was, he was still your father and a part of your life. You may speak freely of him any time you wish."

"I hate the things he did, Tony. Sometimes, I hate him, too."

"*Shh,*" he hushed, drawing her into his arms. "It's all in the past. Forgiven now, if not forgotten. Think only of the good memories, since you had naught to do with the bad."

Her heart turned over in her chest, love welling up inside her. The words hovered on her tongue, her need to tell him suddenly fierce. But before she could confess her feelings for him, he claimed her lips.

Long, long moments later he released her, both of them a bit breathless as they drew apart. "Shall we get dressed and go look for those fish?" he questioned. "Since I don't think I can trust myself in this bed with you for much longer."

She laughed. "I don't trust myself much either. Yes, let us go. I have an appetite for trout."

"Trout, hmm?" he teased. "By tonight, I promise you'll have an appetite for something else entirely."

* * *

Tony rolled onto his back, his body satiated as he fought to regulate his breathing, Gabriella doing the same as she curled against him, equally replete. Stroking his hand over her silky hair, he let her sleep, watched the breaking dawn slowly illuminate the interior of their bedchamber.

Over the past seven weeks, he'd viewed many similar daybreaks, a sharp need he couldn't seem to control bringing him awake, driving him to take her again when he'd already taken her only a few hours before.

He'd certainly made good on his promise to slake his hunger, indulging his sexual craving for her as often as the urge struck. And it struck often, he'd discovered, his desire for her sometimes nearly insatiable as he took her until neither one of them had the strength to do more than collapse, utterly spent, across the sheets.

Not that their lovemaking had been confined to their bedroom, the pair of them exploring farther afield almost from that very first day. While their initial fishing expedition had been just that—a fishing expedition—their next one had turned into something more. Tossing aside their reels after several unsuccessful bites, he'd lain her down beneath a leafy canopy of trees and taken her until her cries of pleasure drifted in the warm late summer air. Two weeks later, after a day's visit to Swaffham—where luckily they had encountered no one they knew—he'd pleasured her inside their coach on the way home, stifling her moans of completion with his kisses so they would not be overheard. He'd even made love to her early one morning in the kitchen while they waited for the tea water to heat, taking her on the long, wooden work table while steam from the kettle billowed wildly into the room.

Yet the need he felt was by no means his alone, he'd realized, Gabriella as seemingly eager for their frequent, fervid couplings as he was himself. Free now to explore that side of her personality, Gabriella's sensual nature had come alive, her innate femininity flourishing beneath his experienced hands, her confidence deepening with each new day and long, impassioned night. An enthusiastic partner, she followed his lead, willing to give and receive pleasure in equal measures. She even had the ability to surprise him on occasion, such as the night he'd awakened to find her stroking and kissing him to arousal, her uninhibited enjoyment plain.

She was everything he could want in a lover, and more than he'd expected to find, despite the undeniable passion he'd felt for her before their marriage. More than that, she was an amusing companion, her company never dull whether in bed or out. She made him laugh and she made him think, challenging him to view issues and events from a perspective he'd never considered. Even more, she made him content, relaxed, and happy in a way he could not recall ever being before in his life.

Of course that's probably nothing more than the result of a surfeit of good sex, he told himself. *What man wouldn't be relaxed and happy after nearly two months of that!* Their honeymoon had been a kind of fantasy—intimate, secluded, and intense, a special time away as they made memories together in this place and this house. But once they arose from their bed today, all that would change. The idyll would be at an end, since like it or not, it was time to go home.

Already he'd put off their return to Rosemeade twice—first when the original four weeks he'd allotted for their honeymoon elapsed and he had decided to stay another week, then again when he'd sent word that he would be away two weeks more. But a note that had arrived a few days ago from his secretary, subtly complaining of his absence, made him realize he could not put reality off any longer. As duke, a great many people depended upon him, his duty to his servants and tenants alone requiring that he stop being a lazy, self-indulgent hedonist and return to his normal life. Certainly Gabriella would be with him, but he knew nothing was going to be quite the same for them once they left this house. Still, he vowed to keep their passion—and their friendship—alive as long as he could possibly manage. *Who knows,* he mused, *maybe we'll succeed in being one of those couples who don't end up hating each other.*

With sunshine now pouring into their room, he knew their time was short. *Once more,* he thought. *I have to have her one last time before this world of ours goes away.*

Gliding his palms over her body, he stroked her, fondling her in all the places he now knew she loved to be touched. She arched, responding to him even in her sleep, mumbling a few unintelligible words as she smoothed a comforting hand over his shoulder.

He kissed her, taking her mouth in a long, thorough exploration while his hands continued to do the same below, her nipples beading into tight little peaks that he delighted to caress, the velvety flesh between her legs growing wet and ready for his possession. Soon he could stand it no longer, rolling her onto her back and parting her thighs. Bracing his weight, he came into her in one deep, smooth thrust. Her eyes opened then, pleasured gasps coming from her lips as he built them both toward completion. Her arms and legs locked around his back, holding on as if the two of them were caught inside a storm.

Cradling her face between his palms, he kissed her again, loving the sounds she made, the scent of her body, the texture of her skin and hair. Then suddenly she came, screaming into his mouth from the force of her release. Not long after, he took his satisfaction with equal ferocity, fists clenched into the sheets as he poured out his pleasure inside her. Closing his eyes, he drifted and let his mind go dark.

"Welcome to Rosemeade, Your Grace," greeted Tony's butler as Gabriella stepped down from the coach long hours later that day. "Everyone has gathered to wish you and His Grace our heartfelt good wishes on your marriage." The older man gave her a smile, an expression that seemed somewhat incongruous on his proper, very distinguished features.

She tightened a hand against her hip to calm her uncertain nerves and returned his greeting, forcing herself not to tremble when she turned to find a small army of people looking her way.

"Dear me, Tony," she whispered, leaning toward her husband as he moved to take her arm. "Are those your servants?"

"Most of them, I believe. There may be a few of the stable lads and gardener's assistants who were told to remain behind."

Most of them! How many does he have? But then considering the size of the house and grounds, she supposed they were needed, each and every one.

Even now, she had yet to completely recover from her first sight of the estate, made only minutes ago as the coach glided through a set of massive wrought-iron gates that bore the Wyvern coat of arms emblazoned on a plaque in gold at its top. What had appeared to be several hundred huge oak trees, each one thick as the coach itself, lined the elegant drive, the combined canopy of green leaves creating a majestic overhang that was both romantic and shady. Yet the obviously ancient trees were nothing compared to the house itself—if one could call the sprawling, many-winged expanse of stone, wood, and gleaming glass a house. More like a palace fit for a king!

Gabriella knew that Tony was a duke and that his family was a powerful, distinguished one with ancestors whose exploits dated back to the time of the Conqueror himself. But somehow, until this moment the magnitude of his status had not fully impressed itself upon her. Not only was Tony rich and titled, but apparently he was in charge of a small city of dependents. *And now,* she thought with a gulp, *so am I.*

Very suddenly she wasn't ready to be a duchess, a part of her wanting to run and jump back into the coach. Instead, she held on to Tony's arm and let him lead her forward. Pinning her most amiable smile on her face, she prepared to do the best she could.

Greeting them all, however, turned out not to be nearly as daunting an experience as she had feared, his servants polite and friendly, their curiosity about her apparently equal to her own about them. Soon enough, the moment was over and she was taken into the house to indulge in another round of wide-eyed amazement.

Only by sheer determination did she stop herself from tipping her head back and turning in a circle to admire the fresco-painted dome that graced the main foyer, the black-and-white marble entrance as large as many people's entire homes. *Gracious,* and to think she had considered Rafe and Julianna's country house large! Compared to Rosemeade, their immense estate was scarcely more than average.

She wondered how many days it would take to adequately explore such a vast edifice as this. Assuming she was allowed to explore. But then why should she not be, since this was her new home now? *My new home!* she thought, as she tried to take it all in. *Mercy, what a world away this is from the tiny garret room Maude and I were sharing in London only a few months ago!* A lump formed in her throat at the memory, together with a sudden pang of longing for her friend. She worried her lower lip between her teeth for a moment as she continued to study the elegance of her surroundings. Then Tony caught her eye.

As if he was aware of some of her thoughts, he gave her a reassuring smile. "Mrs. Armstrong will show you to the family wing and see you comfortably settled."

The lump in her throat sank to her belly. "Oh, you are not coming with me?"

He shook his head. "Not at the moment. I have a number of pressing matters of business to which I must attend. We shall spend some time together later."

"But we only just arrived. Surely you can take a few minutes to come upstairs and refresh yourself."

His lids lowered, a look she now knew well darkening his eyes. "I am afraid I shall have to wait until later to *refresh* myself."

She moved closer, leaning up on her toes so she could murmur in his ear without being overheard. "That is not what I meant, and you know it. I thought you might like to bathe."

He chuckled, lowering his voice in reply. "I'll do that later, too. You can join me. Go on now, and I shall see you at dinner."

With the housekeeper, butler, and a pair of footmen looking on—despite their best efforts to keep their gazes politely averted—Gabriella decided she had little choice but to do as Tony asked, not unless she wished to create a small ruckus on her very first day in residence. "As you wish, Your Grace," she agreed.

Tony gave her another smile, waiting until the housekeeper stepped forward before he turned and disappeared down a long corridor to the right.

"If you'll just follow me," the older woman said, "I'll show you to your rooms."

On the walk to the family wing, Mrs. Armstrong proved a pleasant companion, chatting knowledgeably about the house and grounds and sharing interesting bits of information regarding the neighborhood and the families who lived nearby. Apparently several members of the local gentry had already called in hopes of meeting Gabriella and offering congratulations to her and the duke on their nuptials. She told Gabriella to expect them again soon, now that she and the duke had returned. If they were as amiable as the housekeeper made them out to be, Gabriella looked forward to their visits.

"Here we are, Your Grace," the housekeeper declared as they entered an expansive sitting room decorated in soothing shades of rose and cream. Pretty flocked wallpaper with tiny pink flowers and curling green leaves covered the walls, while delicate silk-upholstered furnishings and airy draperies were arranged to let in light and provide a comfortable sense of space. Various objets d'art, soft Aubusson carpets, and a pair of landscape paintings completed the effect.

The adjoining bedroom proved just as lovely, the even larger room done in pale greens and blues with exquisite satinwood furnishings and plush sapphire velvet drapes. The wide feather bed looked cozy and inviting, just right for long hours spent beneath its luxurious sheets. Across the room was a massive fireplace with a carved marble surround that conjured images of delightful, warm winter nights spent before its gentle glow.

"There is a dressing room and bath as well," the housekeeper volunteered.

"Oh, it's all so beautiful!" Gabriella sighed, turning slowly to once again admire the rooms.

A pleased smile curved Mrs. Armstrong's mouth, her hands tucked against her motherly waist. "I am glad you approve, Your Grace. His Grace ordered the redecorating done just before he left London for your honeymoon. Gave strict instructions, and said all the work was to be accomplished before your arrival."

"Tony did this . . . I had no idea." She laid a hand against her breast, warmth spreading through her veins.

"The duchess's quarters haven't been lived in for quite some while. He thought everything was too dark and old-fashioned and wanted something new."

"It is absolutely perfect."

And thoughtful. And loving. For a moment she closed her eyes. In the weeks since she and Tony had married they had grown close, spending nearly every moment together—awake or asleep. And yet despite their deep intimacy, he had never said the words she longed to hear, never told her he loved her. But this . . . this gift, how could such generosity show anything but caring? How could she interpret it as anything other than an act of love?

Brimming with pleasure, she wanted to run and find him, toss her arms around his neck and give him a kiss of happiness he wouldn't soon forget. But she forced her feet to remain where they stood, cautioning herself that a duchess should never run like a wild hoyden through a house—not even her own house. Besides, the place was so large she wouldn't have the slightest idea where to find him, and, as he'd told her, he had business. *I will thank him later,* she decided. *Tonight in our bed.*

"His Grace's rooms are just through there," Mrs. Armstrong said, indicating a door that stood on the far side of the sitting room.

The information gave her a sudden pause, until she realized that it was only logical that Tony would have his own set of rooms. But just because they existed didn't mean he had to use them. Certainly not the bedroom, anyway.

"Your extra trunks from London arrived some while ago," the housekeeper volunteered. "And everything has been stored away. One of the maids will see to the belongings you brought with you today from Norfolk. You will find hot water in the bath. I can have refreshments sent up as well."

"That would be most welcome. Thank you."

The other woman nodded, then started across the room. Halfway, she stopped and turned back. "Perhaps it is not my place, Your Grace, but I wanted to tell you how delighted all the staff are to welcome you here to Rosemeade. We are so glad the duke finally decided to take a bride, since many of us despaired he ever would. Things have not always been easy for him, but he's the very best of men and deserves to be happy. Having met you, I can see why he changed his mind."

Mrs. Armstrong paused, laying a hand against her chest where a small watch was pinned. "I hope there will be a baby in the next year or two. It would be so good to open the nursery again. Well, I've run on long enough and you must be tired from your journey. I'll send the tea up immediately."

A baby! Gabriella thought the moment the other woman left. She and Tony had only been married seven weeks, far too soon to be thinking about babies. Yet she had always wanted a family. If she found herself expecting so soon, she supposed she wouldn't mind. Considering all the hours she and Tony had spent making love, such an occurrence certainly wasn't out of the realm of possibility. Then again, she would like to have him to herself for a while more. Either way, she decided, she would be glad.

A moment later one of the maids arrived, giving her no further time for reflection.

Chapter Sixteen

FOUR DAYS LATER, Tony signed one of the myriad pieces of correspondence he and his secretary had been laboring to complete, then set the letter aside on one corner of his desk to be franked and mailed. A glance at the clock showed him morning was nearly past and that perhaps it was time he took a break.

Laying down his quill pen, he leaned back in his chair, his thoughts turning to Gabriella. A small squeeze of guilt went through him, knowing he'd been neglecting her of late. Despite his promise that they would spend time together, he'd mostly left her to her own devices, letting Mrs. Armstrong help her get acquainted with the house and grounds. He saw her for meals, of course, and he came to her bed at night, unable to keep his desire for her at bay even now.

Last night she'd changed their routine, he recalled with a little smile on his lips, coming to him with a claim that she wanted to see his rooms. After a cursory inspection and a comment that the space suited him despite it being "very brown and masculine," she'd hopped onto his bed and bounced, giggling with the carefree guilelessness of a child.

"*Just finding out if the feathers are soft,*" she'd teased before she'd leaned back with a naughty sparkle in her eyes that wasn't childlike in the least. He'd joined her there only moments later and had refused to let her leave until her inquiry was well and thoroughly satisfied.

As for her own rooms, he was gratified by her response to them, pleased she was so happy with the renovations he'd had done. He'd wanted everything to be new and bright, with modern furnishings and appointments chosen specifically for her. He supposed he could have left the rooms as they had been and let Gabriella do the redecorating herself, but he'd wanted a fresh start to inaugurate their new life together.

And—as he'd told her that first night while she'd been dusting thank-you kisses across his face as they stood inside her bedchamber—if there was anything she did not like, she had only to say the word. As far as he was concerned, she could tear out everything and start over again, if that was her desire. But she'd shaken her head and professed to love her rooms—every inch of fabric and paper, glass and wood. For a moment, he'd thought she'd been on the verge of telling him something else, but then he'd slipped his hands under her robe and both of them had forgotten all about conversation for a very long while.

Casting a glance at the clock again, he considered the time and his duties. Despite the numerous items that still required his attention, he supposed no great harm would be done if he slipped off with Gabriella for a few hours this afternoon. Warming to the notion, he decided he would ask Cook to pack them a hamper. *Yes, a picnic might be just the thing*. They could ride out to a spot he knew well—a lovely, tree-sheltered knoll near one of Rosemeade's streams, where they could enjoy a fine meal and who knows what else afterward.

Already relishing the idea, he slid his chair away from his desk, but before he could rise from his seat, a knock sounded at the door. "Come," he called.

His butler entered the room, a serious cast to his always proper features. "Pardon me, Your Grace, but a visitor has arrived. The dow—"

"Pray do not be absurd, Crump," interrupted a lilting feminine voice as a slender, elegantly gowned woman breezed into the room. "I am not a *visitor* and do not need to be announced, certainly not to my own son. I used to live here once, if you will recall. I believe you were a footman at the time."

"Yes, Your Grace," intoned the retainer. "First footman, though that was many years ago."

"I trust you will not be nasty and remind me how many. Now, be off and attend to your duties. I want to talk to Wyvern."

The man, who despite appearances was likely the younger of the pair, bowed and withdrew, closing the door behind him. Once he did, Tony surveyed his mother, aware that despite the reality of her age, no one looking at her would suspect that the Dowager Duchess of Wyvern was now in her fifth decade.

Always a beauty, her looks remained nearly unchanged from the days of her youth. Her hair was the same rich, burnished gold it had always been, without a single strand of white. Her skin was still taut and clear. As for her face and figure . . . well, from all reports, she continued to attract new lovers into her arms with steady regularity—just the way she liked.

"So?" she demanded as she glided forward and sank into a nearby chair, pausing for a moment to fuss with the peach-colored material of her skirt. "Have you nothing to say?"

He relaxed back in his chair, steepling his fingers under his chin. "Hallo, Mother. What is it that brings you here?"

Her lips rounded into a moue. "The same as ever, I see, alarmingly direct and to the point. A rather annoying trait inherited from your father."

"Luckily for me, I inherited a great many traits from my father."

She made another face but ignored the comment. "I have come because of this rash, impetuous act of yours. What do you mean by getting married and telling no one beforehand?"

"You had my letter, I assume," he said, his hands moving to the arms of his chair.

"Of course I received your missive, if you call that brief note a *letter*. I was in Prague at the time, else I would have been here sooner. I left to return to England as soon as I read it."

"Why? I should think the news alone would have sufficed without any need for you to cut short your sojourn."

Her lashes swept downward for a moment. "My time abroad was nearly over by then, so the change of plans made little difference."

He quirked a brow. "Ah, got rid of your lover, did you? Or did he get rid of you?"

Her shoulders stiffened. "There is no need to be crude. And my social life is no concern of yours."

"One might say the same to you about the specifics of my marriage. Besides, I should think you would be happy that I have finally wed, given your expressed displeasure over the years at my single state."

Her blue eyes flashed. "Of course I was displeased by your refusal to marry—nothing but stubborn selfishness on your part, if you ask me."

He studied the fingernails of his right hand. "Yes, so you have said before."

"That's right," she returned. "You have a duty to this family to carry on the name, just like all the other Blacks before you. How else do you think the title has managed to pass in a direct line through twenty-three generations?

If I had done as I wished, some cousin would have inherited it long ago."

He listened with half an ear, the speech a familiar one.

"Why else do you think I sacrificed my own my health in order to bring you into the world?" she continued. "Not to mention my willingness to risk my figure. Many women *die,* you know, and worse, get *fat,* but your father needed an heir and, of course, it was my obligation to comply."

She broke off, her brows racing together. "Good God, that isn't why you married that girl, is it? Because you got her with child? If that is the case, I should think you could have bought her off with a few pretty trinkets and a house somewhere in the countryside. Then you might still be free to marry a girl of good lineage, as befits your station, instead of one of such lowering origins. I suppose there is always the possibility of divorce, but just consider the scandal. Then again—"

"Enough!" he bit out in a voice that sounded deadly cold even to his own ears. "You have said more than enough, madam, and I will not listen a moment longer. My wife came to me untouched, not that it is any business of yours, and though she is not yet carrying my child, I hope to change that circumstance in the very near future. As for my decision to wed, it was mine to make and none of yours. Now, I believe this interview is at an end. You are welcome, of course, to stay and refresh yourself before you continue your journey to the dower house."

"Do not think you can put me off, Anthony Charles Edward Black," she intoned after a long pause, her jaw tight, eyes snapping fire. "You know as well as I do that girl you now call your wife is completely unsuitable to be the Duchess of Wyvern. Dear Lord, the things I've heard since my return—that her mother was an actress and her father a murderer, no matter the noble blood that may have run in his veins. You speak of children. Do you not care that they might turn out to be maniacs, not to mention coarse louts with peasant tastes and crude sensibilities? What will you do when the next duke is a vulgar simpleton? Or a madman? Oh, it is simply not to be borne!"

He got to his feet, his fists braced against the top of his desk. "You will be silent," he ordered in a hard, modulated voice.

But she went on, too overwrought to stop. "I know why you've done this. It is because of me. For years you've wished to shame me, to see me suffer for all the wrongs you think I've done. You've never understood the truth. How difficult it was to live with your father. You idolized him, but you were too young to know the real man. I needed more, confined here in this place. I was young and had a right to some pleasure and excitement in my life, especially after I gave him what he wanted—*you, his precious son.*" She drew in a breath and lay a hand against her bosom. "Now you are having your revenge, dishonoring this family and seeing to it I have to share in the disgrace."

"It seems to me you have managed to do that all on your own without any assistance from me, what with your constant parade of lovers," he retorted, his voice a few degrees colder than ice. "Frankly, I do not care how you conduct your life, but you will not interfere with mine, nor that of my wife and the family we hope to have. Now, I do not believe there will be time for you to take that tea, after all. I shall have Crump see your carriage is made ready."

A part of him wanted to rail against her, but he had long since moved beyond such feelings when it came to the woman who had given him birth. He'd stopped loving her so long ago he could scarcely remember the emotion, so that all he felt now was resignation and pity. But anger burned within him on Gabriella's behalf. *How dare she say such things about her! How dare she condemn a girl she had never even taken the trouble to meet!* Not that he wished them to do so. Suddenly he heard a sound in the doorway and looked up to see that it was already too late to prevent such an occurrence.

Framed in the entrance stood Gabriella, an expression of clear discomfort on her face. *Christ,* he silently cursed, *just how much of Mother's venom has she heard?*

Obviously noticing they were no longer alone, the dowager shifted on her chair and pinned Gabriella with an inquiring look. "Your *bride,* I presume," she remarked.

"My pardon," Gabriella said, hesitating a moment before coming farther into the room. "I didn't mean to interrupt, but I was informed we had company and I thought—"

"No need to apologize," Tony stated as he rounded his desk and strode toward her. "We had already finished our discussion. Mother was just leaving."

Rising to her feet, the dowager turned to face them. "But I can take a moment for an introduction."

Reaching Gabriella, he slid an arm around her waist and pulled her protectively against his side. "Fine. Gabriella, this is my mother, the Dowager Duchess of Wyvern. Mother, my *wife.*" He made sure to emphasize the last word so his mother could not fail to take note of his underlying warning.

Innately polite no matter the circumstances, Gabriella smiled and stretched out a hand. "Hello. How do you do?"

"Not as well as I had hoped," the dowager said, making no effort to accept her daughter-in-law's hand before she lifted her gaze again to Tony's. "It is plain to see why you couldn't keep your hand out of the cookie jar. At least I have the consolation of knowing your offspring won't lack for looks."

Gabriella stiffened at his side.

Before his mother could say more, he released Gabriella and stepped forward. *Should it prove necessary,* he decided, *I will escort her out by force.* "This interview is done. I assume you will not be remaining in the country for long given your aversion to all settings pastoral. Perhaps another trip overseas might amuse you, now that the war is well and truly over."

Her eyes narrowed as she took his meaning. "Perhaps. Though the decision would be more easily made were my widow's portion increased a few thousand more."

Forever greedy, he mused. Despite the extremely generous allowance he provided, his mother never seemed satisfied by the amount. He didn't care about the money, though. He'd gladly give whatever it took to see her on her way. "Of course. I will have my secretary send over a cheque."

She inclined her head, obviously pleased at having triumphed in that small skirmish at least. "Well, I shall take my leave now, though I would counsel you to reconsider what we discussed."

"There is nothing to consider. Nothing at all. Your coach awaits you, madam. Pray permit me to see you out."

"Do not bother, Wyvern. I can find my own way to the front door. Good day." With a regal swish of her skirts, she departed.

The atmosphere in the room shifted the moment she had gone, as if a great storm cloud had just blown through. Gabriella raised her gaze to his. "Tony, I—"

"You need not say a word. My mother is what she is and I have found it best not to dwell on her. I do apologize, however, for whatever portion of our conversation you may have heard."

"I heard very little. And honestly, I did not mean to intrude—"

"I know," he said, drawing her into his arms. "And your presence is never an intrusion. This is your home and you are its duchess. You have a right to go anywhere within these walls that you choose."

"Including your personal rooms and this study?" she quipped.

He could tell she was half teasing, but he was not. "Yes, even those, even here," he told her with utter sincerity. "Now," he continued, deciding a change of topic was greatly warranted. "I was wondering if you might enjoy taking an excursion this afternoon?"

Her beautiful eyes lighted with interest. "Oh, but do you not need to work?"

He shook his head. "Not today. How do you feel about a picnic?"

A grin brightened her face, and her arms looped snuggly around his waist. "I would adore a picnic! When shall we leave?"

He smiled. "Within the hour. As soon as a hamper and horses can be arranged." Leaning down, he pressed his lips to hers for a brief but distinctly satisfying kiss. By the time their embrace ended, he'd forgotten all about his confrontation with his mother, Gabriella and the afternoon ahead the only things left on his mind.

Five mornings later, Gabriella sat in her own study and listened politely while Mrs. Armstrong consulted with her about the running of the household. Despite the fact that the older woman had been doing an excellent job managing the staff and the day-to-day activities of the estate for some years, she seemed genuinely pleased to have Gabriella's input.

For her part, Gabriella tried her best. At times she felt woefully inadequate, still so new to Rosemeade that she hadn't even realized there was a dairy, an apiary, and a brewery on the grounds until Mrs. Armstrong asked her questions concerning each. She offered comments and suggestions where they seemed advisable; otherwise she deferred to the housekeeper, trusting her clearly wise counsel.

"That sounds lovely. Thank you, Your Grace," the woman said, making a notation about an addition to one of the dinner menus. "His Grace quite likes apricots, so using them as part of the entremets will be just the thing."

"Apricots are a favorite of mine as well. I shall look forward to trying Cook's dish."

While the housekeeper made a few additional notes to herself in a small ledger, Gabriella took a moment to let her thoughts drift, centering, as they so frequently did these days, on Tony.

Not surprisingly, she and Tony's afternoon excursion the other day had been delightful, the secluded location just right for a picnic. Under the shade of a leafy elm with a pristine blue stream flowing nearby, they'd eaten their meal and talked. He'd flirted with her as well, teasing and tempting her over dessert until their mood had grown abruptly amorous.

Despite her initial concern that someone might happen along, he'd soon convinced her otherwise, enthralling her with kisses and caresses until she'd been too dizzy with need to care who might see. Afterward they'd returned home, then gone upstairs to her bed, where they'd continued to let their passions run free long into the night.

Not until the next morning did she remember that he'd said nothing further about the visit from his mother. Nor had he mentioned her in the days since, resuming his usual routine as if nothing at all had occurred. Part of her wanted to question him, to let him know he might confide in her should there be anything he wished to say. But she remained silent, suspecting he would tell her he had no concerns whatsoever and to leave everything exactly as it was.

As she'd told him, she really had heard very little of what he and his mother had been discussing that day, but the memory of the coldness in his voice was enough to send a shiver rippling through her even now. The fact that he didn't like his mother was clear. The why, however, was not. She couldn't say she'd liked his mother much either, but as she knew, all families had troubles and disagreements. Though to her, this seemed to be more.

"Mrs. Armstrong," she said suddenly, "you have been here at Rosemeade for many years, have you not?"

The housekeeper glanced up, a proud smile on her lined face. "Yes, Your Grace, since I was a girl. I came into service at twelve, started first as a tweeny, then moved up to second upstairs' maid, then first. I even worked in the nursery for a time before I was offered the opportunity to train as the housekeeper."

Gabriella's pulse gladdened at the news. "So you knew the duke when he was a boy?"

The older woman's expression grew soft. "Why, I've known him since the day he came into this world. Swaddled his little rump myself, though I would not dare remind him of that now," she added on a chuckle. "The master was always so bright and full of youthful energy."

"And his mother? What about her? How was she with him?"

The smile fell from the housekeeper's face. "Her Grace was . . . Her Grace. She had many interests that did not include looking after a child, but then very few of the Quality actually take an active part in the raising of their children. No offense intended, Your Grace," she added, casting a worried look at Gabriella.

"None taken, since I find I agree. So she was absent?"

"Yes. She longed for the city and would often persuade the duke—the late duke—to take her to London. Sometimes, they went abroad for several months as well."

"And Tony was left here alone?"

"Lord Howland, as he was known then, stayed with his nurses and the rest of the staff."

"And when his parents returned?"

"Why, he was overjoyed, of course. His father fairly doted on him and seemed to regret the time away. They spent every day together when the duke was in residence."

"And his mother?"

The housekeeper paused for a moment. "Well, he adored her, too. He was such a good boy, always looking for ways to please and amuse her in hopes of earning her approbation." She lowered her gaze, clearly uncomfortable. "Forgive me, but I am afraid I have said far more than I ought and should not continue."

"Oh, but I wish you would," Gabriella urged in a reassuring tone. "I only want to understand. When the dowager duchess called the other day, I could not help but notice a marked distance between her and my husband."

Mrs. Armstrong glanced up and sighed. "Yes, 'tis true, the duke and his mother are not close, though I know His Grace does his best to be generous and considerate despite the fact that she does little to deserve his kindness."

"What do you mean?"

The housekeeper's gray eyebrows drew together as if weighing whether or not to continue. "Well, Your Grace, the dowager is, and always has been, a very vain, selfish sort who expects the world and everyone in it to bow to her every whim. When she first came to live here at Rosemeade, though, she seemed content enough. The late duke loved her to distraction and did everything in his power to make her happy. For a time, I believe they were. But then she discovered she was with child, and that was when everything changed. She simply could not be cheered."

"You mean she didn't want him, her own baby?" Gabriella demanded, aghast at the idea.

"I'm not sure it was so much not wanting the child as disliking having to carry him. She would cry for hours over her cumbersome shape and complain about how dreadfully miserable she felt. When the time arrived for the birth, the delivery did not go well. Her Grace nearly died, and I believe that is why there were never any more children. The duke did his best to pretend all was well after that, but anyone with eyes could tell it was not."

"How sad!"

The older woman nodded. "That's when the affairs started. She was discreet at first, but as the years went on, she became more and more incautious until no one was left in doubt of her faithlessness, least of all the duke. I'm not sure when His Grace knew, since he was only a child at the time, but he was fully aware there were problems between his parents. Then the duke fell ill."

"What happened?" Gabriella asked, leaning slightly forward in her chair.

"He was caught in a downpour and took a bad chill. The ague set in a couple of days later and he came down with a terrible fever. The duchess dismissed the idea of calling a physician. She said it was only a bit of a cold and he would be right again in no time. She left soon after to be with one of her amours. His Grace is the one who ordered the physician once he realized how severe his father's condition had become, but by then it was simply too late. There was nothing to be done. The duke died late the next evening with the young master at his bedside."

"How old was my husband?"

Mrs. Armstrong met her gaze, her eyes filled with sorrow. "Only ten. He wept like a wild thing, shaking his father and telling him to wake up. He wouldn't leave, refusing to accept. We finally had to force him to his room and give him a little laudanum so he could sleep. I think His Grace blamed himself for the duke's death. I think he blamed his mother as well."

Gabriella wiped a trace of moisture from the corner of her eye, remembering the deaths of her parents and how hard it had been to cope—and she had been a great deal older than ten.

"Her Grace arrived two days later, after we sent word of what had occurred," the housekeeper went on. "She stood over the body and didn't shed a tear, Your Grace, and when the young master ran to her for comfort, she . . . she sent him back to the nursery. But that wasn't the worst."

"Why? What did she do?"

"She decided to send him off to school. His father hadn't even been in the grave a week when she told him he would be going. Maybe I shouldn't tell you this, since I don't think even His Grace realizes I overheard, but . . . he begged her to let him stay. He got down on his knees and pleaded with her to allow him to remain here at Rosemeade. He told her he'd be good and wouldn't get into a bit of trouble. He'd mind his tutor and do every lesson he was given. He told her he loved her and asked her to stay and not go traveling again for a while. I was as relieved as the young duke when I heard her tell him he could remain.

"But the very next morning . . . she ordered all his trunks packed, and made us awaken him early to get him dressed and fed. Then with her lover standing right at her side, they put him in the coach. She told him it was time he acted like a man, instead of a weak little boy. He was the duke now and he ought to behave as befits his title and his duty. Lord above, I'll never forget the master's face—he looked so shocked and betrayed. But he didn't cry, not so much as a tear. I think whatever love he felt for her died that day. Maybe she was alive, but for him, he'd lost both parents. I know that was the last time he ever called her Mama."

She drew a rueful breath before concluding her story. "After his coach rolled away, she went off to the Continent with her lover. His Grace didn't come home for six more years, not even for holidays. Once he did return . . . well, he truly was a man grown, the duke in every way in spite of his young years."

Gabriella sat for a long minute, imagining it all, seeing Tony as he must have been then, young and defenseless, without anyone in the world who truly loved him—certainly not the woman who had given him birth. How could she have been so callous? How could any mother treat her son in such a cold, heartless way? It was a wonder he could bring himself to speak to her at all. Gabriella would not have done so, and if she'd known last week what she knew now, she would have sent the woman away with a flea in her ear. She didn't know how Tony could so much as tolerate being in the same room with her—hateful woman!

"Thank you, Mrs. Armstrong," she said. "Thank you for telling me. I can only imagine how abandoned he must have felt. How alone. She is a dreadful woman and I shan't be inviting her here to the estate, nor to the townhouse in London. I wouldn't serve her so much as a cup of tea, I'll tell you that!"

The housekeeper smiled. "Oh, Your Grace, it's glad I am that the duke has found you. You are just what he needs, and we can all see how deeply you care for him. I don't believe he has trusted any woman since he was a boy—I expect that's why he was so adamant about never wanting to marry. But he couldn't resist you, now, could he? Nor you him."

"No," she said. "As I have discovered, His Grace is completely irresistible."

Is Mrs. Armstrong right? Gabriella wondered. Had Tony's refusal to marry all these years been because he couldn't trust a woman enough to commit to such a bond? Because he wouldn't let himself take the risk of falling in love? He'd made no secret of his intention to spend his life as a bachelor. And yet he'd married her, had he not? If she'd needed confirmation that he loved her, she didn't any more. After all, what other reason could there have been for his change of heart and mind?

Still, there was a part of him that remained closed off to her, she knew, inviolate and accessible to no one but himself. Yet trust took time, did it not? And patience. Maybe she only needed to wait and show him her love, until slowly, like water dripping on a rock, the barrier he kept between them gave way.

Besides, she sensed he was happy despite the fact that they spent much of their days apart now. He was busy with his duties, while she had new responsibilities of her own. And there was still so much for her to learn about Rosemeade, and especially about how to be its duchess. She wanted Tony to be proud and have no cause to regret his choice of bride. To that end, she supposed she really ought to return to her review of domestic matters.

"My thanks again for telling me about His Grace. I shall not forget it," she told the servant. "We were discussing menus before, were we not? Shall we continue?"

"With pleasure, Your Grace."

Chapter Seventeen

"OH, YOU'RE HERE!" Gabriella exclaimed as she hurried down Rosemeade's front steps toward the refined, black coach-and-four that had pulled to a stop only moments ago. Her scarlet cashmere cloak fluttered in the crisp December wind, her pleasure impervious to the clouds that lumbered in the overcast sky.

"Gabriella!" Julianna said as soon as Rafe finished assisting her to the ground. The two women embraced, laughing at being together once again; then it was Rafe's turn to wrap Gabriella in an exuberant hug before setting her away for his inspection.

"I need not ask how you are," he said with a smile, "since I can see that for myself. You look well."

She smiled. "I am. Wonderfully, in fact. And so glad you could come for the Christmas holidays. Ethan and Lily arrived not fifteen minutes ago and are already inside with Tony. Everyone else should be here soon, including Maris and William and Harry. I'm so glad Maris decided she felt well enough to travel, what with her being nearly six months along with the baby."

"I had a letter from her just last week," Julianna volunteered, "and she says she's feeling extremely well. A good thing, too, since she would have been quite blue-deviled to have had to miss the festivities."

Without warning, Gabriella felt a light tug on her

cloak. Glancing down, she discovered Campbell Pendragon's intense green gaze on her, his little arms stretched high in clear expectation of receiving his own greeting. "Up, Aunt Gabby. I want up."

"Hello, sweetheart," she said, as she bent down to lift him into her arms. "So you haven't forgotten me then, hmm?"

"Lord no," Julianna replied with a smile. "He's talked of nothing else over the past two weeks, ever since I told him we were coming to visit Aunt Gabriella and Uncle Tony."

The boy snuggled close, grinning as he twined his arms around her neck. She shifted him, finding him amazingly heavy despite his lean frame. "He looks more like Rafe every day."

"And acts like him, too, if the stubborn streak he's developed is any example," Julianna quipped, taking fourteen-month-old Stephanie from the nursemaid.

"You love my stubborn streak," Rafe countered with supposed affront.

"I love *you,* darling. As for the streak. . . ." Julianna gave a teasing shrug before trading adoring glances with her husband.

"Oh, just look at the baby!" Gabriella declared. "Oh, how she's grown. And so beautiful!"

"Ladies, if I might offer a suggestion," Rafe interrupted. "Why don't we continue this conversation inside where it is warm and not threatening to pour rain at any moment?"

Agreeing, the five of them entered the house, along with a small swarm of servants who were working to unload the baggage from both coaches and bring it into the house. In the front hall, they met Tony, Ethan, and Lily, who had been on their way outside to greet them. A fresh round of hugs and welcomes ensued, with Cam passed happily to several different pairs of arms.

They were about to go upstairs to the drawing room five minutes later when Gabriella saw Lily pause suddenly and turn her head. Her pretty red eyebrows drew together as she stared at a wicker hamper that had just been carried inside. "Perhaps I am mistaken, but is that basket mewing?"

Julianna's dark eyes grew wide, turning to hand the baby to Rafe. "Oh, my! In all the excitement, I nearly forgot."

"Forgot what?" Tony asked, shooting an incriminating look at the basket in question.

"We've brought you a special present. Well, Gabriella really, but they're for both of you to enjoy."

Tony frowned harder. "*They?*"

A fresh set of meows resounded. Hearing them, Gabriella smiled and hurried forward. Yanking open a strap, she pulled the top off the wicker hamper. "Kittens!" she cried as she gazed down at two of the most adorable cats she'd ever seen, one orange and the other black. "Oh, they're just precious." Reaching inside, she stroked one, then the other, their fur soft as silk.

"Another one of Aggie's litters," Julianna remarked. "They needed homes and we thought of you. They're both boys, so you shouldn't have too many more."

Tony crossed his arms over his chest. "Thank God for small favors."

Gabriella sent him a look. "Don't be a spoilsport. They're adorable, and I love them already." Carefully, Gabriella lifted one of the kittens into her arms, eliciting a fresh round of meows.

"In that case, I suppose there is nothing else to say, but thank you." Walking nearer, Tony reached out to pet one small, furry head.

Gabriella had just set them down outside the basket when a scrabbling of claws and barks announced the arrival of Rafe's two dogs, Max and Digger. She and Tony reached for the kittens at the same time, but it was too late—the little cats arched their backs and started spitting as a frenzy of commotion broke loose. It took them a couple of minutes, but they managed to secure the dogs and catch the frightened cats, returning them to the safety of their hamper.

"Well," Tony said as he wound a handkerchief around his bleeding hand. "This should be an interesting holiday."

"Would you care for a brandy?" Tony asked two weeks later as he and Ethan walked into his study, afternoon sunlight filtering through the windows to warm the room in spite of the frosty January air outside. Ethan agreed to the proffered drink and took a seat in one of a pair of comfortable wing chairs near the fireplace.

All the other guests had departed a few hours earlier—everyone except Ethan and Lily, who had decided to remain another day due to Lily's having awakened that morning with a queasy stomach.

"I never did get an opportunity to give you a proper toast, what with all the recent festivities," Tony said. "After all, it's not every day a man learns he is to become a father."

A wide smile creased Ethan's face. "True, especially the first time. Lily is so excited. I am, too."

Filling the snifters, Tony replaced the crystal stopper, then crossed to hand one to the other man. After doing so, he sank into the seat opposite. "Congratulations, Papa."

As he and Ethan drank to the toast, Tony let his thoughts drift back over the days just passed. The holiday had proven not only interesting, as he'd predicted, but enjoyable. To make the house festive, a Yule log had been felled and carried inside to burn in Rosemeade's largest fireplace, while ribbons and bells and greenery had been strung in charming displays throughout the house. During the day, Tony had taken the men out riding and hunting, while the women stayed indoors to talk, sew, read, and paint—Gabriella complaining that her watercolors were as shamefully dismal as ever. In the evenings after dinner, everyone gathered for fun and games—singing and playing music some nights, while on others they indulged in cards or guessing games like crambo and charades.

Two days before Christmas, the rain that had fallen earlier in the week turned to snow, coating the ground in a glittery blanket of white. Tony had ordered sleighs prepared, the whole party traipsing out into the cold so they could enjoy the thrill of racing out over the frozen fields. He could still picture the delight in Gabriella's pert violet eyes as he drove the two of them, her cheeks rosy as she huddled warm and secure beneath a thick layer of woolen coaching blankets and her own fur-lined cloak.

Afterward, they'd all trundled inside to warm up over dishes of hot tea, mulled cider, and fragrant spice cakes. And before long, he and Gabriella had found themselves standing beneath a strand of mistletoe. Never one to let an opportunity pass, he'd pulled her into his arms and given her a thorough kissing, one that had elicited hoots and a round of good-natured teasing.

Much later that night, after everyone had retired for the evening, he'd come to her room to continue what he'd started downstairs, taking her mouth in a series of long, drugging kisses that had driven both of them nearly mad with want. Using his hands and lips, he'd brought her to peak time and time again until she was half-delirious from an excess of pleasure. Only then had he sheathed himself inside her warm, willing flesh, joining them in a way that never failed to leave him satisfied.

Later, when he'd recovered enough to think coherently, he'd found himself puzzling over his contentment. After nearly six months of marriage, he'd expected his fascination with her to have begun to wane, having assumed from past experience that his desire for her would have cooled to little more than a barely warm simmer. Instead, he hungered for her as much now as ever—if not more. Enough so that it concerned him at times.

Which is why he had kept his needs under strict regulation since returning to Rosemeade, often using his duties as a way to put what he considered a reasonable amount of distance between them. She was his wife, not his mistress, he reminded himself, and it wouldn't do to be constantly hovering around her skirts, nor delving beneath them.

Yet at night he always went to her, loving her long and well. And even on the occasional night when they didn't make love, he stayed, savoring the sensation of her curled against him, her body a sweet warmth against him as they slept.

Were it not for their household full of guests, he might have been tempted to break his self-imposed rule and keep her with him in bed the whole of Christmas day. Instead, he'd contented himself by watching her eat sweetmeats and sip wassail while she opened a huge mound of presents. Among them had been a diamond and amethyst choker and ear bobs he'd had specially commissioned from London. The jewels had drawn an audible cry of delighted surprise from her lips, followed by murmurs of appreciation from the other women, who'd immediately come forward to see.

For her part, Gabriella had given him a fine pair of leather gloves and a Stubbs painting of a horse, together with three dozen monogrammed silk handkerchiefs she'd taken the time to embroider herself. He'd immediately tucked one into his pocket.

While the dogs had barked, the children laughed, and the kittens—who'd wrapped everyone around their tiny paws just as Gabriella had once predicted—played in the paper and ribbons, Gabriella had sought him out to show her pleasure with a pair of quick but enthusiastic kisses. She had given him kisses and much more in private later that night.

All in all, the holiday had been one of the best he'd ever known—likely *the* best, if he was being strictly honest. But now it was over, as all things, no matter how pleasurable, must eventually be.

Returning to the present, he met Ethan's inquiring gaze. "Never mind me," Tony said. "Just taking a moment to gather my thoughts. Once again, my heartfelt congratulations on your happy news. To your future son and heir."

"To my son," Ethan cheered. "Or daughter. I know I'm supposed to want a boy, but I'd actually like a girl this first time around—a little beauty with red hair and green eyes, just like her mother."

"To your daughter, then."

Raising their glasses, he and Ethan drank.

"I'll be toasting you one of these times soon, I expect," Ethan said, setting down his glass on a side table.

Tony considered the comment. "You're likely right, though I wouldn't mind having Gabriella strictly to myself for a while longer."

"Hmm, I can understand that. Still on your honeymoon even now. That's the way it was with Lily and me, but with a year of marriage behind us, we're ready to increase our family. You will be soon enough, too. I have to admit I was a bit skeptical at first about your nuptials, but I can see the affection between the two of you. I'm glad you found her, Tony. I'm glad you actually fell in love."

Love! Good God! he thought, his heart giving a quick double beat. As he contemplated the idea, an uncomfortable sensation rose inside his chest, one he decided must be an unlikely bit of dyspepsia from the brandy he'd just consumed.

He scowled. "Love? Well, that's going a bit too far. Gabriella and I . . . we suit each other and it's lucky that we do. But beyond that, it's mostly physical and nothing more."

"So you are telling me that you don't love her?" Ethan said, disbelief clear in his voice. "To observe the two of you together, one would imagine otherwise."

"All it proves is that looks can be deceiving. Because of your own love match, that's what you think you see in everyone. But you're mistaken." *Or is he?* whispered a niggling little voice. Despite any further potential disturbance to his digestion, Tony tossed back the last of his brandy, suddenly more in need than ever of its fortifying influence. Ruthlessly shoving aside any doubt, he plunged ahead, his words deliberately calm and assured. "So, in answer to your question—no, I do not love Gabriella."

On the other side of the door, Gabriella stood with her hand frozen against the wooden frame, her breath shallow and nearly stilled inside her lungs. She hadn't meant to eavesdrop—God knows she hadn't—and now wished she could somehow rewind time and not have heard Tony's words.

She'd come to tell Ethan that Lily was feeling greatly recovered—her morning sickness now gone—and to invite him and Tony to join the two of them for a game of whist. As she'd drawn close to the study, the deep rumblings of their male voices had come to her ears. But it wasn't until she'd stood directly on the other side that their words had become clear.

"I wouldn't mind having Gabriella strictly to myself for a while longer," Tony had said.

She remembered smiling at the sentiment, warmth rising inside her as she'd paused with one hand on the door. But then, they'd kept talking, the conversation taking a sudden, horrible turn.

"Love? Well, that's going a bit too far . . ."

Blood had buzzed like angry insects inside her head, a lump of bile rising in a sickening wave within her gut. And then she'd heard the worst. *"No,"* Tony had said in an almost matter-of-fact tone. *"I do not love Gabriella."*

The world had narrowed down in that moment, taking on a strange, unreal quality that made her feel as if she were swimming in a great, frigid river of ice. Her own sense of self-preservation called for her to move away, to cover her ears and run. But she couldn't move; something was holding her in place, forcing her to listen and endure the rest.

"Then why did you marry her if not for love?" Ethan asked.

A small silence hung for a moment inside the room. "You may not know this, but the night of the fireworks celebration, Gabriella and I ended up stranded alone."

"I surmised that might have been the case, but you got her back to Rafe and Julianna's without difficulty, did you not?"

"We made it home by way of Erika Hewitt's coach."

Ethan let out a muffled curse.

"Without belaboring the point," Tony went on, "Erika decided to blackmail me. Either I come back to her bed, or she would tell Society what she had seen, with a great deal of added embellishment, I'm sure. What else was I to do, Ethan? I couldn't let Gabriella be ruined. Had I not married her, no man but a scoundrel would ever have touched her again. She certainly would never have been able to make a suitable marriage."

"So you married her in order to save her from the clutches of your vindictive ex-mistress?"

Another short pause followed. "And also because I wanted her—quite badly, as it would happen. I figured in exchange for my bachelorhood, I got to take her to my bed. Not a bad trade, all in all."

"For you, perhaps. Are you aware that Gabriella loves you?"

Silence.

"Does she?" Tony mused aloud. "She's young yet, so the emotion will likely fade, as will our passion in time. Hopefully, any affection she feels will make the next few years easier on us both. Since we are married, I have to admit I would like a child or two—a son to carry on the title, despite my willingness once to see the dukedom pass into my cousin's hands. Beyond that, I am hoping Gabriella and I might end up comfortably together, perhaps even find a way to remain friends. At the proper time, I expect each of us will go our own way—discreetly, of course, and without the tiresome need for arguments and recriminations."

Go our own way discreetly! she thought. So, he was already contemplating the day when he would have grown tired of her and want to seek out his pleasures in some other woman's bed? When he would no longer feel compelled to pretend an affection for her—at least nothing stronger than a *comfortable friendship*? Although apparently he was not the selfish sort, she thought derisively, since he was willing to let her find solace and satisfaction in the arms of another man. Her stomach churned at the idea, and for a moment she feared she might be sick right there in the corridor.

Somehow she managed to control her emotions and finally force her limbs to move. Easing silently away from the door, she retreated the way she had come. Traversing the house, she reached her room, realizing afterward that she had no clear memory of the journey. Inside her sitting room, she stared vacantly at the trailing roses on the wallpaper—roses Tony had chosen for her. Flowers she had loved until that moment.

Her maid touched her on the shoulder, awakening her from her reverie. "Your Grace, my pardon, but you look quite pale. Are you well?"

Well? Gabriella thought. *I don't think I will ever be well again.* She shook her head. "No, I . . . I have a headache. I . . . would you please send my apologies to Lady Vessey, and tell her I will see her at dinner."

"Of course, Your Grace. May I bring you anything to relieve your discomfort?"

Yes, she thought wildly. *Bring me something that will make it all go away. Something that will change things back to the way they were only this morning when I awakened happy and content in Tony's arms.* And yet, to do so would mean she would still be living a lie. Would still believe her marriage had been based on honest devotion, instead of sacrifice and necessity. Would still believe that Tony loved her, when the most he really felt was lust, a kind of tolerant, lukewarm affection, and pity.

Oh, God, what am I going to do? A single tear trailed down her cheek, pain spreading like an open wound inside her. "Leave me," she murmured. "Leave me and let me be alone."

"Another lemon tart, Lily?" Gabriella inquired several hours later at the dinner table. "You're eating for two now, you know, so I'm sure you can afford the indulgence."

"I'm not sure!" Lily laughed, laying a hand over her still flat stomach. "Although they are exceptionally delicious." She wavered, her gaze studying the contents of the dessert platter. "Well, perhaps half. You can give the rest to Ethan, since he's one of those obnoxious people who can eat as much as they like and never put on an ounce."

"I do have a sound constitution," he agreed with a grin. "Though perhaps you should eat the entire sweetmeat yourself, considering how little food you've been holding down lately."

"If that were my objective, I ought to have eaten more roast duck, but you've talked me into it anyway." With a grin, she helped herself to the treat.

While Lily ate her second tart of the evening, Gabriella sipped her tea and did her best to keep the smile on her face. Even now, she didn't know how she'd managed to force herself out of her room and downstairs for the evening meal.

Earlier, after her maid had left, she'd taken to her bed, lying on her side under a blanket with the curtains pulled tight to block out the afternoon sun. Tony had come to check on her, but she'd squeezed her eyes closed and pretended to sleep, waiting until she heard the door shut behind him before letting loose with a fresh round of tears.

Until tonight, she'd never considered herself much of an actress, but she realized that she could indeed have followed in her mother's footsteps and taken to the stage. The great Mrs. Siddons herself could not have given a better performance.

Assuring everyone that her headache had passed, she'd talked and laughed and done her best to behave as she always did. She'd even endured Tony's kiss, closing her eyes as he brushed his lips over hers, his hand moving over her hair, his fingers across her cheek in a comforting caress, as if he truly did care that she was unwell.

In that moment, she'd wanted to push him away and scream, tell him what a liar he was and ask him how he could have manipulated her into marriage, and worse, into believing that he loved her. But then that particular assumption had been her own doing, she supposed, since she now knew his silence for what it was—the truth.

Frequently over the past few months he'd said he wanted her, praising her body, telling her how much she pleased him in bed. But when it came to love . . . that was one word he had never spoken. Perhaps such an emotion wasn't in him. She thought of his mother and the way she'd abused his young heart. Maybe by doing so, she'd killed off his ability to love and ever let himself trust a woman. Then again, maybe he could love; he just did not love her.

The strain of putting on her act must finally have started to show as dinner concluded a few minutes later, the four of them rising to make their way to the drawing room.

As they walked, Lily slipped an arm through her own. "Are you sure you are well?" she questioned in a soft voice. "You look a bit peaked again."

"I'm fine. A little tired, that's all."

"You're not in the same condition as me, are you? Lord, I get so exhausted some days it's all I can do not to drop down where I am and go to sleep."

"No," she replied. "No, it's nothing like that." At least she didn't believe it was, since she'd finished her menses just last week. And God knows, she didn't need such a complication right now. Then again, perhaps a baby would actually be a blessing—someone to love, who would surely love her back. Still, she didn't honestly think she had conceived.

For a moment, she almost told Lily, desperately needing to unburden the misery that gripped her heart like a vise. But she stopped herself, knowing that once she began, she wouldn't be able to hold anything back, every detail rushing out of her with the force of a flood. And once that happened, Tony would know. Know that she'd listened at his door, however inadvertently. Know, too, how devastated she was by his self-expressed lack of love for her. And she was not ready for a confrontation, at least not yet.

"It's nothing. Truly," Gabriella lied.

The rest of the evening passed; then it was time for bed.

With a silent dread, she let her maid assist her into her nightgown despite the fact that she rarely ended up leaving it on. Tonight, however, she did, burrowing under the covers on her side, hoping he would not seek her out.

But of course, he did, the mattress dipping as it took his weight. Sliding between the sheets, he moved close, placing his lips against the nape of her neck to claim a warm kiss, while he reached to cup one of her breasts inside his palm. Normally, she would have stretched against him and turned to receive his embrace. Tonight, she could not, her muscles stiff, her body for once unresponsive to his touch.

Apparently recognizing her lack of enthusiasm, he stopped and leaned up on an elbow at her back. "What is it? Is something wrong?"

Yes, everything, she cried silently. *Everything is wrong now that you have broken my heart.*

"No," she said. "I am just tired."

She sensed his frown. "Has your headache returned?"

"Yes," she told him, seizing on the excuse. "I don't feel at all well. I . . . I'm sorry."

He stroked his palm over her hair, then kissed her temple. "No need to be sorry. You can't help being ill. Shall I get your maid? Would a compress help?"

"No . . . I just need to sleep."

"All right, then, that's what we'll do." Lying back, he settled his head against his pillow. When he reached to turn her into his arms, though, she resisted.

"Tony . . . I . . . don't," she said. "My head aches too

much. In fact, would you mind going to your room? I think I would sleep better tonight if I were alone."

A long pause followed, his body suddenly tense with what she might have assumed to be hurt had she not known better. She refused to meet his gaze, curling in on herself as she waited to find out what he would do.

"All right," he said in a thick tone. "If that is what you wish. I shall see you in the morning, then."

"Yes. Good night."

"Sleep well, Gabriella."

But as he let himself out of her bedchamber, closing the door softly at his back, she knew she wouldn't sleep at all. Hot tears stung her eyes, a terrible pressure welling up inside her chest. Rolling over, she buried her face in her pillow and gave way to the sobs.

Chapter Eighteen

SOMETHING ISN'T RIGHT *with Gabriella,* Tony decided three days later as he drove his carriage toward Newmarket. Though for the life of him, he couldn't figure out what was amiss.

At first he'd assumed she was ill from the headache that had been plaguing her, though she'd certainly seemed well enough when she'd come downstairs that first morning to see Lily and Ethan on their way. After giving each of them a wide smile and a warm, exuberant hug, she'd stood waving fiercely as their coach rolled down the drive. But afterward she'd withdrawn again, murmuring some excuse about not wishing to keep him from his work.

At nuncheon, and then again at dinner, she'd been polite but reserved, not at all her usual bright self. When he'd tried to question her about her unusual mood, she'd told him she still wasn't feeling well and that she wished to retire early. Her tone had clearly implied she also preferred to retire *alone.*

Despite wanting to query her further, he'd respected her wishes and spent a second night in a row alone in his own bed. He didn't sleep as deeply as usual that night, missing her warmth at his side. He told himself she was still recovering from the after-effects of her headache, but he sensed something more was involved. Given Lily's recent news, it occurred to him that perhaps Gabriella was in the same state. *Is she with child?* he wondered, a glimmer of excitement flaring inside him at the idea.

But when he broached the subject later that evening, she gave him a stare and shook her head. "No, Your Grace, I am not carrying your baby."

"Then what is it, Gabriella? What is wrong?"

Her eyes flashed like a pair of polished amethysts and for a moment he thought she was going to tell him. Instead she lowered her gaze, then pitched her dinner napkin onto her plate and pushed back her chair. "My head hurts again," she murmured. "I am going to bed."

He scowled. "Your head seems to hurt a lot of late."

"Yes, you are right. It does." Turning, she hurried from the room.

He nearly went after her but stayed himself, uncertain of his temper. Striving for calm, he forced himself to finish his meal.

Nearly three hours later, he went upstairs, debating whether or not to join her. Deciding he had every right to be in her bed, he thrust open the connecting door and strode through her sitting room and into her bedchamber. And there she was curled on her side under the covers, the room lighted only by the pale, flickering glow of the logs burning in the fireplace. He hesitated, then pulled off his robe and climbed in beside her. Curving an arm around her body, he pulled her close, kissing her neck and shoulder.

Warm and drowsy, she turned. "Tony?"

"Hmm-hmm. Go back to sleep." But despite his words, he wasn't able to keep himself from slipping his hand beneath the bodice of her nightgown to cup one of her soft, pliant breasts.

She arched, her body responding of its own volition to his familiar touch, her nipples tightening as if seeking the attention of his questing fingers. He complied, fondling her as he took her mouth with a deep, drugging, fervid hunger that made her moan. Muttering her name, he pushed her nightgown up and off her body. As he did, she began to wake, her body stiffening momentarily in his embrace as if only then realizing what she was doing.

But he bent his head and began to suckle her breasts, drawing upon her while he played his hands over her in ways he knew she loved, ways designed to bring her the most intense kind of pleasure. Breath soughed from her lips in quick pants as she writhed against him, returning his touch with bold, erotic caresses of her own.

When the time came, he thrust deep into her body, her hips bucking as they arched to accept his penetration. Wrapping her legs high around his back, she urged him on. When keening cries issued from her throat, he knew she was close, savoring the sound and the sensations as he brought her to a powerful, shuddering peak. He claimed his own satisfaction moments later, closing his eyes as ecstasy ripped through him in a long, hot wave.

He gathered her close afterward, regaining his breath and his sanity in measured draughts. He was drifting off to sleep when he notice the damp on his bare shoulder. At first he didn't understand what it was, then suddenly he did.

"Are you crying? Gabriella? What's wrong?"

But instead of telling him, she shook her head and turned away, rolling onto her side with her back to him. When he tried to comfort her, she refused to let him, drawing more tightly into herself.

Abruptly he felt like a brute, though for what, he didn't know, especially since he had no doubt she had enjoyed their lovemaking. In the end, he lay there on his back, listening until he could tell she had fallen asleep. Only then had he let himself do the same.

By the time he awakened, she was out of bed, dressed,

and downstairs. If he hadn't already made long-standing arrangements to meet with a horse breeder in Newmarket that afternoon, he would have spoken with her to demand, once and for all, that she tell him what was troubling her.

Instead, he kissed her briefly, noticing she would not meet his gaze. "Whatever this is, Gabriella," he said, "you are going to tell me when I return. I'll be back tonight and we'll talk." She said nothing.

Now as he neared Newmarket, he could only hope he would receive a different response tonight.

I have to leave! Gabriella thought. *I cannot stay here a moment longer, especially not after last night.*

She supposed she had the excuse that she had been asleep when she'd first roused to find Tony in her bed, kissing and fondling her with his usual mesmerizing skill. But even drowsy, deep down she had known what she was doing, aware she could have protested his touch and demanded that he stop. Only she hadn't, nor had she wished to do so—his hands and mouth were far too wonderful to resist.

And therein lay her dilemma. Even knowing that he didn't love her, even aching with a misery that went bone deep, she wanted him still. And she loved him, too, no matter how much she wished she could erase the emotion from her mind and heart. If she stayed, she knew a night like the one just past would happen again, and again. It was inevitable. Oh, she might try to deny him, but once he touched her, she would be lost. When that happened, what would she have left? Even her pride would be gone. He would have taken it all. Eventually, she feared such a circumstance might destroy her—especially when he decided he'd grown tired of her and moved on to another woman. If she left now, at least she might still manage to retain her dignity.

Desperate to keep something of herself, no matter how small, she realized she had to get away. Thank the stars for Tony's day trip to Newmarket. Otherwise, she didn't know when she would have had an opportunity to leave—at least not without a terrible confrontation first.

Though maybe he wouldn't care, she considered. He'd told Ethan Andarton he still desired her, but how much longer would that last? Maybe her departure would come as a relief.

Knowing she dare not waste a moment, she directed her startled maid to begin packing her belongings into her traveling valise and a trunk. Obviously, she couldn't take everything, only the essentials. But she would make do. She'd certainly lived on far less in her life, and would manage quite well with what she took today.

Yet even as her clothes, toiletries, and other essentials were being gathered and laid inside her trunk, an alarming thought occurred. *I am running away, but where shall I go?*

Rafe and Julianna would take her in—she knew they would show her sympathy and not turn her away. But they had been Tony's friends far longer than they had been hers, and despite Rafe being her uncle, she did not want to put him and Julianna in the position of choosing sides. The same with Ethan and Lily, no matter how kind the both of them were.

Her parents were dead and she'd lost touch with most of the performance troupe with whom she'd once traveled. All except Maude Woodcraft.

Of course, Maude! How could she not have immediately thought of her old friend? Maude was as good as family, the two of them having once been that close. She could think of no better person to whom she could turn.

Sending down word that she wanted a coach prepared, though not yet revealing her destination, she readied herself for the journey.

* * *

"Good evening, Crump," Tony said as he strode into the house just after dusk. Shrugging out of his heavy greatcoat, he handed it to a waiting footman. "It has been a long day. Please send word to Gull, would you, that I would like a bath prepared and my dinner clothes laid out. And then inform Her Grace that I have returned." Tony paused, casting a glance up the stairs. "On second thought, perhaps I shall tell Her Grace myself. Where is she, do you know?"

The butler got a very peculiar look on his face, his mouth opening, then closing, then opening one more time as he struggled to form his words. "Her Grace is . . . um . . . Her Grace is not here."

Tony frowned. "What's that? What do you mean, she isn't here?"

Crump swallowed visibly. "She ordered a coach and departed just before noon, Your Grace. She . . . um . . . left this for you."

Glancing down, Tony stared at the note in the butler's hand. Feeling his brows grow tight, he took the missive and broke open the wax seal. Gabriella's fine, feminine hand leapt out at him from the page.

Your Grace,

Not Tony? he thought. *What happened to Tony? Obviously, she's far more upset than I realized.* Putting the issue aside for the moment, he read on:

Your Grace,

After much consideration, I have decided I can no longer remain at Rosemeade with you. I need some time away and have taken a coach—I shall send it back once I have reached my destination. I will be staying with a friend and shall be perfectly safe, so you have no need to worry—assuming you would worry, a circumstance of which I am no longer certain. Pray be so good as to not attempt to contact me. I shall be in touch when I am ready.

Yours,
Gabriella

He read the letter a second time, then crushed the vellum inside his hand. What did she mean? *She can no longer remain at Rosemeade with me?* Why the devil not? And what was this nonsense about her being uncertain whether he would worry over her absence? Of course he would worry! "*Pray be so good as to not attempt to contact me . . . I shall be in touch when I am ready.*" As far as he was concerned, she could be ready now, and *would be* if only he knew where to find her.

"Did Her Grace give her direction?" he demanded, already knowing the answer but deciding to ask regardless.

The other man shook his head. "I am sorry, Your Grace. She was quite adamant about not providing that information despite my making several attempts to ascertain her plans. The coachman and I both attempted to dissuade her from leaving, beseeching her to wait until you arrived home, but she would hear none of it."

"No, I am sure she would not." Once Gabriella made up her mind about a thing, there tended to be little use reasoning with her. "It's all right, Crump. I am sure you did your best."

He paused for a moment, pacing a few steps in thought. *Where would she have gone?* To Rafe and Julianna most likely, he conjectured. Or perhaps to Ethan and Lily, though that seemed less probable given their departure only a couple of days ago. There was another possibility as well, that the friend of whom she spoke was no one he knew. She'd lived an interesting and varied life before he'd met her. Given that, she might have journeyed anywhere.

"Have my coach readied. I will ride for London within the hour," he commanded, deciding to begin with the easiest and most obvious choice first. Before he departed, he would write a note to Ethan and Lily. He would also dispatch a pair of footmen to inquire at various coaching inns in hopes of tracing her path. One way or the other, he would find her.

With his plans set in motion, he went to his bedroom to collect a few belongings. As he strode through his sitting room, he caught a glance of hers through the open connecting door. Curving a hand around the door frame, he looked inside, air rushing abruptly from his lungs as a fist lodged in his gut.

Dear God, he thought, *she has left me. And what's worse, I do not even know why.*

Four days later, Gabriella's coach pulled to a halt in front of a quaint cottage located in the western part of Shropshire, not far from the market town of Ellesmere. The powdery white snow that had slowed her journey coated the ground and the roof of the small house, smoke drifting upward from the brick chimney in slow, gray spirals.

Jumping down from the box above, the coachman went to announce her arrival. The door opened moments later, and a woman—who Gabriella assumed must be Maude's cousin Josephine—stood framed in the entrance. Against her hip, the woman held a baby, while below a dark-haired toddler clung to her skirts. Gabriella watched as she exchanged a few words with the coachman before casting a surprised glance in the direction of the coach. "You must be mistaken," she stated, her words carrying on the chill breeze. "Heavens above, do I look like the sort of woman who would know a duchess?"

Her coachman made an inaudible reply, the woman

shaking her head once more. With the assistance of a footman, Gabriella stepped down from the coach. As she did, another woman joined the group, weak winter sunlight glinting off the fiery auburn strands in her graying hair.

Maude! Gabriella cheered silently. But as she walked forward, protected against the wind by her dark green velvet and ermine-lined cloak and hat, her hands warm inside a matching fur muff, she realized with a sinking heart that her friend did not recognize her.

Have I changed so much?

"He says this here duchess is come to see ye, Maude," her cousin declared, another pair of children peering out around their mother's skirts. "A pardon, yer ladyship, but you must've got the wrong house," Josephine said to Gabriella, managing a curtsey despite the clinging youngsters.

"If that lady is a duchess, you should address her as 'Your Grace,' " Maude corrected in a gentle tone, her gaze curious. She stared for another long moment before her eyes suddenly grew wide. "Why, my lord above! *Gabby?* Is that you?"

Gabriella nodded, hurrying forward to be caught inside her friend's reassuring embrace. "Yes," she said. "I'm sorry to surprise you. I would have written to let you know I was coming but there wasn't time."

"That's no matter," Maude said, waving off her remark. "Oh, it's so wonderful to see you! I had your letter about your marriage, of course. Wed to a duke, only imagine! And my, just look at you! You're quite the elegant lady now. It's why I didn't recognize you straight off, you've grown so refined." Maude glanced toward the coach. "Is your husband with you? Tell him to come out so I can meet him."

She shook her head. "He is not with me. Maude, I . . . can I stay?"

The older woman's eyebrows rose. "Here, do you mean?"

She nodded. "If it would not be too much of an imposition. I have some money, so you need not worry that I would be a burden."

"Well, the cottage is small, not what you're used to—at least not anymore."

"I've stayed in smaller. Please."

Maude frowned and drew her close enough so no one else would hear. "Are you in trouble, sweetheart?"

"If leaving my husband counts as trouble, then yes, I am."

Her friend curved an arm around her shoulders. "Well, then, we'll find a place for you, even if I have to sleep on the floor. Now, come inside and tell me everything."

A week later Gabriella sat at a plain wooden kitchen table, three of Josephine's children chasing each other through the room in giggling circles. With a gentle scold, Maude shooed them out, then took a seat opposite and reached for the teapot. After pouring herself and Gabriella each a steaming cup, she helped herself to a biscuit.

"It will be good when Jo's husband returns," Maude said. "She got word just today that he's been released from his military service. These children need a father, though I hope she doesn't end up in the family way again after his return."

"Eight is a great many, is it not? They're all dears, though."

"Hmm. Dears indeed, but a handful nonetheless. Jo appreciates that you've been helping out. She said she was worried at first you'd expect to be waited on, but she's relieved to find you're not so high in the instep, despite your lofty title."

"I like seeing after the young ones," Gabriella replied,

stirring a spoon through her tea. "The littlest, Maura, is a charmer."

"That she is. She's taken to you as well. Her face lights up whenever you are in the room. She'll miss you when you go."

Gabriella frowned, laying her spoon onto her saucer with a click. "Are you kicking me out already? I thought we were all getting along rather well. You haven't even had to sleep on the floor as you feared," she quipped.

"Jo don't mind sharing, though we knock elbows some nights. And you know full well she and I are happy to have you here. But I expect that duke of yours doesn't feel the same."

"I doubt he cares. He's probably in London right now enjoying his newfound freedom."

"I wouldn't be too sure of that. Men have a habit of wanting anything they think they can't have. You're his wife. He'll want you back if for no other reason than that."

"Well, I don't want to go back. Not for a while yet, at least not until I can figure out what I am going to do."

"And what are you going to do? As much as I wish it might be different, you cannot remain here indefinitely. The world doesn't work that way."

"I'll think of something. I just need a bit more time."

But Gabriella knew her friend was right. No matter how much she wished she could keep hiding away here, she'd realized soon after her arrival that her bold decision to run away was nothing more than a temporary measure at best. By now, the coach in which she had traveled must certainly have arrived back at Rosemeade. Tony would be sure to question the servants, who would divulge her exact location. Assuming he cared where she had gone, that is.

But as Maude pointed out, his pride would be injured. If for no other reason than that, he would want her back under his control. She supposed he would send her a letter, demanding that she return home. She wasn't sure what she would do when that happened.

Spirits low, she sipped her tea.

"A coach, a coach, a coach!" whooped a pair of the boys from the front parlor. "Look at the horses and the big, fancy crest on the door. Who do you think it could be?"

Gabriella's gaze met Maude's, a lump forming in the base of her throat, both of them knowing exactly who it must be.

What am I going to do? she thought, as a cold draught of wind swept into the cottage a minute later when the front door was opened and closed to let him inside.

"Who are you?" chirped one of the children.

"I'll bet he's the duke," another one piped. "Are you? Are you really a duke?"

"That's right," resounded a deep, familiar male voice.

"Don't be familiar," reprimanded Josephine. "All of you, upstairs to your rooms."

"But Mama—"

"Now!"

Groans filled the air, followed by a tidal wave of feet pounding against the stairs and floorboards. Moments later, all fell quiet.

"Sorry for that lot. H-how do you do, Y-your Grace?" Jo greeted in obviously awed tones.

"Good day, madam. Pardon the intrusion, but I am given to understand you may have a guest in residence. My wife, Gabriella Black."

"Oh, I . . . well . . . well—"

"It's all right," Gabriella assured her flustered hostess as she stepped out of the kitchen into the front hall. "Obviously, he knows I'm here." Her breath caught as she gazed up at Tony, his hair faintly wind tousled, a hard cast to his jaw. *Heavens,* she decided. *He looks tired and angry.*

His striking blue eyes fixed upon her. "You have not been easy to find, especially given the snowstorms of late. Might we be in private, do you think?"

"The parlor." She gestured toward the room. "You don't mind, do you, Jo?"

"No, no, 'course I don't."

Tony waited, ever the consummate gentleman, while Gabriella preceded him into the room. He closed the doors behind them with a soft click that nevertheless managed to sound intimidating.

"Now, Gabriella, would you care to explain what is going on and why I've had to chase you halfway across England in the dead of winter?"

Her shoulders tensed as she moved farther into the room. "You need not have chased me anywhere. In my letter, I specifically asked you not to follow me."

His eyebrows lowered like a pair of dark slashes. "Yes, I had your letter, but I've never been much of a hand at following dictates, especially when they're of the nonsensical variety. Did you really imagine I would let you leave and not come in search of you?"

"At the time I wasn't thinking of much else but the need to get away."

Some of his anger visibly faded, replaced by an expression of concern and confusion. "And why is that? Everything was fine between us, or at least I thought it was, until those last couple of days. Then all of a sudden you withdrew from me. What has happened?" Crossing to her, he reached out to take her in his arms. "Tell me so I can understand. Give me a chance to make it better."

"You can't make this better," she told him, shrugging free of his touch and stepping away. "Not unless you can change how you feel. I . . . I heard you, Tony. I heard what you said to Ethan, and I—" She broke off, hugging her arms around herself as she fought back the tears that suddenly threatened.

His shoulders stiffened, his arms falling to his sides. "And what conversation is this? What is it you believe you heard?"

"I don't *believe*, I *know*. I stood at your study door—quite by accident, I might mention—and listened to you tell Ethan the real reason for our marriage. That you wed me out of pity because I was compromised and that your mistress, Lady Hewitt, was planning to tell everyone in Town about it."

"*Ex*-mistress," he corrected. "And yes, once she saw us together that night, your reputation was irretrievably damaged. There was nothing else to be done but wed."

"Yes, there was. You could have simply ignored the entire thing and let matters take their course instead of manipulating me into marriage. No wonder you rushed me to the altar the way you did."

"And thank God for it. Had I stood aside," he retorted in a hard tone, "your reputation would have lain in shreds by the end of that week. No respectable family would so much have looked at you ever again, let alone received you into their home. If you believe the business with your aunt was difficult, it would have been nothing compared to that."

"Maybe I would have preferred being shunned to being deceived."

A muscle ticked in his jaw. "And that is why you are so upset? Because I persuaded you to become my duchess? To live a life of privilege and ease that most people would give their right arm to possess?"

Stepping forward, he caught her shoulders inside his grasp. "You're correct, I did not want to see you ruined by Erika Hewitt's spitefulness and cruelty. She hoped to get back at me and was happy to harm you in order to achieve her aim. If keeping you from suffering such a fate was wrong, then I stand guilty as charged. If that's pity, then yes, I suppose I pitied you. But if you want to know the real reason I married you, it was because I desired you—in my bed and in my life. I still want you despite your exasperating, headstrong ways. So, let us put this behind us and go home."

"And then what?"

"Then we'll go back to the way things were. You seemed happy enough before."

"Before the blinders came off, you mean. Before I learned the truth."

"The truth of what? That we get along well together? That we enjoy pleasuring each other in bed? That we are far more compatible than most of the couples I know? Why do you have to question everything? Why can't you simply let things be?"

"Because I can't!" she declared, easing away from his touch. "Because I heard you say that one day you expect we'll grow tired of each other and decide to go our separate ways—discreetly, of course."

He gave a muffled curse under his breath.

"Well, I don't want to wake up every morning wondering if this will be the day you decide you've had enough."

A long moment of silence fell. "Perhaps I said something to that effect," he admitted, "but that's a long way off. Years from now. And if and when it happens, I am sure the decision will be mutual."

"Really? What if it is not? Is that what went wrong between you and Lady Hewitt? The reason she's so spiteful now? Did you decide you'd had enough, but she hadn't? When you're done, will you buy me a pretty trinket, then give me my congé like some discarded mistress?"

"You are my wife," he said between clenched teeth. "It isn't the same at all."

"It will be if you send me into the arms of another man."

His eyes flashed fire. "You will never go to another man."

"Oh, then I must have misunderstood. I thought you said we would each be allowed to seek out our own comfort. Apparently you are the only one of us who is permitted to dishonor our vows."

"I have been faithful to you, Gabriella. Is that what you want to know? Since long before we wed, there has been no one else, only you. If it will allay your concerns, I have no difficulty swearing that I will remain exclusively in your bed. There will be no other." When she didn't answer, he raked a hand through his hair. "I don't understand you. What is it you expect of me? What is it you want?"

I want you to love me! she cried silently. But he did not, and had only confirmed that fact over the past few minutes—making not a single mention of the word, nor any attempt to convince her he might feel something more for her, after all. Yes, he wanted her. True, the two of them were compatible. He'd even promised to be faithful. But still, it wasn't enough. How could it be when only one of them loved? If she accepted this uneven affection, she knew it would eat at her, nibbling away at her heart, at her very soul, one tiny piece at a time until nothing remained but emptiness and sorrow.

Oh God, what am I going to do?

For a long moment, she stared at the flames burning in the fireplace, seeing nothing but an indistinct blur of color. "What do I want?" she said, repeating his question in a soft voice. "Just one thing."

"Yes," he returned. "And what is that?"

Forcing her gaze upward, she looked him square in the eye. "Your Grace, I want a divorce."

Chapter Nineteen

"WHAT!" HE SAID, her words hitting him like a horse's hoof to the chest.

She raised her chin and held her ground. "You heard me. I no longer wish to be your wife."

Fury billowed through him with the heat of flames consuming dry tinder, his jaw muscles snapping so tight he was surprised they didn't pop. He held himself in place, fists bunched at his sides until he forced his fingers open, fighting for control. "You *are my wife,* madam, whether you wish it or not. There will be no divorce."

"But—"

"There are no buts!" He cut her off, his tone cold and scathing even to his own ears. "When you and I wed, it was until death do us part, and that is the way it will be. You may run from me. You may rail against me. You may even hate me. But know this—we are married, and that is one fact that will never change." He broke off, drawing a full breath to steady his emotions. "Now, go and pack your belongings. We are returning home."

Alarm turned her eyes a vivid hue that was nearly purple. "No! I will not go home, not with you. I do not want this."

"I am no longer certain I do either, but such are the vagaries of fate. Pack your cases, madam, or I will see it done for you."

She stood, trembling visibly as she searched for a way out. Apparently realizing there was none, she released a gasp of distress, then whirled on her heels and raced from the room, slamming the door behind her.

He was glad for the privacy as he sank into a nearby chair. *So she doesn't want to be my wife?* he thought. *So she wants a divorce?* Laying his head in his hands for a long moment, he wondered how it had all gone so horribly wrong.

Neither of them spoke on the journey back home, she and Tony sitting across from each other like a pair of strangers sharing a ride. She wanted to weep, but the tears wouldn't come, the pain simply too deep for such mundane things as tears. Nor had she cried when she bid farewell to Maude, Josephine, and the children, putting on what she hoped had looked like a happy smile to calm their concerns.

But Maude had seen through her façade, giving her a fierce, rib-crushing hug. "I will always be here for you," her friend had whispered. "But don't give up hope. Things may yet come right. Try not to despair."

But how can I not? Gabriella wondered, when she and Tony were so distant they could barely stand to exchange a hello?

The journey proved easy, the roads clear, the weather clement, with blue skies to guide their way. To her surprise, however, they did not go to Rosemeade, arriving in London late on the third day. Tony forced her to accept his hand as he assisted her from the coach, but he released her as quickly as possible, following in her wake as she walked up the steps into Black House.

Crump was there, word having obviously been sent ahead in time for him to transfer the household. He gave her a smile as she came inside, a footman moving forward to take her cloak.

"Welcome home, Your Grace," the butler greeted. "Your maid is awaiting you in your room and dinner is being prepared. Will ten o'clock be acceptable to serve?"

"Hello, Crump. Actually, I would prefer to take a tray in my room this evening, thank you."

The butler cast a glance toward the duke.

"Send her meal up," Tony said. "It's late. I will eat in my study."

"Very good, Your Grace."

Divesting himself of his hat and greatcoat, Tony turned and strode away.

Suppressing a sigh, Gabriella allowed one of the servants to show her the way to her bedchamber, since this was her first time staying here at the townhouse. The duchess's quarters were lovely, though not as large as the ones at Rosemeade, the rooms decorated in pale shades of apricot and cream. Despite the soothing hues, however, she spent little time studying her surroundings, too tired and sad to pay them much heed.

A warm bath refreshed her greatly, though, as did a satisfying meal of beef soup, yeasty bread and butter, and a delicious caramel custard for dessert. Sleepy and relaxed, she crawled between the sheets.

Yet sleep didn't come, her eyes remaining open as she waited to see whether or not Tony would come through the connecting door to exercise his marital rights. She'd considered locking it, but feared what he might do if she did. In his present mood, he might attempt anything, even tearing out the lock or knocking down the door. During the trip home, he'd stayed away, requesting separate accommodations for them on each overnight leg of the trip. But maybe now that they were back on familiar territory, he would change his mind. If he did, she wasn't sure how she was going to respond.

The minutes ticked past, the house falling silent as the servants went to bed. Near one o'clock, she thought she heard a low murmur of male voices in Tony's bedchamber as he spoke to his valet. Her heart pounded and she clutched the sheets. Would he come to her? She hoped not—at least that's what she told herself.

When she awakened with a start come morning, she realized she'd had no reason to worry. His door had stayed firmly shut and her bed had been slept in by no one but herself. A tear slid from her eye as she realized this was how things were going to be between them from now on.

Two days later, Gabriella took the coach across Town to visit Rafe and Julianna. She hadn't been sure how she would be greeted when she walked inside their townhouse, but one glance at Julianna's sympathetic face and she had rushed into her arms, the tears she'd held back for days bursting forth. To her surprise, she discovered Lily already in the family drawing room, the two women comforting her as everything poured out.

A mutinous gleam shone in Lily's gaze once Gabriella had finished her tale. "Ethan told me what Tony said—or at least he did once I wormed it out of him. I think it's awful! How could he say he doesn't love you? I wish you'd said something to me that day at Rosemeade. I realize now that must have been the cause of your sudden headache."

"I thought about confiding in you," Gabriella said, "but I didn't want to burden you. Besides, what could you have done? Tony feels the way he feels and there is nothing more to be said."

"Well, I think there is a great deal to be said," Lily went on. "The man is obviously a fool for all that he is my friend. I just may stop speaking to him."

"No, please do not even say that. This is between Tony and me."

"And how *are* things between Tony and you?" Julianna queried in a gentle voice.

"Horrible. We barely speak. God, I don't know how I can bear to keep living under the same roof with him. I would find my own establishment, but I have no money. He has everything."

A moment of silence descended, all three of them thinking.

"Maybe he doesn't have everything," Lily mused. "You need a townhouse, do you not?"

"Yes, but I've told you, I cannot afford one."

"You don't have to. I own a very nice townhouse just across the square. Ethan and I were thinking about selling it, but I'll give it to you. Or let you stay in it, anyway. No charge."

"Oh, but I couldn't—"

"Of course you can," Lily countered. "It's a lovely place and going to waste sitting empty with dust covers on the furniture. All you need to do is pack your belongings and move across Town."

Gabriella bit the corner of her lip. "But think of the talk. Tony would be furious."

"Do you care? You said you wanted a divorce; just think of the talk then. Beside, a great many couples live apart. It won't amount to much more than a nine-day wonder."

She glanced toward Julianna.

"No doubt the Ton will be rife with comment," Julianna said, "but then the Ton is always rife with comment about something. If you are determined to break with Tony, then this seems a sound way."

Despite her friends' reassurance, Gabriella wasn't nearly as sanguine about how matters might proceed. On the other hand, Lily's offer was generous and very, very tempting. The present frosty atmosphere between her and Tony was all but unbearable. If she had her own residence, she wouldn't have to endure his glowering silences nor repine over what the two of them would never have together. And maybe she could move on with her life, finding some way to be content, if not happy, without him. Abruptly, she made up her mind. "Yes, all right, if you are sure," she said.

"Of course I am sure," Lily told her.

"I will need servants—"

"That won't be a problem. Julianna and I can help you assemble an able staff."

"But oh, I hadn't thought. How shall I pay for the upkeep?"

"That's easy," Julianna declared, clearly warming to the plan. "Just send the bills to Tony. He'll pay them, if for no other reason than to stave off further comment."

"Come to that," Lily interjected, "the new Season will be upon us in only a few weeks. I am sure you will need a completely new wardrobe. Once you're moved and settled, I say we shop!"

For the first time in weeks, Gabriella smiled.

Tony scowled down at the correspondence in his hand, just one of several letters he'd received in the five days since he'd been in residence here at Black House. But it wasn't the letter that had put the sour expression on his face—that circumstance came courtesy of Gabriella.

He supposed the two of them should return to Rosemeade, where he'd originally intended for them to stay through the winter. At least that had been the plan until she'd run away and informed him she wanted a divorce.

His hand tightened at the memory, the vellum crinkling dangerously beneath the pressure of his fingers as a fresh spurt of anger rushed through him. He'd been simmering for days, but anger he could handle. It was the swirl of emotions underneath that he found of a far more troubling nature. No matter how he might try to deny it,

Gabriella had hurt him—hurt his pride and something more.

He might tell himself her desertion and disaffection didn't matter, but it did. He'd given up his freedom by marrying her, and done his best since to treat her with kindness and respect, and this is how she repaid him. *Blast it, why did she have to overhear me talking to Ethan?* he silently cursed. Yet like it or not, the deed was done. Now all that remained was to discover a way to move on.

Perhaps he should try to talk to her, attempt to find some middle ground between them instead of living in this dreadful limbo. He didn't know exactly what he might say, but he supposed anything was worth a try.

Thud!

An echoing reverberation sounded from the front hall, followed by a confluence of voices. *What in the devil?* he wondered, laying the letter aside. Rising to his feet, he went to investigate.

A flurry of movement was taking place in the main foyer, the front door standing open as a pair of unfamiliar footmen carried a heavy trunk down the stairs, another set of men outside in the street loading a stack of bandboxes into a wagon. A black barouche waited just behind.

Tony stared at the scene, fists set at his hips. "What is all this?"

An unsettled-looking Crump appeared near his side. "I was just about to find you, Your Grace. It would seem Her Grace is—"

"Yes?" Tony demanded, his brows descended. "Her Grace is what?"

"Leaving," remarked Gabriella from where she stood on the landing above.

Glancing up, Tony took in the sight of her, noting how attractive she looked in a gown of scarlet kerseymere and a warm woolen pelisse. As he watched, she glided easily down the staircase as though she were contemplating nothing more involved than an afternoon excursion to Bond Street.

"What do you mean, *leaving*?" He gave her a fresh glower and crossed his arms over his chest.

"I am taking my belongings and relocating to a new address. That is what I mean."

"If you are planning to return to your friend, you can forget the idea," he restored in a dismissive tone.

She pulled on her gloves. "Actually I am going across Town. Bloomsbury Square to be exact."

"Running off to Rafe and Julianna then, are you?"

"No, I have my own residence now, though it will indeed be located across the square from my uncle and aunt."

His arms fell to his side. "Across the square? How did you—*Lily!* Is she behind this scheme?"

"No. She merely agreed to help me by offering the use of her townhouse. The *scheme* is all my doing. Now, I believe my new footmen have finished loading my belongings. I will bid you good day, Your Grace."

He shot out a hand and took hold of her arm. "You'll do nothing of the kind. You," he ordered, shifting to speak to one of the unfamiliar servants. "Take those things out of that wagon and bring them straight back into the house. *Now!*"

"If any of you obey him," Gabriella called, "I will sack you on the spot. Those trunks stay right where they are."

The men paused for a moment, then remained where they stood, her belongings untouched inside the wagon.

Pressure built inside Tony's veins as if his blood had suddenly turned to lava. "Come with me," he told her.

Gabriella paused, then gave a shrug and accompanied him to his study. Not that he gave her a great deal of choice considering his hand was wrapped like a vise around her arm. The moment he closed the door behind them, however, he released her, worried what he might do otherwise. "Now," he demanded, locking his arms across his chest. "Why don't you tell me what all this nonsense is about?"

"It's not nonsense. I have decided to relocate to my own establishment."

"Your place is here in this house as my wife. You're being foolish and immature and acting once again on impulse."

Her spine grew straight. "I am doing nothing of the sort. I have thought this through and am simply facing facts. Our marriage, if you wish to call it that, is little more now than a sham. Our living arrangements are far from congenial and I, for one, have no wish to continue living here under a constant state of acrimony."

"Your decision, madam, not mine. You are the one who began this state of warfare. And you are the one who can end it."

Her lower lip trembled faintly, then she continued. "By what? Pretending to be your obedient little bride until you decide you've had enough of me? Well, I am not that much of a liar."

A sudden chill washed through him. "So, you want a separation? Well, I suppose it would have come to that at one point or another, so why not now? Fine, if you wish to leave, then leave. You may, of course, forward your expenses here to me for payment. I will see your debtors satisfied."

She linked her hands. "Thank you. Though I had intended to do so anyway."

He shot her a look, his eyes narrowed.

She gazed back, a sudden hesitation in her stance, a sadness in her expression. "Tony, I—"

Abruptly he'd had all he could take. "You what?" he charged. "You said you wanted to leave, Gabriella, then leave!" *Yes, go,* he thought. *Please go. Leave before I do something crazy like scoop you up in my arms and lock you away somewhere in the house where you can never get away from me again.*

Her lips trembled again. "Good-bye, Tony."

"Good day, Your Grace."

Her violet eyes sparkling with tears, she turned and fled the room.

He gave a savage curse, then went to the window, watching until her coach and the wagon containing her belongings drove away down the street.

"Exactly how many of those have you had?" Rafe Pendragon asked Tony a week later as he dropped down into one of the armchairs across from where Tony sat in Brooks's Club.

Tony tossed him a hard glance over the top of his whisky tumbler. "Apparently not enough, since I'm still capable of conversing with you." Catching the eye of a passing waiter, Tony signaled for a refill, downing what was left in his glass before setting it aside.

"You'll only end up with an aching head, you know," Rafe advised.

Better that my head aches, Tony thought, *than other parts of me.* "It's my head," he said. "I'll do with it as I choose."

Rafe shrugged. "Fair enough. I've drowned my sorrows often enough in times past to have no right to criticize."

Tony lifted the new glass the waiter set next to him. "This isn't from sorrow, but from celebration. I'm as good as a bachelor again, don't you know." He swallowed a draught, letting the alcohol do its work. "So, is your new neighbor all moved in?" he demanded in a sarcastic tone.

"Gabriella, you mean?" Rafe paused to accept his own

drink. "Yes, she's settled into Lily's old townhouse with a minimum of fuss. Julianna has been taking the children over to see her every day." He paused and leaned forward slightly. "Look, Tony, about this situation between the two of you. I—"

"Really don't need to say anything," Tony interrupted. "You're her uncle and I can appreciate that you may have your concerns. However, I would ask you to stay out of it. This matter is between Gabriella and me. She may not be living under my roof at present, but she is still my wife and I would thank you to recall that fact, as a friend."

Rafe took a sip of his brandy. "Well, as a friend, I will respect your wishes. As her uncle, I hope the two of you can work out an amicable solution to this very public difficulty. The whole Town is abuzz and half the Ton isn't even back from their country homes yet. Already every other word people say is about the Duke and Duchess of Wyvern—their hasty marriage and even hastier separation. The Society columns are full of little else."

"Luckily, I don't read the Society columns," Tony drawled, his fingers tightening against his whisky tumbler before he raised the glass and tossed back another mouthful. "And you may inform your niece that she can return to her rightful home any time she likes. The decision to leave was entirely her own."

"Maybe you could talk—"

"I'm done talking." He set his empty glass aside with a thump. "Now, is there some other topic on which we might converse?"

Rafe paused, then gave a nod of concession.

"Hello, there. What are you both debating with such serious expressions on your faces?" Ethan asked as he joined them a minute later.

Tony glared. "Something other than my wife's current

choice of accommodation. Although now that you're here, I do have something else to say on the subject."

Ethan shot a glance toward the entrance. "Perhaps I ought to be going—"

"No, have a seat," Tony demanded, gesturing toward an empty chair.

"Now, look Tony—" he began, sinking down onto the cushion.

"Don't 'now look Tony' me. What do you mean by letting your wife give *my* wife use of your Bloomsbury Square townhouse?"

"I don't *let* her do anything. Believe me, she has a mind of her own and she uses it. If she'd asked for my opinion first, I would have told her to stay out of things—"

"Exactly!" Tony agreed.

"But she didn't. She just offered the house. And Gabriella accepted."

"Well, you should have told her to *un*-offer it and advise Gabriella to forget her idiotic notions about moving out. You really should exercise better control over your wife, Vessey."

"Oh, like you do, Wyvern?" Ethan shot back, accepting a glass of port from the waiter, who also paused to replenish Rafe and Tony's drinks.

"Touché," Tony said, saluting the remark before swallowing nearly all the fresh whisky in his tumbler.

"Tony, I'm sorry about your troubles with Gabriella, truly I am." Ethan took a swallow of his wine. "But there is nothing I can do about it—not unless I'd like to start 'batching' it again myself when I put down my foot and Lily tells me to find my own new quarters. She's none too happy with you these days as it is."

Tony's forehead creased. "Oh? And what have I done?"

"Gabriella told Lily and Julianna pretty much everything about the conversation she overheard that day. Lily . . . um . . . thinks you should reexamine your feelings."

"I don't need to reexamine anything. And I'm entitled to my feelings whatever they may be."

"True. Although I might question why you're drinking all that alcohol if your emotions aren't engaged."

Tony thrust out a pugnacious finger. "She ran away to Shropshire, has moved out and taken up residence in your wife's townhouse, and has—according to Rafe's report on the scandal sheets—made the pair of us the most titillating *on-dit* of the new social season. I believe I am entitled to have a few drams."

Ethan and Rafe exchanged looks. "Well, when you put it that way," Ethan conceded.

"What's more," Tony said, swallowing the rest of his drink, "while she's off across Town in her new house, I suppose she expects me to continue honoring my vow of fidelity. Well, maybe I shouldn't. And don't bristle up about it, Rafe. You'd feel the same if Julianna was doing what Gabriella is."

Rafe nodded. "Indeed, I suspect I might. As for discussing such a topic in any further detail, though, I believe I will stay out as you requested me to do. Now, shall we move on to a less volatile subject? Horses, perhaps?"

Ethan agreed with obvious relief, while Tony sipped more whisky and let his friends carry the conversation. As much as it galled him to admit—and in spite of everything Gabriella had done—he still desired her.

At night, he was barely able to sleep, his mind and body consumed with thoughts of her. During the day, she preyed upon him as well, interfering with his work and keeping him from carrying out the most mundane activity without having some memory or thought of her flit through his head. Ethan had suggested that Tony missed her on an emotional level . . . well, he didn't. *No, not at all,* he assured himself. He was quite able to entertain himself intellectually without any assistance from Gabriella.

Yet physically, he was forced to concede that he craved her—needed her with a hunger that was nearly driving him mad. He'd been without her now for weeks. Their last time together had been that night at Rosemeade before she'd run off, and the abstinence was beginning to wear very thin.

What I ought to do, he mused as he sipped more spirits, *is go over there to her new townhouse and demand my rights.* As he'd told Rafe, Gabriella may have left him, but that didn't make her any less his wife. Maybe they were separated, but that didn't mean he'd stopped having needs—needs that required attention! And she could damned well attend to them, or else he might have no choice except to seek out the company of other women. Except he didn't want any other woman—he wanted Gabriella. *And by God, I'm going to have her!* he decided.

Setting down his tumbler with enough force to splash liquor over his fingers, he surged to his feet. Or rather he tried to, finding himself back in his chair seconds later, the room whirling around him, Ethan and Rafe both shooting him looks.

Lord, I'm foxed, he realized. *Maybe going over to her townhouse today isn't such a good idea, after all.* In his current state of inebriation, he'd likely end up saying or doing something he would come to regret. And if he did manage to get in her bed, chances were good he'd pass out before he finished exercising his marital rights. He might be drunk, but he had enough sense left to realize he'd be better off sobering up before he paid a call on Gabriella. He'd go home now and soak his head. But come tomorrow . . . well, things were going to change.

Chapter Twenty

GABRIELLA STRIPPED A feather off an old hat she had decided to refurbish, the new lace and ribbons she and Lily had selected at the millinery yesterday waiting in a small brown paper sack nearby. Under normal circumstances, she would have enjoyed the project, but lately nothing seemed to make her happy, despite a concerted effort on her part to try to be.

Never one to mope, she'd thrown herself into as many activities as possible over the past several days, striving to stay busy and keep her mind off a certain man she was doing her best to forget. But forgetting Tony was proving impossible, as was any attempt on her part to stop loving him. He was in her heart, she realized, and no amount of wishing was going to change that fact. *I may have cut him out of my life with this separation, but I can't cut him out of myself.*

With a sigh, she plucked off another feather and then took up a pair of scissors to snip away a piece of frayed velvet trim. She was gathering up the scraps when a knock came at the door.

"Pardon me, Your Grace," said her new butler. "But His Grace, the Duke of Wyvern, is here to see you. Shall I show him up?"

Discarded trim burst from her hand, stray bits of cloth and ribbon cascading onto the floor. "His Grace! Here?

Yes, yes, of course, send him up." She'd barely had time to tidy the mess and take a proper seat in an armchair when her butler returned, Tony at his heels.

"I believe we can dispense with the formalities," Tony informed the man before he had a chance to speak. "The duchess and I are already acquainted, seeing she is my wife."

Taking the hint, the butler gave a respectful bow and withdrew, closing the door behind him.

"There is no need to be cross with Ford," Gabriella said as soon as the servant departed. "He is only doing his job."

"And so he is." Tony stalked across the sitting room toward a window and peered out. A long moment later, he turned to survey the room, his gaze sweeping over the furnishings. "The house appears comfortable enough."

"It is quite pleasant. Lily chose well when she purchased this home."

His jaw tightened, but he said nothing further, striding over to the next set of windows to once again look out.

Gabriella restrained a sigh, the tension between them palpable. "Have you come then to inspect my new quarters?"

He turned, his midnight-blue gaze steady. "No. I am here for another reason entirely. This situation has gone on long enough. I want you back at Black House. Actually, I insist on it."

This time she did sigh aloud. "And I am afraid I must refuse. Nothing between us has changed and I see no reason to return. I shall stay right where I am."

He strode forward. "You are my wife, and that is reason enough. I should never have allowed you to leave in the first place."

"I don't believe it was up to you to *allow* me or not. Now, if that is all—"

"No, it is not. It has recently occurred to me that I have

certain rights—marital rights—that you are not fulfilling at present."

Her eyes widened. "Pardon me?"

"As you well know, I am a man of hearty appetites and you cannot expect me to simply put those needs aside because you choose to live elsewhere. At least not if you still have some expectation that I remain faithful."

A flush rose into her cheeks.

He pinned her with a look. "Even if you do not care and would see me take my pleasure with another woman, there is a separate matter that requires your specific attention."

"Oh," she said, crossing her arms. "And what might that be, pray?"

"A child." He set a fist against the back of the sofa opposite her. "I have a right to an heir and you, as my spouse, have a duty to provide me with one. I believe a second son would not be unreasonable as well, come to that. And, of course, any female children produced would not count, so we would perforce have to keep trying should you fail to present me with sons after the first two successful pregnancies are brought to term."

A chill swept through her. His words were calm and matter-of-fact, as if he were discussing a business arrangement. And perhaps for him that was all it was—a means of seeing that both his physical and familial needs were satisfied. *How absurd of me!* she thought. For a fleeting instant when he'd first walked through the door, a tiny part of her had hoped he'd come to tell her how miserable he'd been since she'd left, how much he missed her, and to ask—not order—her to come home. She had hoped as well that he might say his feelings for her had changed, and that he realized he loved her, after all. But such ideas were no more than a fanciful dream. All he wanted—and would ever want, she reminded herself—was her body. And now a child, too.

"So you expect me to perform duties that fall somewhere between a courtesan and a brood mare?" she observed.

His brows narrowed at a dangerous slant as though he didn't much care for her description regardless of its apparent accuracy. "I want a *wife* willing to accommodate me in bed and provide me with children—a combination that naturally goes together. Given that, I see no difficulty in the arrangement. Unless you are increasing already? If so, then it would seem one of my requirements is satisfied before we even begin."

Her fingers curled against her hip, the cold spreading outward to the tips so that even her nails felt chilled.

"Well, are you?" he questioned.

She raised her chin and met his gaze. "Am I what?"

"With child? It's been some weeks since we had relations. Have you discovered yourself in a family way during that time?"

Since she had just finished her monthly, she knew for certain there was no child. "No, I am not expecting."

A spark of anticipation flared in his eyes. "Then the matter is settled. You will come home."

"No," she said in a low, flat tone.

"What? Of course you will return. I'll have your things moved back to Black House today. Though perhaps we should go to Rosemeade again for the next month or two as we had originally planned. We will need to be together often, since we are trying for a child."

And wouldn't that make everything perfect—for him? she mused. For her, she would be back at the beginning, utterly dependent upon his wishes, left with nothing—not her heart nor her pride. She supposed she could not rightly deny him a child, and truth be known she did not want to. She deeply longed for children and ached that she had not yet conceived. To remain estranged from him would mean giving up all hope of ever having a family, and that she did not want.

As for the other . . . the sex . . . well, as he said, the two matters did go hand in hand. She couldn't have babies without sharing her body with him, and it wasn't as if that would be such an onus. After all, he was a consummate lover, never once failing to bring her anything but the most exquisite pleasure. Still, she had to keep something for herself, retain some bit of independence that he could not touch.

Taking a deep breath, she steadied her resolve. "I am willing to give you a child, but as for living together again, it is out of the question."

He leaned a hip against the sofa and crossed his arms. "Then I fail to see how this child will ever come into being, since I will require access to your body."

"You can have access. Here."

"What?"

"Yes," she said, warming suddenly to the idea. "You can visit me here at this townhouse. We'll have relations, then you can leave when we're done."

"But that's ridiculous!" he scoffed.

"How so? It seems an eminently workable plan to me and certainly no more inconvenient than keeping a mistress. Surely your former light o' loves didn't come to live with you at your townhouse while you were partaking of their favors? Ours can be of a similar nature, the only difference in our case being that we need not worry about my becoming enceinte, since that is the ultimate objective."

"It's unfeasible," he blustered. "Not to mention the fact that my *visiting* you will only cause more talk. And believe me, there is quite enough of that already."

"Let them talk. You were never worried about the Ton's good opinion before; why should you be now? Besides, if it becomes an issue, you can tell everyone that we are attempting to repair our relationship. The fact that we're meeting to procreate is no one's business but our own."

He glared at her, paced to the window, then swung back. "I don't like it."

She shrugged, her pulse beating in her throat like the wings of a wild bird. "Those are my terms. You may agree or not as you choose."

His jaw worked, his teeth clenched, fists locked at his sides. "So, you want to play at being my mistress, do you?" he drawled in a smoothly menacing tone.

"I want to continue living separately from you," she stated, refusing to yield. "If that requires me to play a part, then yes, I will."

Crossing to her, he planted his arms on either side of her chair, then leaned down so she was trapped by his powerful frame. "If we do this your way, I will give you fair warning that the restraints are off. I'll want you when I want you, and as often as I like. No once a night and no conveniently timed headaches."

Color warmed her skin. "I will see I make myself available. Though I would remind you that I may still have social engagements to keep. I cannot lie abed all day, you know."

His lambent gaze dropped to her breasts, openly tracing their shape. "Don't worry. I won't keep you exclusively in bed. I'll find other places to take you as well."

She swallowed, viscerally aware of him and the images he created. The traitorous woman's flesh between her legs grew abruptly moist. "So, we're agreed then? I will continue to reside here while you live at Black House. You'll come visit me for sex."

His gaze remained fixed upon hers for a long moment, then his expression grew shuttered. "Yes, we are agreed."

"Very well. When shall we begin?"

Good heavens! she thought. *What if he says now?* She would have to let him, would she not? What if he refused to allow her out of this chair? Deciding instead to lift her skirts to touch her before dropping to his knees and sliding her forward so he could take her right here? Her nipples tightened beneath her shift.

"Tonight," he said instead. "Unfortunately, I have an appointment this afternoon I can't break. Otherwise, I'd stay and do whatever it is you're thinking."

"I'm not *thinking* anything," she lied, struggling to regulate her features. "And you can quit crowding me now and be on your way."

His mouth curved in a humorless smile as he straightened to his full height and took a step back. "As you wish, madam. I'll be back to *crowd* you quite a bit more in a few hours' time."

"Until then," she said, striving to sound bored. "I have this bonnet to finish trimming and a pair of calls to make now that Society is beginning to return to Town."

"Enjoy your afternoon," he told her. "Oh, and have a key sent over for me. I don't want the bother of having to knock every time I decide to pay you a visit, whether it be day or night."

"As you wish, Your Grace."

With a nod, he turned and strode from the room. Only after he was gone did she allow herself to react, her muscles trembling, her knees far too weak for her to stand. *Stars above,* she thought, laying a hand across her chest, *what is it I have done?*

Gabriella didn't go out to pay calls, nor did she finish refurbishing her bonnet, stuffing it and the trimmings into a hat box and putting them both away. She tried to take a nap, but couldn't sleep, instead ringing for her maid and asking the girl to draw her a warm bath.

As she was lying in the tub, it occurred to her that perhaps Tony would want dinner. Then again, he hadn't said what time he expected to arrive, so planning a meal around him might turn out to be nothing but a waste. Besides, he wasn't coming here for food and conversation, she reminded herself. He was coming for sex—intent on slaking his pent-up passions and begetting his heir, nothing more. She was a convenience, just another female out of many with whom he had enjoyed carnal knowledge. The only difference was that she wore his ring—though even that apparently meant little now. His mistress and his brood mare, she mused on an increasingly sour note. That is all she was supposed to be.

By evening, she had worked herself into a temper, especially when ten o'clock came and he had not arrived. Then eleven. At midnight, she decided he must have changed his mind, and so she went upstairs to bed.

She was lying between the sheets at one o'clock, about to blow out the small branch of lighted candles on her night table, when her bedroom door opened. She glanced up to find Tony silhouetted in the entrance, his athletic, masculine physique looking even taller and more powerful than usual.

Abruptly, her weariness fell away, her blood thrumming with a disturbing combination of annoyance and simmering desire—a reaction that only increased her pique over the substantial list of grievances she held against him, as well as with herself for her undeniable weakness where he was concerned.

As though he slept with her here in this room every night, he strolled inside and closed the door with a quiet snick of the lock. Approaching slowly, he began to disrobe, hanging his coat and waistcoat over the back of a chair before tugging open his cravat. He freed his cuff buttons, then kicked off his dress shoes. Next came his shirt and stockings before he reached down to unfasten his falls.

She didn't say a word, and neither did he, as she watched him strip to the skin, his arousal a blatant announcement of his hunger for her. His erection twitched beneath her gaze and stiffened even more. Barefoot, he padded across the carpet, pulled back the sheet, and climbed into bed.

"You're late," she remonstrated as he reached for her.

He paused for a second before lowering his lips to her neck. "I don't believe we agreed on a time," he stated, moving up to nuzzle her earlobe. "As I recall, I said I will visit when it suits me." He ran his tongue along the edge of her ear, then blew gently inside. "Earlier did not suit."

She suppressed an answering shiver, his touch as magical as ever. Peeved with him, however, she fought to resist. "Even so, you might have sent a note. I assumed you weren't coming."

"Couldn't wait for me, hmm?"

"Oh no, I could wait," she drawled in a cool tone. "I just do not like being kept waiting, especially when I'm tired. Why don't we get to it then, so you can go home and I can go to sleep."

He leaned up on an elbow. "You just want me to toss up your nightgown and take you, then? I very much doubt you'd enjoy that."

She rolled her head to one side, wanting to make her point by refusing to meet his gaze. "I don't enjoy *this*, since I am being manipulated and used by you."

He caught her chin in his hand and with a gentle, yet inexorable pressure forced her to look at him. "Trying to goad me, are you? Hoping I'll reconsider and stop?"

"Or be done with me fast and leave," she said, wondering at her foolhardy mood. "And while we're discussing matters, there are a couple more on which we need to agree."

"And what is that?" he asked, his voice rough and low.

"How long this is to go on. I think it only fair that once

I conceive, I have the right to call a halt to any further encounters between us—at least for the duration of the pregnancy."

He tensed, then slid his palm down to cup one cloth-covered breast. "So no more of this," he said, gently finding and pinching her nipple between his thumb and forefinger, "once you're with child?"

"No," she said, forcing aside any pleasure she felt at his touch. "No more."

"Well, if you find yourself unwell because of the baby, then, of course, I shall leave you be. Otherwise, I can't promise not to touch, not for all nine months, anyway. I would remind you of my needs." As if to emphasize his point, he let his arousal press more insistently against her hip.

She might have argued further but did not, deciding that was the best concession she was likely to get from him.

"You said a couple of matters." He pressed. "What else do you require?"

"I want . . ." She hesitated, knowing he would think her foolish. "I want my kittens. I had to leave them at Rosemeade and I haven't felt comfortable asking the staff there to send them along. There won't be any difficulty if you do it."

Some of the harshness eased from his face. "Lonely here, are you? You could always rectify that by coming home."

"This is my home now, which is why I want them," she stated. "To me a house is not a home without a few furry bodies in it. So, may I have my kittens?"

"Most assuredly. You had only to ask. I will see them transported as soon as a coach and traveling hamper can be arranged. Now, are we done, or is there more?"

Her pulse gave an erratic beat. "We're done. You may proceed."

She watched as he took a long moment to study her, candlelight highlighting his handsome, sardonic features. Then he leaned down and pressed his mouth to hers, kissing her as he always did, with passion and sizzling intensity. Yet she was determined to resist.

Despite her earlier thoughts of allowing herself to take pleasure in their coupling, she couldn't help but remember the reasons why they were in this bed. He wanted her body—not her. He wanted a baby—not love and a family. She might be willing to let him quench his lust, but giving in to her own desires seemed too great a concession to make. And so she willed herself away, turning her thoughts from his kisses and his touch as she deliberately cooled her response.

Abruptly, he broke off. "What's this then? Why aren't you with me, Gabriella?"

"I'm with you," she prevaricated. "I'm lying right here beneath you."

"Yes, but you aren't *with me.* And you aren't kissing me back."

"I did not realize my full participation was required."

His eyes narrowed. "Well, it is. So you want to act the martyr, do you?"

"No, just acting the brood mare. *Neigh,*" she replied, some of her earlier anger rushing to the fore.

His jaw tightened. "I believe you may come to regret that comment before the night is out."

"Why? What are you going to do?" she taunted. Yet her bravado slipped a bit when she saw the dangerous glint in his deep blue eyes. Suddenly she realized her resistance was only acting as a challenge, one he was now determined to win.

She swallowed. "Tony, I—"

"You what? Claim not to want me? Let's test that theory, shall we?"

Before she knew what he was about to do, he reached

for her nightgown. But instead of drawing it up over her head, he caught the seam in his hands and began to tear. The delicate silk gave way with a tremendous ripping noise as he shredded the garment in two. He tossed the pieces to the floor, the ruined cloth fluttering into filmy pink puddles.

"From now on," he said, "I suggest you dispense with the night attire. Otherwise, you may not have any left to wear. Although you have my permission to put on some of those drawers the more daring ladies are starting to fancy. The ones with the split up the center. And leave on your stockings, too. Nothing on top though." He cupped his hands around her breasts. "I want these bare."

"Tony!" she said in shocked tones, her heart pounding in her chest.

"Turn over."

"What?"

"You said I'm treating you like a brood mare. If that is the case, then I think it only fitting we do this from behind."

"No!" she protested, realizing suddenly he meant to humiliate her, to make her regret her words and her earlier actions.

"Come on." He gave her a light slap on the hip. "Hands and knees. Now."

"Tony, don't," she beseeched.

"Don't what?" Using a force she could not escape, he compelled her to do as he demanded; although she noticed he was careful not to bruise her flesh or cause her harm—at least not physically. "You said to just take you and get it over with," he reminded in a harsh voice. "You didn't say what position I had to do it in. This is the one I want."

She swallowed and trembled, wondering how this had all gone so wrong. But even as she braced herself for his penetration, it didn't come. Instead, he bent over her and began to caress her skin. Scattering kisses, he roved over her shoulders and along the line of her back, while around front, he stroked her, his hands gliding in a warm, winding, seductive path.

"I suppose you won't respond to this either?" he questioned as he fondled her breasts, sliding her tight nipples in and out between his fingers.

She shuddered, her nipples hardening to aching beads.

"Ah, it would seem you're making a liar of yourself already," he declared. "But let's investigate further."

Before she could stop him, his hand dived low, trailing over her belly and thighs, then around to thread through her nether curls as he sought out her most delicate flesh. She throbbed against him, condemningly slick to his touch. As he ran his fingers over her, scattering more kisses against her neck and back, she suddenly knew how he planned to claim his punishment.

He was going to make her beg.

Biting her lip, she held back a moan. But he wouldn't have it, wrapping her hair around one wrist so he could angle her head back for his kiss. Forcing her to yield, he claimed her mouth with raw, dark need, opening her so he could capture her tongue and draw on it, suckling her the way he might a candy stick. She had to moan then, the sound unstoppable as it vibrated against his lips. Smiling, he took more.

While he continued kissing her, he made no pause in his sensual assault of her body, his fingers moving over her and inside her until her mind began to dull, her body writhing and arching of its own accord. Pleasure spread, her skin growing damp and aching.

He stroked her again and abruptly she came, the climax crashing through her—wild and fierce as a hurricane. Shuddering, her muscles trembled as a blissful lassitude stole through her weakened limbs. Half-boneless, she tried to sink downward onto the mattress, but Tony refused, holding her in place as he started the process over again.

"I'm going to make you come," he whispered. "I'm going to make you come until you can't come any more, and then I'll make you do it again even then."

And as he touched and kissed, fondled and licked her over the next long span of time, he did just that, driving her up and over in relentless waves until all she knew was need and Tony—her mind blank to anything but him and the bliss he made her feel.

Just when she thought she couldn't take more, he settled firmly behind her and parted her legs with his knees, opening her fully to his possession. Positioning her hands flat against the mattress, he wrapped one arm around her belly and held her secure.

Curving over her, he kissed her neck. "Have you ever seen a stallion breed?" he murmured. "The mare is readied, then he comes to take her. Often he'll bite her to keep her in place. Shall I kiss you, Gabriella, or would you rather I bite you instead?"

She shuddered and gasped, releasing a keening cry as he thrust inside her, sinking his teeth into her shoulder at the same moment. Ecstasy chased through her veins like liquid fire, threatening to burn her up from the inside out. She arched and took him, her vulnerable position letting him sink almost impossibly deep, deeper than she thought he'd ever gone. Stroking fast and hard within her, he built her desire again, tormenting her with want, his every thrust leaving her needier than the one before. Gripping the sheets in her fists, she held on, arching back now to meet him, to drive him deeper and quicker as she trembled on the brink of pure ecstasy.

She flew over moments later, a scream ripped from her throat as she shook violently within his powerful grip. A blinding cascade of rapture flooded her, making her quake from tip to toe as her mind simply stopped.

When she returned to herself, she was floating on a sea of divine pleasure as Tony made a few last, frenzied thrusts inside her before claiming his own delight. He groaned, then slid down, the pair of them collapsing in a tangle of limbs. Panting and dazed, she cuddled against him, drawing in his scent and his strength. At length, he rolled onto his back, keeping her against him as if loath to give her up even for an instant.

If only he loved me like that! she mused. But then she pushed the cruel idea away and let herself sleep, her final thought the hope that he would still be there when she next woke.

The steady gleam of sunlight roused Gabriella from a deep, almost dreamless sleep. As she woke, the faint sounds of water splashing into a bowl came to her ears. "Lay out my dressing gown, would you, Janet?" she mumbled in a drowsy voice. "I'm just going to lie here a few minutes more, then I'll be up."

"You can lie abed all day if you like," rumbled a low masculine voice. "And Janet brought you a pitcher of warm water before I sent her off. You can ring for her whenever you're ready."

Abruptly, Gabriella's sleepiness fell away, memories of the night just past rushing into her mind. Rolling onto her side, she searched for Tony and discovered him across the room in front of her washstand. He'd slipped on his trousers, she saw, but nothing else—the rest of him boldly, breathtakingly naked.

Letting her gaze roam, she realized she must have interrupted his ablutions, since glistening droplets of water were caught in the expanse of dark curls on his chest, his face moist from a recent washing. Employing a leisurely motion, he rubbed a towel over his face, then did the same below, stroking the cotton cloth over his pectorals and under his arms.

"I assumed you'd gone," she said, curving the sheet up over her breasts.

He draped the towel around his neck and strolled toward her. "Not yet. I have some time this morning. I thought we might take breakfast together."

"Breakfast, is it?" she repeated in a casual tone that belied the unsteady thumping of her heart. "I am sure Cook would be more than happy to oblige you. I, however, have engagements and shall just take tea while I dress."

Before she could rise from the bed, he dropped down next to her, nudging her with his hip so she was compelled to scoot over and roll onto her back.

"I thought you were going to sleep a while more?" he questioned in a silky voice.

"I was, but then I recalled that I promised Julianna I would accompany her on a trip to the millinery. We are to have nuncheon, then make our way to the shops."

Leaning forward, he planted his hands on either side of her, effectively caging her between his strong arms. "Nuncheon's hours off. You have time."

She met his gaze for a long moment, reading the undisguised desire that turned his eyes a deep, penetrating blue. Her blood heated as a liquid rush engulfed her. Resisting her own needs, she rolled abruptly onto her side. "You're right," she declared, beating a fist against the pillow beneath her head. "I do have time. Tell Janet to wake me up in an hour." Having clearly dismissed him, she squeezed her eyelids closed.

Instead he kept his seat.

"Go away, Tony," she said after a full minute had passed, resolutely keeping her eyes closed. "You can see me again tonight."

"But I'm seeing you right now. Perhaps you need another reminder like the one last night." He lowered his mouth to her shoulder and kissed her before giving her a teasing, painless little nip with his teeth.

Her eyes flashed open, her gaze going once again to his. "No, I need no reminders."

"Well then?"

She turned onto her back. "You haven't shaved."

"I didn't have a razor. I will see to it one is sent here, along with a few other essentials I'll need in the future." Hooking a finger around the edge of the sheet, he eased it down to expose her naked breasts.

Her nipples hardened with condemning honesty, her body telling him what she could not conceal. "So?" she said on a husky note. "Do you still want breakfast?"

A feral grin curved his lips. "I do, yes. That is, if you're what's on the menu."

Their gazes locked for a long moment before she gave a muffled curse and reached up to pull him to her. Taking his mouth with a ravishing hunger, she let him have his way.

Chapter Twenty-one

A LIGHT BREEZE wafted through the open sitting-room window of Gabriella's townhouse, the air surprisingly warm for a late March day. Seated at her rosewood escritoire, she watched an orange-bellied robin hop across the greening grass in the small rear garden below, and knew spring was definitely upon them.

The new Season was as well, London abuzz as members of the Ton descended upon the city in force. With their arrival came parties and balls, and a steadily increasing selection of invitations that began to arrive daily at the house requesting her presence at one event or another. Despite the ceaseless gossip regarding her separation from Tony—if one could call what they presently had a *separation*—such chatter was not proving a hindrance to her social success. As the new Duchess of Wyvern she seemed to be more popular than ever, clearly more so than she had been as plain Miss Gabriella St. George.

After sifting through the small stack of vellum cards that had arrived only that morning, she set them aside and returned to penning her letter to Maude. Choosing her words with some care, she related most—though not all—of what was now happening in her life. To be truthful, even Gabriella didn't always feel as if she knew what was going on in her life lately, taking each day as it came, without expectation or plan. She was Tony's wife, and yet in many of the ways that counted, she wasn't. She was his mistress, though she wasn't actually that either—her days and nights passing in a strange, almost contradictory duality of roles.

Since that first memorable evening—and morning—two months ago when Tony returned to her bed, she'd given up any further attempts to deny him. He'd more than proven his mastery over her when it came to all things sexual, her passion for him simply too strong to resist. *And what is the point,* she found herself asking, when I adore all the deliciously wicked things he does to my body?

As for the rest, including her continuing one-sided love for him, she refused to let herself dwell on such difficulties. There would be plenty of time later to repine, she decided, months and years to come in which she could wish for what she did not have and would never be able to find.

Still, in spite of her total capitulation in the bedroom, she was adamant about maintaining her independence when it came to her living arrangements. More than once, Tony had asked her to give up her stubborn ways, as he called them, and return with him to Black House. But always she refused. She might give him her body. She might give him a child. She might even give him her heart, but she would not let him claim her free will or what scraps remained of her pride, knowing how much she would one day need those small dignities in order to survive. And so she went on day by day, not allowing herself to think much beyond the moment or the activity at hand.

She had finished her letter and was sealing it with a few drops of hot red wax when her cat, Hamlet, leapt onto the desk. With his orange tail held high, he paused and gave a loud meow before weaving dangerously close to her open bottle of ink and the candle she'd lighted to melt the wax. Quickly she replaced the stopper and blew out the wick, doubly glad she had done so when his black-furred brother, Othello, joined them.

True to his word, Tony had sent immediately for her kittens after she'd asked him to do so, the lively pair arriving only two days later, rushed down to London by a footman. In the weeks that followed, the growing cats had settled in, claiming their spots on all the best furniture and providing excellent company during those times when she found herself alone.

Rescuing her letter from stray paw prints, she watched the pair leap down again and race playfully across the room, nearly crashing into Tony's legs as he appeared in the doorway.

He laughed as they ran past, out into the hallway. "Considering the antics of those two miscreants, I am surprised you have any breakables left," he remarked, strolling into the room.

"They're amazingly nimble, although they did break a plate in the kitchen last week. Anyway, I'm glad you've come," she said, turning slightly on her chair. "You can frank this letter for me."

Stopping next to her, he shot her a look. "Glad to know I can be of some service," he said, quirking a brow that conveyed his amusement and sarcasm. Leaning across her desk, he took up her pen, dipped it into her inkwell, and inscribed his name on the upper corner. "There, that should suffice. I will, however, expect a proper show of appreciation."

"Oh. Well, thank you."

"You can do better than that."

She paused, sending him a teasing smile. "Thank you very much."

"Minx," he said on a laugh. Drawing her out of her

chair, he wrapped her inside his arms. "Now, madam, you may begin displaying your gratitude."

Cupping his face between her palms, she urged him to bend his head and kiss her, opening her mouth to share a warm, wet side of tongue and lips that was long and bold enough to elicit a growl from deep in his throat. "Acceptable?" she asked as she eased away.

"Not bad." His palms slid downward to cup her bottom, giving her pliable flesh a light squeeze. "Although I can think of other methods you might exercise."

She looped her arms around his waist. "Hmm, well, those methods will have to wait until later. I have an engagement this afternoon."

"Break it," he said, planting his lips against her neck for a drawing kiss.

"I can't," she said, shaking her head. "In fact I need to dress if I'm to leave on time."

"Let me help you *undress.*" He kissed her again, stroking his hands over her posterior in a most possessive, insistent manner. "You can be late."

"It's a lecture. If I'm late, I'll miss it entirely."

"Then miss it. Lectures are notoriously boring. Let someone else take notes." From behind, he began to gather her skirt into his hands, distracting her with a kiss that made her pulse skitter at a crazy pace.

"The servants might come in," she warned, breath growing shallow in her lungs.

"They won't. Not after your footman caught me tupping you against the dining-room wall last week. I think they know now to stay away unless they're called for—at least when I'm around."

Color pinked her cheeks to remember, recalling the servant's astonished expression before she'd hidden her face against Tony's shoulder and blocked out the view. For his part, Tony had barked out a harsh command for the young man to get the hell out and shut the door; then he'd gone on thrusting inside her, reawakening her passion until she'd come in a violent, spasming rush—the rapture too intense to be denied despite any future embarrassment.

"Maybe I can be a little late," she said. "Why don't we go to my room."

"We can, but—wait now, what is this?"

God, how could I have forgotten? "Nothing," she squirmed, suddenly not wanting him to know. But already it was too late, his hands delving beneath her skirts.

"Are you wearing the pantalettes?" he ventured, one palm sliding over the silk before roving inside the garment to find her bare skin.

She'd worn them before as he'd asked, but only in bed. She didn't know what naughty imp had gotten into her today to put them on under her clothes. Beneath his trousers, his shaft leapt to life, straining like a length of steel that threatened to rend the cloth. Suddenly, she realized they'd never make it to her bed. "At least close the door," she whispered.

Lifting her off her feet, one of his hands positioned on her naked bottom beneath the slit in her little silk pants, he strode across and kicked the door. It closed with a slam she was sure everyone in the house heard. But suddenly, she didn't care as his mouth came down on her own, his other hand joining the first to explore her nether flesh.

A thrill went through her as he set her in the armchair where she'd once fantasized about just such a scenario. Shoving her skirts high, he revealed the undergarments, then spread her legs open to reveal her. Dropping to his knees just as she had envisioned, he slid her forward. But instead of taking her as she expected, he claimed her with his mouth, using his lips and tongue in such a way that she couldn't contain her cries of ecstasy, quaking as he brought her to several forceful peaks. Then it was his turn, freeing his trousers to thrust inside.

They ended up on the floor with her on top, Tony working her until she was so limp and languorous with pleasure that she couldn't form a coherent sentence. She was so dazed, in fact, that she forgot all about her lecture, snuggling happily inside his arms. At length, he carried her to bed, where they slept and made love throughout the afternoon and on into the night.

Tony stretched an arm behind his head, lying comfortably against a pair of feather pillows while he watched Gabriella dress. He'd sent her maid away, agreeing to help her with any buttons or laces that might need fastening. At the moment, she was rolling one of a pair of white silk stockings up the length of her shapely leg, the sight doing things to his body he'd frankly assumed impossible at the moment.

"If you keep that up," he drawled, "I may just need you back in this bed."

She shot him a look. "I don't know where you can find the strength." Returning to her grooming, she secured the first stocking with a ribboned garter before reaching for the next. "You are insatiable, Your Grace."

"And so I am," he grinned, feeling well satisfied after their morning tryst. He'd spent the night—an occurrence that was starting to take on the trappings of a routine. Rarely now did an evening go by that he wasn't here, preferring to sleep in her bed far more than he ever did his own.

He frowned a bit at the thought, as well as the realization that Black House felt lonely these days without her in it. Curious, since she'd lived there only for a brief time before taking up residence here. "Are you going to the Hamiltons' fete this afternoon?" he asked, pushing away his former thoughts as he stretched against the sheets.

She nodded. "Yes, I am supposed to meet Julianna and Lily there, so please don't attempt to change my mind."

"I wasn't intending to. Actually," he said, rolling onto his side to lean up on an elbow, "I thought I might escort you."

Her head turned his way. "Escort me?"

These days, he didn't escort her anywhere, the two of them tending to go their separate ways unless it was to meet here at her house.

"Yes. Why don't I stop by around three?" he suggested.

"Oh well, it's most kind of you to offer, but there's no need. Dickey is taking me."

He shot up into a sitting position, the sheets bunching at his waist. "Dickey? Milton, you mean?"

"Yes." She wiggled into her shift. "He's been escorting me to a few parties lately. Here," she said, crossing to stand in front of him. "Help me with my stays."

After she settled the cage of silk and whalebone around her torso, he reached for the laces and began pulling each one tight. "So, you've acquired a cicisbeo, have you?"

"Oh, I hadn't thought of him that way," she replied, sounding genuinely surprised. "Dickey and I are just friends."

Friends, hmm? And is that how Milton feels? Somehow Tony doubted it. Then again, the man was obsessed with gossip and fashion; maybe he was only amusing himself. But did he also plan to keep amusing himself by slowly luring Gabriella into his bed? Tony gave a fierce tug on a lace that elicited an exclamation from Gabriella.

"Careful," she warned. "I like my corset snug, but not so tight I can't breathe."

"Sorry," he muttered, gentling his touch as he finished.

Undergarments now in place, she walked to her wardrobe and drew out a day dress, the lilac sprigged-muslin she selected draping in soft folds around her body as she slipped it over her head.

Climbing out of bed, he went to assist her with the buttons. Before he did, though, he caught and turned her into his arms. Bending his head, he claimed her mouth, pleasuring her with a thorough, infinitely tender kiss that left a dreamy smile on her lips once their embrace was done.

"What was that for?" she asked as he lifted his head.

"I just felt like it." He played his fingers over her back. "As you know, I often feel like it. From now on," he stated, "if you need an escort, you are to tell me. I'll do my best to make myself available."

Surprise shone in her gaze. "Well, I . . . all right. If that's what you wish."

"I do. Now, let me fasten those buttons."

Several hours later, Tony leaned against a pillar on the far side of the Hamiltons' spacious drawing room, a glass of canary in hand as he surreptitiously watched Gabriella. She was engaged in conversation with Julianna and Lily, whose figure was just beginning to show signs of her pregnancy, and a fourth woman whose name he couldn't for the life of him recall. Laughing at some remark, Gabriella flashed a pretty smile, the sight warming the blood in his veins, making him think of the night to come. One of many nights for which he now waited with constant anticipation and pleasure.

But it was more than the nights, he realized, raising his glass to quaff a mouthful of wine. He enjoyed all the time they spent together, the reason perhaps why he was finding himself more and more in her company lately, even on those occasions when it wasn't strictly required.

This afternoon, for instance, he could have used the time to visit his stables. He and his trainer needed to talk about several horses, including a likely mare he was thinking about running in the Derby. Instead, he'd decided to come here today. His offer this morning to escort her to the party had been an impulse, but after discovering she was coming with Dickey Milton, he'd made sure he didn't miss the fete.

He could have insisted on escorting her, he supposed, but knew she would have wondered at his reaction. Frankly, *he* wondered at his reaction, since despite his remark about her having a cicisbeo, he knew she was faithful to him. He kept her so occupied sexually—often taking her multiple times a day—that she couldn't possibly have the time or energy for anyone but him. Besides, he trusted her, knowing with a bone-deep certainty that she would never be dishonest enough to betray him with another man.

So what was worrying him? When he thought about it, their current arrangement gave him the best of both worlds—all the benefits of marriage with none of the inconvenient obligations. Going to her house was like having a mistress—the best one he'd ever had. As sensual and satisfying as a trained courtesan, Gabriella brought him to heights of pleasure that even he, in his vast experience, hadn't realized he could feel. And yet, despite the illusion, there was nothing truly illicit about their relationship, since she was, after all, his wife.

Actually, he ought to be enjoying the situation. He had everything he claimed to want—great sex, as much as he wished, as well as a woman who would legitimately bear his children and ensure the continuation of his line. So why the niggling discontent inside him? Why the longing for something else, something more? He didn't understand himself these days. If only she hadn't started this nonsense about maintaining her own residence. They were practically living together again as it was. If only she would relent and come home, everything would be fine.

But would it?

Surely she could see he had no interest in any other woman. And as for her accusation that he was using her as a brood mare, well, that was patently ridiculous, since he wanted more than children, he wanted *her.* And not just for sex. He liked Gabriella, he always had. She made him smile and kept him amused. When they were together, there was no place else he longed to be. And when they were apart . . . he wished he was with her as well.

He gazed at her again and felt a pressure blossom inside his chest. Too much rich food at nuncheon, he decided. Then he saw Dickey Milton approach, watching as the other man kissed her hand and made some remark that soon had her giggling. He scowled and tossed back the rest of his wine.

As he observed them, he remembered his remark about the possibility of someday letting her go her own way discreetly, and knew he'd lied. He would never let her go. And if any other man dared to touch her, he would make sure the fellow was sorry he had. Very sorry indeed. Accepting another glass of canary from a footman, he sipped the wine and waited.

Nearly a half hour later, Milton made his way from the room. Setting down his glass, Tony followed.

"Milton," he said when he and the other man were well out of earshot. "I would have a word with you."

"Oh, hello, Wyvern, I didn't realize you were still here. I noticed you at nuncheon, then you seemed to disappear."

"I've been around. Had an excellent vantage point, in fact."

Milton tossed him a curious look. "You ought to have joined the conversation. The ladies were regaling me with tales of a ball they recently attended. Some very amusing stuff, I must say."

"Yes, I noticed your rapt fascination, particularly when it comes to my wife."

To his credit, Milton didn't so much as flinch under the nasty glare Tony gave him, returning the look with apparent equanimity. "The duchess is a lovely young woman. I always enjoy her company."

"Well, from now on you can enjoy it a great deal less. I understand you escorted her here today. She won't be needing your assistance in the future."

"Are you warning me off?" he questioned in a clearly astonished tone.

"In a word, yes. I don't want you seeing her anymore. And I don't want you telling her why, either. I'll leave the excuses to you."

Milton stared for a long moment, then released a hearty laugh, the sound traveling over Tony's spine with the irritation of a dull razor. "Well, I don't believe it."

Tony crossed his arms over his chest. "Believe what?"

"You, jealous over your own wife! I never did put much stock in all the romantic tales of your hasty wedding. How you'd supposedly been overcome by love and swept her off her feet. Lust, more like, and something else is my guess. Though clearly the 'something else' wasn't an early baby, as a few of the less charitable among us speculated."

Milton ran his fingers over the ribbon of his watch fob as he continued. "When I heard about your public separation, I assumed I'd been right, and that you'd grown tired of her as you have all your other women. But then you started visiting her at her townhouse—an interesting twist, to say the least. Still, until this moment, I never realized the truth."

"Oh?" Tony said on a near growl. "And what *truth* is that?"

"Why, that you really do love her. Just think, Anthony Black, the most dedicated rake among us, brought to heel by a woman—a sweetly adorable, witty, and beautiful woman, yet a woman nonetheless. I'm going to have to make a huge bet at White's Club before anyone else guesses."

Tony's heart kicked in his chest, the other man's words crashing like a thunderclap inside his head. *Love Gabriella? No, I don't love her.* And yet the more he considered the idea, the more he realized how true it was. When viewed from that perspective, everything he'd said and done over the past few weeks made perfect sense. His moments of anger and despair. His temper, which had never before been unsteady. His obsession to have her—and not just in a carnal sense, but in all ways. He not only wanted her, he needed her, knowing suddenly that without her he would never be entirely whole.

By God, Milton is right. I do love her, he thought. Why had it taken him so long to realize what had been there in front of him this entire time?

"You make that wager," Tony told the other man. "And in the meantime, stay well away from Gabriella."

Milton laughed again. "She and I really are nothing but friends, you know."

"But you wish you were more."

"You have me at that," Milton admitted. "She's a delightful woman and you're lucky to have her. Although at the moment, you don't have her, do you? Seeing that you're living apart. Well, good luck winning her back, since I get the impression she doesn't believe you care."

"Well, she's wrong. Now, do us both a favor and take yourself off."

Milton chuckled and strode away, apparently not the least bit offended.

Chapter Twenty-two

GABRIELLA SNUGGLED AGAINST Tony, her body warm and replete from a most thorough bout of lovemaking. *But then Tony is never anything less than thorough*, she mused, *always making sure I am well satisfied before he takes an equal amount of pleasure for himself.*

To her surprise, he'd brought her home from the Hamiltons' party, telling her something about Dickey Milton needing to leave early and him volunteering to take the other man's place.

There'd been an odd, unusually intense expression on his face while they took his coach across the city. More than once he'd appeared on the verge of saying something, but then he'd stopped and kissed her instead. As so often happened, his kisses led to more. By the time they reached her townhouse, both of them had been so hungry for the other, they'd just barely made it up the stairs to her bedroom before taking each other in a frenzy. He'd stripped them both after that first coupling and settled her beneath the sheets, where he'd proceeded to do it all again—only this time he'd been slow, almost reverent, as he brought her to a trembling, soul-stirring climax.

Now, here they were, with night darkening the world

outside, all thoughts of the ball she'd originally planned to attend gone from her brain.

"Are you hungry?" she asked, sliding her palm across his chest before threading her fingers into the black curls that grew there. "We missed dinner, you know. I'm sure Cook could make something simple for us. Or we could always raid the pantry."

He captured her hand and brought it to his lips. "Hmm, we'll eat. But first there is something I want to say. Something I ought to have told you long ago."

"Oh? And what is that?"

"Gabriella. Sweetheart," he said, gazing directly into her eyes. "I love you."

For an instant, she didn't think she'd heard correctly, sure a moment later that she must have imagined the words. *Maybe I am actually asleep and this is a dream,* she mused. "What?" she asked aloud.

"I love you," he repeated. "I only just realized it myself or I would have said something earlier."

She swallowed, her heart threatening to beat up into her throat, repressed joy fluttering like a pair of gold-edged wings around her heart. "And when did you decide this?" she asked, marveling that she could speak at all.

"Just today. I suppose I'm not used to the idea, so it didn't occur to me sooner. But I know it's right, and I want you to come home."

The wings stopped fluttering, the tiny glimmer of hope she'd felt dying an abrupt death. Suddenly cold, she sat up. "Home, is it?"

"Yes," he murmured, running his palm over the bare skin of her back. "Now that we're reconciled, there seems no reason for you to remain here. I'll have your belongings packed up first thing come morning."

Tossing back the covers, she rose from the bed and crossed to her wardrobe to pull out a dressing gown.

Wrapping herself in the heavy folds, she struggled to get warm, knowing it would be a long time before that happened. She tightened the tie at her waist. "You presume a great deal, Your Grace, based on a few simple words. You will leave my belongings right where they are. Now, shall we go have that dinner?"

He sat up, his eyebrows angled like a dark pair of swords. "Didn't you hear what I said? I love you, Gabriella. I want us to be together."

"No, you want me to be in your house, just as you have wanted this entire time. It's an old argument and one I am not interested in continuing."

He looked astonished. "Are you saying you don't believe I love you?" When she didn't reply, he continued. "My God, that is what you are saying. Why?"

"How can I not when I heard you tell Lord Vessey the exact opposite? *'Love? Gabriella?'* she mimicked. *'No, I don't love Gabriella.'* Well, you made your feelings very plain that day and now you expect me to believe you've had a complete change of heart?"

His jaw tightened, a muscle ticking near his eye. "Yes, I do."

"Do you want to know what *I* think?" she said, anger bringing her the rush of warmth she had craved earlier. "I think you are so determined to bend me to your will and get me back where there will be no further scandal that you will try anything, even this. You had no compunction in seducing and manipulating me into marriage, and now you are doing it again. Well, I will not allow it. I will not let you use my feelings for you against me by saying what you know I so desperately want to hear."

"And what are those feelings?" he asked in a quiet voice. "Are you saying you love me, then?"

"Of course I love you!" she returned, her voice quavering with barely checked emotion. "I can't believe you haven't known all along. My God, why else would I have married you if not for love? Why else would I have been so distraught hearing what you said to Ethan? What other reason could possibly have driven me out of my home when I had been so happy? Or at least stupidly imagined myself to be."

Her voice caught on the last, tears threatening to rain down her face. Somehow she held them back. "I am not falling for your blandishments this time and I am not coming home. *This* is my home now," she stated, pointing a finger at the floor. "And this is where I will remain."

"Gabriella, I—"

"No, no more. I've let you back in my bed. I've played along with this . . . whatever these past weeks have been and I'll keep playing if that is what you demand. I promised to give you a child and I will honor that commitment. But this other, I want it to cease. No more talk of my moving back to Black House or Rosemeade. And no more false promises of love."

"They aren't false," he interrupted in a rough tone. "I really do love you."

For a long moment she stared, wanting to believe him in spite of everything. Yet something inside her refused to take the leap, afraid if she did and he changed his mind once again that the loss would break her. She looked away. "I'm going to go downstairs now and have dinner. You may join me or not as you wish."

Instead, he sat motionless in the middle of the bed, his skin pale beneath his usual swarthy complexion. A trick of the candlelight perhaps, she decided. Or maybe a result of suppressed rage over her having caught him out in his lie. Whatever his emotions might be, she could not let them sway her, would not let *him* sway her. Fitting a pair of slippers onto her feet, she opened the door and went out into the hallway.

Ten minutes later, she sat at the dining-room table waiting for a meal she did not want. She heard a single creak and the quiet sound of his footfalls on the stairs. Her shoulders tensed as she prepared herself to face him. But as she listened he walked not toward the dining room, but away. A minute later, she heard a murmur of conversation as one of the footmen opened the front door, then closed it behind him. Tony had left.

It's for the best, she told herself. *But if it is, then why do I feel as if I've just cut out my own heart?* Unable to hold them back any longer, she let the tears slide hot and wet down her face.

As soon as he arrived home, Tony saddled a fresh horse and rode out with no clear direction in mind. In spite of the late hour, he couldn't bring himself to go inside and upstairs to his bed, knowing how lonely the house would feel, how empty his bed would be without Gabriella there to share it.

For the first time in my life I am in love, he mused. *And the woman I adore doesn't believe me.* He gave a mirthless laugh at the divine irony of the situation and spurred his mount faster, tossing a coin to the toll keeper as he headed past one of the gates that led north from the city.

"*Love Gabriella? No, I don't love, Gabriella.*" The words he'd said, the words she'd repeated tonight, haunted him now. As if he'd awakened from a long sleep, he realized that he had loved her even then, had probably loved her for a very long time before that. Only he'd been too obstinate, too blind, to recognize what had been in front of him all along. Worse still was her admission that she loved him but could no longer bring herself to trust or to believe him. He'd taken her love without even being aware, then crushed it—crushed her. And now he was left with the aftermath. Maybe it would be better to leave her alone as she wished, let her lead her life without him.

Perhaps he should even grant her the divorce she had once said she wanted. But selfish as it might be, he knew he could never let her go.

Out of the city now, he rode hard, the cold April night seeping through his coat sleeves and ruffling his hair. At length, he sensed his horse's weariness and slowed the stallion to a walk. Only then did he realize he'd ridden halfway to Rosemeade. For a long minute, he debated whether to continue toward his estate or go back to the city. In the end, it was the fact that Gabriella was in London that decided his direction. With a soft command, he swung his horse around to retrace his path.

Gabriella slept little that night and even less the next, awakening tired and dejected. She'd heard nothing from Tony, not a word since he had left the other evening. Perhaps it was over. Maybe she had finally driven him away.

Ringing for her maid, she allowed the girl to assist her into a blue-and-white striped day dress, then made her way to the morning room for a cup of tea. As for food, she wasn't sure she could tolerate more than a single slice of toast, her stomach queasy, her appetite barely existent. She was woolgathering over her tea fifteen minutes later when Ford appeared in the doorway.

"Good morning, Your Grace," the butler said, walking into the room. "These just arrived. I thought you would want me to bring them up."

Her eyes widened at the vase of flowers he held. And not just any flowers, but long-stemmed roses—three dozen at least—their petals so vibrantly red they rivaled the richest, darkest wine she had ever seen. Their luscious perfume filled the air, compelling her to take a deeper breath to savor the fragrance.

Heavenly, she sighed to herself.

"There is a card," the butler informed her after he set

down his burden, turning to hand her a small white card. With a bow, he departed.

Aware of her heart beating, she opened the note.

These reminded me of you. Sweet and passionate and undeniably beautiful. For your safety, I have removed the thorns, since I know I have hurt you enough already. Please forgive me.

Your servant,
Tony

She stared at the roses, the hand that held the card limp in her lap. *Forgive him,* he asked. For what? For claiming he loved her and not meaning it? Or for everything else that had passed between them? She noticed he'd signed the card "Your servant," with no further exhortations of love. Yet what did he really mean?

In the past he'd given her many gifts, but this was the first time he'd ever sent her flowers. Would it be the last? Were these a parting of sorts? Confused and not knowing what to think, she crushed the card in her hand. But just as quickly, she smoothed it out again, reading the words one more time.

Unable to stop herself, she stood and crossed to the flowers. Cupping one blossom with a gentle palm, she leaned near and closed her eyes. With Tony in her thoughts, she breathed deep.

Another bouquet of roses arrived the following afternoon—vivid, perfect pink this time—together with a new note. It read:

These may be lovely, but they cannot begin to compare to you.

Your servant,
Tony

Gabriella set them next to the first arrangement and wondered if he would visit her.

He did not—nor did she see him that night when she attended the theater with Rafe and Julianna. Instead of watching the play, she spent the entire time glancing toward his box in hopes of finding him there, but he never appeared.

The next morning, however, another gift was delivered to the door—a box this time. Ford carried it upstairs and set it on the breakfast table before her. Only after he left did she yank open the big yellow silk bow and lift the lid to reveal a huge assortment of confections: candied fruits, delicate meringues, marchpane, clusters of sugar-coated comfits, taffy, and little honey cakes.

Something sweet for someone sweeter.

Your servant,
Tony

What is he trying to do? she mused. *Seduce me again?* Unable to resist the temptation of a honey cake, she bit in. As she did, though, she vowed she would not give in to him.

Every day for the next week, he sent her a gift, each one accompanied by a card that he always signed "Your servant." On the eighth day, however, the note said something different.

May I call upon you?

Tony

She sat for a long time in indecision before turning over the card and writing, "Yes."

The following afternoon, Tony drew his carriage to a halt in front of Gabriella's townhouse. After jumping to the ground, he gave his waistcoat a sharp tug and fought the tight feeling in his stomach.

In all his years, Tony couldn't recall ever being nervous when calling upon a woman. The fact that this particular woman happened to be his wife made his reaction that much more singular. Reaching into his phaeton, he retrieved the nosegay of flowers he had brought for her, then navigated the short flight of steps up to the front door.

Instead of using his key, he allowed Ford to grant him entrance. After exchanging greetings, he was informed that Her Grace was in the sitting room expecting his call. Giving one last tug to his waistcoat, Tony went to find his wife.

She was seated in a pool of lively April sunshine, a pensive expression on her face as she gazed out at the garden below. A spark lit briefly in her eyes as she turned to find him in the doorway. "Tony."

"Gabriella. May I say you look a picture." And she did, her flawless, translucent skin aglow in a gown of shell-pink silk, some delicate lace edging the garment's short, capped sleeves. Perhaps it was because he hadn't seen her in over a week, but he thought she looked more beautiful than ever. "Is that a new dress?" he inquired, abruptly in need of something to say.

"Yes, it's part of my new spring wardrobe. The one Lily and Julianna helped me select." She stood, her hands crossed before her. "I hope you don't object to the cost—"

"Not at all," he assured. "If this is an example of your purchases, then I must say it was money well spent."

Her expression softened, her hands falling to her sides.

"Here," he continued. "These are for you." Stepping forward, he extended the flowers he'd brought.

"Violets! Oh, aren't they lovely!" Cradling them in her hands, she brought the bouquet up to her nose to sample their fragrance. "Wherever did you find them so early in the Season?"

"I am acquainted with a most excellent florist. It was a simple matter to obtain them." Actually, locating such a large quantity of blossoms had not been easy at all, but he saw no need to tell her that. "I thought their color might complement your eyes," he went on. "But I see now that nature gave you the far more interesting shade."

She lowered the flowers. "Tony, what are you doing?"

"What do you mean?"

"The flowers, the confections, all the gifts you've been giving me lately."

"Do you not like them? I can find something else—"

"Of course I like them. How could I not? But. . . why?"

"Do I really need to explain?"

She took a long moment to answer. "Yes, I believe you do."

"All right then. It is my hope that I can show you what you will not let me say. It occurred to me that I never gave you a proper courting, so let me give you one now." Catching hold of her hand, he brought it to his lips. "Please, Gabriella, let me woo you a bit."

A faintly alarmed expression crossed her face as she pulled her hand from his grasp. "You courted me," she defended. "We did all the usual things."

"No, we played at doing all the usual things. What I did was seduce you, and you are entirely right to chastise me on that score. Now, enough of such talk. Go put on your pelisse and let me take you for a drive."

"Now?"

"Of course, now. I brought the high-flyer phaeton. I thought perhaps you might enjoy a spin around the city. We can go to the park as well if you wish, but I warn you it will be crowded, even this early in the Season."

His earlier nerves returned as he watched her hesitate. *Surely she isn't going to refuse me?* he thought. But to his relief, she nodded. "I will only be a few moments."

He wanted to go after her, but held himself in check. Despite his decision to court her, restraining his desire for her was not proving easy. But he would do it if it meant winning her love, and more important, her trust.

He knew she would let him back in her bed if he asked. She'd already told him she would honor her pledge to give him a baby. But if he went to her now, he knew she would think that was all he wanted—proof in her mind that his claim of love was nothing but lust in disguise. *Well, I will show her—I have to show her.* Anything else was unthinkable. And at least she had said she loved him. Surely that gave him some hope.

Her quiet footfall signaled her return. He shifted to find her in the doorway, stunningly pretty in a feathered bonnet and spring-weight, white pelisse. A familiar rush of desire swept through him, but this time he was aware of more, a swell of emotion that had nothing to do with physical need and everything to do with his heart.

How could I not have known? he wondered. *How could I have failed to realize how much I love her, when she is as necessary to me now as breathing? And I've all but driven her away.* But he was going to fix that. He had only to find the means to convince her to let him.

Striding forward, he extended his arm. "Ready?"

She laid a gloved palm on his sleeve and nodded. "For a carriage ride, yes."

Each morning after, Gabriella rose from her bed, telling herself that today she would refuse to see Tony and put an end to this foolish "courting" of his. But then he would show up on her doorstep with some gift in hand—flowers or confections, or sometimes a pretty trinket—and in spite of her best resolve, she would melt and agree to whatever it was he had planned.

They went driving and riding and for leisurely strolls in the park. He took her to Astley's Amphitheater and the British Museum. He even escorted her shopping on Bond Street one afternoon, carrying her packages while she browsed for new linens for the dining room and silver candlesticks for the front hall. She'd thought that last might drive him away, but he'd been perfectly amenable to whatever she wished to do, waiting with seemingly unlimited amounts of patience while she mulled over her choices and made her decision.

In the evenings he was there as well, escorting her to balls and soirees and fetes where he always made a point of dancing with her at least twice, then taking her in to supper when she would allow him to do so. At both the theater and the opera she sat in the Wyvern box, and one evening the two of them dined in royal style at Carlton House with the Prince Regent himself.

At the end of that night, Prinny clapped Tony on the back and asked him what it was he thought he was doing, lavishing such marked attention on his own wife when he and everyone else in Society knew such things simply weren't done between married couples.

As he answered, Tony turned his head and met Gabriella's gaze. "Why, Your Royal Highness, I am merely demonstrating my affection. You see, she does not believe I love her."

Prinny gave a shout of laughter, greatly amused. "And quite right she is to doubt you, considering what a rake you've always been. Your duchess is a wise woman."

"Yes, sir, she is. But not, however, in this particular regard."

His remark earned another laugh from the prince, and a frown from Gabriella.

Am I wrong? she'd found herself wondering later as

she lay alone in her bed. *Does Tony truly love me, and I am doing nothing more than torturing us both with my lack of faith? Or is Prinny right, and I am wise not to believe Tony?* Her mind had chased round and round in a terrible quandary until sleep finally gave her a few hours' relief.

Now, as she sat sipping her morning cup of tea on the first day of June, she realized she might need to make her decision for another reason entirely. She was pregnant.

She'd been wondering for nearly two weeks now if such might be the case, but she'd waited, trying not to become too invested in whatever the outcome might reveal. But when her second monthly in a row failed to arrive, she knew she must be with child. Besides, she'd had other symptoms—unusual tiredness, sore breasts, and a queasiness that didn't allow her to do much more than sip a little weak tea most mornings.

She should have been overjoyed at the prospect—and she was—yet she couldn't help but wonder how Tony would greet the news. And how it might change this current relationship of theirs. Although maybe for all their sakes she should simply give him what he wanted and move back to Black House, even if she might still harbor doubts about the honesty of his protestations of love.

A strong part of her longed to do exactly that, longed to let herself pretend so she could be with him as his wife. And more, so she could stop missing him. For in spite of all the hours they spent together each day, the nights without him were long and lonely. At first she'd assumed he would continue to seek out her bed, but after that last terrible fight between them, he had not returned to her. She didn't know if he was punishing her, was punishing them both, or thought she no longer desired him.

And yet another disturbing possibility existed—one that made her cringe to consider. *What if he has stopped wanting me altogether?* she worried. But if that were the case, his attentions to her made little sense—unless he was only being stubborn, determined at all costs to win his point. Then again, maybe the truth was that he did really love her, just as he said.

Oh, God, I don't know what to think, she realized, setting her teacup into its saucer with a sharp clink. *But at least I have the baby,* she reassured herself. *No matter what might happen, at least I have our child.*

The music stopped two evenings later, the last lilting notes drifting away as Gabriella and Tony finished their waltz. Numerous couples around them began to separate and make their way from the dance floor. Slipping out of his arms, Gabriella turned to do the same, then reached out to clutch him again as the room suddenly whirled around her.

"Here now, what is this?" Tony asked, catching her close.

As quickly as the sensation had begun, however, it stopped, her head clearing as her balance turned strong and steady once again. *Gracious,* she thought, *what* was *that?* Even as the question formed, she knew what *that* had been—her pregnancy. But she hadn't told Tony about the baby yet, and a crowded ballroom was no place to share such news. She did plan to let him know, though she still hadn't decided exactly when.

"Heavens, I'm not sure," she dissembled. "The heat perhaps. It is rather close in here, do you not agree?"

He sent her a look of concern. "A little, but no more than the usual Ton squeeze. Are you sure you are well?"

"Quite sure."

"Because if you are coming down with something—"

"I only need a cool drink and a bite of supper. All that dancing has left me famished." And she was—battling nausea in the mornings only to find herself starving come nightfall. Now she knew how Lily had been feeling these past few months.

"If you are sure?" he questioned.

"I am." She forced an extra-bright smile. "I feel fine." And she did—for a woman who happened to be in a delicate condition.

Tony smiled back, apparently deciding to accept her explanation. "If I know our hosts, their staff is probably laying out the buffet by now. Shall we see if we can sneak in a few minutes early?"

She nodded. "Yes, let's."

Tony was right, and although they were the first to arrive, several other couples and small groups drifted in only moments after they found a table and began to eat.

The meal eased her hunger, but to Gabriella's consternation, she found herself smothering yawns by the time supper concluded over an hour later. As she and Tony exited the dining room, he bent close. "You look ready to drift off. Why do I not call for our coach and take you home?"

Covering another yawn with her gloved hand, her eyes watering a bit, she agreed.

Inside the coach, Tony drew her against his side so she could use his shoulder as a head rest. Too sleepy to object, she settled against him with a relieved sigh, relaxing deeply for the first time since she had last slept in his arms.

The vehicle was motionless when she awakened, awareness returning to her in an easy slide. Tony was holding her, his arm cradling her close like a warm, snug cocoon. "Are we there?" she asked.

"Yes, but there's no hurry."

"How long—"

"A little while. I didn't want to disturb you; you were sleeping so peacefully." With a finger, he brushed a curl away from her face. "You looked like an angel."

Gazing at his deeply handsome face and into his intense blue eyes—their color turned nearly black in the low light—she felt a rush of desire quicken inside her. "Kiss me, Tony," she whispered.

An answering half-smile fanned over his lips. "With pleasure."

Gathering her even closer, he touched his mouth to hers in an embrace that was passionate and tender, warm yet restrained, as though he was set on relishing her like some rare delicacy of which he had just been invited to partake. Caressing her, he sipped and savored, his tongue gliding and exploring in ways that soon turned her blood to steam, her heart beating like thunder beneath her breasts.

Threading her fingers into his hair, she kissed him back, giving herself the right to express everything she felt, everything she desired. Opening her mouth, she drew him in, leading him deeper into a fervid aerie of passionate delights that left both of them struggling for breath and her for sanity. Yet soon, even that much was not enough, her body hungering for more—much more.

"Would you like to come inside?" she asked, quivering as he cupped one of her breasts inside his palm for a gentle caress.

He kissed her twice more, skimming his mouth over her cheek and down the line of her throat, pausing to run his tongue over her wildly thrumming pulse. "*Hmm,* do you want me to come in?"

"Yes," she admitted, her voice husky with need. "My bed is empty without you."

He raised his head, his gaze warm as he met her eyes. "Does this mean, then, that you believe me now? That you trust I love you? Because I do, Gabriella. I love you so very, very much."

A small measure of her passion faded, doubt rushing in to replace her pleasure. She stared, knowing she should just say "yes" and let their lives go forward. Tell him what he wanted to hear whether she truly believed it or not. But something within her refused to say the words, her tongue and her promises silent.

The light died in his gaze as suddenly as it had come, his arms sliding away. "I see." He swallowed and looked away. "Well, perhaps it is still too soon. I think you should go inside and up to bed now." His face was shuttered, jaw drawn tight as if he were in pain.

"Tony—"

Reaching over, he shoved open the door and leapt out, then reached up a hand to assist her from the coach. In silence, she accepted and allowed him to see her to her door.

Once there, he gave a curt bow. "Good evening, madam. I wish you sweet dreams."

"Tony, please. Come inside and let us talk."

He shot her a caustic glance. "About what? I think we've said it all."

Behind her, a footman opened the door as Tony turned and stalked to his coach. After a curt order, the coachman flicked the reins and set the horses in motion.

She watched until the coach disappeared, only then retreating inside. With her footsteps like lead, she went up the stairs to her bedroom, all too aware he would not be joining her. Once inside, she slumped onto the mattress, her mind replaying the memory of his expression. He'd looked . . . crushed, like a man who'd just had his heart twisted from his chest. Had she put that look on his face, in his eyes? Had she hurt him that much? And if she had, then it could mean only one thing. *He does love me!*

Oh, God, what have *I done?* she whispered to herself.

Chapter Twenty-three

TONY PACED ACROSS the Pendragons' upstairs drawing room two mornings later, dejected thoughts tumbling through his mind.

"How about a cup of tea?" Julianna suggested. "Or would you rather I send for something stronger? A brandy, perhaps?"

At first he didn't respond, then abruptly he stopped and turned to face her. "Thank you, no. Unfortunately spirits will not cure what ails me."

A little frown settled between her delicate brows. "Well, at least have the tea and some cakes. You look as if you could do with food, and several hours' rest as well. When is the last time you slept?"

"Yesterday, I don't know." He waved off the question with a hand. "All that isn't important right now. I came here because I didn't know who else to ask. You're her friend and her aunt. You know her better than anyone else."

Julianna folded her hands in her lap. "If 'her' is Gabriella, then I would say her friend Maude knows her quite a bit better than I. But I suspect you do not wish to wait long enough to contact Miss Woodcraft."

"No. Besides, she would likely tell me to get stuffed and take a swim in the Thames."

"I rather doubt she would make either of those suggestions," Julianna replied, her lips twitching for a moment. "Nor do I believe she would be unwilling to help you. But what is it that has occurred? Something new besides the separation, I assume?"

He strode across the room, going to the window to gaze across the square at the Vesseys' townhouse—Gabriella's townhouse. For a moment, he looked for some sign of her before turning away. "She doesn't believe me. I've told her I love her and she does not trust a word of it."

Pausing, he strode back and dropped into a chair, reaching up to drag a hand through his already disheveled hair. "I don't know what else to do. I've tried everything. Flowers, candy, jewelry. I've sent her notes and poems. I've been courting her this past month like some lovesick swain—appropriate, I suppose, since that is precisely what I am."

A moment of silence fell before Julianna spoke. "You poor thing! You really do love her, don't you?"

"What!" His head came up. "Yes, I love her, but obviously even you don't believe me. How much plainer must I make it?"

"None. And I *do* believe you," she said in a soothing tone. "But even you have to admit, after what you said to Ethan, she has valid reason to doubt."

"Christ!" he swore, then just as quickly apologized. "Please do not remind me of that accursed conversation. How I wish I could take back that blighted day! If I could, everything would be right between us." But it wasn't. *Heaven help me,* he thought, *I've made such a mess of everything!*

Quiet despair crept over him, a soul-deep sadness that tore at his vitals in a way he'd never before known. "Perhaps I should just grant her the divorce she says she wants. Accept that this marriage is over between us and let her go. Maybe without me, she might be free to find some happiness. And I want her to be happy. More than anything, I need her to find joy."

Julianna made a dismissive noise. "Well, she won't be happy divorced from you, I can tell you that. In spite of whatever difficulties the two of you may be having at the moment, I know Gabriella loves you. A divorce would devastate her."

A breath of hope rose again inside him. "Then why will she not believe me? What can I do to make her see how deeply I care? And I do, Julianna. I never thought I would love a woman the way I love her. Hell, I can't even abide my own house these days because she isn't in it."

Julianna smiled. "Then we must find a way to convince Gabriella of your devotion and coax her back home. She's just scared, you know. Afraid of being hurt yet again."

"Well, she won't be," he defended. "And I will prove it to her if she will only give me the chance."

"Let's see," Julianna mused, tapping a finger against her chin. "Obviously none of the usual cajoleries will work, so you'll need something stronger, something she will find impossible to refute or ignore."

"And what might that be? I mean, how do you prove an emotion?"

"By example, generally. Or in extreme circumstances, such as this one, by doing something you would not ordinarily do. I think you need to make a grand gesture."

"A grand gesture? And what would that be exactly?"

"Oh, I couldn't say; that will be up to you to decide. But I know you will think of something, since you are a man of extraordinarily persuasive abilities. Just remember that she loves you, Tony, and everything will come right."

Everything will be well, Gabriella repeated to herself five days later as she walked into the Duke of Raeburn's crowded London ballroom. Tonight's gala festivities were rumored to be one of "*the*" events of the Season, drawing at least half the members of the Ton—the better half, she'd overheard someone boast a few days ago.

Nevertheless, she'd almost decided not to come. But when she mentioned her reluctance to Julianna, her friend had convinced her to change her mind.

"But you must come," Julianna stated. "Everyone will be there. It's even rumored they will be having fireworks, ordered by the prospective bride, Lady Jeannette herself. You wouldn't want to miss that."

"Oh, I don't know. It sounds lively, but I haven't been feeling much like having fun lately."

"No, you've been quite blue-deviled, so a rousing party seems just what you need. I will not accept no for an answer. Rafe and I shall take you up in our coach, so all you need do is enjoy the evening."

But now as she strolled across the ballroom, she had serious doubts that she would enjoy anything tonight. Julianna was right, though. She did need to shake off her mopes. Contrary to her usual optimistic nature, she had been seriously blue-deviled of late. Of course, dealing with bouts of morning sickness and unexpected waves of weariness didn't help matters. Mostly, though, she was despondent over Tony.

Since that night in his coach, she hadn't been able to get his face out of her mind, continuing to see the expression of hurt in his eyes, to hear his earlier declaration of love. Obviously she had wounded him deeply, since he'd stopped calling upon her after that. Nor was he sending his usual assortment of gifts and cards to her, leaving her to wonder if her lack of faith had injured him so much that he'd decided to wash his hands of her, after all. Yet she knew she owed it to them both to make one last attempt to repair their faltering marriage.

After a nearly sleepless night, she'd realized it no

longer mattered what she believed. She loved Tony, and that fact alone compelled her to give him her trust—and her devotion. If he honestly loved her, then all would be well. And if he did not, then she would spend her life striving to change his mind. Her life was with him—for better or worse, just as the vows said—and with him she would remain. Now, she had only to convince him to let her come back—to his arms and his bed and his life.

Which was another reason she had decided to attend the ball tonight, so that she and Tony might have an opportunity to talk. She'd considered going to Black House, but hadn't been able to work up enough courage. But maybe she could get him alone, or at least see if he would agree to escort her home, and then she would tell him—not only what was in her heart, but also about the baby. He had a right to know he was going to be a father. No matter what, she would never deny him that.

Stopping at the refreshment table, she reached out to get a drink.

"The lime punch is quite good," said a shy voice from nearby. Turning, she gazed at a pretty blonde in spectacles, her hands twisted into the folds of her plain white gown.

"Lady Jeannette, is it not?"

The girl shook her head. "Oh no, I'm Violet. M-my sister is over there." She nodded across the ballroom where an exquisitely dressed, stunningly coifed blonde beauty held court among a group of enthralled gentlemen and ladies. As the other girl turned to display her lovely profile, Gabriella saw the marked resemblance between the two sisters. Without Violet's glasses, they were so close to identical she wondered how anyone could tell them apart.

"That's right, you are twins," Gabriella said. "I met your sister only briefly in the receiving line."

"And Raeburn? Did you meet her betrothed as well?"

Lady Violet asked, her gaze moving to linger on a tall, handsome man standing on the ballroom's other side. Without knowing it, intense longing shone in Lady Violet's eyes as she beheld the duke.

Heavens, Gabriella thought. *Does she have feelings for him?* But then she shook off the thought, aware she had her own duke to worry about. "The lime punch, did you say?"

Violet turned back. "Y-yes. Forgive me, Your Grace. I did not mean to intrude upon you."

"You haven't. Not at all." Taking a cup, she sipped her punch, finding it as refreshing as promised. A moment later, she saw Ethan with a very pregnant Lily at his side. "It's been lovely talking, but if you will excuse me, some friends of mine have just arrived," she said, setting down her cup.

"Of course. I see my friend Eliza as well." Lady Violet waved to a mousy-looking girl attired in a dreadful pea-green gown. The mousy girl waved back.

Parting, Gabriella made her way toward Ethan and Lily. Only moments after reaching them, Tony appeared. Her pulse hurried faster as he made her an elegant bow.

"Gabriella," he said, his voice low and smooth as whisky. "Would you do me the honor of the next dance?"

"Of course, Your Grace."

After a couple of minutes' conversation with Ethan and Lily, she and Tony made their way to the dance floor. As the music began, he led her into a waltz, the sensation of being held again in his arms wonderful, even magical. Neither of them spoke, so many thoughts and emotions whirling around in her head that she feared she might not be able to express them all, or at least not adequately.

"Tony, I . . . I wonder if we might speak later. I . . . I have things I need to say."

A mild frown creased his brow. "I have things to say to

you as well. In the garden perhaps, before tonight's fireworks?"

A lump caught in her throat as she forced herself to nod her head in agreement.

But nearly two hours later as she stood on the terrace, she feared she might have made a mistake. For one thing, there were far too many people out-of-doors for any sort of private conversation, guests making their way from the townhouse so they could enjoy the coming show. For another, she was worried over what he might be planning to say. *Mercy,* she mused, *surely he hasn't decided to end things between us?* She didn't know what she would do if he had. Plead, perhaps?

But then the time for indecision was over as Tony strode across the stone terrace toward her, the light from the house casting his gorgeous features into prominence. When he reached her, she tried to draw him away, wanting to be alone. Only he resisted, taking her arm instead to pull her forward so she stood in a pool of golden illumination that she imagined must look like a kind of theatrical footlight in the gathering darkness.

"Tony, let us go back inside," she urged.

"No, not yet," he said. Turning, he raised a hand to draw the crowd's attention. "Everyone," he said, projecting his deep voice. "I have something to say, something of extreme importance that I would like all of you to witness and share."

Witness and share! What is he doing? Confusion rippled through her, then a twinge of alarm. Subtly, she tried to pull out of his grasp, but he held tight, clasping her hand so she could not possibly get away. Trembling, she held her place, her heart beating out a crazy tattoo.

"As I am sure all of you know, my wife and I have lately been living apart."

"Tony," she hissed under her breath. "*Stop this!* What are you doing?"

But he ignored her, retaining his hold upon her as he continued to speak. "This has been a situation of great distress for us both, but I am hoping all that will end tonight."

End tonight! Oh, dear Lord, is he going to cast me aside? Publicly? She closed her eyes and struggled not to faint. Sensing him changing position, she opened her eyes enough to peek, her gaze growing wide when she found him on one knee before her, her hand clasped inside his.

"My dearest Gabriella," he intoned. "I want to say what is in my heart before you and all these good people. I am doing this without shame or pride, so there can be no misunderstanding and no more doubts. I love you with everything I am and all that I possess. Since we met, there has been no one else. There *can* be no one else because you are the only one. My only true love."

She couldn't breathe, her lips parting in astonishment at his words.

"I used to say that I would never beg—woman or man—but I am here before you tonight begging you to forgive me for any hurt I have caused. Beseeching you to believe me when I tell you that I love you and cannot live another day knowing we are apart. Wherever you are, that is where you will find my heart. Where you go, that is where I long to be. If you cannot bear the sight of me, tell me now and I will leave you in peace. But if you return my affection, pray end my present misery and say you will be mine."

Gabriella's breath caught in her chest. "Oh, Tony. Oh my love," she whispered. Tugging him to his feet, she threw her arms around him. "Of course I will be yours. Don't you know, I already am."

His lips met hers in a fervid, ardent kiss while around them people broke into thunderous applause. She barely heard the commotion, however, too overwhelmed by the joy and relief in her heart.

At length he broke their kiss, pressing his cheek to hers so no one else would hear. "Forgive me if I embarrassed you with this, my love," he whispered. "But I did not know what else to do. I could think of no other way to reach you."

"No, no it's all right," she told him. "I've been so stubborn—too much so and for far too long. Everything you said tonight was so beautiful, but you had only to wait a few minutes more and I would have come to *you,* to say I love you. To ask if I may come home."

He squeezed her closer into his embrace. "Of course you may."

"I don't want to be anywhere but with you either. And I was wrong for not believing you, not trusting you when you told me how you felt. I'm sorry, so sorry, love."

"Don't be. You were right to do what you did. You were right all along. I've been such a fool!"

She smiled and stroked his cheek. "We both have."

"Hey, you two. Are you done cooing?" Ethan asked, grinning at them. "I think they want to start the fireworks."

"Tell them to wait a minute," Tony ordered. "I have one more thing to do." Reaching into his waistcoat, he drew out a small, black velvet-covered box, then turned to take Gabriella's hand. "My love, I didn't do this right the first time. We rushed to the altar and not for the reason that should have counted most." Opening the box, he drew out a shimmering gold ring. "Gabriella St. George Black, will you marry me? Again? I want us to wed for love this time, so there will never be any doubt between us. We can even post the banns and hold a big church wedding, if that is what you want."

Tears slid down her cheeks. "I don't need all that, I

only need you. But yes, I would love to marry you again. Our anniversary is soon. We could do it then."

He wiped his thumb across her damp skin and kissed her. "Read the inscription first."

She took the ring, turning it so she could make it out even in the low light. *"For eternity you hold my heart."* Flinging her arms around him again, she kissed him, uncaring who watched.

Pulling apart from him a good minute later, she let Tony exchange her old ring for the new one. She was admiring it when a fresh thought struck her. "Oh, I nearly forgot."

"Forgot what?"

"My news. But maybe I should wait until we are alone."

"No more waiting," he said, slipping his arm around her waist. "What is it?"

"Sweetheart, you're going to be a father."

"What! Are you with child?"

She nodded, a huge grin on her face. "I am. Why else do you think I've been dizzy and falling asleep at balls lately?"

Letting out an exuberant shout that made everyone stare at them again, he picked her up and whirled her in a circle, both of them laughing with happiness. Bending low, their lips met in a warm, rich kiss, while above the night sky filled with whizzing rockets and colorful showers of light.

But Tony and Gabriella needed no such displays, reveling in a celebration all their own.

Chapter Twenty-four

Rosemeade—Bedfordshire, England
January 1817

"WHAT ARE YOU doing up?" Tony murmured in a tender scold. "I thought you promised me you would rest."

Gabriella turned as he joined her in front of the elaborately carved rosewood cradle that had been used by every Wyvern baby for the past two centuries. "I was resting, but I awakened and just had to see him." Reaching down, she stroked a fingertip over one tiny cheek, the day-old baby making sucking motions with his lips for a moment before falling back to sleep. "He's so beautiful, I can't believe he's finally here."

Tony slipped an arm around her waist and hugged her close, dropping a kiss against her temple. "He is indeed, our little Jonathan. Though he certainly gave you several rough hours, and me as well. I've never been so scared in my life as I was waiting for him to be born. You were amazingly brave, braver than any man who ever did battle."

"I didn't have much choice," she quipped. "He was coming whether I was ready or not. I was so relieved, though, to have you with me through the delivery. I'm glad you didn't let the doctor shoo you out."

"He couldn't have budged me. Besides, Rafe and

Ethan were both at the birth of their children. I wasn't about to be left out of mine." He brushed a soft kiss over her mouth. "Thank you for our son, my love."

Smiling, she kissed him again.

A soft tapping came at her bedchamber door a few moments later, Julianna poking her head around. "So you are awake. I thought I heard voices and decided to come see." Julianna strolled forward, stopping before the cradle. "And how is the new Marquis of Howland? Oh, just look at him sleep! Aren't they adorable when they're so little like this?" She paused for a moment as the three of them looked on. "You know, Tony, I think the baby has your nose."

"The Wyvern nose, you mean. The heir always seems to have it. The picture gallery is full of ancestors with that exact same nose. Jonathan is apparently holding true to form."

"Well, I'm glad he is. It's a beautiful nose," Gabriella declared.

"Handsome, love. Handsome," Tony corrected with a grin.

"Are you all in here admiring the baby?" Lily asked, walking in on silent feet. "I thought Gabriella was sleeping."

"She's supposed to be," Tony reminded his wife, pinning her with a look.

"I've barely been able to do more than sit and waddle around this past month," Gabriella complained. "I needed to be up on my feet for a while. It's been so wonderful, though, having all of you here at Rosemeade again for Christmas and the Twelfth Night celebration. You made everything so merry."

"We wouldn't have missed it," Julianna said. Lily nodded in agreement.

"Wouldn't have missed what?" Ethan asked, careful to

keep his voice lowered. Rafe entered the room behind him.

"The holidays here together," Lily explained.

"Ah, that. It has been exciting," he said. "Especially toasting the New Year, then watching Tony go white as a sheet when Gabriella set down her cup of syllabub and informed us all that she was in labor."

Tony sent his friend a dark look. "I doubt you did much better when Lily gave birth to your daughter."

"He didn't," Lily volunteered with a chuckle in her voice. "Drank half a decanter of brandy before he felt calm enough to come in the bedroom."

"It worked, didn't it?" Ethan defended. "When Louisa arrived, I was steady as a rock."

Lily linked her hand with his. "You were. Tough as granite."

Appeased, Ethan leaned over and gave his wife a quick kiss. "And where is our beautiful daughter? Upstairs in the nursery, I assume?"

Lily nodded. "I fed her, then put her down for a nap not ten minutes ago."

"Stephanie and Cam are supposed to be doing the same," Julianna said, "though I know Cam often finds ways to avoid his nap time and sneak back into the playroom. By the way, Rafe, when I told your son about the new baby, he wanted to know when *he* was going to get a little brother of his own. Apparently, Stephanie is far too boring to play soldiers."

Rafe smiled and slipped an arm around his wife's waist. "Well, I'd be happy to oblige him and have another," he said with a grin. "Maybe you and I should leave so we can work on the matter."

"Rafe!" Julianna exclaimed, her eyes twinkling despite her reproof.

He gave an unrepentant chuckle.

"Rafe is right about one thing, however," Julianna

said a moment later. "All of us should leave so Gabriella can get some rest."

"Yes, indeed," Lily nodded. "Giving birth is hard work. We will see you later, Gabby."

After the four of them retreated from the room, Tony insisted on helping Gabriella climb beneath the sheets. Relaxing against the pillows he'd stacked behind her head, she waited while he tucked her in, carefully drawing the sheet and blankets up to her shoulders before bending low to press a lingering kiss against her lips. "Sleep well, love," he murmured. "I shall be back to check on you in a short while."

"Don't go," she said, reaching out a hand to stop him. "Stay. I'll sleep better if you're with me."

And it was true. Since their reconciliation last June, she and Tony hadn't spent a night apart. Not even when she'd been so huge with child she could barely sleep, restless and uncomfortable and surely keeping Tony awake. And he'd slept with her last night after the birth, she needing him there to cradle her as she drifted into a happy but exhausted slumber. This was only a nap, she knew, but she wanted him with her nonetheless.

After a brief hesitation, he walked around to the other side of the bed. Toeing off his shoes, he slipped in next to her, taking her in his arms. "Rest now," he exhorted. "The baby will be awake again soon enough wanting a meal. Sleep while you can."

Settling her head on his shoulder, she closed her eyes, but opened them again a few moments later. "I didn't tell you before, but I had a note from your mother."

A small silence fell. "She didn't say something to upset you, did she?"

"No. Actually it was a very nice note. She apologized for not welcoming me to the family properly, then went on to ask if she might stop by one afternoon to see the baby. Apparently she is at the dower house again. I haven't written back. What should I say?"

"What do you want to say?"

She paused, playing her fingers over one of the gold buttons on his waistcoat. "I'm not sure. She has been so hateful to you, I hesitate to agree—and I won't if a visit from her will cause you even a moment's distress. But she is Jonathan's grandmother. I suppose she ought to be given the chance to see him."

"A visit from her will not trouble me in the slightest. I have you, Gabriella, and that is all that matters. What is past is past. Your love and our life together—those are the things that concern me now. So long as she doesn't upset *you,* she may come to the house."

"Then I'll tell her to call. In a few days maybe, once I am feeling a bit stronger. She is family, after all. And family forgives."

"Have her here whenever you like. And you're right. Families forgive each other, even if they don't always agree. Now, enough talking. You need to rest."

"All right," she murmured, tucking her head more comfortably against his shoulder. A minute passed. "Tony?"

"What?" he said, his voice a mixture of amusement and exasperation.

"I love you."

He angled her face up so he could gaze into her eyes. "I love you, too, and never doubt it. You and Jonathan are the best things that ever happened to me. There was a time when I thought myself content to remain a bachelor, but I know now I would never have been truly happy. How could I, when I would never have known the joy and pleasure of starting each day gazing at you? When I would not have realized the delight of holding you like this in my arms? You're my world, Gabriella, and I want no other."

"Nor do I." Smiling, she blinked back happy tears as his mouth claimed hers for a long, blissful kiss. At length, they parted so she could settle her head against his shoulder once more in an attempt to sleep. Her eyes had just closed and she was relaxing when the baby started crying.

"See what you get for not resting when I told you to?" Tony admonished.

With the baby's healthy wails filling the room, Tony helped her sit up against the pillows. "I can sleep later," she said. "Right now, I don't need anything more than you and our son."

Acknowledgments

To Charlotte Herscher, Signe Pike, and Helen Breitwieser for their unflagging trust, professionalism, and support during the writing of this book. Thanks for giving me the quiet time I needed.

Again to Charlotte, wishing her great happiness and success in all her future endeavors. You'll be missed.

To Linda Marrow, Kim Hovey, and Kate Blum for all their wonderful efforts on my behalf.

To fellow author, Monica, who really gets it. Thanks for being such a great friend.

To my brother, Rick, and my nieces, Kelly and Olivia. Hugs for cheering me on.

And finally, to my three feline office "assistants"—Christofur, Violetta, and Georgianna—who make sure I've always got company when I write.